Propontis

Thasos
Samothrace

Lemnos

TROAS

Lesbos
Eresus   Mytilene
Pyrrha   caicus
             AEOLIS   LYDIA

Scyras

Chios

Hermus
Sardis

Andros   IONIA
                Ephesus

Samos

Tenos   Maeander

Icaria

Mikonos   CARIA

Naxos

SEA

Rhodes

MAIN MAP

Crete

SICILY

NILE
DELTA

1000 km
600 miles

Sappho's Leap

Sappho's Leap

A NOVEL BY *Erica Jong*

W. W. Norton & Company

NEW YORK | LONDON

Copyright © 2003 by Erica Jong

All rights reserved
Printed in the United States of America
First Edition

Excerpt from "In Praise of Dreams" in *View with a Grain of Sand*, © 1993 by
Wisława Szymborska, English translation by Stranislaw Baranczak and Clare
Cavanagh © 1995 by Harcourt, Inc., reprinted by permission of the publisher.

For information about permission to reproduce selections from this book, write to
Permissions, W. W. Norton & Company, Inc., 500 Fifth Avenue, New York, NY 10110

Manufacturing by the Haddon Craftsmen Inc.
Book design by Brooke Koven
Production manager: Julia Druskin

W. W. Norton & Company, Inc., 500 Fifth Avenue, New York, N.Y. 10110
www.wwnorton.com

W. W. Norton & Company Ltd., Castle House, 75/76 Wells Street, London W1T 3QT

1 2 3 4 5 6 7 8 9 0

FOR MOLLY & KEN

Once all our storytelling was imaginative, was myth and legend and parable and fable, for that is how we told stories to and about each other.

—DORIS LESSING
Walking in the Shade

Sappho was born on the Greek island of Lesbos and flourished circa 600 BCE. One complete song and approximately two hundred fragments of her work remain. On the strength of those fragments—most of which describe erotic love—she has inspired lovers and poets for 2,600 years. The music of her songs has not survived.

Many of the facts of her life are disputed. But her metaphors have never ceased to live in the minds of those who came after. Plato called her the "tenth muse," already predicting the way her fragments would inspire future generations. The most famous of many dubious legends about Sappho describes her jumping off a cliff on the island of Leucas because of unrequited love for a beautiful young ferryman called Phaon.

In my dreams I paint
Like Vermeer van Delft
I speak fluent Greek
And not only with the living.
—WISŁAWA SZYMBORSKA
  "In Praise of Dreams"

arcano è tutto
fuor che il nostro dolor.
All is hidden
except our pain.
—GIACOMO LEOPARDI
  "Ultimo canto di Saffo"

I am become a name:
For always roaming with a hungry heart.
—ALFRED, LORD TENNYSON
  "Ulysses"

Contents

Contents

PROLOGUE

On the Cliff

The future
Will remember us.
—Sappho

WHERE TO BEGIN my story? The minstrels counsel us to begin in the midst of things where excitement is at its peak. Well, then, imagine me, trudging in a whipping, cold wind to the top of the Leucadian cliff where the sanctuary of Apollo still stands. It is said they practiced human sacrifice here in ancient times. The place still has that air, the old odor of blood. All the magic places on earth have that smell.

There are little clumps of stunted pine trees along my way and these golden sandals I wear are no match for the rocks that roll and skitter under my feet as I climb. More than once I have twisted my ankle and fallen. My knees are as raw as when I was a climbing girl.

I have been at sea for many days and, climbing to the top of the white cliff, I still feel the rocking of the ship under my feet.

I am unimaginably old—fifty. Only witches live to be fifty! Good women die in childbirth at seventeen as I nearly did. By fifty I should be dead or a crone—with my dark looks and my somewhat crooked spine—which I have always disguised with capes of multicolored silk. My youth is gone, but my vanity is not. How can I still dream of love at fifty? I must be mad!

My black hair, which used to glisten like wet violets on an ebony altar, is now a steely gray. I have stopped letting my slaves dye it. I do not like to look at my reflection these days. Even the thickest paint cannot disguise the wrinkles. Yet I have my wiles, my perfumes, my potions, my magic salves as much as Aphrodite has hers. I can still make someone love me—if only for a little while.

In the past it was the charm of youth I conjured with. Now it is the charm of fame. And I am skilled with my lips, my hands, my voice. I know the perfumed secrets of the courtesans of Naucratis, the clandestine rituals of the dancing girls of Syracuse, the obscene melodies of the flute girls of Lesbos.

So many stories about me. My legend confused with the legends of Aphrodite. Did I leap to my death for the love of a handsome young ferryman? Did I love women or men? Does love even have a sex? I doubt it. If you are lucky enough to love, who cares what decorative flesh your lover sports? The divine delta, that juicy fig, the powerful phallus, that scepter of state—each is only an aspect of Aphrodite, after all. We are all hermaphrodites at heart—aren't we? The delta is soft as Aphrodite, the phallus stiff as Ares' spear. And no one wears anything for long but a coat of dust. Only the songs of passion linger.

The beautiful ferry boy liked my fame. Like all beautiful ferry boys, he dreamed of being a famous singer. He would make up songs as he rowed. So what if his songs were banal? So what if he borrowed from me and every other minstrel back to Homer? He was beautiful and his voice was black honey. His ringlets were ebony. His eyes were agates. His chin had a beguiling cleft.

The islanders probably think I am desolate because some lover abandoned me. What rot! I toyed with him more than he toyed with me. He was the plaything of a week. My real despair came because Aphrodite withdrew her favors. Aphrodite needs nothing from me. She always has new singers to celebrate her. So what if they are my students, acolytes, and imitators? So what if they learned everything they know from me? The goddess of love favors the young. She always has.

Forever fresh-faced, forever nubile, how can Aphrodite know what it means to lose beauty and youth, inspiration and passion? The gods are cold. They never experience the loss of beauty, so they laugh at our sorrows. I used to love Aphrodite as she loved me. Now I find her love as hard as these rocks beneath my feet. She has turned her beautiful young face away from me.

Age seizes my skin
And turns my hair
From black to white:
My legs no longer carry me
Lightly, nimbly
Dancing like young fawns.
What can I do?
I am not eternal
Though my songs may be.
Can pink-armed Dawn,
Who could not save her love
Erase these harbingers of age?
My youth is gone.
Still I adore
The sun.

Up, up, up. The air gets thinner and the sea churns. From the sea, the cliff looks like a large loaf of barley bread torn off jaggedly—as if by Poseidon's huge blue hand. Around the base of the promontory, the sea roils azure, gray, green, and savage white like the teeth of wild animals. But as you trudge up the cliff with the rock rising before you and your heart pounding in your throat, all you see is the white dust under your feet, the scraggly bushes tilting at the wind, and the little animals darting away with their little lives—lizards, rabbits, feral cats. Often you see the bones of animals and bits of their fur. Nature is not kind.

The boat that brought me here is anchored on the other side of the island. I think of all those I have loved—my difficult daughter, Cleis; my difficult mother, for whom I named her; my honey-voiced *hetairai*; Alcaeus, my first and last love; Praxinoa, my beloved slave-girl, whom I freed to become an amazon; Charaxus, my foolish lovesick brother; Larichus, my other surviving brother, who sold himself into slavery because of a whore's tricks; Eurygius, my dead baby brother, whose tiny hand I almost touched in the Land of the Dead; my late drunken husband Cercylas; my lovely golden Egyptian priestess Isis; Aesop, my philosophy tutor; Necho, the Egyptian pharaoh who set me free to discover my life; Penthesilea and Antiope, my amazon guides; Phaon, my most recent conquest and would-be muse—and nothing seems worth living for. I will grow old and people will turn away from me in disgust. Nobody likes the smell of an old woman—not even other old women.

All my songs have been released into the air. They are sung far and wide—from Lesbos to Egypt, from Syracuse to Ephesus, from Delphi to Epidaurus. The frenzy that predicts the conception of a song will never be mine again. I am barren and naked as this cliff I climb.

When I reach the top of the promontory where the wind flails my cheeks and the gulls shriek and glide, I stand for a moment balanced between life and death. The ghostly rows of white islands in the distance seem to beckon to me from Erebus. I can imagine the icy waters of Acheron lapping at my toes. I tease the gods and myself by leaning, stepping back, and then leaning forward again. My revenge on the gods will be to take command of my own death, to cut the strands the spinners believe only they can cut, to reweave my destiny as if I were Penelope.

But Penelope lived to see her Odysseus once more. Will I ever see my love again? Where is he? Alcaeus of the golden words and golden hair. Alcaeus, who could make me laugh like no one else. (Of course, the one who can make you laugh will also make you cry. That must never be forgotten.) If Alcaeus came back to me now, I would not have to jump! Or am I lying to myself? I know that love is no cure, but rather the disease itself.

I lean over the cliff till the backs of my scraped and bloody knees tingle. I wish I were a kingfisher flying over the flowering foam. My limbs are loosened as if by love and I sway on the edge of the abyss. My beloved students Atthis and Anactoria are with me. My late mother Cleis is here, as is Cleis, my living daughter. She always found a legendary mother to be a heavy load. Perhaps she will be lighter without me. Alcaeus' shieldlike chest rises before my eyes. I will pretend I am jumping into his strong arms! I will conquer death by embracing death.

When a woman is standing on a cliff about to jump into the wine-dark sea, her life does tend to flash before her. But the times get all mixed up. The boat I sailed with Alcaeus when I was sixteen fades imperceptibly into the boat I sailed with Phaon when I was fifty. It is all the same boat on the same ocean. The ocean is called time.

My feet slip, my heart pounds. I start to teeter over the edge. For a moment, I am not so sure about this final leap. I need feathers, I need wax, like Icarus. My knees are weak. My head spins. The dead are waving at the end of a long, torchlit corridor. My father, my grandparents, my mother. I feel myself being carried inexorably back to my childhood on my native isle of Lesbos.

Since at every moment of our lives we stand on the brink of eternity, this is as good a place as any to start the story of my life.

I

Legends of Aphrodite

Brightness. With luck we'll shelter in
The harbor, solid ground
For our storm-tossed ships.
—Sappho

THE LESBOS OF my childhood was an enchanted land. Between Eresus and Mytilene, there were gentle hills with shrines to Aphrodite surrounded by orchards. Not stony and bare like so many other islands, Lesbos was green and mossy; shimmery with silver olive leaves, round with golden grapes. Its arms embraced two deep bays that seemed like lakes but mysteriously opened out into the sea through narrow birth canals. Lesbos was a female island humming in the masculine tumult of the sea.

It was said that our singers were so great because in ages past the severed head of Orpheus had washed up on our shores, still singing. It's as good an explanation as any. The fact that Orpheus could sing after the maenads tore him limb from limb tells you something about the power of song. The singer can be dead and go on singing. Even his lyre went on reverberating after his fingers were scattered among the hills and had turned to dust.

The island was also known as a meeting place between east and west. We were just a ferry ride from the coast of Lydia. Travelers would marvel at the greenness of the hills, the sweetness of the grapes, the excellence of the wine, the fineness of the barley bread, the beauty and the freedom of the women. We were known for treating our women far better than women were treated in Athens or Sparta. But that was hardly well enough!

We were also famed for our festivals in honor of Aphrodite. The Adonia, our midsummer festival, brought all the female singers together to vie in making songs to commemorate the death of Aphrodite's young beloved, Adonis.

The first time my mother took me, I was perhaps ten or eleven. I stood in awe, transported by the festivities, gazing at the women on the roofs of their houses planting seeds that withered in the hot sun. I imagined Aphrodite, whose bare feet make the grass and flowers grow, bent weeping over her beautiful boy, trying to bring him back to life. She cries to her maidens:

> *Beautiful Adonis is dying.*
> *How can we save him?*

But even as she asks, she knows the answer. A gash in his thigh lets life leak out of him. The boar's tusk has opened his leg as if it were a womb and the ground is clotted crimson with his blood. Everywhere the sticky drops fall, fierce red anemones spring up—even out of season.

Tear your garments, maidens, and weep for Adonis! I wanted to sing out. But I was afraid. All those swaying choruses of girls in white seemed to exude music I would never know. Later I realized that I had first felt the thunderbolt of poetry at that festival and I reclaimed those very words and wove them into a song. At every Adonia in the wide world, maidens in white now sing my song to Adonis. *Weep for Adonis, weep!* Oh, I am also weeping as I tell this, but am I weeping for Adonis or for myself?

I loved Aphrodite from the first and steeped myself in her legends. My mother told me that in ancient times her rituals were bloody and cruel, but I only half believed it.

"Foam-footed, born of the waves—this is all a later whitewash of the so-called goddess of love," my mother said. "She was, in olden days, a bloodthirsty goddess, neck ringed with skulls of infants, holding aloft severed phalli still dripping with blood." My fierce mother always delighted in telling such gory details—the more frightening, the better. "She came from much farther east than Cythera," my mother continued, "and her triumph was a triumph of death. Without death, there is no life. The ancients believed this even more passionately than we do. They plowed the furrows with pigs' hearts and placentas to make the corn grow again. They rutted in the seeded trenches with beautiful boys who were later sacrificed to the goddess."

"Why did they sacrifice these boys?" I asked, horrified, thinking of my brothers.

"Because the goddess required it, Sappho. Gods and goddesses demand blind allegiance. At one time even Aphrodite required human sacrifice. She sacrificed her consort of a year just as the gods sacrificed Adonis. Blood flowed into the trenches and the corn grew high. Our soil is rich because of all that blood."

"Would my brothers have been sacrificed if we lived in those times?"

"Best not to ask such questions. Today we are more civilized. Later singers made Aphrodite seem almost blameless. They said she was born when Cronus pitched the testicles of his father, Uranus, into the sea. Thus her legend: that she was born of foam. Never forget that the foam is semen of the gods—a potent brew!"

But I would never forget my mother's words. Beautiful golden Aphrodite had been born out of semen and delighted in the blood of sacrifice. If my mother said so, it must be true.

You CANNOT understand my life unless you understand my special bond with Aphrodite. She was my goddess, the one who tutored and set traps for me, the one who placed temptation in my path. I knew her first when I was changing from a girl into a woman.

I am lying in an orchard. Bees are buzzing through the apple blossoms and I am looking up at the sunlight sifting through the leaves and daydreaming about becoming the greatest singer the world has ever known. The times are treacherous. We have been through a decade of war with the Athenians and peace is slowly returning to the vineyards and the shipping routes of Lesbos. The young people hardly know what the adults are warring about. And some of the adults themselves hardly know. People are concerned with what always concerns them: love, hunger, money, power. Song is last. Except for the singer.

The island of Lesbos is ruled by Pittacus, sage and benevolent tyrant. Or so he has come down through history. I found him neither so benevolent nor so sage. The aristocrats were feuding, as usual, over their rights as landowners and cupbearers. But I'll come to politics later. I am young—too young to be a wife, but not too young to *think* of being a wife—and I am lying in the orchard, dreaming of my destiny. Above me are the gods, making bets:

APHRODITE: *A woman singer can be as great as any man—I'll prove it through my devotee Sappho—lying dreaming in the orchard there.*

ZEUS: *Perhaps she can be great, but I bet she will throw it all away for the love of an unworthy man.*

APHRODITE: *Impossible. You grant her all the gifts of song and I'll prove you wrong. No man could humble her.*

ZEUS: *Any man could.*

APHRODITE: *You could, maybe, but I mean a mortal man—even an irresistible mortal man.*

ZEUS: *Then make him irresistible. You have the power. And I will give her all the gifts. Then we'll see who's right. Pass the nectar.*

To win the bet, Aphrodite went down to earth disguised as an old crone. She walked among the people. Many men scorned her, and women too. She was amused by how stupid mortals were. Could they only recognize the gods when they sat on rainbow-colored thrones and wore purple? It seemed so. Aphrodite searched all of Lesbos for a likely man. Finally she found a handsome young ferryman called Phaon, who plied the waters between Lesbos and the mainland of Lydia. He treated her with courtesy, as though she were beautiful, and refused to let her pay for the ride. He was so solicitous that for a moment she forgot she had turned herself into a crone. Smitten by his beauty and deference, she decided to bestow the gift of eternal youth upon him.

At the end of the ferry crossing, she presented him with an oval alabaster box containing magic salve.

"If you smear this on your lips, your chest, your penis, women will find you irresistible—and you will never grow old," the goddess said.

"Thank you," the ferryman said, suspecting her true identity despite her rags. She flashed her dazzling smile and disappeared.

So I was given gifts of immortal song. And Phaon was given gifts of eternal youth and heartbreaking beauty. And all the while, the gods were laughing.

I divide my childhood into before the war and after. The war caused us to flee Mytilene and move across the island to Eresus, my mother's birthplace. My grandparents were the only stability I knew. I think of my grandmother with her smell of lavender and honey. I remember my grandfather, fierce in battle but with a special tenderness for me—the only granddaughter.

My father, Scamandronymus, was a distant myth, always coming and going surrounded by men with bronze-tipped spears. When the war claimed him, his death and homecoming as cold ashes in a jar forced me to grow up far too quickly. A father who never grows old remains a legend to his daughter. For me he was forever young and handsome, more god to me than father. Whenever I thought of him, I flew back in time and became six years old again. I could see him picking me up in the air and whirling me around. "Little whirlwind," he would call me. Little whirlwind I became.

I knew he loved me better than my brothers. They were his legacy, but I was his delight. Some nights when I was little, I would wander the house in the dark middle of the night, hoping that my footsteps would wake him. (Like most warriors, he was a very light sleeper.) Then, when he woke and came to find me, I would throw my arms around his neck and ask him to carry me into the courtyard. There, beside the gurgling fountain, we had our deliciously private conversations.

What did we talk about? I cannot remember much—except that once I asked him if he loved me better than my mother. Charaxus, Larichus, and Eurygius were younger than I, and boys. I *knew* he loved me more.

"I love you *differently,*" he said. "I love her with the fire of Aphrodite. But you I love with the nourishing love of Demeter, the intoxicating sweetness of Dionysus, and the warmth of the fires of Hestia. The love for a daughter is serene; for her mother it can be a torment."

This gave me pause. "And do you love me better than my brothers?"

"Never will I tell," he said, laughing. But his eyes said yes.

During the years when the grapes were ruined, the barley fields blasted, we lived among slaves and grandparents in my family's villa in the countryside. We were always in fear that the brutal Athenians would come to slaughter all the men and enslave the women and children. I knew from my earliest days that I could go from free to slave in one turn of fortune's wheel. We were told that Athenians tipped their spears with sickness from rotting corpses, that they had no qualms about killing children—even pregnant women. We were told that nothing held them back from slaughter. They lacked our Aeolian sense of the beauty of life. They would stoop to anything for conquest. Or so our elders said. We had no reason to doubt this. Even children feel the uncertainty of war. They may not understand what adults understand, but they feel the insecurity in their very bones.

I remember my brothers Larichus, Charaxus, and even the sickly littlest one Eurygius playing at being soldiers in the pine groves above the sea. I remember how they thrashed each other on the head with wooden swords as if they were Homer's heroes. Little boys love war as much as little girls fear it. I was the oldest and the ringleader. I used to bring them to a cave where we could hide if the Athenians came to enslave us.

I was both intrigued and frightened by the idea of marauding Athenians. Fear and desire warred in me. In the cave we ate bread and cheese, making the crumbs last. I adored my younger brothers and knew I was charged with the responsibility of protecting them. I had no idea how difficult that would become as we grew older.

Larichus was tall and fair, and vain of his beauty. He longed to be

Pittacus' cupbearer, which indeed he would become. Charaxus was short and stocky and always a devil. He devoured every morsel before any of us could eat. He was greedy for bread, for wine—and eventually for women. His greed for women would become his downfall. It almost became mine. And Eurygius? Just saying his name makes tears spring to my eyes.

I always knew that I was cleverer than my brothers. My father knew it too.

"If the time ever comes that your brothers need you, Sappho, promise me that you will put all your cleverness at their disposal."

"I promise," I told him. "Whatever they need they shall have from me." How did he know to tell me this? Had he read the future? Later, when he was dead, I thought so. My father had astonishing powers.

I know now that parents often tell the stronger child to take care of the weaker ones. Does that enforce the weakness of the weak? Sometimes I think so.

THE BOYS PLAYED at war before they knew of women. Women would come soon enough—though not ever for my baby brother Eurygius. He died before he grew to manhood, breaking my mother's heart, even before my father's death broke it again.

SO THE WAR informed our lives—perhaps my mother's most of all. For she lost her love and her youngest child.

"We are told the war is being fought over the Athenians' trading rights on the mainland," my mother used to say. "But I see other motives. In Athens women are little more than slaves, and in Sparta they are only breeding stock. These barbarians are drawn to Lesbos by the beauty and freedom of our lives, but they will try to destroy precisely what they admire and make us more like them. They are in love with chaos and with night. We must fight them with every breath in our bodies."

My mother's hatred of the Athenians later became her excuse for grasping power through men. She wanted to use her beauty before it failed her. I understand the panic of aging women now—though I disdained my mother for it then. Men had always loved her. She was said to look like the round-breasted, jet-haired goddess of the ancient Cretans. With my father gone and four young children to protect, she seized upon the tyrant Pittacus as her life raft and he obliged by floating her. Oh, how contemptuous I was of her wiles! I didn't realize she was saving her own life and mine.

It was true that women in Lesbos had far more freedom than women in Athens. We could go out walking with our slaves, meet each other at the market and at festivals. We were not completely housebound as women were in Athens. And our slaves were often companions and friends to us.

In fact, it was my slave Praxinoa who alerted me to my mother's intention to journey to Mytilene for Pittacus's victory feast—a great symposium such as no one had seen since before the war.

"Then we'll follow her!" I said.

"Sappho, you will get in trouble and so will I."

"I refuse to be left in Eresus, where I know every house and every olive tree," I said. "I long for adventure and if you love me, Prax, you'll go with me!"

"You know I love you. But I fear the punishment. It will fall more upon me than on you."

"I'll protect you," I said.

Praxinoa had been given to me when I was only five and she could refuse me nothing. We were more than slave and mistress. We were friends. And sometimes we were even more than friends. We bathed together, slept together, sheltered from the thunder in each other's arms.

"Your mother will kill you—and me."

"She'll never know, Prax, we'll be so secretive. We'll shadow her to Mytilene. She'll never even guess we're there, I promise you."

Praxinoa looked doubtful. I insisted she go with me—flaunting all the rules by which I had been raised. Even in Lesbos, two girls, free and slave, seldom left the family compound without men and without an entourage.

So we set out from Eresus together on the road to Mytilene. We traveled far enough behind my mother's procession to be invisible to her. Sometimes we even lost sight of the last stragglers in her entourage. We walked and walked in the morning shade, in the noontime sun, in the slanting late sun of the afternoon. It was twilight of the second day before we came anywhere near the villa of Pittacus, and we were exhausted. My mother traveled in a golden litter carried by slaves, but Praxinoa and I had to lean on each other. And sleep on the hillside with the goats.

We were bedraggled and dusty when we arrived. Nor had we bargained on the guards who barred the flower-strewn path to the tyrant's villa.

"Who goes there?" demanded the first guard, a tall Nubian with the face of an Adonis. Five other men, huge, with muscles and terrifying bronze-tipped spears, stood behind him. They glowered and looked down at us.

"I am Sappho, daughter of Cleis and Scamandronymus. We come from Eresus," I said bravely.

"We have no orders to admit you," the first guard said, blocking our way. We were hustled to the side of the road and seized roughly by two of the other guards.

"Sappho—I think we should be going home," Praxinoa whispered, shaking.

"Sir, if you'll unhand us, you'll be rid of us," I said. With that, they let us go and we started to run away from the villa.

"Who are you running from, little one?" It was a tall young man with a yellow beard and the scarred cheeks of a warrior. He was older than I—a mature man of at least twenty-five.

"I wasn't running."

"I know running when I see it," the man said, his eyes twinkling as he teased me. Those eyes looked deep into mine. "I am Alcaeus, who scoffs at war and heroes. I dropped my shield and fled the last battle. For this Pittacus means to banish me. I am supposed to be ashamed. But I defy shame. There's no shame in loving life above death. We are not stupid Spartans, after all. Otherwise, I would be dead. What use would that be to the gods, who will not die themselves?"

"Alcaeus the singer?" I asked the handsome stranger. My heart pounded in excitement just to behold him. I wanted him never to leave my sight!

"The same."

"I know your verses by heart."

"Well, don't just stand there trembling—sing one!"

> Dog days—our throats are dry,
> Our women bleed for love,
> Our parched brains rattle like gourds,
> Our knees creak.
> Douse your voice with wine and water—sing!

"You think to make it better than it was!" he said in his arrogant way. But later, at Pittacus' symposium, I found out that he had truly liked my version better than his own, because he sang it just as I had rephrased it. He'd be damned before he'd admit his admiration for me. Yet I loved him helplessly from the moment I met him. It was his confidence, his self-possession—even his hubris—that so appealed to me. Eros had pierced me through the heart with his sharpest arrow.

Alcaeus looked like the sun god—an aureole of golden hair, a golden beard, and golden hair curling on his chest. He seemed to have power enough to pull a chariot across the sky. How could I know in an instant that our lives were linked? He walked with a swagger that made me long to open my legs to him—virgin though I was. Except for my father and grandfather, I had never even *liked* a man before.

"Come—let's get you two cleaned up!" he said to Praxinoa and me. And then, to the muscular guards: "Let us pass! These two are with me—my serving maids."

The guards jumped aside to let us pass.

The winding path to the villa was carpeted thick with rose petals, shaded by white linen canopies embroidered in gold thread. You could hear flutes playing within and smell the aroma of grilled fish. The perfumes of the women floated on the hot night air. Dozens of magnificently dressed aristocrats could be seen circulating in the inner courtyard with their admirers and sycophants. Some of the women wore gold crowns. Some of the men wore laurel wreaths of gold. We were hardly well enough dressed for such elegant company.

Alcaeus hustled us to the *gynaikeion* or women's quarters and directed the slaves to dress and veil us all in cloth of gold like doe-eyed virgins from the East. Our faces half hidden, our eyes blackened with kohl, we felt strange and exotic. When we emerged, Alcaeus laughed at us.

"You look like temple virgins from Babylon," he said, "ready to earn your dowries from strangers. Now stay close behind me in my shadow, but disappear when I tell you to. Do as I say!"

Following Alcaeus like simpering servants, we gaped at the many splendors of the house. The feasting rooms had couches in semicircles where guests could recline and eat and drink. (In Lesbos, men and women drank together.) The art and artifacts came from all over the known world—golden statues from Lydia encrusted with precious jewels, Egyptian granite statues of cats and gods, protective lions from Babylon. The wall paintings were the most seductive I had ever seen. In truth, they embarrassed me at first. A painted flute girl was playing a man's painted phallus as if it were a musical instrument. Three men were making love to a *hetaira* and to each other. Did nobody notice but me? The guests were so sophisticated that they ambled past these scenes as if they were invisible. From time to time, I glimpsed my beautiful mother, but, distracted by the important guests, she didn't notice me in my disguise.

Tables were piled high with loaves of barley bread, all the fish of the sea—including crabs and eels—and roasted vegetables piled like gifts gleaming with golden olive oil. There were pyramids of fresh fruit surrounded by fields of tangy cheeses and low bowls of burnished bronze honey. Little tables were brought before the feasters, who half reclined while they ate and drank their fill. Too afraid to eat for fear of dropping our veils, too afraid to speak to each other, Praxinoa and I shadowed Alcaeus. Before he went to recline and eat with the others, he stationed us in the courtyard behind a huge *krater* for mixing wine and water so we could not be seen.

"Don't move till I come to get you," he said. Neither of us had any intention of moving. We pulled our veils across our faces and froze.

As we hid in the courtyard, we could marvel at the magnificence of the feast. We could smell the food but not taste it—and in truth we were starving.

"I'm dying of hunger," I whispered to Prax.

"Shhhhhh," she said. "Suck on this." She stuck her finger in my mouth.

The feasting went on and on. It seemed it would never end. Finally, a battalion of household slaves swept the floors of fishbones and torn bits of bread. The spilled oil was wiped from the mosaic floors and hands were washed clean by the beautiful serving girls carrying bowls of water. The serving tables were whisked away. A huge mixing bowl was brought and an endless supply of flower-scented wine was ritually mixed with clear, pure water. Incense was ignited by invisible hands. It drifted heavenward like smoky prayers. Each guest received garlands and chaplets of flowers and dill. There was a pause as all the party wondered who would first break the silence. Competition at a symposium was always fierce, and skill at making songs was considered a sign of the gods' favor—particularly here in Lesbos. Guests were frightened that when their turn came they would be seen as tongue-tied clods.

I had observed many symposia at my parents' house—though none as luxurious as this. Always I held my tongue, wanting to sing but fearing I was too young, too green, and would make a fool of myself.

But Alcaeus was unafraid. He leapt in first and he amazed me by singing his song just as I had sung it. He leered at me flirtatiously as he did—but nobody knew at whom he was leering. Then he recited scurrilous satires about Pittacus and his cohorts, delighting in the outrage of the other guests.

I feared for Alcaeus. He called the company "empty braggarts" almost as if he were daring them—or Pittacus—to strike him down. Standing before this glittering company, he made fun of their clothes, their manners, their hauteur. It was clear that he despised them, and I trembled for him. "*Let us drink!*" he cried:

> *Why do we wait for the lamps?*
> *There is barely an inch of day left!*
> *Zeus gave us wine to forget our sorrows—*

One part water to two of wine.
Pour in a brimful and let the cups jostle
Like courtiers before a king:
Base-born Pittacus, tyrant of our ill-starred city,
All of them loud in his praise!

Pittacus was drunk and merry, but his ears pricked up as he heard Alcaeus slander him, then describe Lesbos as "my poor, suffering home-land." This was open treason at the symposium. The guests trembled to see what the leader would do.

But Pittacus was as wily as Alcaeus was brash. He listened. He absorbed it all thoughtfully without reacting. Was he pretending the slurs and insults did not apply to him? He even joked with his hench-men as if he didn't care about being criticized. But there was little doubt he noted it. He was no fool. He knew a traitor from a sycophant immediately. That was the source of his power.

Then Alcaeus did an even more outrageous thing. Suddenly he dragged me out in front of the whole company and bade me sing then and there as if I were a flute girl or a *hetaira*. With a theatrical flourish, he thrust his precious lyre—his marvelous wooden *kithara*—into my hands.

The audience gasped and tittered. Who was this girl, this veiled exotic "visitor" from the East?

I was terrified—not only because my mother was there and Pittacus, but because I was only a girl, and an uninvited girl at that. My heart was pounding in my throat. Somehow I opened my mouth and my tutelary goddess saved me:

Sacred tortoise shell,
Sing!
And transform yourself
Into a poem!

I began. The unseen muses filled my mouth with words.

Once I began, I found to my surprise that I forgot all about my fear. It was there at Pittacus' symposium that I first felt my power to tame an audience, to feel them beating and breathing in the palm of my hand. Little by little I entranced them, and I entranced myself. When I sang, I became tall. When I sang, I became all the voices in the room. When I sang, the air ignited.

No one had ever told me I was beautiful. My mother was the beautiful one. I was small and dark and exotic. But when I claimed the stage that evening, I found I had the power to seduce the audience into a trance. I could feel their hunger, their lust, their throbbing need, and I could express whatever darkness and distraction they were feeling. It was as if their feelings filled me and I became their mouthpiece.

I still don't remember what I did that night. The music entered me, and with it the spirit of the goddess. I swayed and sang and raised my arms in supplication. I was possessed.

Immortal Aphrodite—
Rainbow-throned
In the shimmering air—
Weaver of webs,
I pray
Do not shackle my heart
With sorrow.
Fly to me
From your father's house
In a whirling of sparrows' wings,
Your chariot descending
Over the dark earth
As you smile
Your sly, immortal smile
Asking whom I desire
So desperately this time,
Asking whom to persuade to love me,
Promising to turn
Indifference to passion
To make her pursue

When she longs to flee . . .
Oh Aphrodite, give what only you can give,
Be my ally, my co-conspirator!

The room fell silent, then burst into mad applause. Where the words and music came from, I don't know—but fueled by the applause, I made up songs for all the guests. Finally, I sang this for Alcaeus:

You came, and you did well to come—
I needed you.
You have torched my heart
And set fire to my breast.

Everyone was shocked and titillated. My reputation—both as a singer and as a scandal—was made!

Alcaeus took me aside after that.

"You little minx," he said, "you are so hungry—you want to devour the world. I know ambition when I see it, but I have never seen it blaze so high in a girl."

"Sir, I don't know what you mean."

"Of course you do. Your belly is full of fire. I know because you're just like me. But don't think to fall in love with me. The truth is—I prefer boys."

"You flatter yourself if you think I am in love with you. I love only Aphrodite—my goddess."

"Then you are in for a difficult life. Devotees of Aphrodite die young."

"According to whom?"

"According to Aphrodite herself!"

"I am not afraid of Aphrodite, or of you, or of anyone!"

"Listen to you! What a funny little thing you are!"

"Is this your way of wooing?"

"Certainly not!" Alcaeus said.

"I think I pique your curiosity because I am so like you."

"Now you flatter yourself!"

"I think you wanted to shock the company and make them whisper about you."

"I think *you* wanted to!"

It was just then that my mother appeared, her face a mask of rage.

"You have disgraced me, yourself, and your entire family. Go home this instant—and take your little slut with you!"

Until that instant, I had not thought of Praxinoa. She would bear the brunt of this. I felt so terrible!

"Please, Mother, forgive me! And know that Praxinoa had no part in this!"

"Go home this instant! I'll deal with both of you later."

BANISHED BACK TO Eresus for my presumption, having to witness dearest Praxinoa beaten, branded, and shorn for her part in the adventure, I was returned to my grandparents' house as a humiliated prisoner. I had hurt my only friend with my thoughtlessness. Carried away by my lust for Alcaeus, I had gotten my darling Prax into terrible trouble. Not only was she branded—a fate she had escaped till now—but she was sent to work in the kitchen as a punishment, and forced like all kitchen slaves to wear a horrid wooden hoop called a gulp-preventer around her neck to keep her from tasting the food. I hated myself for that. What sort of friend was I? I had promised to protect her!

My mother came and went between Eresus and Mytilene with her retinue of slaves. She was so angry with me, she did not speak to me for weeks. The slaves whispered that she was taking comfort with Pittacus, who had sent my father to his certain slaughter. My mother knew that her safety depended on the kindness of power and she would use her beauty to soften it as she always had. Since I did not have her beauty, I could only make myself beautiful with my songs. And now I was condemned to silence.

But my grandparents were inclined to be lenient with me, as grandparents so often are. After a few days, I was able to walk down to the sea by myself. There I had my slaves build me a little tent where I could sing and dream:

> *Wreathe your locks*
> *With sprigs of anise,*
> *Binding the stems*
> *With your soft hands.*
> *For the happy graces*
> *Gaze on what is garlanded*
> *And look away*
> *From the bare heads*
> *Of even the loveliest maidens. . . .*

I was dozing in my tent one moonlit night when suddenly I was awakened by a rough whisper: "We sail for Pyrrha tonight—are you with us, Sappho?"

I woke, rubbed my eyes, looked up at the sunny beard of Alcaeus, and thought I saw a vision of Apollo.

"We sail now or never!"

I had been dreaming of him, and here he was!

"Now," I said and bounded out of bed.

Did I stop to ask why he wanted me if he liked boys so much? Did I think of my mother, of my grandparents, of Praxinoa? Of course not! I was sixteen!

I followed Alcaeus and his men to the harbor, where, after neglecting the proper sacrifices to the gods for fear of attracting attention, we boarded a square-rigged merchant ship to take us from Eresus to Pyrrha. The black ship had two fierce blue eyes emblazoned on its prow as if it could see into the future. I leapt aboard without a backward glance.

If this was dreaded exile, I welcomed it. My real education as a singer had begun.

2

The Groom Comes

Raise high the roof beams!
The groom comes like Ares.
—SAPPHO

WE LIVED IN EXILE in the woods above Pyrrha on the other side of
the island. Alcaeus and his men were plotting to rid Lesbos of Pittacus.
They hated him for his shrewdness and cleverness. Or perhaps they
hated themselves for their own lack of it. The truth was that Pittacus
had outwitted them. They cursed his bloody ways while they themselves plotted bloodily.

Alcaeus had once been allied with Pittacus against the previous
tyrant Myrsilus, but Alcaeus and Pittacus had fallen out—the gods
alone knew how. Pittacus was the sort of leader who switched allegiance according to his own convenience. He had no aristocratic scruples to hold him back. That was the crux of the problem.

At the bottom of the hatred between Alcaeus and Pittacus was a
contest between an old way of life and a new. Noble families like
Alcaeus' and mine used to rule these islands and command these
waters. Since the war with the Athenians, a rougher breed of men was

coming to replace us. Our families were aristocrats who were raised to leisure and the lyre. Warfare was an art to men like my father. Men like Pittacus, on the other hand, were raised to commerce and manipulation. Pittacus would never drop his shield in a display of aristocratic pique like Alcaeus. Pittacus was the consummate politician. He knew how to tell people one thing and do another. He knew how to lie with straight face. He was a passionate orator who believed only in the sound of his own voice. Unencumbered by antique ideas of honor, he was invincible.

ALCAEUS HAD done the unspeakable: mocked Pittacus in witty verses, which were now gleefully repeated all over the island. Ridicule enrages tyrants even if they pretend to be above it.

Pittacus now wanted nothing more than to destroy Alcaeus so he could suppress rebellion and cement his own rule. But he did not dare to kill him for fear the older nobles would mutiny. Exile, therefore, became his solution.

I myself resented Pittacus for taking my mother and reducing her to what I considered whoredom, even if she had sought it herself. The greatest aristocrats of Greece had loved her. Minstrels had sung of her. Artists had painted her. Philosophers had based their theories of love upon her. Noble warriors—my father chief among them—had died for her, and now she was the mistress of a commoner. Even if she was not ashamed of her fall, I was. I was furious on behalf of my poor dead father. Or was I jealous of my mother's effortless success with men? She could both infuriate and reduce me to tears simultaneously. All my feelings about her warred with each other. I loved her so much that I also had to hate her!

"THERE IS only one person who could lead us to Pittacus when he is not surrounded by guards—and that person is your mother."

"You ask too much, Alcaeus, if you ask me to betray my mother."

"I said nothing about betrayal."

"You didn't say betrayal, but you meant it."

"Nonsense. Forget I asked. But remember it is Pittacus who has made you fatherless. He would sacrifice you in a flash. Your mother too. He has no loyalty. He considers loyalty a toy. All he has is a potbelly and a ravenous appetite."

"From what I've seen, all men consider loyalty a toy. My father comes home as ashes in a jar, but I am supposed to be happy that he died gloriously—whatever that means. I hate all these glorious deaths. I hate death. It was my father who decreed I should be raised, not set on a hilltop to die like other girl babies. I loved him. And he adored me. I owe him and my mother loyalty—even if loyalty is no longer the fashion in Lesbos." So I said, but somewhere in my rebellious heart I must have *burnt* to betray my heartbreakingly beautiful mother!

Alcaeus cajoled. He beguiled and nagged. He stroked my cheek, my arm, my thigh. He made up songs for me. At last I agreed to accompany his treacherous expedition. I told myself that I would only watch, not become part of the bloodshed. Even after his reckless behavior at the symposium, I thought I could control Alcaeus. I thought I could control *myself.*

Together in the woods we talked and talked, and the more we talked, the more I fell in love with Alcaeus. I loved his looks, his poetry, his wild talk. Men with eloquent tongues have always swayed me.

"Before the gods, all was shapelessness, chaos, and darkness," he said, "a black-winged being whose unblinking eyes saw everything. Then the wind came, made love to the night, who hatched a silver egg, giving birth to Eros—without Eros there would be no creatures on the face of the earth. . . ."

"But Eros was born of Aphrodite, who himself was born of the sea foam that bubbled when the testicles of Uranus were tossed into the sea by his son, Cronus," I said like a dutiful mother's daughter.

"Believe whichever version you wish, but know that Eros is the root of all. . . . Eros blows through our lives, leaving chaos in its wake . . . and Aphrodite laughs."

"I will not believe any philosophy that dishonors Aphrodite," I said solemnly.

"Aphrodite dishonors herself," Alcaeus laughed. "And so do her devotees."

"Blasphemy!" I protested.

WHEN WE had been together for a time—long enough for me to see Alcaeus ravish beardless sailor boys—I asked innocently, "When did you last make love to a woman?"

"Women are too complex," he said, "too unknowable. Sometimes I long to make love to a woman, and then I think how much *work* it will be to satisfy her. I get *tired* just thinking about it."

Did he say this to shock me or to deny his own attraction to me? Anyway, it did the trick. I left him alone. Sometimes I wished I had the courage to seduce him. I didn't really believe he was as unmoved by me as he claimed.

Maybe I wasn't conventionally pretty, but I knew I had a kind of power. When I had played the lyre at the symposium, people had stared at me as if I were a great beauty. I would catch Alcaeus staring at me from time to time. Then he'd remember that he was supposed to be indifferent to me and he'd turn away. He seemed to be torn between fascination and derision. He was always trying to impress me with how worldly he was and how many exotic lovers he had conquered.

"I have been to Naucratis in Egypt, the city of the Greek traders in the Nile Delta where Lesbian wine is traded," he began. "I have been with Egyptian prostitutes who are skilled at beguiling the Greeks with their mouths and hands. In Babylon, I have seen the Temple of Ishtar, where women copulate with strangers for the glory of the goddess, where they set up little tents or huts in the precincts of the temple and remain for weeks at a time to earn their dowries. *There is healing in a woman's delta,* the Babylonians believe."

"Are you saying this to shock me?" I asked. "Because if you are, I can match you obscenity for obscenity. *Delta, daleth, kusthos, sacred space, zone of Aphrodite, the triangle of our beginnings, the source of all our blessings, the three-cornered passage to our end.* There! You are not the only learned sensualist on this island!"

Alcaeus ignored me and went on with his exotic descriptions of foreign travel. "Not for nothing do the Egyptians smear blood on doorways to symbolize birth and death. They worship the divine delta, that all-seeing eye. The Babylonians do the same."

"You seem quite fascinated yourself," I said. "Strange that you sought all these exotic women out if you really prefer boys," I said teasingly. This encouraged him to try to shock me even more.

"All manner of sickly men would come to try their luck with these temple virgins. I watched all this and took the most beautiful women as my partners, but I always returned to my pretty boys with a great sense of relief."

"I wish *I* were a boy," I said, "so I could experience these things."

And I meant it. I *did* want to devour the world and all its pleasures as Alcaeus immediately had known. But maybe I was also thinking that if I were a boy, he'd make love to me.

I TRIED out this theory on the night before we set sail on our murderous expedition. We found ourselves alone in an olive grove in beautiful Pyrrha. The hills embraced us with their calming green. The olive leaves fluttered their small silver flags. I had made my obeisance to Aphrodite, had burnt incense heavenward, had sung hymns of my own making to my tutelary goddess. Then I dressed myself as a shepherd boy just for the fun of it.

Alcaeus watched all this with a smirk upon his face. He openly laughed at both my devotions and my disguise. Then he challenged me.

"You know, little whirlwind, there is only one way to honor Aphrodite truly."

"How?"

"I cannot tell, I must *show* you."

I looked at him in childish perplexity. Then he pulled me under the silvery trees.

"Here in Aphrodite's grove, we must do Aphrodite's bidding," he said.

I jumped back.

"Are you *afraid* of your own goddess? You'll never become a singer that way," he teased.

I felt my heart race. My knees began to knock. My delta grew wet.

"Are you challenging me to grant you the gift of my virginity?" I was always too direct, too incapable of artifice.

"What a quaint way to say it!" Alcaeus said with a laugh, making me blush furiously.

"I am ready," I said bravely, closing my eyes and opening my arms, "but I thought you liked boys!"

"Aren't *you* a boy? You *look* like a boy! After all, boys are less trouble in the act—and afterward. They are less apt to whine and cling, less apt to try to trap you forever. Poor darling, you're shaking," Alcaeus said, wrapping his arms around me.

"I'm ready," I trembled.

"Let's lie under these tender green branches and drink a little wine and water. We don't have to do anything but hold each other," he said. (They always say that.)

His arms enfolded me. His heart thundered against mine. We stared into each other's eyes as if they were torches lighting a pitch-black room. His lips found my lips. The inside of my mouth and the inside of his became one. His huge legs wrapped around my tiny waist. The inside and the outside of my body became one.

Aphrodite smiled down on us and blew her hot breath into all the orifices of our bodies. What was hard and strong opened into what was soft and warm. We moved together like dolphins playing in the waves, tail chasing tail, head nuzzling head. Then we became like horse and rider. There was no beginning of each other and no ending. We were one animal, one demigod, with four legs and two pairs of wings.

So *this* was the thunder of Pegasus—poetry's racehorse! So this was where Aphrodite's softness and the flinty arrows of her devilish son became one. Soft became hard, hard soft, outside in, inside out.

Time vanished. Space collapsed. The stars shone in the day sky. If we stayed together, the sun would never be quenched at night. We would make light with the heat of our bodies and spin off another universe between us. Our loving was that powerful.

At last, under a dawn sky of red and violet, we staggered back to the boat from our idyll in the olive grove. My insides were sore from Alcaeus' rough love. I wanted to feel sore forever. The sailors stared at me and smirked as if they knew.

"My darling boy," Alcaeus joked. "I'd almost think you were a *girl!*"

THE NEXT NIGHT, we slept aboard ship but did not touch. The wind whipped and whistled in the rigging and the oars slammed against the side of the boat. Several of them floated away. Two men were lost off the bowsprit as if mythical monsters were nearby and the whole sea had turned into Scylla and Charybdis. In the shrieking of the wind, in the screeching and tearing of the ropes, the gods were heard:

"*Alcaeus is your first true love,*" Aphrodite sang in the voice of the wind, "*but he doesn't know it yet.*"

"Then come and guide him," I whispered.

"*When the time is right,*" she said. "*Love you as I do, I cannot hurry fate. The spinners spin as slowly as they will.*"

"Unfair Aphrodite!"

"*I have been called unfair before,*" she laughed and disappeared.

> Aphrodite has everything,
> Can renew her virginity
> With one immersion in the sea.
> What can I give her?

All night the ropes of the ship cried like skinned cats. All night the stars hid behind clouds. The boat rocked precipitously. We were sorry we had not beached our boat and slept ashore in the shelter of the great sail.

The next morning, it was improbably clear and bright. Dawn's fingertips touched our unfurling sails with rose. We sailed around the island to Mytilene with three of Alcaeus' men as a practice run. Two would go ashore with him to do the bloody deed. Another and I would remain to watch the ship. We were to seek harbor in a hidden inlet near Hiera, waiting for word from them. But before we reached Hiera, when we were hugging the shore between the Temple of Dionysus at Brisa and the beginning of the Gulf of Hiera, a black ship fitted with a great black sail began following us.

At first Alcaeus dismissed this as coincidence, but soon it became clear that we were its quarry and it was swifter than we.

A race began along the rocky coast. As the black boat came closer, we saw that the sailors wore satyr masks, shields with the emblem of Pittacus, and brandished bronze-tipped spears.

"Pirates!" was Alcaeus' first thought, but these were no ordinary pirates. Pittacus had sent the boat. Politics played a part in this piracy. I prayed to Aphrodite.

"You are praying to the wrong goddess," Alcaeus barked. "She doesn't give a damn about this sort of thing. Try Athena. She's a warrior! She's the one who rescued Odysseus!"

Of course he would joke grimly at a time like this.

For a while it seemed that, using only our sail, we could outrun the black ship before the wind. Alcaeus' sailor boys were good, but not good enough. We had lost too many oars and the black ship had oars aplenty and slaves to man them. The waves were rough and rose on either side. Alcaeus had sung of all this in his songs.

Look before you sail, he had famously sung, *once at sea, you have to ride what comes*. This was not the time to remind him of his prophecy.

I remember the swell of the waves, the slop of seawater over the sides, and our boat seeming to go backward, as in a nightmare. The black boat was irrevocably gaining on us. The smells of wet wood, pitch pine, and the sea always bring back those terrifying moments. The enemy boat came out of the spray with its fierce eyes staring and its sea-worn battering ram like the tusk of a mythical beast. It approached, gathering speed from its oars, until its bowsprit was poised to pierce our virgin hull. The satyrs crouched on deck, ready to leap aboard our ship and take us.

"Jump!" Alcaeus commanded as the satyrs from the black ship rushed to capture him. I looked at him one last time, tears blinding me. But I could still blurrily see his beloved face. I jumped overboard and began to swim as if furies were behind me.

"We'll meet again," he screamed, "in this world or the next!"

I swam like mad for shore while my breath still held.

Because I had loved him but never wholly possessed him, he stayed in my mind like a myth through subsequent adventures. When we met again, we were both older, but were we any wiser?

SHIPWRECKED, PARTED from Alcaeus, swimming for dear life to the shore of my green island, I found myself unmoored from time. I became weary, exhausted. My breath felt as if it would fail me. Then, just as I thought I was going down, a sharp nudge in my buttocks awakened me and I looked down to find myself buoyed by dolphins. These playful creatures leapt and dove around me, lifting me up when I was most exhausted. They ferried me to shore on a deserted coast and left me there to brave the elements.

A search party had been sent out for me, led by my grandfather, but of course I did not know this at the time. I lived on the sandy coast for days, until my lips were parched and I was so hungry I took to eating crabs that I caught and cracked open. My chiton torn into rags, my skin burned from the sun, I hardly looked like a woman at all—let alone the boy I was masquerading as—but rather like a strange human crab scuttling along the beach.

I came to know why our ancestors worshiped Poseidon, god of the sea-blue mane, above all other gods. The sea is the source of life for an island people. But it is even more capricious than golden Aphrodite who was born from it, bearing its wildness. The ocean's roar nearly convinced me to abandon Aphrodite for Poseidon. Perhaps it was because I wavered in my fidelity to the goddess that she cursed me. Aphrodite is a goddess who tolerates no disloyalty. Actually, that is one of the great characteristics of the gods—fierce jealousy of each other. The gods are babies with the appetites of grown men and women. That's why they torment us so.

I do not know how long I lived on that timeless beach dreaming of Alcaeus to keep myself alive. Day gave way to night, and night to day. I built a hut for myself and learned to catch fish in my bare hands. I wove leaves for my hat and rushes for my bed. After fear left me, I was proud that I could endure this life. And then I was saved yet again. My grandfather arrived with his men in a small boat, expecting to find me dead. They had been circling the seas in search of me, and fear for my fate had made my grandfather furious instead of tender.

"Pittacus would have you killed for conspiring with Alcaeus," he screamed. "You are a little fool who hurts no one but herself and her family. But I have saved you. I have made a pact with Pittacus to marry you off instead. . . . I have found this certain Cercylas of Andros who seeks a wife of noble family. He has agreed to take you despite your rebellious nature."

"Despite my rebellious nature!" I spat. "Are you my grandfather or my jailer?"

My grandfather's brow lowered in ferocity. Whatever pity he might have shown me was now undone. We sailed back to Eresus, without exchanging a word.

So I was to be married to someone ugly but sufficiently rich to crush my spirit. It was thought that weaving and raising children would substitute for the gifts of the muses, and that, buried in domesticity, I would have no time for political plots or love affairs. Or singing.

Marriage and death were not so dissimilar in those days. When I look back on my marriage procession, I think that it might as well have been a funeral march. My mother, my grandparents, my brothers, and I journeying yet again from Eresus to Mytilene, where I was to be given to the ancient Cercylas.

Strangely, I was less angry with my grandfather than I was with my mother for abandoning me to this ghastly marriage. How could she conspire in exiling her only daughter?

I had demanded this of her as she bedecked me for my marriage—a necklace of golden grapes and quinces, matching earrings that dangled to my shoulders, a golden diadem that held my lustrous hair.

"I would rather you were married than dead, Sappho."

"I see little difference between the two states."

"Because you are young and think you know everything. But husbands can die and liberate you."

"That's something to look forward to."

"And you have other gifts that can free you. The way you held the audience at that symposium was extraordinary. Underneath my fury I was proud. It reminded me that when I was pregnant with you, a priestess made a prophecy—that you would be known in times to come."

"Now you tell me!"

CERCYLAS THE hideous was fifty if he was a day, and he wore a girdle to bind his paunch, which otherwise would have wobbled. His hair was sparse and draped over his baldness, fooling nobody. He smelled strongly of perfume and sweat. And wine. Like a barbarian, he loved to drink his wine unmixed with water.

He also seemed to be the sort of man who rehearsed his jokes before a symposium and then claimed they came to him at the minute as gifts of the gods. (This turned out to be true!) When, at the wedding ceremony, he gravely said to my grandfather, "I take this woman for the ploughing of legitimate children," my brothers and I could not help but giggle. By the time the guests pelted us with nuts and fruit, I was still terrified of the fate to which I'd committed myself. I thought of Alcaeus—our passionate lovemaking and equally passionate arguments—and I looked at Cercylas as in a nightmare.

The feasting went on and on. It began at noon and continued until midnight. The wine from my grandfather's vineyards flowed like water. The food was rich and abundant—breads, fish, fowl, meats, sweets of every description. There was singing and dancing, the procession to Cercylas' house, more singing and dancing, more heaps of delicacies.

At last, at midnight, the horrible time had come. Choruses of maidens singing sweet epithalamia I myself had written accompanied us to the bridal chamber. Cercylas was by then so drunk, he reeled and staggered. I steeled myself to the pain of allowing Cercylas into that sanctuary where only Alcaeus had lovingly trespassed before.

I ate the wedding quince and Cercylas removed my girdle as ritual dictated. The maidens choired. I begged for another chorus. They choired again. Cercylas' eyes began to close.

"Sing again!" I begged the maidens.

"Damn you, Sappho," Cercylas raged, "I will have your maidenhead!"

What maidenhead? I thought.

At last we were left alone. Cercylas stripped off his clothes and appeared in all his hideousness. Taking a pomegranate from the many fruits arranged in a bowl at the foot of the bed, he pressed six red seeds into the bridal sheet and hung it up in the window for all to see. Then he collapsed in a drunken swoon.

> *Raise high the roof beams!*
> *The groom comes like Ares,*
> *Towering above mortals*
> *As the poets of Lesbos*
> *Tower over all the others!*
> *Lucky bridegroom!*
> *We drink your health!*

I lay awake in bed and pondered my fate as Cercylas snored. I felt like Persephone transported to the Land of the Dead to be the bride of Hades. I wept until I soaked my bed with tears. I thought of Alcaeus somewhere far away, banished for his treachery.

Then I slept and Aphrodite spoke to me in a dream.

She was dressed as a bride herself and was singing the epithalamium I'd written.

Raise high the roof beams! she sang, smiling wickedly. *The groom comes like Ares. . . .*

I cried and cried inconsolably even in the dream.

"*Don't cry, my little Sappho,*" she said, like a loving mother calming an infant. "*A husband is merely a means of transport between childhood and woman-hood. If it is love you want, passion you want, that always happens outside the bridal bed. . . . The bridal bed is where you sleep, but you will find your lovers everywhere— on beaches, in palaces, in apple groves, olive groves, under the shining moon. . . . It will be full for you—full of lovers, full of love, full of inspiration!*"

"But I only want Alcaeus!"

"*He is not the only man on earth. Come, now, Sappho—I have had many* men—*Ares, Adonis, so many others—I have forgotten their names, women too. Life is meant for pleasure. There is more to life than your first man. . . . Your life is just beginning, not ending. It will be rich and full . . . lucky bride! You will be free and full of life!*" Then she drifted off and I slept like the tired child I was.

I have only had one husband, so I have to judge all husbands by him. The truth is he was not an evil man. He was only weak and common and a drunk. He believed that a wife should stay indoors and tend to the looms and the slaves and the larder—except on religious holidays. If you wonder why women were so damned religious in those days, know that the festivals were the only times we got out of the house! I figured pretty quickly that my songs in honor of Aphrodite were my tickets to freedom. Once I grew famous enough to have my presence demanded at festivals, weddings, distant rituals to foreign gods, Cercylas could not hold me back. He was clever enough to know that my renown reflected glory on him. Besides, I left him alone with his dearest love—the wine he drank and drank until he fell headfirst into a delirium.

3

Walking Through the Fire

Do I still long for my virginity?
—SAPPHO

IF MARRIAGE WAS death, then Syracuse was reincarnation: a city without peer in the greater Greek world, a city of festivals and temples, of wealthy aristocrats, wretched slaves, mean hovels, and shining palaces.

Syracuse stood on the eastern coast of the isle of Trinacria, where Odysseus blinded the savage cyclops and incurred the everlasting wrath of Poseidon. With that one sharp stick in the eye of Polyphemus, Odysseus nearly doomed himself to eternal wandering. But fortune found him again and he was able to return to Ithaca and find his family still alive and waiting. Even his ancient dog Argos waited until Odysseus returned home before he expired with old age. Maybe the gods would take pity on me as they had on Odysseus. I could only pray for that as I sailed far from home to beautiful Syracuse.

Syracuse was founded by the Corinthians, who worshiped Artemis. It was in Syracuse that virgin Artemis changed Arethusa into a rushing stream of water so that she could escape the advances of Alpheus, the lecherous river god. Arethusa's spring still gushed into a fountain here, and a famous temple to Artemis had stood in Syracuse from the beginnings of time. A temple of Athena faced the Great Harbor, while a Temple of Apollo faced the Little Harbor. There were also two huge amphitheaters on the mainland, beyond the agora.

The oldest sections of the city jutted out into the dark blue sea on a peninsula connected to the mainland by a narrow strip of land. The major palaces were here. Cercylas established our house in the very center of this quarter. We also had a farm in the countryside that provided us with all the meat, cheese, and fruit we required. Trinacria was a land even more bountiful and green than Lesbos—which did not mean I was not often hideously homesick. I dreamed myself back in Lesbos almost every night. And I dreamed of Alcaeus and wondered what had become of him. I did not have to wait long. I had only been in Syracuse a few months when a letter from Alcaeus reached me.

> *My funny little Sappho—*
>
> *What shall I do without your laughter? What shall I do without your love songs? I am alive—just barely—though my heart is empty without you. We were caught by Pittacus, detained for months while he tried to cook up the most desperate charges against us. Several of my men were tortured brutally, their naked bodies dragged over carding combs. Thank the gods you were no longer with us. Pittacus could not decide what to do with me. He couldn't bring himself to kill me and he couldn't let me remain in Lesbos, so he banished me to Lydia, where I find myself most amused at court. Don't be jealous, little one, but the slave-boys here are even more delicious than in Lesbos—boys with tawny pricks that soar like birds, boys who cannot wait to pleasure a notorious warrior like me. And yet I think always of Sappho—violet-haired, holy, honey-smiling Sappho. I wish to say something to you, but shame prevents me. I have heard you are married off to an old buffoon. If I am responsible, forgive me. I shall find a way to come to you.*
>
> *Trust in our love!*
>
> *Alcaeus*

I hid the letter, written on the finest Egyptian papyrus, among my most treasured possessions—my golden necklace of quinces, my dangling golden earrings with the trembling flowers and leaves, my scrolls of favorite poems, my *kithara*. In the days that followed, I was to read the papyrus so many times I smudged it with my eager fingertips. I touched it with my lips thinking my lips were touching his. In a way, they were.

What is more personal than a letter written by a hand you love? Words, breath, kisses. Papyrus can transmit all these. Alcaeus' scrawled letters kept me alive. Kissing the papyrus was almost like kissing him!

This is the mystery of words. Simple things made of reed and plant fibers, and yet they reproduce our heartbeats and our breath. Mouthfuls of air trapped in timelessness. The miracle of writing!

I had learned to make letters on clumsy wax-covered wooden tablets when I was a child. Then, when I was older, I was allowed animal skins to write on. They always betrayed the bloody odor of their origins. Papyrus was so much purer. I loved the feel of chaste papyrus sheets on which you could spill your heart's fresh blood!

As long as Alcaeus was teasing me about boys, I knew he still loved me. Boys were his defense against the fear he felt at giving all his love. I could play this game as well as he. And so I took a reed in hand and I began:

I am greener than grass and I seem to be a little short of dying . . .

Then I began to write to him about my life in Syracuse, but whatever I wrote seemed somehow not good enough. How could I intrigue and seduce him from this distance? He was surrounded by the amusements of a splendid court and I was living with an old buffoon! I wrote, but judged myself so harshly I could send nothing. And papyrus was not cheap! I covered the sheets with my words, then threw them in the fire, cursing myself for my profligacy. I wanted to woo Alcaeus with my words, but something held me back. What was I afraid of? If I gave my whole heart to him, perhaps I would never get it back.

And yet what use is having a heart if you do not share it? In this futile way, my thoughts went around and around like puppies chasing their tails. I wrote my shapely words, then burnt them. Such was the torment of my mind.

MY GRANDFATHER and Cercylas had bargained with Pittacus to bring me here—as far from Alcaeus and his political plotters as they could. Or so they thought. How could I outwit them all if I was so afraid to write to Alcaeus?

Having equipped me with two houses, slaves, litters of gold, looms, Cercylas went about his business growing richer. Because of my dowry, he now had Lesbian wine to trade with as well as his ships. He and my grandfather had made a good business putting the family's wine business together with Cercylas' ships. Thanks to me! Sold off in marriage to an old sot so all could prosper! Woman's fate! My hunch was that Pittacus was getting rich on my fate as well.

> *Say what you will—*
> *Gold is the child of Zeus.*
> *Neither worms nor moths eat gold.*
> *It is much stronger*
> *Than the heart*
> *Of a man.*

I was to learn early that men can agree on very little but using women to cement their alliances and enrich themselves. Or using them as they used Helen—as excuses to fight wars.

IF I HAD judged by my wedding night that I would never be bothered by my husband, I judged wrong. Usually he was too soaked in wine to bother me at night and I happily departed for my own quarters. But some mornings, he awakened in a fit of passion and came after me. Usually I got away, but on one occasion he *almost* managed to make love to me.

He smelled of fish and onions—and his breath was sour from the wine of the night before. He groped between my legs, pawed my breasts, and released his white force before he had a chance to enter me. Given the wobbly condition of his equipment, it was unlikely the marriage would ever be consummated—not that I cared.

Praxinoa had been restored to me before my departure for Syracuse and she had almost forgiven me for the troubles I'd caused her. When I discovered I was pregnant, she tried to forgive me entirely.

"A baby! What fun we'll have with your baby, Sappho."

"Almost as much fun as I had making it with Alcaeus!"

"*Alcaeus!*" Prax exclaimed.

"Surely you don't think that old sot Cercylas was—or is—capable."

"But what will he think?"

"Cercylas is usually so drunk that he hardly remembers the night before. I'm sure he'll be happy to take credit for any child I may bear." I said this with great bravado, but I had my own misgivings. I needn't have. It was true that Cercylas never remembered anything in the morning.

"What a great lover you are!" I had said on several mornings, and he seemed to believe me. Was it possible men were so easy to fool? I asked Prax about this.

"Am I crazy, Prax, or can any husband be fooled with flattery?"

"You're not crazy. They believe what they want to believe and they hear what they want to hear. I know; after all, a slave is privy to everything. And I've learned the self-delusion of husbands is extraordinary."

"I love you, Prax," I said.

"I know you do. But your love is careless."

"Then you still have not forgiven me."

"I know you mean well," Praxinoa said, "but you forget that we are not the same. You get away with things I never could chance."

I looked at the angry red brand on Praxinoa's forehead and I knew she was right. Praxinoa's bouncy black curls were reduced to stubble on her skull. Her huge brown eyes were sad.

"I brought you a wedding gift," she said.

"What is it, Prax? Tell me!"

"Something every wife needs." From under her creamy linen chiton, she produced a cunningly made leather dildo, an *olisbos* three times the size of anything Cercylas had.

"The groom comes like Ares," she said, laughing.

"We'll use it together!" I said.

"Only you'll be dreaming of beautiful Alcaeus," Praxinoa said, "and I'll be thinking only of you."

WHEN WE were girls, Praxinoa and I had discovered pleasure together and had shared it in total innocence. We explored each other like little kittens playing and grooming. Many nights we fell asleep contented in each other's arms.

Without Praxinoa, I would have been lost; she was my only friend from home. For the longest time, I had no word from my mother, who had abandoned me to this horrible marriage. I sorely missed my brothers, who had been my playmates and protectors throughout my whole childhood. I was still not much older than a child—even though, as a married woman, I was expected to put my toys away. And I did—all except my *olisbos*!

Living with Cercylas was like sharing space with a sponge. Fortunately, I was rich enough now to greatly embellish the women's quarters on the upper levels of my town and country houses, to give Praxinoa and me the privacy we craved. But I certainly came to know why women so dreaded marriage. It was not only leaving the warmth of home and going away with a virtual stranger, but also having to completely make a life in an unfamiliar place. Without a slave who had tended and loved me from childhood, I would have been utterly friendless.

It turned out that Cercylas was thrilled to take the credit for the baby. He remembered nothing about our wedding night or any subsequent nights. He probably would have been amazed to discover that he'd never succeeded in doing the deed, and I had no intention of enlightening him. Cercylas walked through his life in a fog, and that was useful to me. Let him claim paternity if it would enrich the child.

MEANWHILE, ZEUS and his daughter were lounging on a cloud, looking down:

ZEUS: *Where are you going with this twisted love story? This was not our bet at all. If Sappho has only to choose between a drunken old husband with a paunch and a poet who prefers boys, she's hardly typical of all mortal women.*

APHRODITE: *That's what you think! Besides, I'm only warming up. The girl is young. She hasn't experienced many of the delights of Eros except with Alcaeus and Praxinoa, and now with her* olisbos—*which doesn't really count. I know what I'm doing. Wait.*

ZEUS: *Maybe she needs* me. *I could transform myself into a beautiful young maiden and have my way with her.*

APHRODITE: *Don't you dare.*

ZEUS: *Just to spice up the story. At this point we need a rape or a war. A rape* and *a war! Let's go!*

APHRODITE: *Male madness is a terrible thing.*

ZEUS: *Where would you be without it?*

My reputation as a singer had preceded me from that fateful symposium at Lesbos. In Syracuse I found myself often asked to perform my hymn to Aphrodite at festivals and weddings. My songs had already become my means of escape. Every time I was asked to perform, I nursed the hope that I would encounter Alcaeus at some symposium. Alas, he was never there!

If my marriage had been better, would I have performed as much or composed as many songs? Would I have been as eager to travel? For I performed throughout my pregnancy and often I felt I carried a muse inside me. I first knew my daughter as a glowing presence under my navel that inspired song. She gave me authority, turning me from Persephone into Demeter, from maiden to mother, from girl to woman.

A priestess named Jezebel of Motya had attended a lavish symposium Cercylas and I had hosted in Syracuse. There I had again sung in honor of Aphrodite. Jezebel, who knew Greek and many other languages, was much taken with my songs and asked me if I would honor her god Baal with my performance.

"Gods cannot so easily be traded," I told her. "Aphrodite is my tutelary goddess."

"True," she said, "but you have yet to see the power of Baal."

Jezebel was tall, had ringlets of red hair, and wore only purple embellished with shimmering gold. She had invited me to visit her native island Motya and I had readily accepted the invitation in order to get away from Cercylas. Perhaps I would meet Alcaeus there!

Motya lay around the coast from Syracuse, about two days' sail westward. It was an island famous for its salt flats, its manufacture of purple dyes from murex shells, and its strange religious customs. This island had been settled in ancient times by small, wiry desert nomads from Canaan who were known as merchants, seafarers, explorers. It was said that they still worshiped Baal in a mysterious rite called "Walking Through the Fire."

The Canaanites were cousins to that desert tribe who believed in a single god. Like the Egyptians under Akhenaton, they had succumbed to the madness of reducing their pantheon to only one.

One god? Why have *one* god when only a plethora of gods can fill the multifarious needs of human beings? The gods are so disinterested in human affairs that they wander off among the rosy clouds of Olympus, ignoring us and pursuing their own pleasures. We must tempt them with the sweet smoke of sacrifice, sing songs to them, weave golden garments for them—and still they care little if we live or die. Our petty fears strike them as absurd. And who can blame them? They are immortal. We are not. We pass before their all-seeing eyes like mayflies. We are little more than a distraction to them.

Jezebel's island people traded with the Carthaginians and also had close ties with the Phoenicians. They were said to be savage and wild. I could hardly wait to meet them! All I had to hear was the rumor of ancient rites and my curiosity blazed.

ACCOMPANIED BY Praxinoa, several manservants, and a captain, I set sail for Motya when I was almost six months pregnant. The boat rocked; seasickness claimed me, but the prospect of bizarre religious festivals was always tantalizing. The weather was not good, and, beating against the wind, it took us more than a week to make a passage that normally took two days.

We arrived at sunset on the seventh day and found Motya strange and beautiful. It had enormous windmills whose sails glowed orange and red in the flames of the setting sun. We dropped anchor and made our way by cart across the stony causeway that connected Motya to the mainland. We saw the huge salt flats that gave the island its riches, and we smelled the rotting murex shells from which purple dye had been extracted. These two industries had made the Motyans rich. The whole known world yearned for purple dye to make royal garments and depended on salt to preserve fish. The Motyans fervently believed that only sacrificing to their god Baal had made all this plenty possible.

We were taken to Jezebel's house to refresh ourselves and prepare for the fire ritual the following morning.

"I promise you will be inspired to sing when you see how we honor Baal," Jezebel raved.

That night we purified ourselves with ritual baths. We drank only water. Our stomachs grumbled, but our hearts were pure.

Early the next morning, Jezebel and her attendants led us to the home of a family who had earned the supreme honor of sacrificing their firstborn.

"Do you always sacrifice the firstborn?" I asked in horror, "or only at times of trouble?"

"We do it to *prevent* trouble. Our god is good to us because we feed him only the freshest flesh."

Outside the house of the chosen family, a procession was forming. People had been gathering since daybreak, carrying musical instruments—mostly drums and bells—and wearing gorgeous rainbow-colored robes. As the sun rose over the sea, they beat their drums and rang their bells to summon the parents out of their palace by the sea.

"How do they choose the family?" I whispered to Jezebel.

"They must be noble, newly married, about to have a child."

Eventually the mother appeared, carrying an infant of not more than a month old. It kicked and cried as if it knew its fate. The mother comforted the child by putting it to her breast. She nursed the babe continually as the procession snaked toward the tophet at the edge of the city. The crowd was wild and disorderly, playing loud instruments.

"To drown out the screams of the child," Jezebel said.

As the procession swelled with participants, the drums sounded louder and louder.

"How do the mother and father bear it?" I asked.

"With utter calm or the god will not be pleased."

When the procession arrived at the sacrificial area, the celebrants all began to kneel down before a brazen image of the deity. It was a human form with a bull's head and outstretched human arms. In the belly of the god, priests were stoking a blazing charcoal fire.

Jezebel then went forward and invoked Baal with these words:

> We bring a babe to purify in fire—
> Fire which is life and death and change.
> Grant him immortality as you grant
> Immortality to our storied city.

She then presented each parent with a clay mask wearing a hideous grin. Both mother and father wore one. I imagined myself and Alcaeus standing there, about to sacrifice our firstborn child, and I nearly swooned. A tiny mask was also proffered for the baby, who tried to push it away with his little hands. There were endless prayers and supplications during which the baby screamed and screamed. I couldn't bear to watch or hear. I covered my eyes and ears. When I peeked through my latticed fingers, the babe had gone shrieking into the arms of the red-hot god. My empty stomach lurched.

Inside me, I felt Cleis kick for the first time. The sky seemed to tip into the sea and my knees grew weak. Though my stomach was empty, I retched. Until that moment, the child within me was no more than a notion, no more than a dream. Now it was a real baby and I was its mother. I imagined giving birth, only to relinquish the baby to the flames.

I leaned on Praxinoa, my head spinning. "Why did you let me come?" I asked her.

"How could I stop you?" she said. "Whenever you have a chance to get away from Cercylas, you can't resist!"

"Next time, I will resist," I said.

"You say that now," said Praxinoa, "but I know you."

The image of a baby devoured by flames repeated itself over and over in my head. My head itself felt as if it were on fire. Now the baby in my belly seemed to be kicking my heart.

"Feel!" I said to Praxinoa, bringing her hand to my belly.

Praxinoa felt my belly, felt the tiny foot kicking. A tear came to her eye.

"Oh, Sappho!" she said.

"I will tell you a secret," Jezebel said, "if it will make you feel better. The parents have substituted a slave-child captured in a raid on the mainland. All things are made of fire and return to fire. The flames will only purify this child. It is an honor to be fed to Baal."

"Slaves can work for you," Praxinoa said, "but they shouldn't have to die for you." She looked at Jezebel with considerable ferocity.

"The universe is made of fire and returns to fire," Jezebel said, "so it is better not to grow too attached to living things."

"Is that true for everyone—or only slaves?" Praxinoa asked defiantly.

"Does she always express herself with so much audacity?" Jezebel asked. "I would not accept it if I were you."

"Praxinoa is free to express whatever she feels," I told Jezebel.

"Then beware," said Jezebel, "that you are not nurturing an asp in your own bosom."

I decided to let that warning pass without comment.

"I am afraid your god does not inspire me," I said later.

"I would say that more quietly if I were you," Jezebel said. "He hears everything and he speaks in flame."

"I cannot love a god who demands the incineration of infants."

"Do you expect to make no sacrifice for your god?"

"I honor Aphrodite with song, with sweet-smelling incense and chaplets of herbs, but she never demands blood."

"You say that now," said Jezebel. "Perhaps you have not seen her in all her aspects. In my experience gods are capricious and need appeasing.

For centuries we sacrificed our own babies. Then we began to substitute slave-babies and our island continued to prosper, but perhaps my kinsmen are fooling themselves. Baal knows everything. Perhaps we are risking our lives by playing games with the all-seeing gods."

I WAS TO think of this conversation often in the next few months as I grew bigger and bigger with child. Would I substitute a slave-child to save my own kin? Was I as hypocritical as the Motyans? I didn't know. Fortunately, Aphrodite no longer demanded human sacrifice—or so I naively thought at the time.

Praxinoa and I returned to Syracuse across a glittering sea. The winds were fair and we made better time than we had on the outward sail. Being aboard ship made me think constantly of Alcaeus. I had been writing to him in my head ever since his letter arrived, but I had not yet sent him my reply. Everything I thought to write seemed foolish. Whenever I reached for reed and papyrus, I grew frightened. How could I let him know of his impending fatherhood? It was too large a thing to put in a letter. It should be whispered across a pillow. I remembered our lovemaking and I ached for him. Praxinoa rubbed my back while I thought of Alcaeus. I didn't tell her who I was thinking of, but I think she knew.

My love,

I have just witnessed a wretched ritual in which a child was sacrificed to appease a savage god. I thought I knew human nature, but until now I did not understand the war between creation and destruction that is waged in every human heart. The ceremony was all the more painful to watch because of the child I carry which belongs to both of us.

I wrote this letter in my head as we returned to Syracuse by sea. I promised myself that in time I would send it—as soon as I got the wording right.

4

Gold Flower

Hesperus, bringing all that the shining Dawn scattered,
You bring the sheep, you bring the goat,
You bring the child back to its mother.
—SAPPHO

BUT I NEVER did. Back in Syracuse, I thought of Alcaeus with every sunrise and sunset. I wrote him many letters in my mind. But still I could not bring myself to send him anything I scrawled on papyrus. Why, I did not know. I wanted to contact him, yet could not. Was it because I feared my letter would fall into unfriendly hands? The household was full of potential spies. Was it because I feared my letter would never reach him? Was it because my pregnancy was too great a thing to be communicated except mouth to ear? What if Cercylas discovered that the child I carried was not his? I was full of trepidation. It seemed I walked above a great abyss. Away from home, far from all the certainties I knew, I became addicted to soothsayers like all the other Syracusans, who were a most superstitious lot.

But I cannot blame my love of prophecy only on the ways of Syracuse. We all consult soothsayers at the times in our lives that are most precarious. Pregnancy is surely such a time. Will you live or die?

Will the babe live or die? Will your life change utterly? (Of course it will, but you hardly want to credit that!) Soothsayers beckon to us because we get so few answers from the wandering gods who delight in withholding their gifts. Magic attracts us when our humanity seems most frail.

There was no lack of magic in Syracuse. The city teemed with diviners and oracles. Some were obvious charlatans. Others put on amazing demonstrations using birds and herbs and incense, red binding cords, lead manikins, cauldrons of green and purple fire.

One day I found myself in the humble hovel of one Cretaea, sitting on a packed mud floor around a fire filled with lead manikins with huge phalli. These priapic manikins represented the beloveds of her clients.

Cretaea had three wobbling wens on her sagging chin, eyes and hair the color of pitch, and long fingernails stained red with henna. She chanted:

Where are my magic spells? Where are my charms? Wreathe the golden bowl with crimson wool, that I may bind a spell upon my love! Let me learn fire spells to summon him! Let me make a lead manikin complete with his beautiful phallus so that it may be stiff only with me! Let it wilt with disuse whenever he approaches a boy or another woman! Hail, grim Hecate, attend me always! Make my love drugs as potent as Circe's or Medea's! Let him smell the juice of my delta even in that far land where he dwells!

This was the love incantation devised by Cretaea to assuage the fears of her clients. Elusive Hecate was her goddess—creature of mists and magic, who delighted in the sacrifice of puppies. As she chanted, Cretaea's fingers raked the air like claws. She was unimaginably old and ugly and demanded to be paid in golden *oboloi*. She sold me a lead manikin with an enormous erect phallus on which she had inscribed the name *Alcaeus*.

I wrapped the manikin carefully in clean linen and secreted it in my chiton. Having learned her incantation by heart, I went home and repeated the spell over and over myself. I bound red cord around a golden bowl. I burned a fire in it and sprinkled in minerals to make it burn green and purple. I put the lead manikin in the fire so that Alcaeus' phallus would burn hot only for me. And then I waited.

Within the week I had another letter from Alcaeus! It began with this poem:

> *Scheming Cyprian goddess—*
> *Bring me the one with the violet hair.*
> *Her I love better than all the boys of Lydia.*
> *But my legs are tangled in ropes of fear*
> *And I ride out the storm of Eros*
> *Without the one I love!*

Sappho, my love,

When I think of beautiful green Lesbos, it merges in my mind with a vision of violet-haired Sappho—or Psappho, as you call yourself in our beautiful Aeolic dialect. My thoughts go back to that other exile in Pyrrha when you were with me, hanging on my every word, adoring me, adored by me. I miss you—or do I miss your adoration? I feel responsible for you. I remember the beauty contests of Lesbos—the kallisteia—*where the young girls swayed like mobile caryatids in their columns of white linen.*

> *Lesbian maidens in trailing robes*
> *Walk up and down, being judged for their beauty.*
> *Around them, women choir to Aphrodite. . . .*
> *O Lesbos, you sprout beautiful women*
> *Even as you grow the vine and the olive tree.*
> *Soft syllables shake the silvery olive leaves*
> *As the wind whispers*
> *Sappho, Sappho, Sappho. . . .*

You have something more beautiful than beauty. You are wholly alive. I think of your smile, your quick retorts, your ability to match me line for line. And I think of our lovemaking, of your sex, which becomes a living thing, when I enter it, of your pulsing wetness, of the song between your thighs.

Damn Aphrodite! I refuse to be bound in the snares of a woman's hair. Boys are simpler. You take your pleasure and walk away. Where is my Sappho? Why do you not answer me? Alcaeus is dying of love for you. Must he come to get you?

OH, YES! I thought, come to get me. Rescue me from this horrible exile. Take me with you wherever you go! My feelings for Alcaeus burned hotter than that god with the fire in its belly. I loved him. I longed for him, but his teasing me about his beautiful boys even in the midst of his ardent love letters piqued me. I had always lived in tidal waves of changing emotions, but pregnancy had made these feelings even more pronounced. As the baby rocked in the sea of my womb, I rocked in a sea of tempestuous emotions. I cried easily. I laughed easily. I scoured the city for soothsayers and witches who could tell me the fate of my baby. I saw them all. Then I went back to Cretaea a second time to ask her why I was so diffident about writing to Alcaeus. I could make no sense of my reluctance. What held me back?

"Shall I tell the father about his babe?" I asked the hideous old witch on my next visit.

"The answer to that question will cost you three more golden *oboloi*," she said.

"On top of what I have already paid?" I asked.

"Yes!" said Cretaea.

"All I have is one *obolos*."

"Then I cannot help you," said the hag.

I sent Praxinoa running home for more *oboloi*. Cretaea and I waited together in silence, staring into the multicolored flames. Once Cretaea had the *oboloi*, she stroked them covetously with her reddened claws and answered as ambiguously as any oracle:

> *Am I the father of the child she carries*
> *Underneath her bosom?*
> *A warrior asked. And the wind whispered no*
> *But the leaves rustled yes*
> *And the doves cooed maybe*

> *And the bronze cauldrons rang*
> *Like funeral bells.*

"What does it mean?" I asked in a panic. "Does it mean my child will die? Is it yes or no? Shall I tell him or will it hurt the child?"

Cretaea stared at me with her rheumy eyes. "That is all the spirit said. The interpretation I must leave to you."

"Tell me!" I cried.

"I would tell you if I could," Cretaea said, smirking.

"Give my mistress back her *oboloi,* then!" shouted Praxinoa.

"*Oboloi* returned carry a curse," Cretaea said craftily. "Let me only say, heed the leaves in the trees of your garden well. They will tell you."

THAT NIGHT, under a full moon, Praxinoa and I sat in the courtyard of our house and listened to the leaves fluttering in the wind. At first they seemed to say yes, then no, then yes again. How could we tell?

I called for papyrus and reeds and wrote this letter to Alcaeus at the court of Alyattes in Sardis:

> *My love—*
>   *Why has it been so hard to tell you that the child I carry is yours? Heavy with the fruit of our love, I understand life in a way I could not when we were together. I feel the baby kicking and it is the memory of your love, kicking at my heart. . . .*

What a sappy letter! I would have to make a song to express how I really felt and so I burnt the papyrus and broke the reed!

BUT WRITING to Alcaeus was hardly the only challenge I faced. As my confinement approached, I grew more and more frightened. The cemeteries of Syracuse were crammed with the bones of women who had died in childbirth. Childbirth was more dangerous than the battlefield. Oh, I longed for my virginity now as if it were my native land! How could I have opened my legs—not to mention my heart—to Alcaeus? I was terrified of dying. If I died, what would become of all the songs I had yet to write? I understood the virgin goddesses then, understood Artemis and Athena, understood women who refused the sexual life for the life of the mind. Why had I fallen into the trap of loving a man? Why was dear Praxinoa not enough for me? I had made a terrible mistake by following Alcaeus. Perhaps that was why I could not write to him. Underneath my rapture was rage for having to face a fate he would never face! I *wanted* him to worry about me. I *wanted* him to fret. Let him be as miserable in his own way as I was in mine!

Praxinoa and I made daily offerings to goddesses who ruled childbirth—Artemis and Ilithyia. We also remembered Asclepius, the god of medicine, in our sacrifices. We would have sacrificed to Baal if we had believed it would do any good! That was how terrified we were.

Thighbones wrapped in fat, rare birds, beautiful garments woven with our own hands—these were some of the things we offered to the gods. No babes walked through flames in Syracuse—though there were certainly those who sacrificed puppies to Hecate on altars at crossroads. Yet mothers had no choice but to endure torture—emerging only if they were blessed.

Cercylas seemed tamed—not only by my pregnancy but also by my absence in Motya. He was so relieved at my return that he prostrated himself before me, embraced my knees, and kissed my feet.

"I know in my deepest heart that we'll soon be adorning the door of our house with an olive crown," he said—like the pompous fool he was. An olive crown was symbolic of a son, while a tuft of wool meant a girl and her future toil at the loom.

"I would much prefer a tuft of wool," I said.

Cercylas laughed, thinking I had made a joke.

PREGNANCY CAN be a time of troubling dreams. I had them all. The trip to Motya certainly hadn't helped. Cretaea's prophecy was also troubling. I dreamed again and again of a baby given up to the arms of a red-hot god and devoured by flames. I couldn't banish the image from my mind.

The last part of pregnancy is probably best forgotten. Birth is a battle to the death between two clinging souls. We come apart so we may come together. If women knew what birth cost, they'd forswear love forever.

When my time came, it was announced by a fit of prodigious hunger. I remember eating a whole chicken baked in honey the night before my water broke.

Praxinoa called the midwife as soon as my pains began. Then the pains stopped and Praxinoa foolishly let the midwife go. Of course, when I needed her, she was off delivering another babe.

The women's quarters of my house were filled with useless helpers—slaves, nurses, sweepers, cooks—but no midwife. Everyone had an opinion. I myself had no idea what to do, and my first taste of motherhood was a chaos of conflicting advice.

When at last the midwife returned, I was given herbs to ease my pain—which again stopped the labor. Then the pains began again in earnest and I traveled to another world. Odysseus in Hades' realm was not as lost among shades as I was, laboring to bring my babe to birth. I wailed until my throat was sore. I could not *believe* the pain! I was certain I would meet my own ghost among a crowd of wailing women who had died in childbirth.

Every mother has experienced this—though none remember. Forgetfulness is the gods' blessing. I do remember that finally two helpers seized me by the shoulder and two by the legs as if to shake the baby out of me! It didn't help. Then I was seated on a birthing stool and told to push with all my might.

"Damn you, Artemis!" I yelled. "Damn you more, Aphrodite!"

When at last the head of the baby was seen between my legs, the women began to shout the ritual cry of joy—the *ololuge*—but the baby seemed to be *stuck*! Was it bad luck to cry for joy before the birth was complete? Was I doomed? Was the *child*? I hardly cared by then—if only the pain would stop! Another great wave of pain obliterated my mind— and suddenly, miraculously, I pushed the baby out!

The midwife had prepared goatskins to place the newborn babe upon. It was customary that the goatskins be filled with warm water, then pierced so that water leaked from them. The idea was that the skins would slowly settle under the weight of the babe, extracting the afterbirth by tugging the cord of flesh. But this time the cord was wrapped around the infant's neck! Once it was cut, the goatskins were useless. The midwife had to extract the afterbirth with her bloody hand.

Covered in blood, looking more like afterbirth than baby, the child was put into my arms. It was a little girl! Her sea-blue eyes blurrily sought mine. Her little sex a pale pink shell. Her red, wrinkled feet had walked to us through the air. The midwife was strangely silent.

Then I heard the old witch whisper to Praxinoa, "Don't let her grow too attached—perhaps the father will not agree to raise the child."

"Out!" I screamed. "This child will be raised no matter what that idiot says!"

"I promise you life," I whispered to the most beautiful creature I had ever beheld. "It is all I can promise you." I thought of the infant girls exposed on rocky hilltops and wept. "No one will sacrifice you for your sex, little stranger," I sobbed. "And I shall call you Cleis like the one who gave me life."

I yearned then for my mother as I had never yearned before.

"Put a tuft of wool on our front door," I ordered the midwife.

"But your husband?" she asked.

"My husband has nothing to do with this," I said.

Cercylas came in to worship at my throne.

"She looks like me!" he cried. "The little darling."

She'll have more brains, I thought.

As soon as I was well enough, Praxinoa and I went to give thanks to Artemis for my survival and the child's. We left the goddess a beautiful purple chiton and a purple cloak with a wavy blue border that looked like the sea.

At the temple of Artemis, I watched the mother of a woman who had died in childbirth dedicating an entire chest of golden treasures to the goddess. Was she mad? The gods had taken her daughter and she was still attempting to pacify them!

"There is as much carnage in birth as in war," the woman said. "At least the goddess spared my granddaughter."

How do women give up their babies to the midwives to be set on rugged hilltops? I will never understand it, any more than I understood the savage rites of Baal. We pretend to be civilized, but only blood sacrifice quiets the murderer within.

And tell me why Artemis, who never lets Eros loosen her thighs, should be the goddess of childbirth. She, who is a virgin hunting on the peaks of solitary mountains, holds the fate of all pregnant women in her hands. Is this just? Is this fair? Zeus of the thundercloud who rules the world has plenty to answer for!

ZEUS: *Blasphemy!*
APHRODITE: *Philosophy! You never could tell them apart.*

I was astonished by the love I felt for my baby. This little lump of flesh, with the blurry blue eyes and the pink fingernails that resembled the translucent shells of undersea creatures, remade my view of the world. I was less than before—now merely a mother—and much, much more: the maker of this marvel. I knew how the gods felt creating life.

> *I have a beautiful daughter who is*
> *Like a gold flower. I wouldn't take*
> *All Lydia or even*
> *The whole lovely island of Lesbos for her.*

Contemplating my daughter, her pink fingers like the dawn, her transparent skin, the perfect bivalve of her sex, I fell in love with life all over again. I would even trade her for my songs. She was my best creation.

DURING THE time when Cleis was a small baby, I played Penelope, sitting at my loom but weaving my own wiles. The baby lay in a basket at

my feet. When Cercylas appeared, I seduced him with my imperson-
ation of traditional womanhood. Of course, I didn't nurse the baby
myself. Two wet nurses did that on different shifts, day and night. And
my share of household slaves increased.

Cercylas fell in raptures over the baby. He was already saving up a
dowry for her and planning her nuptials. But more and more he had to
travel to Egypt for the wine trade with my brother Charaxus. They
stayed for months at a time in Naucratis, where the Greek traders
could worship their own gods while enjoying the Egyptian prostitutes
and luxuries. Good riddance! I was happy to be the queen of my own
household.

Because Cercylas was so advanced in age, both his parents were
dead. I had no wretched in-laws to obey like most young wives. That
was another blessing.

Before Cleis was born, I had been terribly impatient with my
mother. Now that began to change. What I had once seen as her obsti-
nacy, I saw as her protectiveness. No woman can understand her
mother until she becomes a mother. I would have given anything to see
my mother now.

Repeatedly I sent messages to her through traders plying the seas
between Syracuse and Lesbos. She sent greetings back—together with
a beautiful sea-green cloak, emblazoned with gold, for baby Cleis. Of
course, it was big enough for a five-year-old child, but I draped it over
the baby in her crib and said, "Your grandmother wove this for you with
her own beautiful fingers just like yours."

THEN MY MOTHER arrived. She came by boat on the broad back of the
sea with her slaves and serving women. Not only had Charaxus gone to
trade in Egypt with Cercylas, but Larichus had joined him—young as
he was. My youngest brother Eurygius was dead. A fever brought from
the lingering skirmishes on the mainland had carried him off. My
mother's baby was gone, so she came to stake her claim on mine.

We were so happy to see each other that we wept. Then she ran to
baby Cleis—four months old by now—and drenched her face with

tears. She gazed and gazed at the baby as if her eyes would shortly go blind and she had to memorize this moment.

"How strange," she said. "I haven't felt this way since I first saw *you*. I feel as though she were my own child. Blood of my blood and bone of my bone. It almost feels as though she's *mine*."

Our reunion was ardent, loving, and passionate. But within days we began to quarrel.

My mother had ridiculous old-fashioned ideas about babies; she dictated to the nurses, who grew huffy and snappish. She preached about adding solid food to the baby's diet of milk. She wanted honey-barley water given to the baby before bed; she insisted the baby would sleep better. She rearranged the nursery and the women's quarters; she criticized everything I did. Eventually I got so furious at her for meddling that I accused her of marrying me off to an old sot to better her own financial situation.

"It was only to save your life, Sappho, that I sacrificed myself to Pittacus and married you off to his friend Cercylas. You are such a child and so naive about politics, so unaware of how women are sacrificed— do you think I would let you move all the way to Syracuse if there were any other way? Would I relinquish my only daughter? How can you say that? How can you be so blind? Pittacus knew about your conspiracy with Alcaeus. He was not inclined to be lenient until I interceded. Do you think I enjoyed making love to that bag of guts? Do you think I lusted for that red face and that pendulous belly? Do you think his fat ass made me think of your beautiful muscular father? How dare you fault me for saving your life the only way I could?"

"So you let me be raped by Cercylas!"

"I hardly think that sot had the power to rape you. Better a rapist with a little prick than a satyr with a battering ram. Besides, the world is based on rape! Europa was raped. Thetis was raped. Even Leto, the mother of Apollo, was raped. And she was one of the titans! Only Penthesilea, queen of the amazons, was killed, not raped. She would have been *happy* only to be raped. Grow up, Sappho—and look around you. This world was not made for women. Lesbos was once the home of the amazons. Look at Lesbos now—under Pittacus! You're better off with an old, impotent, pliable lush of a husband than with no husband at all! A dumb rich husband who travels is what you want—and what you got! I refuse to feel sorry for you, Sappho."

"At least you had a husband you *loved*!"

"Yes, I loved him. Yes, I was bewitched by passion. Yes, I was enthralled by his beautiful legs, his chest like the shield of Achilles, his glinting green eyes. And he had four children by me and forty more by slaves and concubines. And he never missed an occasion to make himself glorious in battle until he came home in a jar, leaving me to the mercies of his parents—and Pittacus.

"You should see the way that man is covering Mytilene with images of himself! He has the sculptors make him resemble Zeus—or Poseidon! Long beard, sage eyes, a philosopher's knowing smile. He doesn't just want to be a tyrant; he wants to be a sage! And a singer! He has that young fool Pherecydes of Syros writing songs, aphorisms, and philosophical treatises for him to put his name on! It's not enough to be absolute ruler—he wants to be a singer *and* a philosopher! Don't they all!

"I had my suffering too, Sappho, little whirlwind—ohhhhh, whenever I think of your father I still want to cry. And rage! And rage and cry! Aphrodite cursed me too. Passion is a curse, and lack of passion is a curse! Don't think you are the only one to know the capriciousness of Aphrodite and her scheming little son with the poison-tipped arrows!"

I started to cry. "Will it be any better for the little one? Will it be better for Cleis? Will it *change*?"

"I doubt it greatly," my mother said. "Women don't know where their own interest lies. If we ever joined together like the amazons of old, we might do something about our plight. But we paint and smile, stagger about simpering in golden sandals, let ourselves be bought for collars and earrings and slaves and houses. A sorry lot we are—always fighting among ourselves for men's praise. Once we loosen our thighs for love, we can be defeated. Artemis and Athena had the right idea— perpetual virginity! Once Alcaeus took your maidenhead, you were doomed!"

I was amazed. How did she know?

"Mother!"

"You don't want to hear the truth, Sappho. Rape is our destiny. But rape is better than murder. The amazons always put up with rape if it saved them from being murdered. They kept the girls and gave the boys away—to their own rapists, usually. They were practical. Then they made their girls strong. They were wise. At least you have your golden flower, your little girl—as I had you."

She bent down to the baby and lifted it gently in her arms as if it were a crystal egg—utterly fragile, utterly precious.

"I think of all the daughters who died in childbirth, all the grand-daughters who died trying to come to this world of darkness and light—and I rejoice for you—despite the pain of life, despite the treachery of men. . . . It is not so bad—this gift the gods gave us. It is a mixture of pain and pleasure, of sweets and bitters, like all gifts, but it is ours to keep awhile and revel in."

She lifted up her little namesake and smiled the smile of the blessed.

5

The Priestess of Isis

I ran fluttering
Like a girl
After her mother.
*—*SAPPHO

NEW MOTHERHOOD is a time of tempestuous emotions. Even though my own mother was here with me in Syracuse, even though I had Praxinoa at my side, my mind was full of fantasies and fears as I fell more and more deeply in love with my baby.

My mind was a seething cauldron. Tenderness for my baby warred with terror for her fate. I understood why babies have often been sacrificed—from the beginning of time. Their little dented skulls show us the thinness of the membrane between life and death. Their new unsteady breath reminds us of the slender difference between being and nonbeing. Only a sigh of air released from the new wet lungs divides them. A baby's fierce life-cries sometimes sound like death-cries to the anxious mother. All of existence hangs on a thread during those early days. I never stopped thinking I would walk into Cleis' nursery in the middle of the night to find her still, stopped, mute, a little lump of putty without air.

A gift so newly given may be snatched back by the gods. It seems tentative, provisional, fragile. We know the gods are nothing if not capricious. What they give with golden hands, they may take away with bloody ones. From one minute to the next, their will may change. Until you know this in the pit of your gut, you are no parent. Persephone's dark bedroom awaits us all. Demeter's desperation for her lost daughter, kidnapped by the king of death, could be the fate of any mother.

I was always glad that I had borne a daughter. Her beauty and fragility never ceased to stir me in that secret place where fear and desire mingle. But as Cleis grew, I also wondered what it would be like to be the mother of a son—a little Alcaeus who would smile and coo for me when I unfastened his loincloth, a little boy whose tender phallus would come to overmaster him and guide his fate, a little hero offered up to Ares to be killed on the battlefield, to be transported home as cold ashes in a jar. No! It was too horrible to think about. I was grateful for my daughter. At least she could be kept off the battlefield—until she came to the battlefield of birth.

Still, my mother and I left nothing to chance. We used all the magic at our command to ensure the baby's life. This time I did not go back to Cretaea, but instead we found an Egyptian priestess who was reputed to be able to read the future.

In the ancient quarter, not far from the fountain of Arethusa, lived the one who called herself the priestess of Isis. My mother and I visited her with little Cleis in our arms.

THE PRIESTESS' HOUSE was full of cats—which are sacred to the Egyptians. They leapt about, meowed, rolled over like dogs, urging you to rub their soft bellies. There must have been at least twenty living cats I could see and surely more in hiding. Against every wall stood small sarcophagi, which held the mummified remains of other cats. I later learned that every cat the priestess had ever loved was here. Despite the fact that Egyptians are very clean, the smell was overpowering. I guess, with that many cats, even the most meticulous practices cannot remove the odor.

A female slave led us to the inner courtyard.

"The priestess will see you soon," she said.

My mother held the baby. I busied myself with observing the decorations of the priestess' courtyard.

Isis is the name the Egyptians give to Demeter. There was a statue of her in the middle of the courtyard and one cat stood unceremoniously on Isis' shoulder. Isis is usually depicted as having horns—the way we Greeks depict Io. Cows are sacred to Egyptians and cannot be eaten.

There was a fountain with lotus flowers in one corner of the courtyard and the sound of running water gentled the air. Most soothsayers, I had found, live in squalor and seem to grub for bits of gold—but this one had obviously grown rich in the practice of her craft.

"How much money did you bring?" I asked my mother.

"Enough," she said, gazing down into the baby's face as if it were a precious jewel that twinkled on her finger.

A slave who had greeted us padded into the courtyard on bare feet. "The priestess will see you now," she said, "but first you must purify yourselves." She led us to a tinkling fountain, bade us wash, then dried our hands with clean linen. She anointed our hands with sweet-smelling almond oil.

We were led into a small chamber draped with red silk where the priestess sat on a throne. I had expected an old crone, but this priestess was young and beautiful, with shaved eyebrows and jewelry that seemed like liquid gold.

"You bring a babe for me to bless," she said, speaking Greek with only the smallest hint of an Egyptian accent.

"Yes," my mother said. I was silenced by the priestess' beauty—her long almond-shaped golden eyes, her tawny skin, her aureole of red-brown ringlets, her breasts plainly rising and falling under her silken chiton, which fell into a hundred rainbow pleats of red and purple. I could not help but stare. My breath caught in my throat.

"Are you wondering about my eyebrows?" she asked. No, I was wondering about her beauty, but did not dare to say so.

"I have shaved them in mourning for my favorite cat, Sesostris. He died some days past. He is being mummified and a splendid golden sarcophagus is being made for him. He is the only babe I will ever have. If I could reincarnate him I would, but alas, not even priestesses have that power. Tell me, what can I do for you?"

"I need to know the fate of my child," I blurted out, "and my fate."

"A tall order," said the priestess. "One fate at a time. Show me the baby."

My mother reluctantly handed over Cleis. The priestess held the baby tenderly and gazed down at her. She gazed for a long time but said nothing. Then she handed the babe back to me. I was almost afraid I would drop the infant, since my knees were weak from the priestess' beauty. Her tawny oval face seemed to hold the secrets of the universe.

"Usually I sacrifice a bird and read its entrails, but the words of the goddess are so clear, I do not have to.

"Isis says that you and this child will someday return across the sea's broad back to a land you love, that you will be a singer and a teacher there, that you will teach the air to resound with your syllables so that they will forever echo, that you will be a muse to all who come after you, all except your own daughter, and that when you die, your name will live forever."

"But what about baby Cleis?"

"She will grow and prosper," the priestess said. "She will have her own renown and she will live to bury you. That is all a mother can ask."

The prophecy was so clear and precise that I immediately doubted it. I knew that soothsayers, like oracles, sometimes spoke in riddles. I knew it took a strong and clever mind to understand them correctly. But on this day my mind was far from strong! Not only was I crazed with worry over my child, but also the beauty of this priestess had weakened me. Already confused by my tumultuous feelings for my daughter and Alcaeus, I was further confused by my sudden feelings for this priestess. Her skin was golden, her hair a mass of ringlets, her arms and legs long and sinewy, her aroma that of frankincense and myrrh. My breath caught in my throat. My knees seemed to sway under me. I could feel the sweat under my arms and the moisture between my legs. If she had touched me, I would have swooned and fallen over backward on one of the soft pillows that lined the room. My mother steadied me. She quickly took the baby out of my arms.

"Sappho!" she said, as if to awaken me from some reverie. Syllables formed in my mind:

Love, that loosener of limbs,
Makes me tremble to the root.

I did not say these words aloud.

"Where are you, Sappho?" my mother asked again.

"The girl is flower-picking on Parnassus," the priestess said. "She will come back to us by and by."

The baby suddenly cried as if it knew it had a rival. My mother hushed her, rocked her, comforted her. I knelt before the priestess with my hands on my knees in the Egyptian style.

"I do not even know your name," I said, prostrating myself.

"You can call me Isis," the almond-eyed beauty said.

"Isis, tell me the prophecy again," I asked.

"I never repeat my prophecies," she said. "If you want a more complex and confusing prediction, go to Delphi, spend your money needlessly. Leave me! I have no time for those who question me!"

LOVE IS a fever, a contagion, a storm among the old oak trees. I went home with my mother and my daughter, but in my mind I remained with Isis.

Praxinoa knew instinctively that something had changed.

"Sappho—you walk like someone in a dream. What has happened to you? What did the soothsayer say?"

"Only good things, Prax."

"Then what has come over you?"

"Nothing, I'm fine, I promise you."

But Praxinoa knew me too well to believe me. She sensed that strong winds of change were blowing in our lives. She watched me carefully after that and I felt her uneasiness. My love for Alcaeus and the baby she could almost accept, but love for another woman—never.

I knew I would try to see Isis again as soon as I could leave the baby and evade my mother and Prax. The priestess had my heart to twist and throw away. Or was it some other organ?

The next day, like one possessed, I went to court the priestess. I wish I'd known that Praxinoa was trailing me and reporting to my mother!

IsIs WAS NOT an easy prey. I waited in the antechamber again, amid the cats. This time my heart pounded and my chiton was drenched in sweat. I waited an hour or more. Eventually, the priestess saw me.

"You are agitated," she said, "despite my prophecy."

"You are the most beautiful creature I have ever seen."

The priestess laughed. "You think that if you hold me in your arms and stroke me like a cat, your soul will purr. It is Aphrodite you love, not I."

"How can you say that? I ache for you. I would give everything I have for one taste of your mouth."

"Even your child?" Isis asked.

"Everything but that," I said, my heart pounding.

"At least you are honest with me," said Isis. With that she kissed me, her tongue reaching into the moistness of my soul, her slender fingers entwined in the damp tendrils of hair behind my neck. I shook with desire like an oak tree in the wind. Oh, Praxinoa and I had played with each other and pleasured each other as small girls. This was the first time I had been kissed by a grown woman. A kiss can be more intimate than any other form of touch.

"Now go," she said abruptly.

"Go? How can I go when I adore you?"

"Go home to your babe and your mother," the priestess said. "This is no time for play. Come back when you can bring an offering from your deepest well."

"And what would that be?"

"That is the riddle you must solve before you may love me," Isis said.

• • •

Was I mad to have fallen in love so precipitously? Was I getting even with Alcaeus for his beautiful boys? Was I terrified of the responsibilities of motherhood and looking for an escape? Or was I in love with my daughter, my own reflection, and seeking another woman as a double? All these questions raced around and around in my head like Isis' cats.

I thought of "an offering from your deepest well." What did it mean? Did she desire my firstborn child, like a priestess of Motya? What else could I give that had great worth? My lyre? Surely she did not desire anything as worthless as gold. And why did she say that I loved Aphrodite and not her? I loved her as passionately as I loved Aphrodite. I thought of her all day and dreamed of her all night. Her tawny flanks, her shaved eyebrows, her eyes the color of cats' eyes, her long thin fingers whose soft pads I longed to feel on my skin—all these visions and imagined sensations haunted me. I began to study everything I could about the Egyptians and their lore to understand her. I was determined to make her mine.

The Egyptians believed that Isis was the oldest of the old, the giver of life, the mother-goddess from whom all creation arose. They addressed her as *"mistress of the gods, thou bearer of wings, thou lady of the red garments, queen of the crowns of South and North, mother in the horizon of the sky, mistress and lady of the tomb, giver of enchantments, giver of milk and blood and all things which flow. . . ."*

Isis was first among the gods. She gave birth to Horus, the sun. Without her light-giving womb, the earth would be dark and nothing would grow. She had swallowed Osiris the savior and brought him back to life. He was reborn as Horus, whereupon he grew to manhood and mated with his mother so that life could continue. The annual flooding of the Nile was caused by Isis weeping over her dead son. Her overflowing eye was also a delta. Her symbol was a circle surmounted by a horn.

I prayed to know how to please the priestess. Suddenly it came to me. She had lost her beloved cat, Sesostris. If I could replace that animal, surely she would love me. I went to her house and found one of her handmaidens.

"Tell me what Sesostris looked like," I asked her.

"He was like no other cat in the world—his coat was red-gold. One eye was pure blue, the other agate, and his claws were the longest of any cat I have ever seen. He understood Greek and Egyptian and Phoenician. He cried like a human baby. And when you stroked his fur, lightning was made in the sky and clouds parted, bringing rain. We thought him no ordinary cat but a messenger come to earth to tell us the will of the gods. My mistress loved him better than any being on earth."

I rewarded the girl, bade her keep silent about my inquiries, and went home to ponder my predicament. Alcaeus was in my mind, and my baby, and Isis. I dreamed mad dreams in which I was in bed with all three of them. I sweated in a fever all night and suffered the chills all day. I was wild. I longed for more messages from Alcaeus, and yet I feared that if they came, they would distract me from my pursuit of the priestess!

In the days that followed, I sent my slaves all over the city and the countryside to find a cat who resembled Sesostris. Only Praxinoa refused to go. The other slaves found cats with golden manes and cats with agate eyes, cats with blue eyes and long sharp claws but none with precisely the right combination of features. My house swarmed with cats, yet I was in despair. I had convinced myself that unless I could fulfill the priestess' desire, she would never love me.

The cats that had taken over our house appalled my mother and Praxinoa.

"And what will you do if one of these wild creatures scratches out the baby's eyes?" Praxinoa asked. "Sappho, you are mad. Banish these cats to the garden or your babe will not be safe and I myself will not stay in this house." She sulked like a wounded lover. Whenever I entered a room I heard her whispering with my mother.

I gave in and made a compound for cats in our garden. My slaves brought fresh fish every day and laid it out for the cats. Before long all the cats of Syracuse had visited our courtyard. But another Sesostris was nowhere to be found. It was true that he must have been a most unusual cat. I could not find a cat that understood Greek, let alone Egyptian or Phoenician!

In despair and defeat, I went back to the priestess.

"I have tried to find another Sesostris to replace the one you lost," I admitted, "but he is nowhere to be found. There are cats with golden manes and agate eyes, cats with blue eyes and long claws, but none that understands Greek, let alone Egyptian and Phoenician. What you have lost is irreplaceable. I cannot restore it to you. Yet I love you with my whole heart. May I sing what I have composed for you?"

The priestess nodded her head.

Love shook my heart
Like a fierce wind
Troubling the oaks on a high mountain.

The priestess listened deeply. Then she rose. "Come," she said, "let me show you something."

She led me through the courtyard and into the house where her women were weaving. She led me through the baths and the banqueting rooms. She led me down a damp and narrow stair. There, under the house, she had stored a huge, carved stone sarcophagus in which she planned to be buried. Against the wall there was a life-sized likeness of her face that would eventually form the mask of her mummy. Painted by the most skillful artist, it would preserve her youth forever as the minerals of the embalmers would preserve her flesh. The sarcophagus was uncovered. She climbed inside. I stood there puzzled. What was I supposed to do? She peeked out mischievously and beckoned for me to follow.

The coffin was larger than it seemed. There was just room enough for two. We lay down in it together so our bodies were touching at every point.

"We will be dead a long time," Isis said, as she touched my face with silken fingers. Her body smelled of lotus flowers, jasmine, and myrrh. She drew my tongue into her mouth and stroked my body with her cool hands. She touched the tips of my nipples, which rose to meet her fingers. She sucked them with her sweet mouth.

Then she lowered her head to my navel, ran her tongue around and around in it until it was brimming. She stroked my thighs until I pounded with desire. I had never felt so cavernously empty inside, so ready to be filled up.

"There are many things you may bring me besides another Sesostris," Isis said, as she brought her mouth to my hot center. She ran her tongue around and around the flesh nib that hardened for her. Then she insinuated a slim finger into my liquid core, rocking and rubbing until I came like the Nile in flood. A warm toasty smell suffused the sarcophagus and my legs felt as if they were floating in space.

"We have landed on the moon," said the priestess of Isis. "Let us see if we can return to the sun."

Then she began to show me how she liked to be touched. She loved the lightest touch, a teasing caress that made the golden hair of her arms stand on end. She had an amazing tongue, which she used on me as I used mine on her. I imitated her touch. My tongue became her tongue. Head to foot in the sarcophagus, we pleasured each other as if we had all eternity to do it.

"When I am embalmed and lying in my coffin, I will remember this warmth. We may not be eternal like the gods, but when we make love we experience a foretaste of immortality. Take what you want, Sappho, for what you desire you truly are."

"Immortality is what I want."

"Then take it with your songs. They will bring you immortality."

> *You came when I lay aching for your touch*
> *And you cooled my burning heart.*

"Make a song of that—and bring it to me. That is the gift I will receive."

"I wanted to bring you back your favorite cat as a gift of love. I despaired when I could not."

"You brought me something more precious," the priestess said, "your honesty. You have the gift to transcribe the heart. Use it! Every day you neglect it, you deny the gods."

. . .

IN THE DAYS that followed, I wrote a song for the priestess every morning and brought it to her every afternoon. Sometimes we made love in her sarcophagus, sometimes in the boat she kept ready at the harbor. Her slaves would row us into the open sea, hoist a sail if there was wind, and as we rode the seas in the will of the wind, drinking honeyed wine and eating figs and dates, I would play my lyre and sing my songs to her. She would lie back on pillows as the songs entered her and she would try to memorize their words and music. Then we would pleasure each other under the sun or stars.

"We are fortunate to be living in this age," Isis told me. "In times to come, people will fear Eros and hate all pleasure. There will be a dark age in which all the sweets of life will turn bitter. It will last a very long time."

"How do you know this?"

"I have read the entrails of the future. I am glad I will not live to see them. Music will die because there is no music without Eros. People will live for gold and conquest and only dimly remember that humans did not always live that way. Even your songs will be misunderstood. All songs to pleasure will be seen as evil. Music itself will be suspect. Everything will be measured by how much gold it brings."

"Only fools measure everything by how much gold it brings! Not civilized people."

"Darling Sappho, sweet Sappho—it's better not to know what the future holds. Soothsayers are sad because they know the future but do not know how to change it."

"Songs can change the future," I said. At the time I believed it.

"Songs can do everything but that," the priestess sighed.

6

Messages from the Barbarians

> *Wealth without virtue*
> *Is not a harmless neighbor.*
> —SAPPHO

I WENT HOME to see the baby, Praxinoa, and my mother. The coming barbarians retreated to the back of my brain. They will all be like Cercylas, I fleetingly thought, interested in only the grosser sensations of life—and in gold. I shuddered to think of a world filled with men like Cercylas. Then, as often happens when you are thinking about a distant person, news of him arrived.

A messenger from Naucratis came to my house bringing a papyrus scroll written in Egyptian hieroglyphics.

"Your brother sends you news of your husband, Cercylas, late of Naucratis," the messenger said.

"Late?" I asked. My mother ran to my side, carrying baby Cleis.

"Is he dead?" my mother asked hopefully.

"Read for yourself," the messenger said, handing me the sheaf of hieroglyphics. I could read some, but I was not sure of the whole contents of the missive.

"Let me see," my mother demanded. But she too was hardly fluent in Egyptian. For many centuries, we Greeks had no alphabet, until we borrowed the Phoenician, adding vowels. Some scrolls were written left to right, some right to left, some alternating directions on alternate lines. And Egyptian hieroglyphics were not so widely understood as they had once been. In Egypt itself, hieroglyphics were best understood by priests and priestesses.

"I will bring it to Isis," I said. "She will tell me everything."

Praxinoa gave me a filthy look. "You certainly trust your new friend—perhaps more than you trust me," Prax said.

"I don't know what you mean, Prax," I said.

"I think you do," said Prax. "I hardly think you are going back to her to decipher hieroglyphs—whatever you may say."

"Then come with me, Prax, to assuage your envy."

"I think I will!" said Prax.

So Praxinoa followed me to Isis' house through the crowded streets of Syracuse.

It was almost midday and the sun was hot. We ran along the quay past the fishmongers touting the remains of their catch, the wine vendors with their sealed amphorae, the oil vendors with their pretty little decorated jugs—*lekythoi*, we called them—for serving fine oil. The herb sellers' stands were redolent of dill. The fruit and vegetable sellers shined their multicolored gleaming wares. All the aromatic beauty of everyday life seduced us.

We arrived at Isis' domain and had to wait, as usual, to be admitted as she saw her full complement of clients seeking advice about the future.

Finally, we were admitted to her chambers.

Isis solemnly took the scroll and unrolled it. She read it once, then read it again.

"What does it say?" I asked impatiently.

"Let me read," Isis said. "It is from your brother Charaxus in Naucratis. It was clearly written by an Egyptian scribe."

"*My beloved sister,*" he writes. "*It is my unhappy duty to tell you that your beloved husband Cercylas of Andros breathed his last yesterday. As you may know,*

Naucratis is renowned for its great Egyptian physicians. We called one named Anhkreni, who had attended the great Pharaoh Necho himself and was known for cures of all digestive ills. He made many potions—herbs compounded with mother's milk, essences of grass, of tortoises, of dung—but Cercylas was too far gone. His liver had hardened like a great rock and his eyes and skin were yellow. Cures availed us not. All our best efforts failed. I fear that trading in the fabled wines of our native island only hastened his end. He could not keep out of the amphora once it was unsealed and each night he drank until he dropped. Many times he was warned of his overfondness for the elixir of Dionysus, but he could not refrain. He drank his wine unmixed and would not hear of diluting it. The riot and lustiness of Naucratis had an ill effect on him. The flute girls and acrobats played on his weaknesses in order to steal his gold. I feared it would come to this. Take heart! I share your grief. Your loving brother, Charaxus."

My heart took flight when I heard this missive. It felt like a bird straining to fly out of my chest. Free! I was free of Cercylas! And then I immediately felt guilt for rejoicing at his death.

"I know how you grieve, Sappho," Isis said. "Let me comfort you."

"Go home, Prax," I said, "and tell my mother I will return soon."

"How soon?" Prax asked bitterly, but, grudgingly, she did as she was told.

Isis AND I went away to our private cave under the house and laughed until we cried.

Isis' arms were round and muscular yet slim. The space between her breasts smelled of roses and oranges. After our ecstasies of mutual release, I leaned over to kiss her there. She pulled away.

"You must go to Egypt," she said gravely, "and protect your legacy."

"My brothers would not steal from me."

"Perhaps they would not, but they might love women who *would*. You know how weak men can be. If you go, I will join you as soon as I'm able."

We went back upstairs to Isis' consulting chamber. There her clients waited impatiently to hear the future. As if time didn't go quickly enough, humans feel they have to hurry it with prophecies.

Waiting among Isis' followers was a fat bearded man, dressed like a Lydian nobleman, and covered in golden trinkets—chains, hanging seals, rings, all manner of gewgaws. He looked at me steadily. His eyes seemed to penetrate my chiton.

I looked away. Then I looked back at him. He nodded at me.

"You are the singer Sappho?" he asked.

I was thunderstruck. I didn't immediately answer.

"Alcaeus of Lesbos would have news of you."

"And who are you?" I asked.

"I am Cyrus of Sardis," the fat man said. "I met Alcaeus at the court of Alyattes, where he is much in favor."

"Alcaeus of Lesbos?" I asked. "Where is he now?" The excitement in my voice immediately alerted Isis.

"Who *is* this Alcaeus of Lesbos?" she asked.

"If you ask me, he is smitten with a certain singer called Sappho," Cyrus of Sardis said.

Isis looked stricken. "Tell me who he is!"

"Only my singing teacher from Lesbos," I said to them both.

"Know then that he is now the favorite of the king of Lydia and enjoys much power in the Lydian court from which I come. He advises the great king of Lydia about how to spend his gold. He has been sent to Delphi to consult the oracle on behalf of the king."

"That oracle knows nothing!" Isis said, her eyes flashing in anger. "She is a fraud!"

I had never seen Isis so upset. Was she upset about a rival lover or a rival oracle?

"The priests control her every utterance," said Isis. "They drug her and keep her in a state of twilight consciousness, then bring her out to babble nonsense so they can exact tribute. The whole shrine at Delphi is a fraud!"

Cyrus threw up his stubby hands. "I have no doubt that better oracles exist, but the great King Alyattes swears by that one. He says that the sacred mists fill the mind with visions of times to come. He has sent Alcaeus there to divine the future of his empire."

"Then he is a fool," Isis said, "and he will come to grief."

"I have no doubt you are right," said Cyrus, "but who can argue with great rulers?"

Isis stormed out of the waiting area and left me alone with Cyrus of Sardis.

"Tell me—is Alcaeus well? Is he happy?"

"Not happy without you, my lady."

At this my heart leapt. I may have been momentarily besotted with Isis, but still I longed to see Alcaeus. The strength of my feelings for both of them confused me.

"How can I find him?" I asked Cyrus.

"He will doubtless pass much time in Delphi, awaiting the oracle's words."

"I cannot be with my daughter here and in Delphi and Egypt at the same time," I sighed.

"Perhaps you require a courier to do your bidding? I could be your courier, courtier, right-hand man about the house. I could bring your messages to Alcaeus. Perhaps I could convince him to follow you here or meet you elsewhere. Say the word. Your wish is my command."

Why did this Lydian stranger make me suspicious? How could I be sure he really knew Alcaeus as well as he implied?

"I will think about your offer," I said. "Come call on me when you have seen Isis and know your future better."

Cyrus prostrated himself before me, his gold gewgaws jingling. There was something about him I didn't like.

"The world is a dangerous place, Lady Sappho," said the stranger. "In Babylon, Nebuchadnezzar is preparing who knows what bloody horrors. In Egypt, Necho seeks to return that land to its former glory. Alyattes of Lydia seeks to rule the whole known world—and he has the gold to do it. The Persians are gathering force and want to overmaster all their neighbors. The Greeks are in turmoil both at home and in their colonies. The gods have abandoned us to charlatans and false prophets. We have fallen far from the purity of Homer's heroes. A woman needs a protector and I can be that for you. Syracuse is great, but it is not the only city on earth. A fabled singer like yourself can tour the known world singing and earning untold riches—Delphi, Athens, Ephesus, Dodona, Naucratis, Samos, Chios. As our world crumbles into gold dust, the newly rich everywhere seek poets to sing their praises. They will pay dearly for the privilege. I can do this for you—trade your songs for gold—if only you let me."

"I sing to honor Aphrodite, not for gold."

"Ah—that may have worked in the old heroic days, but now gold is the only measure men believe in. Your scruples hold you back. They will impoverish you. You dream of the gods—but the gods are dead. They cannot intervene on your behalf. Only gold gleams where the gods used to be."

I thought of how I might answer him, but before I could say a word, Isis' handmaiden appeared to usher him into her chamber.

I was so troubled by the choices Isis and Cyrus had proposed that when I got home I asked Praxinoa for her counsel.

"A slave cannot tell her mistress what to do," Praxinoa said angrily.

"Even if the mistress asks?"

"Why now?" Prax asked. "You have Isis to counsel you and also your mother. You hardly asked *my* counsel when you bedded Alcaeus or Isis." I looked at her in shock. Had I been so indiscreet? I myself had told her about Alcaeus. But she also knew everything about Isis.

"What do you know of my life?" Prax asked in a fury. "I know everything about you and you know nothing of me! You do not even know where I come from. My parents found me on a mountaintop near Eresus, where I had been abandoned by my father. They raised me tenderly till the age of six, then sold me to your grandfather. I feel lucky to be alive even if I am a slave. I am lucky not to be in a brothel or on a treadmill. My choices are not your choices. You are free."

"Free! What does it mean?" I asked. I had never felt so trapped by my own conflicting feelings.

"It means making choices," Praxinoa said, "even if you do not know what choices to make. But you are confused because you have too many choices. You think you can love your child, love Isis, love Alcaeus, and be comforted by me when no one else is around. You want everything. You accept no limits. But the gods have been watching you and judging your hubris. Come! Look at what the gods have done to your daughter!"

She led me to the nursery, where we found my mother and the wet nurses huddled over baby Cleis. The baby was burning with fever. She squalled and cried and would take no nourishment. Was she doomed to follow Cercylas to the Land of the Dead?

We bathed her in tepid water to bring down the fever, made sacrifices to the gods, called the most learned doctors. All my confusion of choices dwindled to a point. Would the child live or die? Past and future disappeared. There was only the squalling of the baby and its fever, the smell of baby vomit and shit, the eternal present.

Philosophy disappears at moments like this. Twenty adults hover over a tiny child, importuning the gods for help. I remembered that the Egyptians had the best spells for protecting infants and I sent Praxinoa for Isis. She grumbled, but she went.

After what seemed an interminable pause, Isis appeared, resplendent in her pleated silken robes. She shooed all the helpers out of the room, and began to work a piece of raw linen into seven bulging knots, hang it about the babe's neck, and chant:

> *This is a spell*
> *For a knot, for a fledgling:*
> *Are you hot in the nest?*
> *Are you burning in the bush?*
> *Is your mother not with you?*
> *Does your sister not fan you?*
> *Is there no nurse to offer protection?*
> *Let there be brought a pellet of gold,*
> *Forty beads, a carnelian stone*
> *With a crocodile and hand on it*
> *To drive out this demon of desire,*
> *To fell these enemies from the dead.*
> *You shall break out! This is a protection!*

Horus child, I am Isis.
I protect the lives I make.

Isis produced the gold pellet, the forty beads, and the carnelian stone with the crocodile and hand upon it. She chanted the spell again. And again. She laid the beads upon the baby's body. Then she laid her hands all over the baby's body while she slowly repeated the spell. Time slowed to a crawl. As we stood and watched in amazement, Cleis began to gurgle and smile. I felt her brow. It was cool. The illness had been cast out.

"So much for the power of *your* gods," said Isis. "The older gods of Egypt still prevail."

I knelt before her and kissed the hem of her garment. Then I fell asleep with my baby in my arms, vowing never to be parted from her again. Rocking my baby, smelling the sweet smell at the top of her head, at the back of her neck, I promised her all my love, all my protection. Both Isis and Alcaeus receded from my thoughts as I merged my soul with my child's. All night I sang to her and rocked her. When the dawn came up, I was exhausted but at peace. As long as she needs me, this will be my life, I swore.

The next morning, Isis sent a messenger for me.

"Tell Isis I cannot leave my child."

"Isis says what she gave, she can take away," the messenger said.

"Don't go," said Prax. "This is an empty threat. She has restored the babe to health. She cannot take away the gift."

But I was not so sure. I agonized. Should I go? Should I stay? Was Isis a witch who could give life, then snatch it back?

"I'll be back before you know it," I said, handing the baby to my mother. I ran to Isis in a sweat.

When I arrived at Isis' house, I found she had dismissed all her clients. She was in a rage.

"Love is not a tender emotion," Isis said and bit me on the neck, drawing blood. "It is wild as the beasts of the jungle. I save your daughter, and still you yearn for other lovers. Who is this Alcaeus? Are you planning to leave me for him? How many other lovers do you have? Are you cheating on me even here in Syracuse?"

"No, Isis, not at all. There is no one but you. Alcaeus taught me all I know about my art. I have unfinished business with him."

"You are in love with him!"

"Not at all—"

"I think you are planning to leave me and seek this Alcaeus in Delphi. I heard everything you said to Cyrus!"

"You yourself said I must go to Egypt and make sure my brothers do not steal my family's wine trade from me."

"Then why were you speaking of Delphi with that coarse Lydian?"

"I am not going anywhere. I have a daughter here who needs me. I must get home to her now." I started to go, but Isis held me back.

"Sappho—I have known the love of women and the love of men—I can promise you men are never to be trusted. They think only of their dominance, their mastery, their desire. . . ."

Then she dragged me onto the floor and she made love to me as violently as a man, coaxing moans out of me again and again with a golden *olisbos,* biting me on the neck, the breasts, the lips of my sex until I was covered with blood and saliva and all the outpourings of love. I did not think it possible for one woman to take another by force, but she showed me it was. I was lucky to escape with my life. I ran home again, desperate to see my daughter.

I DON'T WANT to report what happened next. It still hurts my heart to think about it. When I returned, the baby and wet nurses were gone—as was my mother. They had taken a ship for Lesbos. My mother left a note:

Pittacus has offered us his protection. I take my namesake for her own good. Don't try to follow or you will hurt your own child more than you have hurt her already. Someday I pray you will understand.

Praxinoa was weeping in distress. She was inconsolable.

"What have you done?" I screamed in a panic. "What did you tell my mother, Prax?"

"She questioned me about Isis and Alcaeus. She wouldn't leave me alone until I confessed everything I knew. She threatened flogging and I knew she meant it. Oh, Sappho, forgive me! I never thought she'd take the baby. I tried to stop her—really I did."

WHEN YOU LOOK back at your life from the edge of a cliff, the obstacles you faced seem self-created, the adventures imagined, the heroism less heroic than it seemed at the time. When my mother kidnapped my baby, I felt as Demeter must have felt when her daughter was scuttled away to Hades' realm. A black cloak was drawn across my face and I could not see the sun. I raged. I wept. I blamed my mother at first, then Isis, then Praxinoa, then myself. But I had put Praxinoa in an impossible situation and I knew it. Jealous of Isis, still angry with me for disappearing with Alcaeus and letting her be punished for it, how could she protect me when my mother pressed her? No one was to blame for my mother taking the baby but me. In a daze of lust, I had lost the most precious creature I had ever known. I had given my mother every excuse to treat me like an irresponsible child. I had provoked Praxinoa with my usual carelessness.

What use was it to *say* you loved? You had to show it. I wanted desperately to chase my baby across the sea, yet I knew that in Lesbos both my life and hers would be in mortal danger. Without me, Pittacus would protect her for my mother's sake. The pain I felt was unbearable, but it was possible that my daughter was safer without me.

"Let's run to the harbor—perhaps we can still stop them!" Praxinoa said.

We ran like the wind, our sandals clattering over the cobblestones. In the market, I knocked over a stand of ripe pomegranates, then fell into the heap of red fruit, which stained my chiton as if with blood. I picked myself up again and ran. The pomegranate seller shouted curses after me. Carts blocked our way. Donkeys laden with fruits and spices slowly crossed the narrow causeway to the harbor. It was like a nightmare in which you try to run, but your way is blocked no matter where you turn. Crowds of people surged from the harbor. Some had just arrived and were balancing all manner of baskets and parcels on their

heads, in their hands, on carts overflowing with their ragtag possessions. We pushed through the crowd, smelling the sweat of mingled
humanity. Finally we arrived at the water's edge to see the boat for
Lesbos disappearing into the distance, its sails red in the setting sun. I
collapsed on the dock and wept the tears of the damned.

7

Gold, a Shipwreck, and a Dream

I don't expect to reach the sky.

—SAPPHO

I WENT INTO a long black tunnel after that. After the loss of my daughter I could not eat for weeks. I barely touched a drop of water. I slept and slept to escape the curse of consciousness. In my dreams the baby was restored to me. I could smell her sweet smell and press her to my breasts. Life seemed worth living again. Then I awoke and found myself newly bereft.

It was an excruciating punishment, to dream of her with me and wake up to find her snatched away. If I'd had the courage then, I would have drunk poison or opened my veins. But something always stopped me.

"Your mother may relent and come back," Praxinoa said, trying to comfort me. I doubted that. But maybe we'd find a way to get back to Lesbos. Perhaps there would be a revolution and Pittacus would be expelled from power. As long as there was the remotest chance of seeing my daughter again, I could not take my own life. Not then.

I had no wish to see Isis. Because she knew that I was through with her, she sent me endless gifts. I returned them all—except for a golden cartouche with her name written in hieroglyphics and a golden cat curled on top of the symbols in sweet sleep. Praxinoa took great pleasure tossing it into the sea.

Eventually Cyrus came to find me. I had not thought of him or his stories about Alcaeus since my mother had decamped with my daughter. In my misery, I had scarcely thought of Alcaeus. It seemed my life was over and love would never be mine again. I slept all day and paced all night. The sun seemed black, the nights were haunted. If it had been up to me, I would never have admitted Cyrus of Sardis through my door, but Praxinoa thought he might distract me from my grief, so she let him in.

"Send him away!" I said.

"He claims he has news of Alcaeus."

"I don't care," I said. "I only care for news of Cleis. I'm sure he has none of that."

"Sappho—hear what he has to say. It may even lead you to your daughter."

"I doubt it," I said gloomily, but by then Cyrus stood at the door with a long scroll in his hand.

"A letter from Alcaeus of Lesbos," he said. "For you."

"Go away," I said.

"Aren't you even a tiny bit curious?"

"No," I said. "I am only curious about my baby."

"The letter is in Greek," he said, waving it. He came closer. I could see it was in Alcaeus' hand.

He brought it to me. In fact it was not a letter to me, but my name was mentioned several times. Cyrus was beseeched for news of me and how I was faring in Syracuse. "If you should meet the lovely violet-haired Sappho," it said, "tell her she is always in my thoughts." He also reported that he was on the way to Delphi to consult the oracle for the Lydian king.

"If we journey to Delphi, we can also consult the oracle for news of your daughter," Cyrus wheedled. "And there is money to be made in Delphi. People are so bored waiting for the oracle that they pay well for entertainment. Perhaps also we shall find Alcaeus there. In fact, I'm sure we shall!"

"Go away!" I said.

Cyrus went away that time, but he proved to be persistent. He came back again and again, always with new temptations. If I would agree to sing at a certain symposium, he could guarantee me my weight in gold.

"Sappho—I know who will pay, and pay well, for songs. I know the rich all over the known world. I met them all in Sardis—ahhh, I should have bought land near the palace in Sardis when it was still cheap—but that is another story."

"Go away!" I screamed.

"Her weight in gold?" Praxinoa asked. "She's a tiny thing, but we could use the gold."

"What are you talking about?" I asked.

"You may not have noticed this in your despair, but ever since Cercylas died, no money has been coming in from the ships or the wine trade. We owe everyone. We have been trading the produce of our farm for bread and wine, but soon we may lose the farm. Cercylas was improvident. It appears that even when he was *alive* he had enormous debts. While you have been sleeping, I've been managing all this. You'd better sing for your supper or there'll be no supper."

"How can this be true?" I asked.

"I don't know the how of it—but we do have debts. Every morning the merchants are at our door, looking for payment. I have held them off till now, but if there is a way to get gold—you have no choice."

"I concur," said Cyrus.

"But if I sing for gold, my goddess will desert me."

"But if you don't, your stomach will be empty. And mine," said Prax. "Sappho, you have never been very practical—so let me be practical for you, for us both. We need the gold. We need to go to Egypt to protect your legacy, and that will be expensive. If we can earn some money here and earn some more in Delphi—then that's what we must do. We no longer have any choice in the matter."

Cyrus was trembling with excitement. "She's right!" he said. "I can arrange for you to sing at a symposium tomorrow night! Get your songs ready! I shall bring the golden litter for you at sundown!"

"Wait," said Prax. "How much will she make tomorrow?"

"That's hard to say," said Cyrus.

"What about her weight in gold?" asked Prax.

"A figure of speech," said Cyrus.

"Then my mistress will not sing."

"Are you crazy, Prax? I thought we needed the money," I burst out.

"Shhh," said Prax. And then to Cyrus: "If you will bring me half her weight this afternoon, I will let my mistress sing."

"You drive a hard bargain," said Cyrus. "I'll bring my own scale."

"I'd rather use mine," said Prax with obvious satisfaction. "Sappho—go get your repertory ready. Hurry!"

When Cyrus returned later that afternoon, he and Prax argued over weights and measures. I heard them shrieking at each other as I was trying to rehearse my songs. Eventually, I was summoned out of my chamber to sit in a swing hooked up to an elaborate scale. Prax was loading one side of the scale with weights. Cyrus was removing them. Both of them were accusing each other of cheating.

"You'll break me!" Cyrus was protesting while Prax loaded on the weights.

"My mistress is the biggest bargain of your life!" Prax countered. The weights went on. The weights came off. I myself climbed on and off the swing while they argued over whose mechanism was better and whose weights more accurate. It was excruciating. All the while I was tuning my lyre.

"Can I go now?" I asked, as they seemed to be reaching some sort of compromise.

"Go rehearse and rest and make yourself beautiful," said Cyrus. "You never know how a symposium can change your life."

Cyrus came back at six leading a golden litter carried by four burly slaves. The canopy was purple linen embroidered with gold and matched the costumes of the slaves. Praxinoa and I climbed into the litter, which took us through the busy streets of Syracuse. We came into the courtyard of a great villa. Before anyone could see me, Cyrus and Praxinoa led me to private dressing quarters to robe me in royal purple, paint my face elaborately, and perfume me for my performance. Then I waited for the dinner to be over and the floor swept before I appeared with my lyre.

Cyrus introduced me as the "legendary Sappho of Lesbos." I emerged from the shadows, surrounded by slaves bearing torches and sweet incense. I started with my "Hymn to Aphrodite," which had so moved the company at Lesbos. Even before I came to the whirling of wings and the chariot descending, I could feel the audience warming to me. What a wonderful feeling! I enchanted myself as I enchanted them! I was in love with the sound of my own voice, in love with their applause and laughter. When I had softened them up with Aphrodite, I moved on to other songs of love.

> *Some say a host of horsemen*
> *And some say a line of ships*
> *Is the most beautiful thing*
> *On the dark earth—*
> *But I say it is what you love!*

> *Helen deserted her husband*
> *And daughter*
> *And sailed to Troy*
> *When the goddess of love*
> *Called her.*

Here I paused and waited for the audience to remember all their own impossible loves. How I knew to do this I cannot say, but I knew it intuitively and it enabled me to manipulate my listeners. I embodied their hunger and yearning perhaps because deep within me there was so much yearning for Cleis and Alcaeus. My desperation fueled my singing.

> *I would rather see the bright face*
> *Of my beloved*

Than Lydian chariots
And full-armed infantry.

There was a catch in my throat because of my recent losses, and the audience felt it. I had become the orphaned, yearning part of them. I felt their pulse and became one with it. Though I had rehearsed all my songs before the symposium, I decided which of them to sing when I met the audience and appraised their hunger. I even improvised for the crowd. Did they lust for young girls? I sang of young girls. Did they dream of sweet-cheeked boys? I sang of them. Did they dream of marriage for their daughters? I dazzled them with epithalamia. I tugged on their heartstrings by ending with this refrain:

The moon and the Pleiades are set.
It is midnight and time spins away.
I lie in my bed alone.

And they rewarded me with thunderous applause.

Later, when I walked among the guests, I was amazed at how well I had taken their measure.

"You speak my own thoughts," one woman said.

"No—you speak mine!" said her husband.

"I am honored to be your mouthpiece," I said. And I was. But I was also thinking of the gold.

Cyrus of Sardis charged ever more gold for my performances. And the more he charged, the more the people thought they were worth. They bragged to their guests about how much they had paid for my performances. It was a point of pride that I was so expensive.

But Aphrodite appeared less and less frequently to me. I knew she was angry. My gifts had been given to honor her, not to earn a fortune. I knew she would take her revenge, but I could not imagine what it would be. She had already humbled me with the loss of my daughter and Alcaeus. What more could she do to me? I trembled to contemplate her wrath.

What does the singer learn? Enchantment. We love the gods for their powers of enchantment and we seek to summon them by imitating these powers. We burn incense; we utter incantations in order to become like the gods, in order to attract them. But if the motivation is false—gold, not godliness—the gods will know. Eventually our powers will fail. We will not be able to attract the muses to replenish our song.

I knew these things, but I banished them from my consciousness, as I tried—unsuccessfully—to banish thoughts of baby Cleis and my beloved Alcaeus. Driven by the desire to hoard gold to protect myself, I followed Cyrus' lead. Or was it that I loved performing so? I was intoxicated with my own singing. Each time I ventured to transport the crowd, I transported myself. Perhaps their laughter and shouts of encouragement were dearer to me even than their gold. When the floor was swept for my performance, when I took up the lyre and cleared my throat, when I saw the spectators sitting rapt, I was transported to another realm. Yes, the truth is, performing made me feel equal to the gods because I could so manipulate the feelings of my spectators. I thought I was as powerful as Aphrodite. I thought I held the keys to her enchantments. I sang of her, but secretly I sang of myself.

That much-quoted line—*I don't expect to reach the sky*—was written in a fit of remorse after one of these lucrative symposia in Syracuse. It was the night before we sailed for Delphi and I was disgusted with what I had become.

"I began by honoring the gods," I said to Prax, "and now I honor gold. Something terrible will surely happen."

"What can be worse than what has already happened?" asked Praxinoa.

THE VOYAGE to Delphi was harsh. Fog banks stalled us. Storms pummeled our vessel. The gods tossed us around like corks in the sea. I had never been prone to seasickness before, but on this occasion I was.

We have all heard the minstrels sing the adventures of Odysseus—but the women in the legends of our founders sit and spin. Penelope weaves and unweaves. Helen is captured for love—but where is there one woman who sets out on the sea to earn her wisdom? I would be that woman.

From Trinacria to Delphi was fierce open ocean, unbroken by islands. There was no way to hug the shore, to stop overnight, to stop for provisions, to stop for rest. It was cloudy that night; the captain could not steer by the stars. After a time we realized that he had no idea where we were headed. We were as likely to wind up in Hades' realm as at Delphi.

Still worse, the captain and sailors had heard that we were rich in gold and they were determined to have it and then throw me into the sea. When I protested that all my gold had been left in Syracuse, they did not believe me.

"Surely you must have some aboard," the captain said.

"Not enough to content you—but if you take me back to Syracuse alive, I will show you my hoard of gold and give you all you wish."

They debated among themselves, thinking this was a plot to outwit them. But Cyrus intervened, denuding himself of all his golden ornaments and promising more upon our return to Syracuse. I think they were divided among themselves about what to do. The captain attempted to convince them to follow Cyrus' plan, promising them riches beyond measure if they returned to Syracuse—which was easier said than done. The wind had begun to blow in great gusts and a heady storm was brewing. All future plans were forgotten as we clung to the craft for our lives.

I thought I had known rough seas—at Pyrrha, sailing to Syracuse, at Motya—but I had never known the full power of Poseidon before this. The boat heeled so far over that men were lost overboard with every pitch. I clung to the side of the ship as the waves buffeted me, but it was only by entangling my feet in the lines that I managed to stay aboard. Alcaeus had taught me this—and it saved my life.

The captain was lost, and most of his men. Overboard they went—their pockets filled with Cyrus' gold, which had no power to save them. The bottom of the sea must be paved with gold, I thought, and the bones of those who died diving for it.

ZEUS: *I would let her perish right there—unlikely heroine that she is. . . .*
APHRODITE: *You have no patience. This woman will be a myth for three millennia if you let me finish her story.*
ZEUS: *I see no point. . . .*

APHRODITE: *You never see the point of women's lives unless they bear you children.*

ZEUS: *I can even do* that *myself. Drown Sappho, give me Cleis. I'll sew her up in my thigh, give birth to her again, and then we'll start fresh with her story.*

APHRODITE: *I will not silence the only woman's voice that reverberates through time.*

ZEUS: *Who cares?*

APHRODITE: *I care! And so will others.*

ZEUS: *Then* you *save her.*

APHRODITE: *I will, with Poseidon's help—if not with yours.*

ZEUS: *Poseidon! My brother always* was *a pest. Look what he did to Odysseus.*

Praxinoa was struck by a wooden crosspiece from the mast ripped loose by the wind. She was knocked unconscious. Cyrus of Sardis held on for a time, then went the way of his gold. I clung on through the storm, wishing for unconsciousness but remaining damnably awake. Then, by the grace of the gods, I slept.

I dreamed I was Odysseus being pummeled by Poseidon and not knowing which way to turn. Then the white sea goddess, Leucothea, appeared to me as she had to him.

"*Get clear of the wreckage, Sappho,*" she said to me, "*for it will kill you more surely than the sea. Ride the steering oar as if it were a horse. Take this magic veil and cover yourself and Praxinoa with it. It will protect you both as you make your way to shore.*"

"But there is no shore!" I said. "This is open sea all the way to Delphi."

"*Trust me,*" the sea goddess said.

I ditched my heavy clothes and stripped the sleeping Praxinoa naked as well. Catching her up in the magic veil, straddling the steering oar as I'd been told, I paddled with all my might. Out of the corners of my eyes, I seemed to see white dolphins pulling the magic veil, but perhaps this was a dream.

When at last I reached the sea-lapped shores of a tranquil island and put Praxinoa gently down, I was certain I was dead. Were these the Elysian Fields?

Three women were dancing gracefully together on the edge of the sea. One was Helen, her luxuriant red hair still singed by the burning towers of Troy. The second was Demeter, with her crown of fruits and flowers, and the third Athena, with her battle helmet. They were all voluptuously naked and fair. They seemed to welcome me.

"Is it best to live for love?" Helen asked. "We have been discussing this. Can you resolve it?"

"Motherhood is what I live for," said Demeter, "and so must all women."

"Intellect is best," Athena said. "Love and motherhood will drag you down into the mire like animals. Only virginity and a warrior's pride can save a woman from her fate."

"But without love we are only half alive!" Helen exclaimed as if she were Aphrodite.

They danced around and around as their argument went around and around. They seemed to have been dancing forever.

Praxinoa awoke. She couldn't believe her eyes.

"We are among immortals!" she cried—half in delight, half in fear.

"Then join our debate," said beautiful half-immortal Helen, with her breasts like ripe pears, her pubic thatch like fire, her white thighs the color of cream rising.

"Shall we live for love or motherhood or intellect?" the daughter of Zeus and Leda sang. Her voice was as beautiful as her face.

"Motherhood and all its joys and woes," Demeter sighed. "Without it there would be no people on the face of the earth."

"The brain above the heart," Athena said, "or we are all beasts of the field."

"Love," said Helen, "for love alone inspires all things to grow—even children and the glory of war."

"Look where love took you," I said, "and the world!"

"I would do it all again!" said Helen. "I regret nothing!"

Praxinoa was laughing, laughing, laughing. I was afraid she would offend the immortals.

"Look at you all," she said, "arguing like free women—not even dreaming that liberty is at the root of your choices. What if you were slaves?"

The dancing stopped and the three lovely ones looked quizzical and perplexed.

"Liberty is at the root of all we want," said Praxinoa, "for only free women can participate in this debate. Choice is the luxury of the free."

The goddesses and Helen danced away. Praxinoa and I woke up on a sandy beach with salt on our lashes and seaweed in our hair.

8

At the Navel of the Earth

I know the number of grains of sand and the extent of the sea;
I understand the deaf-mute and hear the words of the dumb.
—THE ORACLE OF DELPHI

AFTER THAT MEETING with immortal beauty, motherhood, and wisdom, our luck turned. The weather grew fair and bright. Helen and the goddesses had vanished, but we were picked up by a Phoenician ship bound for Delphi and continued on our journey there as easily as if the gods themselves had decreed it. Cyrus of Sardis was gone. Our gold was gone. But Delphi was the source of all wisdom, so we were hopeful about the future. There our luck would surely change! There we would surely find Alcaeus and a prophecy about Cleis! If what Cyrus had told us was true, Delphi would reverse our fortunes and make us whole. But we were soon to discover that Cyrus had *not* told us all we needed to know.

Across the sea to the Gulf of Corinth, the weather continued beautiful and breezy. Our hearts pounded in anticipation. Delphi was the oldest of the old. It was said that gods had been summoned there long before the olympians ruled the earth. Gaia had been worshiped in Delphi by Cretan priests and priestesses. Dangerous chthonian deities had been defeated and destroyed at Delphi by Apollo the lawgiver and his *prophetai*. In Delphi wisdom ruled if it ruled nowhere else in the whole civilized world. We were going to the fount of all wisdom and civilization, the place where we could truly learn what the spinners had in store. No wonder we were so excited!

We left our boat at the foot of Mount Parnassus and gazed up to see its top buried in billowing clouds.

"This is the place where we will learn our destiny!" I said to Praxinoa.

"It's a long way up," Praxinoa said.

Everything about Delphi was calculated to fill you with awe. The climb up Mount Parnassus made you so short of breath that you could not help but see gods and goddesses in the mist. The owls' screeching and the hollow footsteps of giants who had come before you intensified the atmosphere of the supernatural. Often the sky filled with tumultuous black clouds and lightning flashes as if indeed Zeus were hovering near. Then all at once the skies would open up and radiant rainbows would arc across the mountaintops. The sun would pierce the clouds. You knew then you were in the presence of Apollo.

Three springs rush through a cleft in the sacred mountain. There at the confluence, where the mist rises almost as thick as fog at sea, is Apollo's chosen spot. Some say it is called the great *omphalos*, or navel, of the earth because of the hills that rise around it, trapping sacred mist and intoxicating vapors. Some say Delphi was already a sacred place in days of old, when our ancestors worshiped the earth goddesses who were later dethroned by Zeus and his children. It feels like a sacred place—as if magic can be worked there. The heart beats faster, the limbs grow cold, you draw breath with difficulty and not only because of the altitude. As you climb the sacred way, you see other pilgrims— the rich riding in their slave-carried litters, the barefoot poor begging worn-out sandals and crusts of bread, the prosperous city merchants aping the manners of the aristocracy.

The temple of Apollo is built over this vaporous cleft in the living rock. Apollo's statue—all ivory and gold—stands wreathed in mist as if the god himself were there. The Pythia, we were told by other pilgrims, sits on a tripod over the abyss, crowned in laurel, chewing laurel leaves and raving in fragments of various dream languages. She inhales sacred fumes in a special chamber only priests can enter and then she rises on her tripod to rave again.

"You will think you hear Egyptian, then Phoenician, then Phrygian, then bits of Greek—then gibberish," said one rich pilgrim from Samos whom Praxinoa and I met coming down the mountain after his audience with the oracle. "The Pythia tantalizes you by seeming to speak sense, then sinking into nonsense. There are many complex rituals to perform before you are allowed into her presence—or even into the presence of her priests. But you might as well turn back here, because women are not allowed to see the oracle."

"But the oracle *is* a woman!" I protested.

"Still, women are not allowed into her presence," the pilgrim said.

"That seems illogical," I said.

"Well, women are illogical," the man said, displaying what passed for male logic.

"What can we do?" Prax asked. "We *must* see her."

"Then grow a phallus!" the pilgrim said, laughing as he continued down the mountain as we were climbing upward.

"We will disguise ourselves as men, Prax. Don't worry." For the Samian pilgrim, growing a phallus was a joke. But this joke gave me a good idea.

"We'll dress as men," I said. "Who will be the wiser?"

"The oracle will know," Prax protested.

"As long as her priests don't know, we'll be fine," I told Praxinoa. As usual, I pretended to a confidence I didn't really possess.

EVERYONE CAME to Delphi: founders of cities; would-be bridegrooms—no brides, of course, due to the prohibition against women; generals who wished to pursue wars against their king's neighbors; tyrants like Pittacus who wished to overtake cities and rule their inhabitants; wise men, stupid men, stupid wise men.

Some waited and waited. Some bribed the priests and got ahead in line. Some bribed the priests and got nothing. The system was complex and unknowable. You almost had to be an oracle yourself to figure out how to *see* the oracle.

The theory was that Apollo knew his father Zeus' will and that the oracle could interpret what Apollo knew. The process was far from simple. The oracle only worked on certain days, according to a schedule the priests delighted in changing as capriciously as possible. Just as the Oracle of Olympia "spoke" through sacrifice of animals and the examination of their entrails, just as the Oracle of Dodona at Epirus "spoke" through the whisperings of wind in the oaks, the cooing of doves, and the striking of the golden bowl (which was really brass under a golden wash)—the Oracle of Delphi "spoke" through the priests, who translated her ravings into ambiguous verses. Since the future is ambiguous, prophecy itself must be ambiguous. We see the future intermittently through mist.

"Some say the Pythia was once a laurel tree!" said a pilgrim who climbed with us awhile. "Just as the Oracle of Dodona was once an oak, a laurel tree once spoke at Delphi."

Praxinoa made a disbelieving face at him.

"The ways of the older gods are strange indeed," the climber said, huffing and puffing as we outdistanced him.

"How do you know these things?" asked Prax, looking down at him.

"Everybody knows these things," the man opined.

Praxinoa sniffed. She was not an easy one to convince.

Climbing the mountain, we looked everywhere for Alcaeus, but alas, we did not see him.

"I suspect he is waiting at the top to see the oracle," said Praxinoa.

"Or maybe he never came here after all. Maybe Cyrus of Sardis lied," I said. It seemed more and more possible that poor dead Cyrus was a fraud.

As we trudged ever upward, I thought about all we had to do, and it seemed overwhelming. First we had to raise more gold, since it was clear that the predictions of the oracle would not come cheap. Then we would have to procure disguises and find our way into the sacred precincts to beg for a prediction about Cleis and Alcaeus. And we seemed to have plenty of competition for the oracle's attention. People we met on the climb warned us that many had grown old awaiting the oracle.

"If you think it is easy to get a prediction out of the Oracle of Delphi, think again!" the pilgrim from Samos had warned. And it was true. Even before we reached the top of the mountain, we could see a long line of suppliants snaking around and around. Some men had been waiting months and had even pitched tents on the mountain passes while they took turns waiting in line. However many bags of gold they had brought, it seemed that someone had brought more or had been waiting longer. The priests went among the people in line, extracting tribute. The system seemed very corrupt. The treasuries of Delphi contained riches from all over the known world.

As we reached the very top of the mountain, people who had seen the oracle told us all sorts of things. Some were angry. Some were satisfied.

"She tells nothing," one young man from Chios reported. "She sputters and foams at the mouth. It is the priests who tell you what she says, but their verses are so ambiguous that even then it is hard to understand them. The meaning of the oracle is wrapped in clouds like this mountaintop. You pull away one layer, but behind it other layers remain."

"What did she tell you?" I asked.

"She told me she knew the number of grains of sand and the depths of the sea. I had no idea what she meant."

"She was telling you she encompasses all knowledge," I said. "She was telling you her prophecies are wide as the desert and deep as the sea." The man stopped and stared at me.

"I think you're right!" he said. "She talks in riddles!"

"Not riddles," I said, "metaphors. She talks in a symbolic language—like a singer or poet. You can understand her only if you don't think literally."

"Then you are an oracle too!" the Chian said.

"In a way, I suppose you could say I am."

"For everyone but yourself," Prax teased.

The man from Chios got very excited. He called his friends and traveling companions. "She's an oracle too," he said. "Repeat what you just told me," he directed.

"Only if you pay her," said Praxinoa.

"How much?" asked the Chian.

"An *obolos* will do," said Prax.

And this was how, in the weeks that followed, we raised enough money to see the oracle herself.

PRAXINOA HAD LEARNED her lessons well from Cyrus of Sardis. As the word got out that I was a sort of oracle who could interpret the mysteries of the oracle, Prax kept raising my price. I began by explaining the utterances of the oracle, but before long, people were coming to me and bypassing the oracle. The wait was shorter. The priests did not have to be propitiated. Only Praxinoa had to be paid.

Of course, Delphi was the haunt of many soothsayers. Oracles beget oracles. The ones who wait keep busy with sacrificing, with divination by birds, by entrails, by flames, by wind, by smoke. The ones who have seen the oracle require help in interpreting her pronouncements. The whole precinct reeks of magic, and where there is magic—or the promise of magic—gold always changes hands.

Many wisdom-seekers had brought beautifully crafted golden objects to donate to the treasury at Delphi. It was our pleasure to divert these into our own hands. When we were certain we had collected enough *oboloi* and golden trinkets to please the priests and attempt entrance to the oracle's divine presence, we borrowed turbans and caftans from some clients from the East, glued false beards and mustaches on our female faces, and made ready to breach the inner sanctum, the *adytum*. We knew, of course, that there would be many more complex rituals to perform before we were allowed into the Pythia's presence—or even into the presence of her priests, the *prophetai* who interpreted her will.

"Aren't you afraid that the seekers we have counseled will tell the priests we are women?" Prax asked.

"Why would they? We could retaliate by exposing them for having cheated the oracle and her interpreters. I think fear will silence them. If you say nothing, nothing will be said to you. We owe no loyalty to these priests, these *prophetai* who profit by the oracle's wisdom. If we act as if everything is normal, they will do the same."

So we prepared to see the oracle. First we had to purify ourselves with water from the Castalian Spring, then with oil infused with perfume of rare mountain flowers. Then we had to sacrifice a fine heifer, catch her blood in a pure golden bowl (of our own provisioning), and give it to the priests to examine. They got to keep the bowl. Then we had to share the sanctified meat with Apollo—and of course with the hungry priests. After that we stopped at the treasury to leave our golden offerings and watch them duly catalogued in the papyrus rolls. Then we retreated from the priests to change into clean robes and turbans.

Did I forget to say that before all this we had to abstain from sex for three full days and nights? How can I have forgotten? Prax and I were at that age when three days and three nights were an eternity. We had always found comfort in each other's arms—except during the days when I was besotted with Isis. But now we kept our eager hands off each other. We were determined to elicit a prophecy that we could *use*.

Meanwhile, wherever we went in the sacred precinct, fingers were outstretched to relieve us of *oboloi* and of gold. We watched our fellow suppliants shed golden objects as if they were eagles molting. Many suppliants were turned away even after observing all the rituals. Others were made to wait longer and longer and were finally dismissed. But somehow our luck held and the priests moved us along in the final line that snaked around the innermost sanctuary.

They say there are many Pythias—that they take turns uttering prophecies. Some wags even say that the Pythia is no woman but a priest in women's garb. Others claim the Pythia is no virgin, but, in fact, a former prostitute who has passed the age of erotic love. I can only relate what I saw on my first audience with the Pythia. If it was a show, it was a damned good one!

To my eyes, the Pythia, who wore a wreath of laurel and held a laurel branch, appeared first as woman with the face of a mad dog—a very hairy mad dog whose face was almost hidden but whose mouth moved like a separate animal. The Pythia frothed at the mouth, tore at her linen, rubbed herself between the legs, and said whatever she pleased like a child babbling nonsense syllables. The *prophetai* stood around her like sentinels and did not show any emotion as she raved. Her words were hard to understand. Some of them made sense. Some of them did not.

"Oho. Oho. Oho. Who comes now? Speak, stranger. Are you the Pythia's friend?"

"Yes!" I replied.

"The sea opens, but it does not close. The waves are green but also white. The waves are wine. The waves overflow their immense amphora. . . . The gold of Lydia will hardly shine the lilies . . . they shine themselves. . . ."

As she spoke, vapor rose from the narrow crevice that traversed the sanctuary. I felt drunk as I inhaled this vapor, or was I again imagining?

I looked at Prax. She looked at me and opened her eyes wide. If only we could speak.

Most of what the oracle says makes no sense or the priests would be out of a job. First they are silent and solemn. Then they eagerly hover around her, interpreting her smallest gasp, her longest ululation. I swear they must interpret her farts!

The priests were impressed that the Pythia addressed me directly.

"Very rare," said one.

"Rare, indeed," said another.

"May I ask if the Pythia knows Alcaeus of Lesbos?" I asked.

"Indeed," said one of the priests, "he is drunk on prophecy. He laps up prophecy as some men lap up wine. He was here some months ago for the king of Lydia, the great Alyattes, son of Sadyattes, son of Ardys, son of Gyges, who overthrew Candaules, who was too enamored of his own fair wife. . . . A man who loves his wife too much must come to grief. . . ."

"All very good customers," said another priest.

"You mean—very pious kings," another priest said.

"That too," said the chief priest.

"He asked a few questions about the future of his king," said the chief priest. And then he asked many questions about Sappho of Lesbos—a well-known singer."

"He did?" I asked.

"That he did," said the priest.

"And what did the Pythia tell him of this Sappho of Lesbos—whoever she may be?" This last question came from Prax.

At this the Pythia began to foam at the mouth and sputter syllables: "Psa, Psa, Psa, fa, fa, fa, ha, ha, ha!"

"What does she say?" I asked.

"Shhhhhhhh," whispered the chief priest. "Listen!"

"Cypris guards this girl," said the Pythia—as clear as you or me. Then she erupted again in a shower of nonsense syllables. Cypris, of course, was another name for Aphrodite, who was born out of the sea at Cyprus.

"What does she say?" I asked again.

The Pythia burbled, bubbled, hissed. The mist grew thicker and thunder rumbled above the gorge as if Zeus himself were giving orders to his son Apollo. I swear I felt earth shake under my feet—which was indeed possible since Delphi was in a region of earthquakes. There was a beating of wings as if Aphrodite had just flown in, drawn by sparrows with whirring wings and gentle doves who cooed like lovers.

"What? What did you say?" the Pythia asked, seeming to hear voices from above. "Who are you? Are you Apollo or another god?"

"This is grave," said the chief priest. "She only interprets Apollo's will. If other gods are here, it is a miracle. It will strain her brain and sap her strength."

"Let me hear!" I shouted.

The Pythia blathered and blathered, occasionally saying a word I could understand. I understood "The Cyprian says . . ." and then "Great Zeus says . . ." and then again "Aphrodite is greater than any other god—for even gods obey her!"

Then she sputtered unintelligibly for some time, while the priests listened intently, writing down her words on wax-covered wooden tablets, which would later be transferred by scribes to papyrus rolls.

"What is she saying of Sappho?" I shouted. "What? What?"

"Calm yourself, man," said the chief priest. "We must study and compare our notes on the oracle's utterances. We must go to our sacred grove and pray for the right interpretation. We cannot be rushed in our sacred duties. This is not child's play. This is prophecy. This is the god speaking."

"Indeed," said the second priest. "We must sacrifice again, drink wine, and ponder. Apply again tomorrow."

One by one they shuffled off. Probably they were going to finish the remains of my roasted red heifer. For a moment, Prax and I were left alone in the presence of the oracle. She looked up, stopped sputtering, cleared away her wild hair, and looked suddenly like a beautiful woman. I swear she could have been Aphrodite come down to earth!

She winked at us and smiled:

> The net has been cast, the little fish dart in the sea.
> Your daughter is safe; she will greet you again as a woman.
> Egypt awaits and your foolish brothers.
> You must be the salvation of all your kin.
> You will save them all with immortal song!

The mist now rose in a thick cloud, covering the Pythia's face. Or was it Aphrodite's?

A guard came and hustled us out of the sacred place.

9

Aesop at the Orgy

Don't let Doricha boast
That he crawled back for love
A second time.
—SAPPHO

WE STAYED in Delphi for a while after that, piling up gold, trying to see the Pythia again. To no avail. The priests assiduously kept us away no matter how we bribed them. We also looked everywhere for someone who had met Alcaeus when he was in Delphi and could report to us of him, but we never found such a person. Then, just as we had decided to seek passage to Naucratis in Egypt, a sign of Alcaeus' presence was sent to us.

By now we could afford to stay in a luxurious guesthouse, staffed by slaves, full of private gardens, fountains, and rich wall paintings. Our room had been decorated by a skilled Egyptian painter with paintings of suppliants bringing offerings to the Pythia. One of the females in the procession was small, had blue-black hair twined with violets and gold thread, and carried a lyre. She was walking behind a golden-haired warrior in full battle dress.

My heart sang. I was sure the painting depicted Alcaeus and me. All our play in Pyrrha came back to me. I remembered his twining violets in the hair of my delta and kissing the nether lips tenderly. I remembered him telling me that the corners of my eyes turned up like no other in the world. I remembered him discovering a mole on my finger and finding it beautiful. He kissed it again and again. I remembered him saying to me as we lay in bed, "No one, not even Aphrodite, escapes desire."

Then my mood crashed and turned black. What a fool I was, to find portents in wall paintings. This was no sign of anything at all. It was sheer coincidence. I was grasping at straws because I missed him so.

AFTER DELPHI, we were lucky to get as far as Crete in another Phoenician boat with a captain who knew of my fame as a singer. On the way, we even stopped at Aphrodite's island, Cythera, where we fervently worshiped at her shrines without a flicker of response from her. Praxinoa knew how excited I was to be visiting the very island where Aphrodite was born from the foam.

"Perhaps she will appear to us," said Prax, "as she did at Delphi."

"I dream of it," I said. "Somehow I feel that only she can restore Cleis and Alcaeus to us."

"Then pray for that," said Prax.

"I will," I said.

So I prayed and sacrificed and sang my "Hymn to Aphrodite," but the response was silence. Always before, I had felt Aphrodite's daily presence in my life, but now she seemed absent even on the island of her birth. I sang to her and she returned a strange stillness. The predictions of the Oracle of Delphi haunted me. Was I never to see Cleis until she was full-grown? Was Aphrodite to retreat now that she had appeared to us in Delphi in the guise of the Pythia? Who could tell? It was all too terrible to contemplate.

From Cythera, an Egyptian ship took us as far as Naucratis on the Nile Delta. I entertained the Greeks who were sailing to Egypt, and by the time the voyage ended I had replenished still more of my gold. I asked the traders on board of the fate of my brothers Charaxus and Larichus, but they only laughed and would not enlighten me.

"You'll see what has become of your brothers soon enough," one trader told me. "It happens to most of the Greeks in Naucratis. It probably accounts for the untimely passing of your late husband."

COMING INTO the Nile Delta by water is an unforgettable experience. Where the lands of the Greeks are rocky and precipitous, Egypt looks newly reclaimed from the sea. Silty and marshy from constant flooding, the land is so fertile that the Egyptian farmer has only to sow his seeds when the waters recede, wait for them to grow, and harvest his fields as a gift of the Nile.

The Egyptian gods are the oldest of the old and some sages claim they have given birth to our Greek ones. The Egyptians were also the first people to divide the year into seasons, the seasons into months.

The great Egyptian pharaoh Necho, who admired the Greeks inordinately, had made the city of Naucratis a sanctuary for Greek traders from Chios, Samos, Rhodes, and Mytilene. Necho had been born a commoner and had difficulty earning the respect of his people, but once he did, they worshiped him as a god. In part this was because of his open-mindedness and his famous tendency to leaven work with play.

"Just as a bow cannot be strung all the time or it will break, people cannot always work or they will go mad," he famously said. This was his justification for making Naucratis into a city of luxury and love. It certainly lived up to that reputation.

The harbor was filled with brothels of every description—some cheap, some ruinously expensive. There was a slave market where beautiful Nubian girls were being auctioned.

Praxinoa and I stopped to watch the show with the trader we had met on the boat.

"Don't worry, most of these girls will earn their freedom soon enough. In Naucratis, women go free while men are enslaved. Ask your brothers, Lady Sappho."

"I have no idea where I will find my brothers."

"Find out where Rhodopis lives and you will find your brothers."

"And who is this Rhodopis?"

"She is the most beautiful courtesan in all of Egypt. Her name means 'rosy-cheeked.' She used to be called plain Doricha and was the slave of a Samian called Xanthes, but she is a slave no more and with her freedom she changed her name. Aesop, the fable maker, used to be a slave in the same household, but he is also free now. He entertains her guests with fables in her palace. He is as handsome as Rhodopis is beautiful, but where she has low cunning, he has true cleverness. She manipulates men with her wiles. He elevates them with his philosophical fables."

"Are my brothers enslaved to some Circe?"

"Some say they are, Lady Sappho, but that's not for me to say. Love is enslavement, as we know. And Rhodopis trades on love."

"They were not here for love. They were here to trade the wines of my family's vineyards and increase our fortunes!"

"That's all I know—more I cannot say."

"I think I will like Naucratis," Praxinoa said, "where slaves go free." She looked at me and laughed.

Praxinoa had become so much more to me than a slave that I could hardly believe she still thought of herself as one. On the voyage, she had grown her hair long like a free woman, covered her forehead brand with a beautiful Lydian ribbon of scarlet and gold given us by the admirers of my songs. I had even taught her to play the lyre to accompany me.

"Soon I shall be more Sappho than Sappho," she joked when I taught her.

"Praxinoa—you are free whenever you want to be free. I cannot, I will not hold you, though I would sorely miss you."

"Let us meet Rhodopis first," she said, "but when the time is ripe, I'll hold you to your promise."

BUT IT WAS not so easy to meet Rhodopis. She lived in a huge palace, which looked to be a warehouse as much as a dwelling, and was surrounded by guards. Strangers were not encouraged to visit. Adjoining this structure was a millhouse where slaves went to purchase flour for their masters' households. This place was somewhat easier of access—especially in the early morning hours.

The following morning, Praxinoa and I entered there, pretending to be purchasers of flour.

The air was white with flour dust and the millstone made a dull grating sound. There in the clouds of dust I saw six stooped creatures—neither male nor female, neither man nor beast, wearing yokes and plodding around in a circle making the mill wheel turn. I stopped to look at these pitiful emaciated creatures. Suddenly one of the wraiths looked up and shouted, "*Sappho!*"

A man wielding a whip brought it down upon the shoulders of the wretch. Now his white bent back was crossed with rivulets of crimson blood.

"Sappho!" the man called again, as if impervious to the pain. I ran to him and the whip caught me on the cheek, flicking out a piece of my own flesh. The blood mingled with the flour on his back, on the floor, making a murky paste. My cheek stung, but I was more indignant at the outrage. The man with the whip was ready to strike.

Suddenly I looked at the pale wretch with the bloody back and saw it was my brother Larichus! He gave me a look of such sadness it nearly cracked my heart. The man with the whip raised it again as if to strike.

"Out!" he cried.

Praxinoa grabbed me by the hand and dragged me away as fast as she could.

"We cannot leave Larichus here!" I said.

"We cannot liberate him now," said Prax.

"Larichus—we will return for you!" I vowed.

"If I should be alive," he muttered. My brother continued to turn the flour-encrusted mill wheel, his blood streaking the whitened floor. The man with the whip flogged him again. I felt the whip as if it had fallen on my own back. I followed Praxinoa out of there in a daze.

Down near the harbor, there was a young Egyptian physician who plied his trade for visiting Greeks. His name was Senmut. As he stitched the wound on my cheek, I asked him if he knew my brothers Charaxus and Larichus and indeed the courtesan Rhodopis, formerly known as Doricha.

"They are your brothers?" Senmut asked. "Then I pity you."

"What have they done?"

"What many men have done before them. They came here with their sister's husband to trade the wine of their native land. At first they prospered. Much wine is consumed in Naucratis, as you can imagine. Then they began to frequent the brothels of the town and they fell under the spell of Rhodopis when she was still Xanthes' slave. She begged them for her freedom, in fact she swore that if they paid Xanthes a certain sum, they could share her and she would be theirs alone. They fell for that old trick. It is a familiar game here in Naucratis, but they knew nothing of it. Rhodopis and her so-called owner have sold her over and over again to a variety of men. But that is the least of it. At her symposia, they gamble with weighted dice and Rhodopis always wins. She plays for gold if they have any, for property, for ships, for slavery if that is all she can get. She has enslaved many men—not only your brothers. She repeats this game endlessly—always with new victims. Charaxus first bartered away his own brother. Then he became a slave himself. But slaves in Rhodopis' house disappear soon enough and in Naucratis there are always new victims. The black ships disgorge them. They don't live long."

"Then we must save my brothers soon!" I said.

"I wish you luck," said Senmut dubiously.

"How shall we get into Rhodopis' house?"

Senmut laughed. "You'll come with me. It's easy to get in when she has a symposium—just very hard to get out!"

THE NOBLES of Lesbos would have been appalled by what went by the name of a symposium at Rhodopis' house. Where we competed for our skill at making songs, her guests competed for their skill at tossing dregs of wine at each other. There were small knots of people playing at dice and other groups watching flute girls disrobe. (Later in the evening they would copulate with mules.) The wine was plentiful—it tasted like my grandfather's wine from Lesbos—but no sooner did I taste a drop than Senmut stopped me.

"Eat and drink nothing here," he said, "if you value your life."

I spat out the wine into my hand. It had a strange smell.

"Where is Rhodopis?" I asked.

"I don't see her yet. Sometimes she appears only very late, when the revelers are all quite drunk."

But then I saw a woman who had to be Rhodopis. She was tall as Athena and beautiful as Helen. Her hair was gold and was bound to her head with ropes of gold. She wore an undyed, transparent linen sheath, which fell in folds to her golden sandals. If Aphrodite came to earth, she would look like Rhodopis—ropes of golden hair, brilliant blue eyes, round breasts with rosy nipples, white thighs, golden nest of tousled hair between them. You could see her beautiful breasts and honey-colored delta through the linen. She floated like a goddess and she smelled like one too. All the flowers of the East had perfumed her hair, her breasts, her navel. She came straight for me.

"Sappho," she said, "I have been expecting you for some time. Alcaeus of Lesbos said you might turn up here. We have business to discuss." She spoke as if I were her ally, not her enemy. I was stunned that she even knew my name, and still more stunned that she knew Alcaeus. From the moment I met Rhodopis, I was jealous of her—yet also strangely attracted.

"What have you done to my brothers?"

"What have they done to themselves? I have done nothing to them."

"You enslaved Larichus, and Charaxus too, I presume."

"I did nothing of the sort. I only loved Charaxus and cosseted him. Whatever he gave was of his own free will. Come, Sappho, you know yourself how women are slandered by men. Don't believe those who gossip about me." She looked at Senmut defiantly. "Charaxus is overseeing the Lesbian wine for this symposium. He will appear by and by. Come, drink, enjoy yourself."

I pretended to drink but did not. Praxinoa never touched wine, so she was safe. There was a sudden sounding of flutes and a ringing of bells. Babylonian dancing girls whirled out, wearing bells on their fingers and wrists and ankles. They carried sticks of incense that scented the room. They began to dance as if they were making love to the air. Their perfume was so strong it made you reel.

As they whirled among us, I scanned the crowd, looking for my brother Charaxus. Like Larichus, who had once poured wine for nobles in Mytilene when we were young, Charaxus had been a handsome fellow. He could not possibly be this puffy serving man in a wine-stained chiton, pouring for the assembled guests and bowing low to those who were his betters.

"Charaxus!"

"Sappho—thank the gods you have come to deliver us! This Circe has bewitched us!" Charaxus exclaimed.

"So it seems. And what of our poor other brother?"

"I would rather pull a millstone with him than be humiliated by serving wine at the symposium."

"Perhaps you should have thought of this before," Praxinoa said.

"I did. I warned Cercylas we were in danger of being robbed, but she bewitched him as well. He and I purchased her by borrowing against the next wine harvest in Lesbos. Now she is free and we are slaves to her. It happened faster than anyone might have imagined. I could not write this in my letter. And it gets worse. Now Rhodopis claims she owns part of our family vineyards! We shall never be free of her!"

"Grandfather's vines were hardly yours to barter with!" I hissed. "You had no right to trade them for your whore!"

"I did not mean to!" Charaxus said. "I was tricked. Sappho—if you ever loved me, save me!"

"It sounds like the story of the eagle and the arrow," said a handsome, dark-skinned man who walked up behind us. "Do you know it?"

Charaxus was glad to have the subject changed.

"Please tell," I urged the stranger, whose huge black eyes met mine as if they would devour me. Praxinoa did not look happy. She never looked happy when I had an admirer.

"An eagle perched on a high rock, watching the movements of a hare he wanted to eat. An archer, who saw the eagle from a hidden place, took an accurate aim and wounded the eagle mortally. The eagle gave one look at the arrow that had entered his heart and saw in that single glance that its feathers had been furnished by himself. 'It is a double grief to me,' he exclaimed, 'that I should perish by an arrow feathered from my own wings.' So much for men and their promises. They forever skewer themselves with their own arrows."

"Who *are* you?" I asked the beautiful man, who was clearly as attracted to me as I was to him.

"I am Aesop, who was born a slave," said the man, "free now as your brothers are not. Would you rescue them?"

"Of course I would, however self-deceived they were! I have been taught to honor family—however foolish its members are."

"But should she rescue them at once or let them learn and suffer for a while?" asked Praxinoa. "Perhaps they need to be taught a lesson."

"Then you must teach them not to be wounded by their own arrows," Aesop said to me. "All of my fables are about this. Most men have no worse enemies than themselves. A man stumbles and falls not on his sword but on his own phallus. All our heroes prove it—Odysseus was more waylaid by women than by war. A slave is the keenest observer. He has no choice if he is to survive."

"I have lived your words," said Praxinoa.

"Rhodopis once had such perspicacity," Aesop went on. "But she has forgotten her humble origins and this makes her vulnerable. Would you defeat her? With my help you can. I can even help you rescue your foolish brothers."

"Why would you do this for me?"

"Why not? I would do anything to prove that my fables are true. What better fable can I make than the fall of Rhodopis? I would make an example of Rhodopis for the world to see. She has decided she is a queen and can rule the world. Those who cannot be content with themselves come to a bad end—as in my fables. Every time I prove my fables true, I ensure my immortality. Besides—I like you." His eyes kissed mine again. Praxinoa now looked disgusted.

"I would like to know the secret of immortality."

"The secret is memory," said Aesop. "If people remember and repeat your words, they endure. If they forget them, they do not. As a teller of tales, what I most wish for is to have my stories repeated—even stolen and claimed by others. As a singer, you must wish for your listeners to say: Let me learn that song before I die!"

ERICA JONG

"Rhodopis is too powerful to be brought down," I said.

"On the contrary, she is too powerful *not* to be brought down."

"I don't understand."

"What would you say her ruling passion is?"

"Vanity. She thinks her beauty is invincible."

"Exactly. And she has put all her eggs in that basket. But we know that beauty is not invincible, because it fades. There is always another beauty more beautiful. Rhodopis knew that once—now she has forgotten."

Aesop was tall and tawny—he looked half Thracian, half Nubian, and he had a pointed beard. His eyes were huge. They gleamed like black olives soaked in oil. The brand on his forehead was there for all to see. He never pretended not to have been born a slave.

"How did Rhodopis lose her brand? Some clever Egyptian surgeon?"

"No, the brand is hidden beneath the golden ropes that bind her hair across her forehead, but she has forgotten it is there. She does not know herself. Even the Delphic Oracle would be no use to her."

"We have seen the oracle!" I exclaimed.

"And what did she tell you?" Aesop asked audaciously.

I hesitated.

"Never mind," said Aesop, "you will tell me by and by."

While we'd been talking, the palace had grown darker and darker. The dancing girls had extinguished all the candles and torches. What light remained came from the tips of their incense sticks flickering like fireflies in the gloom. More figures began to mass in the darkness. As they came closer, I could see young women dressed as maenads, bearing thyrsus wands of fennel with ivy looped around their stems. The maenads wore bloody animal skins with ragged edges. Satyrs with grinning faces and huge phalli made of leather flanked them. Unseen musicians began fiercely to play drums and flutes.

The satyrs and the maenads started to dance—first in coy pursuit of each other, then in earnest, their dance turning into rough play, the maenads attempting to rape the satyrs with their wands, the satyrs attempting to rape the maenads with their phalli of leather. At first it was a show, a pantomime, but as the guests became aroused, the dance became violent and uncontrolled. The maenads and satyrs dragged the guests into the dance even against their will. I saw a satyr ravish a female guest—first with his leather *olisbos,* then with his own phallus. I saw a group of maenads bind a male guest with ropes of ivy, rape him with their thyrsus wands, then tear his eyes out with the clasps from their garments. Instead of disgusting the crowd, these bloody rituals excited them. The drums played louder and louder. Blood flowed with the wine. The Babylonian dancing girls aroused the mules with their mouths and fingers.

I watched this scene with astonishment. It was exciting and yet also repellent. My delta throbbed and grew moist, but my mind reeled back. I thought of my brothers in slavery, and when the maenads sought to draw me into their bloody dance, I resisted.

I wanted nothing more than to escape this chaos. Praxinoa took one arm, Aesop took the other.

"Where is Senmut?" I asked. Perhaps I felt safer knowing a healer was near.

"He left long ago," Aesop said. "Let's follow if we can."

"And leave my brothers?"

"We will plot their liberation later," said Aesop. "We cannot free them here and now."

It was not easy to proceed through the mass of frenzied bodies. At the periphery of the room were the dancing girls and their mulish consorts, blocking the exits. I was terrified that we'd be crushed, but Aesop led us away as if we were tunneling through pulsing flesh. I closed my eyes and followed where he guided us with his firm hand. Bodies flung themselves at me. Wine and blood were offered to my lips in golden cups. I heard screams even from beneath my feet as we struggled across floors inlaid with writhing bodies.

"Sappho—don't go," muttered one reveler as I was dragged over him. "The feast is just beginning." I looked down at him. He lay on the floor in a delirium of drugged wine, not even noticing that two dancing girls were pulling the rings from his fingers and the golden clasps from his clothes. They looked at me and winked. Their perfume was overpowering. What did it smell like? Flowers, yes. And incense and amber, but there was also something else more hypnotic still. One of them reached up and put a mushroom cap to my lips.

"Ambrosia of the gods," she said. "*Taste.*"

I was tempted—if only to know the secrets of Rhodopis and her symposia.

Aesop pushed the girl's hand away, and with it the mushroom. She laughed and devoured it herself. "More for me!" she muttered as if in a dream. Aesop and Praxinoa pulled and pushed and dragged me out into the air. At the last moment, I longed to stay.

Finally we smelled the sea, looked up, and saw the stars. The air was fresh. Had we all died and been transported to another realm?

"Where *are* we?" I asked Aesop.

"In the world of my fables," he said, "and your songs. The only world there is. Follow me." Aesop was tall and muscular, with broad shoulders. I let him shepherd Praxinoa and me out of Rhodopis' nightmare.

10

The Pharaoh's Slave

Even the wildest can be tamed by love.

—AESOP

WE SLEPT for a long time. I awoke in a fury. Why should I save my brothers when they couldn't save themselves? They had squandered not only their patrimony but mine. They had injured me as much as they had injured themselves. Let them rot in Naucratis! They deserved it!

I told Aesop how I felt. He understood.

"But would you be in Naucratis if it weren't your destiny to save your brothers? Poseidon flung you up on the Nile Delta for some reason."

"First they marry me off to an old sot. Then they gamble away my grandfather's wealth—and mine. Why should I help them?"

"Only to help yourself," said Aesop. "Anger will not suit your purpose here, but tranquillity will. Teach your brothers a valuable lesson. Later they may be a credit to you."

We were in Aesop's quarters with Praxinoa. The maenads and satyrs of the night before still danced in my brain. I could still smell their perfume.

"I have a plan," Aesop said. "Last night I told you about Rhodopis, but I didn't tell you all. She has another secret wish besides the wish to control men with her beauty. She wants honor in the eyes of the gods. She wants to dedicate an altar at Delphi with iron spits for sacrifice. She wants reputation as well as fame. All whores want to be ladies, and all ladies want to be whores. You think you have nothing that she wants, but here you are wrong. She wants what you have—"

"What do I have? Two brothers in slavery, a dead husband, a ruined fortune, a broken heart from having lost my only daughter!"

"You have aristocratic birth and bearing and the power to sing. Rhodopis longs for those things above all. You are much more powerful than you suppose. Now tell me about this daughter."

"She is like a gold flower. I wouldn't take all of Rhodopis' wealth with the pharaoh's added in exchange for her."

"Then how did you lose this treasure?"

"My own mother took her." I began to cry.

Aesop put his strong arms around me. "If I could heal your heart, I would," he said.

"No one can heal it but Cleis herself, and she is far away in Lesbos, my native isle."

"Then I will take you there."

"I cannot go. I am exiled from Lesbos on pain of death!"

"She tells the truth," said Praxinoa.

"Why were you exiled?" Aesop asked.

"Because I plotted the downfall of the tyrant."

"Then you are brave," Aesop said. "I see it in your eyes. If I could, I would restore your child to you. But until that day arrives, we can still be allies. We can restore your fortunes, liberate your brothers, and then go off in search of your child. I can help you with all this. I can be your guide. I know Egypt and all its quirks. I know that the Egyptians long to be Greeks, and the Greeks long to be Egyptians. I am well connected here. Listen well. We can begin by creating a rival symposium in Naucratis. It will be so exclusive and authentic that all the Egyptian nobles will vie to attend—and eventually so will Rhodopis. We will keep guests away rather than bid them come—the secret of success. All men long to go where they are not welcome. Even in Naucratis, we heard of your symposia in Syracuse. We heard you were accompanied by a Lydian nobleman who earned much gold for you. What became of him?"

"The sea swallowed him, as he deserved."

"But the sea cannot have swallowed what he taught you."

I thought of poor fat Cyrus with his vulgar flair. He was immense. He had rolls of fat around his middle that jiggled when he walked. All fed to the fishes! He spoke Greek badly, Egyptian badly, even his native Lydian badly, but he had a kind of brilliance.

"Cyrus knew one thing—how to get the rich to part with their money."

"And what was he selling?"

"He was selling *me!*"

"Not quite. He was selling something else. The dream of nobility. The dream of nobility is also valuable in Egypt. After all, Egypt has fallen from its former glory. This great country invented everything from the names of the immortal gods to sculpture to statecraft, and now it flounders on the banks of its life-giving river. Once the greatest nation on earth, it is now only one among many. The pharaohs once were gods married to sister goddesses—now they are only men. Ever since they displaced the great mother Isis, the supreme life-giver, the goddess from whom all being arose, they have declined in power and sunk to the level of other nations. All countries decline when they debase their female goddesses—this a secret that you, Sappho, must understand."

THUS IT BEGAN. Aesop and I became allies. We took over an ancient palace on the edge of the desert and filled it with treasures. We hired and trained the finest flute girls. You might wonder where the money came from—for I could not have bought all this luxury with the remains of my gold from Delphi and from shipboard singing. But Aesop had a secret—the first of many. It turned out he was private advisor to the pharaoh. The pharaoh was willing to pay richly for Aesop's fables about animals with their morals about people.

"It is better to get rich with your brain than with your body," Aesop said, laughing. "Rhodopis will learn her lesson. It will be good to watch. Meanwhile, I suggest you let your brothers continue in slavery for a while. Only those who have been in slavery appreciate freedom."

Here Praxinoa sighed and exchanged knowing glances with Aesop.

I was still uncertain of the plan. I had lost Cleis, lost Alcaeus—how could I risk losing my brothers? But I trusted Aesop's wisdom. He had a calmness that I lacked. He was protective as my brothers were not. Perhaps he was also in love with me from the very beginning, but he was too clever to reveal it all at once. He sought, instead, to win me with philosophy. He was wise.

Alcaeus was still in my heart. I thought of him. I dreamed of him. I longed for the day when we might be reunited. In the meantime, there was work to do, and Aesop could help me do it. My family's vineyards must be saved. My brothers must be taught a lesson and then freed from slavery. I had to put one foot in front of the other and suppress my longing for Alcaeus and my dreams of my daughter.

THE NOBLES of the pharaoh's court attended our first symposium and fell in love with my singing. Afterward, they came back, bringing friends and courtiers. The rumor began to spread that the slave Aesop and the singer Sappho had the most exclusive symposia, and the elite of Naucratis—even the wealthiest Egyptians—were curious to come. We refused them. We invited only the highest nobility. We let the others only dream of our invitations.

After a while, the pharaoh sent for us. Necho asked if I could tutor him in song accompanied by the *kithara*. He wanted to be able to improvise when the myrtle wand was passed to him. He longed to organize authentic symposia at court.

"I will try, Sire," I told the pharaoh, "but the gift of song comes from the gods alone. I can teach you to play the lyre. I can teach you to pluck the strings. I can teach you songs of other singers. But you must be touched with divine fire to create your own songs. It is not something I can give. The gods alone give it."

Nobody had ever refused the pharaoh before. He was intrigued by my honesty. It made him desire my instruction more.

"Egypt was once the fount of all civilization, but the world is changing now. You Greeks *own* poetry and fable. The Lydians have invented coinage and commerce. Soon, I fear, the Persians will move against us all. I know I can only protect my people if I learn the newest arts of music, literature, and war. I *command* you to teach me, Sappho."

"I have but one request, Pharaoh. A bewitching courtesan of this town has enslaved my brothers and I fear they might die in her harsh service. Do not liberate them yet, but have your minions prevail upon their jailers to grant them lighter duties, so they may at least survive."

"I will happily cause that to be done," the pharaoh said.

"Then I will teach you with all my heart," I said.

So I became teacher to the great pharaoh. It is not so simple to be a teacher to one who has the power to put you to death. He had many wives and concubines, but nevertheless he believed that the practice of song also required the practice of making love. I held him off for a time, quoting the wise Aesop's words: "It is better to earn your fortune with your brain than with your body." But one night, when we had been composing impromptu verses to each other for hours and playing in harmony in his private chambers, the pharaoh commanded me to strip naked and lie upon his lion-footed golden couch.

This frightened me. I was not at my best naked. Even with Alcaeus and Isis I had resisted total nakedness. My twisted spine was not a sight to inspire ecstasy—or so I thought. Nevertheless, I did as I was told on pain of death. The threat of execution greatly concentrates the mind.

The great pharaoh approached me, took off his golden girdle and tunic, his golden chest plate, his linen kilt and loincloth. He roared like a lion. He pounded on his own bare chest. But when he came and lay between my legs, his great rearing serpent—circumcised, of course, in the Egyptian fashion—suddenly went limp.

He looked down at himself. Then he looked at me. "Sappho—you have bewitched me! You will die the most slow and lingering death a woman has ever known!"

I knew he meant it. I knew the pharaoh had had concubines boiled in oil for the very offense I had just committed. When a pharaoh wilts, it is certainly not the pharaoh's fault. The fault is always the woman's. That's what it means to be pharaoh, after all.

Aphrodite—if you ever loved me—save me now, I prayed. But nothing happened. I kissed my life good-bye. *Let my death be swift,* I prayed. *Let Aphrodite grant me that if nothing else!* I was doubtful Aphrodite would save me. She had been silent for so many moons. It was clear she did not approve of the direction my life was taking. I imagined my fate—boiled slowly in oil like a fish until I died in agony. Only Aesop left alive to tell my story—if the pharaoh indeed spared him, which was uncertain.

Suddenly the pharaoh's serpent reared again. It lifted proudly like a bird in flight. It sought the wet nest between my legs.

"Can you make a song of this?" I challenged the pharaoh.

"Can you?"

> *You came when I lay aching for your touch*
> *And you cooled my burning heart.*

He stopped, midstroke. "Even the phallus of a god hesitates before a muse," he said with no irony at all. Then he ravished me like a conqueror and fell in love with me like a schoolboy.

The more powerful a man is, the more he can be humbled by love. I learned that in Egypt and it helped me thereafter. Men claim they want obedience from women, but I have found that they prefer mastery—as long as it is *cloaked* in compliance. A woman who is bold and challenging, who knows her own strength, can rule the rulers of this world.

The pharaoh was concerned that his low birth would cost him the respect of his people. That was why he needed Aesop and me as his advisors. Aesop counseled him to take a golden footbath and have it fashioned into a beautiful statue of the goddess Io. When the people bowed down before it, he reminded them of its humble origins.

"It used to be a footbath in which you cleansed your muddy feet and spat and vomited, and now you *venerate* it! Things are seldom what they seem!"

It was doubtless because of the pharaoh's insecurity that he built so many sphinxes and colossal statues all over Egypt. He instituted a system of taxation in which every person had to account his entire income to the pharaoh's minions on pain of death. One-tenth of each person's income had to be paid to the state. With this tribute Necho built the mightiest monuments in Egypt. But even the monuments he built did not assuage his fears about the future. He needed to be constantly reassured of his greatness. This became my role—and Aesop's.

There are many kinds of slavery, I discovered. The slavery of the millstone is one kind, of the brothel another, of marriage to a man you loathe another. But the slavery of being needed by a powerful man is the most insidious. Whatever my life had been before I met Necho, my life now *was* Necho. It was a strong drug—this business of being indispensable to the pharaoh—but it was not freedom. And a singer needs freedom. So does a woman. I had no time to worry about Cleis or Alcaeus, or indeed my brothers or Rhodopis. I was constantly at the command of the pharaoh.

We traveled all over the land inspecting the pharaoh's building projects—up and down the Nile and through the deserts. We spent a great deal of time planning the tomb of the pharaoh, with its massive columns built of huge blocks of golden stone. If the pharaoh's life could have been extended by the lives of all those who perished through being crushed by the stones of his tomb, he would have lived forever. Yet he was never content. He was always anxious about invasions from his neighbors. He feared the Persians, the Lydians, the Hittites, the Phoenicians, even the Greeks whom he cultivated and imitated. He worried that the great civilization of Egypt was on a downward spiral. For three thousand years, the Egyptians had ruled the earth. Their warriors were the strongest, their painters the most skilled, their poets inimitable. Their sculptors could carve the most adamantine stone. Their goldsmiths could fashion the most beautiful ornaments. Their linens were the finest. Their wooden furnishings the most ingenious. They could save the body from corruption by means of mummification. They could build structures that made the whole world gasp. But now the other kingdoms had learned their arts—and the monarchy of Egypt was wracked by disease and death. Necho would not have been pharaoh in Egypt's glory days and he knew it. He was undone by doubt.

I learned so much from being his teacher—so much about men and so much about life. I learned that even the great are insecure, that even the rich feel poor, that even the loved feel unloved. Women get many things from love. It was true that the pharaoh's lovemaking did not stir my lust but rather my lust for power. I loved being needed by the ruler of a nation. I was beginning to understand my mother.

PAINFUL THOUGH it was, I let my brothers remain in slavery for half a year—after which I appealed to the pharaoh for their freedom and dispatched them back to Lesbos to repair our fortunes. I never told them that I had been responsible for saving their lives, but I think they knew.

"When you see your beautiful golden niece, Cleis, tell her that her mother loves her with all her heart." Tears rolled down my cheeks as I mentioned my daughter's name. Cleis would be walking by now, perhaps talking as well. Had it been more than a year since I had seen her? Would I even recognize her if I met her? It was too agonizing to think about.

My brothers kissed my feet and blessed me for their deliverance. They had been humbled, as Aesop had predicted.

"Sappho—you are the leader of our family now. If only you could come home with us, what joy we'd know. We will send for you as soon as you are pardoned. We will work tirelessly on your behalf."

Larichus kissed me on both cheeks. "Bless you," he said. And then he whispered in my ear, "I will never forget how you saved me from the treadmill."

EVEN RHODOPIS had fulfilled her wish to journey to Delphi, where she had dedicated an altar and twelve huge spits for roasting sacrificial oxen. She was very pleased with herself and requested an audience with the pharaoh.

"Why should I meet this trollop?" Necho asked.

"Because she comes back from Delphi and may have picked up portents of the future," Aesop wisely counseled.

We studied Necho's face for news of his mood—something you always do with tyrants.

"Send her in!" he thundered.

Rhodopis appeared, looking as fetching and rosy-cheeked as ever. She minced toward the pharaoh in her high-heeled sandals. She bent over double and kissed his feet. She flattened herself before him, showing her comely bottom beneath transparent linen.

"Get up!" the pharaoh said rather peevishly.

"Sire, I have come from the great *omphalos* of the earth at Delphi."

"So we hear."

"I have dedicated an altar and consulted many sages there. They say the Pythia has stirring news for Egypt but will only give it to an appointed emissary of the pharaoh. Other great leaders send their emissaries there—Alyattes, Nebuchadnezzar, the Persian and Hittite kings. All were waiting there for the Pythia to speak. Egypt is the only nation with no representative at Delphi. I fear for Egypt, Sire. I volunteer my services without charge."

At this, the pharaoh perked up. The richer they are, the more they like gifts from subjects.

Aesop cleared his throat nervously.

"Sire, we must discuss this generous offer. Why not let the ladies withdraw?"

Rhodopis and I were taken to a small room adjoining the pharaoh's throne room, where, watched by courtiers, we whispered to each other.

"I have met a friend of yours," Rhodopis hissed tauntingly, "another well-known exiled singer."

"Alcaeus?"

"The same. He may travel with beautiful boys, but he beds down with beautiful girls. This I know for a fact."

"You lie!"

"Hardly. I have experienced the pleasures of his couch and, as Aphrodite is my witness, he is a lover even goddesses would die for."

Of course I knew this. I was stung with jealousy. I didn't mind that Alcaeus took pleasure with boys, but his taking pleasure with Rhodopis made me rage inside. I tried not to show it.

Aesop now called us back to the pharaoh's presence. We left the antechamber and appeared again before Necho.

"Thank you, Rhodopis, for your most generous offer, but Sappho and I will journey to Delphi on behalf of the pharaoh," Aesop said. "Sappho knows Delphi as well as Rhodopis does, if not better."

I held my tongue. Words could not contain my joy. Perhaps this time I would find Alcaeus in Delphi and he and I would discover some way to return to Lesbos and our daughter. I could not bear to believe the oracle's prophecy that she would grow to womanhood without me. How could she grow up without a mother's loving gaze? And how would I live without her?

11

At Sea

Evil wishes, like chickens,
Come home to roost.
—AESOP

AFTER WE HAD left the pharaoh's quarters and were outside where we could talk, I asked Aesop, "How did you convince him to let us go?"

"I thought *you* convinced him by piquing his worry about the Persians and Lydians."

"*Rhodopis* did that," I said. "I hate to admit it, but she *is* good for something. She frightened him with her descriptions of other leaders sending emissaries to the oracle. He is clearly afraid of what they might learn at Delphi, afraid they might find some advantage over Egypt."

"A man will show his Achilles' heel to a woman. With other men, he will pretend to be invincible," Aesop said.

"Rhodopis knows that, if anyone does," I said. "I must grudgingly admit I admire her. Sometimes I think I am even a little in love with her myself. She has such *fire*. She has the gifts of Aphrodite. I can even understand my brothers being drawn to her. I am drawn to her myself. Isn't it remarkable that erotic attraction has nothing to do with goodness or kindness? Goodness and kindness can, in fact, kill it. Damn Aphrodite! Damn her sneaky son."

"So you wish you were more like Rhodopis," Aesop said.

"Yes!"

"Her blond beauty is not nearly as particular as your raven looks. Trust me. This I know."

"Then you find me beautiful?"

"In a completely singular way," said Aesop. "Part of your beauty is your deep intelligence. Your eyes are limitless. They seem to see everything."

I became uneasy at his admiration. "So do yours," I told him. "You are the greatest teacher I have ever had."

"I would rather be your lover than your teacher," he said. "But I will take whatever I can get."

I let this go. It was uncomfortable to hear of his yearning for me, since I still yearned for Alcaeus. I knew that Aesop loved me, but I tried to ignore it. I changed the subject.

"But may I remind you that you were *not* completely right about Rhodopis? She has *not* fallen to her fate. If anything, she has prospered."

"*Not yet.* Wait, Sappho. You are too impatient. Rhodopis stands on the edge of a snake pit. She simply doesn't know it."

"The siren and the snake pit!"

"Wait and see how my prophecy comes true!"

I shrugged. "I'll believe it when I see it."

"My fables always come true—just like your songs."

"So you are sure your fables are prophetic?"

"Absolutely sure. Aren't you sure your songs always please the gods?"

"Of course I am!" But I was far less sure than I claimed. I wished I had more of Rhodopis' brash confidence.

I had, in fact, composed a blistering song about my brother Charaxus and how he was duped by Rhodopis, but I was not entirely satisfied with it and I ripped the papyrus to bits. Years later, fragments of this song were found by my followers and used to prove slanderous things about my brother and me. It is not enough to rip up your rejected drafts. Burn them!

• • •

IN THE WEEKS that followed, the pharaoh outfitted a sailing ship for us and gave us fifty of his most muscular Nubians to row it, his greatest admiral to navigate, and all manner of cooks and servants to wait upon us. He had organized many colloquies in which he and his counselors prepared the most detailed questions for the oracle. We were to ask this—then we were to ask that—then we were to be sure to ask the other. There were great debates about the Pythia and how best to get her to pronounce the future. Some of the pharaoh's ministers wanted to come along for the ride. Who could resist a trip to Delphi? At first I was afraid the pharaoh would allow it. But as usual, Aesop's wisdom came to the rescue.

"As the Pythia is Greek and speaks Greek, she may be offended by barbarians. Not that your highness' advisors are not wise. They are very wise—wiser even than Greeks—but they do not speak the Pythia's tongue. Let us be careful not to offend her."

The pharaoh thought and then he agreed. "It is best not to offend the Pythia," he said.

"The Pythia is unusually fond of gold," Aesop said. "And so are her minions. We have to be prepared."

So the pharaoh's goldsmiths made a variety of cunning objects with which to propitiate the oracle—statues of gods and goddesses, birds, cats, horses, camels, sphinxes, basins, wine jugs, goblets, golden disks made to resemble the sun.

"We will represent you faithfully," Aesop pledged.

"Of that I have no doubt. But it pains me to let the woman Sappho go. Return her to me unharmed and whole, or I will hunt you down and have you killed most lingeringly."

"If the gods will it, Pharaoh, it shall be," Aesop swore.

EGYPT HAD changed me. It was not only the blossoming of my friendship with Aesop and what I learned about powerful men from the pharaoh, but the way power had shifted in my own family. I became the deliverer of my brothers and I planned never to let them forget it. Since they had not plotted against Pittacus, they could easily return to Lesbos. Someday I would need them again. I would remind them I might have left them to their fate!

But my daughter was never out of my thoughts. By now she would be walking, uttering nonsense syllables, and babbling. I had missed her entire infancy. I rarely spoke of her for fear I would be overwhelmed with sadness, but I went to sleep with her and woke up with her. In my dreams I held her. Her sweet infant smell was always in my nostrils.

We were only a week out of Naucratis bound for Delphi when Aesop and I became aware that the mariners kept descending into the hold of the ship for long periods of time and returning on deck looking drunk and disheveled. The ship's hold was not a pretty place. The oarsmen defecated there, as did the pigs and goats we carried for food. No one would go belowdecks who did not absolutely have to. We heard laughter echoing from below and often screams of glee.

Aesop interrogated the captain.

"I am sure that nothing is amiss," he said, "but let me check for myself."

With that, the captain disappeared into the hold and did not return for several hours. The oars were as idle as the sails. We drifted with the current.

Aesop and I were worried. We didn't want to follow the captain into the hold for fear of insulting him, or questioning his authority, but we were alarmed.

"Shall we go and see for ourselves?" I asked Aesop.

"Let us be discreet."

"How long shall our discretion last? Till we go down with the ship?"

"I'm sure there is no cause for concern," Aesop said.

"I think we should go down now," I countered.

AESOP AND I proceeded cautiously down the companionway that led into the bowels of the ship. The lower you went, the more it reeked. We heard the sound of drunken laughter.

Who should we see in the hold but Rhodopis, who had unchained the oarsmen, seduced both slaves and officers, and was looking extremely pleased with herself.

"Sappho! Aesop!" she called. "Welcome!"

Cracked wine bowls were strewn around. The captain had passed out drunk. Amid these sleepy beasts, Rhodopis rose like Circe.

"Welcome, you two," she said. "What fun we'll have in Delphi."

"You are not in charge here," Aesop said gravely.

"Am I not?" Rhodopis answered. "Who is in charge on the sea? Only Poseidon! I command Poseidon as Aphrodite commands even the gods! Who's to say I am not more Aphrodite than Aphrodite!"

"This is the pharaoh's ship," I said quietly. "I will not comment on your hubris in challenging the gods."

"I hardly fear your gods," said Rhodopis. "Besides, the ship belongs to whomever the men obey. I feel sure somehow that they'll obey me. The captain is my special friend." She pointed to the comatose captain.

"As the pharaoh is mine," I said.

"But not here. Absent friends are of little use," the siren said. "Now, shall we speak of our itinerary? I thought we should make way to Samos, Chios, then Lesbos—where, I promise you, Pittacus shall be apprised of your arrival. Then I can continue on to Delphi without worrying about the pharaoh's favorite. What do you think, little Sappho?"

But Aesop spoke before I could get a word in. "Sappho shall be glad to see Lesbos again—and her daughter. You cannot scare her with such a threat," he said mildly. "Whatever the gods decree, she will accept. We will let you be our guide."

"Good," Rhodopis said. "First of all, I want your quarters. I am not so fond of being belowdecks."

"Your wish is our command," said Aesop.

I looked at him as though he were mad.

Rhodopis was obviously pleased. A smile turned up the corners of her mouth. "You know, Sappho," she preened, "Charaxus promised to marry me."

I laughed. "Of course, that's why you enslaved him and my other brother."

"It was just a little joke between us—what is the difference anyway between slavery and marriage?" Rhodopis asked.

Now Aesop really had to twist my arm to keep me silent.

"Will you attend me at my marriage, Sappho?"

At that I burst out laughing.

"Laugh all you want," Rhodopis said. "I know what I know."

"You can discuss all this when we reach Mytilene," Aesop said calmly. "Now I think we should focus on sailing or we'll never reach shore in Lesbos—or anywhere. Do try to rouse our captain, Rhodopis."

But Rhodopis had another matter on her mind.

"Since I shall have you as my sister-in-law, Sappho, perhaps it's time for you to teach me the secrets of the symposium—or whatever it was you were teaching the pharaoh."

Aesop pinched me again, then trod on my toe for good measure.

"I shall be delighted to do so," I said. "Come up on deck and I shall teach you all I know."

There on deck Praxinoa also awaited us. She had been napping while all this transpired. She could not have been more amazed to see Rhodopis.

"Praxinoa—fetch my lyre. It seems I have a new student."

We drifted on the sea. I taught Rhodopis the rudiments of song. Aesop tried to rouse the crew and captain and get them to resume their duties, but they were too far gone. They slept while the ship floundered.

"We would be better to study navigation than to study singing," I told Rhodopis. "Otherwise we may never reach Lesbos or Delphi—or indeed anywhere but the Land of the Dead. If you only knew the bad luck I've had sailing, you'd never have stowed away with me!"

Calmness had come over me, as it always did when I shared my craft. If the gods were with us, we'd be safe; if they were not, we were lost. All the rest was madness.

"We'd better be allies," I told Rhodopis, "or we may not last the voyage at all. I have been shipwrecked time and time again, set upon by pirates, doomed to float forever in the blistering sun, the cold moon. The sea is cruel even to stowaways."

After she'd heard about my shipwrecks, Rhodopis hastily excused herself and went belowdecks to help Aesop in rousing the captain and crew. It was no easy matter. They had drunk her drug-laced wine and could have slept for days.

Praxinoa and I scanned the horizon as the sun set. Was it our imagination, or was another ship approaching?

No doubt of it. Little by little a red-sailed ship came into view. On the deck were men with curly beards, brandishing bronze spears. They were as alert and ferocious as our crew was drugged. They easily lassoed our battering ram, dragged us to them, and boarded us.

A tall beautiful young man with an aureole of red hair and a hauntingly familiar face approached me. At first I thought it was Alcaeus and my heart lurched.

"Antimenidas of Lesbos, fresh from Babylon and the service of the great Nebuchadnezzar," the beautiful man introduced himself. "We have seen the Hanging Gardens, expelled from Jerusalem the Jews who believe in circumcision and one god, followed the spice routes through the desert to the great red city of the Nabateans, and now we are sailing back to the civilized world where men speak Greek."

"And women, sir. We are Sappho and Praxinoa of Lesbos."

"Sappho! I am the brother of Alcaeus!" Antimenidas exclaimed.

Whereupon the three of us fell into each other's arms weeping. It might not be Alcaeus, but it was indeed his flesh and blood. I wanted to throw my arms around Antimenidas simply because he looked so much like Alcaeus!

"When have you last seen your brother?" I asked.

"At the court of Alyattes, whence he was dispatched to Delphi."

"And where is he now?"

"The gods alone know," Antimenidas said. "I trust he is alive, else I should surely have heard. He could be in Delphi, in Sardis, in Syracuse, in Ephesus—who knows?"

"Your brother is indeed alive," a teasing voice said. It was Rhodopis emerging from belowdecks, wearing her most seductive smile, her strong perfumes, and nothing else. "Would you have news of him? Come closer. I'll tell you all I learned of him in Delphi."

I looked at Praxinoa in a panic. All we needed was for Rhodopis to seduce these new sailors.

Aesop now came on deck, took in the scene, and asked Antimenidas for a private word with him. Antimenidas' men were about to search the ship for treasure, but he detained them.

Aesop and Antimenidas spoke for a long time. There was much persuasion and argument.

Finally they seemed to have reached an agreement. Praxinoa and I watched in amazement as Antimenidas gave orders to his men in a savage tongue I did not understand.

The men promptly took Rhodopis, gagged her, bound her hand and foot until she resembled an Egyptian mummy. She made guttural sounds through her gag. We just stood there gaping. She flashed her eyes at me as if to say, *You've hardly seen the last of me!* Then she was carried onto the other ship. Rhodopis was off our hands!

We rewarded Antimenidas' men with a share of our golden offerings. We even gave them some of our comatose crew, piled like so many corpses after a battle. Wouldn't those Egyptian sailors be amazed when they awoke and found themselves on the way to Babylon rather than Delphi!

Antimenidas' men were delighted to get Rhodopis—not to mention the gold. They bowed low before Antimenidas and thanked him profusely. Wait till they found out what a handful she was! Then they reboarded their ship.

Antimenidas embraced us warmly and wished us well before he too departed.

"If you see my dear brother, give him all my love," he said.

"Of that you may be sure," I said, feasting on Antimenidas' face, which was so like my beloved's. Watching him wave and sail away, I remembered my departure from Alcaeus and it reopened the wound of missing him.

"What did you tell Antimenidas?" I asked Aesop.

"I merely reminded Antimenidas of something he already knew. Nebuchadnezzar is very fond of blond courtesans and Rhodopis might fetch a large price in Babylon. On the way there, they might also have some fun."

"So you sold Rhodopis to the Babylonian king?"

"I would never sell another human being into slavery—I merely suggested how much she'd be worth as an ornament for the Hanging Gardens. Besides, Rhodopis never remains anyone's slave for long. She knows how to turn a master into a slave. Some women only know how to turn slaves into masters."

"I hope you are not speaking of me," I said.

Aesop gave me an ironic look.

WE FINALLY roused our captain and made our vessel shipshape again, but I must admit I rather missed the obstreperous Rhodopis. The boat seemed empty and sad without her and Delphi somehow seemed a duller destination than Babylon. I would have liked to see the fabled Hanging Gardens myself.

12

Among the Amazons

Wild women astride their horses' wings
Ride on the moon's pale rings.
—*The Amazoniad*

Once more we were bound for Delphi. Officially our mission was to represent the pharaoh and hear a prophecy for him. Secretly, of course, I wished to find Alcaeus and win his stubborn heart. Why I thought I'd find Alcaeus in Delphi this time when the last time I had not, I do not know. Perhaps it was because Rhodopis had met him in Delphi and that made me think I would too. It made no sense at all. In my fantasy I dreamed that when I met Alcaeus I would tell him Cleis was his daughter and we would return to Lesbos together to confront my mother and Pittacus and claim our child. None of it made much sense. But do even the most vivid dreams make sense? Aesop was too wise not to feel the weight of things I was not telling him.

"Who waits for you in Delphi, Sappho?"

"No one but the Pythia and those who serve her."

"Why do I doubt that?"

"Because you think too much, Aesop. You never take things as they are."

"Because I know that things are seldom what they seem. You and Rhodopis seem to be linked in love—if not for each other, then for some man. He is my rival for your love. Who is he?"

"There is no man. Don't be absurd."

"Rhodopis is a beauty who subdues every man who looks upon her. She has the capriciousness of Aphrodite and her golden looks. Doesn't that rankle?"

"Not at all. My mother was a beauty. Where did it get her? An unfaithful husband and the love of a tyrant. Even Aphrodite found beauty a trap. I would rather sing of her than *be* her."

So I said, but when I looked into my heart, I wished I resembled Rhodopis. She was tall and stately where I was short and twisted, golden and shining where I was dark, full-bosomed where I was flat. If I had my power to sing and Rhodopis' beauty, the whole civilized world would be mine for the taking. I had done well for a plain girl, but I never forgot I was a plain girl. If I were more beautiful, Alcaeus would not have sailed away from me. That was the whole point. I thought of Rhodopis bound up like a sacrificial lamb and I laughed.

"Why do you laugh such an evil laugh?" Aesop asked. "Are you thinking of your nemesis, Rhodopis?"

"Absolutely not!"

"Beware of what you wish for—you may get it!"

"Not this, not ever, even the gods cannot grant it."

"The gods resent such challenges," Aesop said, "and they delight in showing them to be false."

"When did the gods appoint you to be their prophet?" I asked Aesop.

"When they appointed you. We share that fate."

"Ridiculous," I said and stared at the sea.

And yet I thought if wily Isis were here, she might make a lead figurine bound hand and foot and inscribe it *Rhodopis*. Then we could chant evil curses upon it to make sure Rhodopis never came out of slavery again.

Rhodopis would have to be clever indeed to get free of the great Nebuchadnezzar, who was said to be mad. Yes, his Hanging Gardens with their blossoming terraces of trees would someday be judged one of the Seven Wonders of the World, but he was ruthless and bloodthirsty and he spared no one—man or woman—his rage. He had defeated the Egyptians at Carchemish. He had captured Jerusalem and laid siege to Tyre for thirteen years. He was said to be planning a great wall in northern Babylonia to keep out invaders. He was building great high piles of rocks everywhere in the hopes that piles of rocks conferred immortality—if this wasn't a form of madness, what was? The Egyptians preserved the flesh through mummification, the Babylonians built great ziggurats, and Aesop and I hoped our words were immortal. What foolishness! I began to despair. What was I doing on this great gray sea, far from my daughter and Alcaeus? Where were the ones I loved most dearly? Thoughts of Rhodopis had polluted my mind. I was consumed with jealousy of her and the desire to curse her. Every curse I dreamed up came back against me and blackened my mind.

Even absent from me, she was present. This is the paradox of jealousy; it feeds more on phantoms than on reality.

WE SAILED and sailed and sailed. Black as my mood was, no mishap came to us on this portion of the trip. The captain informed us that we should eventually be stopping at the island of Crete, where the great civilization of the bull-dancers and their labyrinths now lay crumbled to unceremonious dust. I had heard the legends of Theseus and the minotaur and thought them as little based in fact as the legends of the amazons or the legends of the cyclops whom Odysseus met and blinded. But I was to be proven wrong.

EARLY ONE MORNING, when fog crept over the face of Poseidon's realm, we came ashore on a rocky coast alive with birdsong. The men dragged our galley up upon the strand, and Aesop, Praxinoa, and I set about searching for fresh water while the men cleaned the ship and mended the sails and rigging.

We walked a narrow rocky path, which wove along the coast. Sometimes the path turned into wading stones and beneath the surface of the shallow sea we could see what seemed to be the drums of fallen columns. Golden mosaics glistened under the water. There were the remains of an ancient town under our feet.

A sudden thunder of hooves at the top of a little hill and there appeared a girl on horseback holding the mane of a snow-white horse. Her hair was as silvery white as her horse's. Her toes glistened with golden rings. She wore a chiton of silver chain mail that winked at the sun. As she came closer, it was clear that she had but one breast. And her mare had tiny wings upon its flanks—or was this some sort of ornate harness?

She raised her spear as if to throw it straight at my head. Then she stopped. She shouted a volley of words in a strange tongue and three other warriors rode up behind her, dressed as she was dressed, brandishing spears.

"We mean no harm!" I shouted. But it was no use. The women warriors advanced, dismounted, bound our arms behind our backs, blindfolded us, and dragged us onto the backs of their horses. They galloped us around and around in circles—clearly to confuse whatever sense of direction we had—then carried us over hill and meadow until we were bruised and dazed from the ride. We were then dragged off horseback and stowed in a dank cave like so much meat for winter.

I heard groans.

"Praxinoa? Aesop?"

They were there—but barely able to do more than whimper.

How long we remained in the damp I cannot say, but when we were finally dragged from the cave, the sun was high in the sky and we were parched. My eyes stung from the sun when they were unbandaged. The beautiful woman warrior stood above me. In a circle surrounding us were at least twenty little girls of eight or nine who were clearly getting a lesson in the treatment of prisoners. One of them came up behind me and started to unbind my hands.

Suddenly Aesop found his voice. "And they say there are no amazons!"

The woman warrior found her Greek.

"They say the amazons were defeated! But as you see, we flourish!"

I had a million questions. My mother had been a great teller of tales about amazons. Now I wondered if she had ever met one.

"I was named Penthesilea after our great queen who fought in the Trojan War," said the beautiful warrior. "But of course she was slandered, as women always are. Achilles did not kill her. On the contrary, he fell in love with her and sought to make her his concubine. She preferred to die. Her women prepared a mock death for her—with herbs they alone knew. She was due to be awakened at a certain hour and revived. But the Greeks captured her maidens in order to rape them and she stayed in a stupor past the appointed hour and perished needlessly. I will make sure nothing of the sort ever happens to me. In those days the amazons lived near the Black Sea. Some migrated as far as Lesbos, Chios, and Samos and intermarried with the native peoples. They lost their faith. They forgot the cruelty of men. Our nation settled here in Crete after Theseus returned to Athens. We never forgot how he abandoned Ariadne, who had given him the secrets of the labyrinth, and we vowed never to let ourselves be tricked by the sweet words of men."

"But where do you get your children?" I asked Penthesilea.

"Girl babies are exposed on hilltops all over the Greek world," she said. At that moment I heard Praxinoa gasp. "There is no dearth of them—only a dearth of those that treasure them. Disguised amazons are busy rescuing these girl babies on every island, in every *polis,* on every seashore. Sometimes we capture a man and get him to be our breeder." She looked knowingly at Aesop. "We have ways."

"And what do you do with the boy babies who are born?"

"Why do you suppose that *any* boy babies are born? We have gone far beyond that primitive stage of civilization!"

"Then what do you do?"

"Oh, there are pessaries to filter out the male seed. We have our ways."

I looked at her in disbelief. Praxinoa looked at her in wonderment.

"We try to keep our secrets from the world. I should be more circumspect. It was fine in the old days when we had a large supply of flying horses to subdue our enemies, but now the horses' ranks are much reduced. They give birth to fewer and fewer colts and many of those are born without wings or with only vestigial winglets. This is the plague that most concerns us. If we still had our equine allies, all would be well. But I have told you too much already."

With that she gave a sign to the little girls, who swarmed around Aesop and led him away to another cave. Praxinoa and I were left with Penthesilea, who began to rage.

"If you saw those stunted winglets, your heart would break. We believe that someone is poisoning the mares' milk, but we have no way to prove it. Who would harm a winged mare? Only a beast would do that—or a man."

"Then are there no good men?" Praxinoa asked eagerly.

"I don't want to debate that old, old question. It bores me. It should bore us all by now. Let's just say they are a different species. We have decided that life is easier without their distractions. We fight for survival. They fight for glory. We fight for our daughters. They fight against their sons and fathers. If you have lived too long in their world and have adapted to it, you may not even see their follies. I pity you. Come, let me show you our world."

Aesop and I were fascinated with the amazons, but Praxinoa was even more intrigued. Her eyes widened as Penthesilea spoke. She was utterly dazzled with amazon lore from the first.

We were to discover that the amazons lived in the most elaborate caves we had ever seen, caves dug deep into their craggy landscape, caves decorated with pictures of their victorious exploits, caves more beautiful than the houses of the greatest aristocrats in Lesbos or in Syracuse. From the outside of these caves, you could see nothing of amazon civilization, but within, all was beauty and refinement. Many of the caves extended far, far into the bowels of the earth. The amazons always anticipated attack from the world of men, and their caves were their protection.

Penthesilea led Praxinoa and me into a special cave where infants were nurtured in a communal nursery. The walls were hung with the whitest linen. The floors were thickly padded with sheepskins so the infants could crawl. Dozens of babies crawled on fluffy sheepskin rugs. Young women, each of whom was responsible for three babies, tended them. Seeing the infants, I ached for my own Cleis.

"We believe that mothers should visit and love their babies but not bear total responsibility for them. They love them better when they are less burdened. The daughters also have less need to renounce their mothers when they reach the terrible age."

"What is the terrible age?"

"The terrible age is thirteen. From thirteen to seventeen, our girls are not allowed to see their own mothers. They are paired with a substitute, whom they call *Demeter,* and she becomes mother, mentor, teacher to them. If they must fight against an older woman, they learn to fight against her. There are rules for fighting—very specific rules. We allow both verbal and philosophical debate, but we also teach the martial arts. Our young women learn to wrestle with their Demeters and debate with them. They learn that disputes may be resolved with words or with physical contests and they may choose either—as long as the rules that govern the contest are strictly obeyed."

"How wise! How wonderful!" exclaimed Praxinoa.

Penthesilea picked up one of the crawling babes and put her in my arms. She was a round little thing of six months, with golden curls and green eyes. I smelled the damp ringlets at the back of her neck and I began to cry.

Penthesilea looked at me incredulously. Praxinoa explained. "Her own baby was kidnapped at a few months of age."

"And where is she now?"

"In Mytilene with her grandmother."

"It is probably the best thing that could have happened to you both."

She put her arms around me. "Now you can learn to be an amazon mother—loving but not clinging on to your daughter for dear life," she said.

"I suppose I might have been an amazon," Praxinoa said triumphantly. "For I was found on a hilltop!"

"It's not too late!" Penthesilea crowed.

She took us next to the amazon temple, a circular structure surrounded by fluted columns. In the center was a heroic sculpture of the amazon goddess Melanippe. Carved out of the blackest basalt—a skill I had believed only the Egyptians knew—it was an image of a nubile woman with the head of a beautiful mare. Her mane was made of golden strands, soft and supple as real hair. Around her waist, she wore the magic amazon girdle of purest gold—the one that Hercules supposedly stole from Hippolyta. Instead of feet, she had hooves with golden horseshoes. From her back grew gigantic golden wings. White-haired priestesses who offered her fruit, honey, loaves of barley bread, and golden cups of dark red blood attended her.

"Every month we offer our own blood to the goddess. It keeps her alive. But the priestesses must all be past the age of bleeding. It is their job to collect and offer the blood, not to provide it. They are the goddess's nursemaids. It is a great honor offered only to women past childbearing."

Praxinoa and I must have looked strange because Penthesilea quickly added, "Oh, yes, I'm sure you've heard we sacrifice captured men to our goddess. But it is not the truth. Most of the things said of us are not the truth. We are said to grow faint and weak at the sight of warrior men. The truth is they grow faint and weak at the sight of us! We do not maim little boys, nor do we worship Ares and Artemis or couple in the woods at random with tribes of marauding men. We do not seek out war and conquest—though at times we have to fight to preserve our community against outsiders. Men try to humble us by spreading rumors about us. If that doesn't work, they resort to rape. The truth is that strong women in armor arouse irrepressible ardor in most men. Then, surprised and distressed by their own emotions, they can think of nothing but how to destroy us. We turn their vision of the world upside down—and men can tolerate anything but that."

As she spoke, she led us to another cave, where colts were nurtured. They too lay on sheepskin rugs, and some were nursed by amazon mothers whose single breasts gave copious amounts of milk.

"We are attempting to nurture them with our own milk in the hope it will solve the mystery of their withered wings."

"Did your horses always have wings?"

"That is a fascinating story. Early in our history, when all the amazons lived near the Black Sea, we were already skilled in riding and training the fleetest horses. It was said by our enemies that our horses must have wings—so swift were they. But whether this was legend or fact, it is impossible to say. Then, somewhere back in the days of the first great queen Penthesilea, the hero Bellerophon mounted and tamed the winged horse Pegasus in order to kill the monster Chimaera. Bellerophon himself was greatly aided by the amazons. In fact, his steed Pegasus was able to shelter for a time among the amazon mares on the sacred island of Aretias, where our steeds were bred and trained. When he departed, all our colts had wings, and for a long time after that we bred the horses with the greatest wings and greatly increased their size and span. We were afraid of no one in those days. We could fight, we could fly, we were like goddesses upon the earth. Then, little by little, our colts began to be born with smaller and smaller wings—or sometimes none at all."

"Then you must attract Pegasus to your mares and keep him with them—if only for a night!"

"But how?"

I had a vague memory of the legends of Pegasus, born of the wisdom of the moon goddess, flying on the wings of her inspiration from ancient Egypt. Didn't Pegasus have a female counterpart called Aganippe? Wasn't she the winged mare who haunts our dreams? If only Isis were here to instruct me! Isis would know how to attract the ancient mate of Pegasus, then Pegasus himself!

"Let me pray over this dilemma," I said to my amazon guide. "Perhaps the answer will come."

Penthesilea looked eager to believe me. "Our best minds, our greatest philosophers have considered this question, but sometimes only an outsider can see clearly."

"But I will need to consult with Aesop, my advisor, whom you have taken away."

"The bearded one?"

"Yes."

"He is a man and cannot be trusted. Even the kindest men are confused by their emotions. They are incapable of thinking rationally. It's not their fault. Unless they are castrated, their brains do not function properly. Fumes, which rise from their testicles, blind their eyes and muddle their brains, poor things. They can't help it."

Praxinoa was quick to appease her: "Perhaps Penthesilea is right, Sappho. Let's not press our luck." It was clear she didn't mean it but was afraid of what the amazons might do.

"Sappho? Are you Sappho of Lesbos, the singer?"

"I suppose I am."

"At last! It has long been written in the book of the goddess that you would come to us! Had we known who you were, we would have welcomed you more fittingly!"

THE WORD went out by drum, by flute, by runner that the prophecy of my arrival had been fulfilled. The amazon queen Antiope wanted to make a feast for me. Throngs of little girls led the way for me, pulling apart roses so that I might walk on their tender petals. I was taken back to the circular temple of Melanippe, but this time choruses of maidens swayed and sang, welcoming me. The priestesses offered me cups of honey and blood as if I were the goddess herself. I felt obliged to taste the sacred offerings. The honey tasted like the honey of all flowers, but the blood tasted like iron ore scooped from deep in the earth. It jolted my consciousness as if I were becoming divine. It made the pathways in my brain spark like lightning.

At the feast I sat with Antiope the queen, trying to understand what she wanted from me—for no one, not even an amazon queen, makes a feast without some secret wish.

"It is time," she said, "that someone tell the truth about our nation. Clearly the goddess has sent you to write *The Amazoniad*."

I paused and thought. I didn't want to disappoint the queen. I never forgot I was her prisoner—however honored for the moment.

"I am no Homer, Majesty, my songs are brief and searing, outbursts of a moment's passion. I do not narrate myths of the founding and passing of kingdoms. I do not tell of battles, but of love."

"Then it's time to branch out, to stretch, to become our female Homer," the queen said. "Perhaps you have not had the proper subject till now. But I will help you. I will send all my most seasoned priestesses to you—the ones with the deepest memories. They will tell you what you need to know, act as your scribes, wait upon you day and night. And you will write our history in Aeolic Greek so all the Greek world will know the truth about us! Thanks to your art, the slanders spread about us shall perish!"

The amazon queen was surely wise in statecraft, but it was clear that she knew little about writing. Slanders stick where compliments are soon forgotten. How to put this gently to the queen?

"Majesty, the most honeyed words soon melt away, while barbs lodge in the throat."

"Nonsense—I will tell you what to write and you will write it. I am queen, am I not?"

"Surely you are the greatest of queens."

"Good. This is how I see *The Amazoniad*. It begins with our fore-mothers near the Black Sea in the dawn of time. It tells the story of our rise and conquests, our horsemanship, our animal husbandry, our great beneficence from Pegasus, our being chosen by our goddess Melanippe to lead womankind to enlightenment and glory, our struggles against marauding tribes, our holy wars, our great exploits, our improvements in civilization, not to mention the increase in human happiness under our reign. Do you see?"

"I do, Majesty." What could I say? If I were a mathematician, she would have me measuring her throne room for carpets; if I were an astronomer, she would have me tracing the route of Pegasus through the night sky. If I were a painter, she would have me depict her as the goddess Melanippe flying over the earth! What good was poetry unless it could glorify power? I could not say this, so I merely nodded and agreed.

1 3

The Amazoniad

Sing in me, Muse, of woman and her curious fate
Oppressed in every nation but the great
Tribe of the amazons, by men misunderstood,
Slandered as evil, seeking the highest good.
—*THE AMAZONIAD*

OF ALL THE punishments that can be visited upon a singer, composing at the behest of a powerful queen is the worst! The truth is, we don't
know where our ideas come from. They issue from the lower depths—
some say the higher reaches—of our souls without our conscious
knowing. A muse or goddess intercedes for us with the daimons of memory and desire and we retrieve what we can—mere fragments of the
greater picture we suspect is there. Whatever we bring up from the
depths is always less than we had hoped, compromised by our poor
powers of expression, our imperfect retrieval, the amnesia for the
dream-state that afflicts the waking. If only we could stay asleep we could
retrieve it! But we cannot stay asleep and compose. And so we stumble
on with our imperfect lyrics, always suspecting better ones are hiding
from us beneath the waves.

Besides, I was used to improvising, not writing. My songs emerged
from the heat of the audience as much as from my brain. That alchemy

of singer and listener was lost here in the dreary solitude of the cave. I hardly knew how to compose songs this way.

The priestesses who were sent by Queen Antiope to assist me in creating a great work to glorify the amazons meant well, but they had no idea what I needed. I needed a muse! They came with both wax-covered wooden tablets and papyri ready to take dictation and write down every passing thought that flitted through my brain. They outfitted my cave with lamps, with tables to write on and couches where I could recline and babble all my dreams for them to take down. They filled my head with myths and legends, hoping to inspire me. One elderly priestess named Artemisia tried to remember all the details of the early battles she had fought, but she was losing her memory, so to disguise that fact she confabulated:

"I remember the Battle of Scythia before we settled in Parthia . . . or was it Ephesus?—Yes, it was Ephesus. I remember the shrines to Astarte—or were they shrines to Selene, the moon goddess? Anyway, we won. We defeated them because our hearts were pure. . . ." Artemisia had scraggly white hair and a long thin face studded with wens. As she sat in the shadows of my cave, she looked to me like an ancient sibyl on a jug made by Etruscan hands such as I had seen in Syracuse.

The younger priestesses, Leucippe and Hippolyta, one a tall redhead and one a short brunette, shook their heads, knowing Artemisia's recollections were wrong, but not quite knowing what to do for me. They had no idea what I needed either. They kept giving me generalities about the glorious amazon foremothers when what I needed were specific details, anecdotes, and incidents. Without detail there is no vision of the past. As a singer and maker of songs, I knew that one searing image was worth more than all these generalities. I could say that Aphrodite was beautiful and it meant nothing. But if I described her as looking like my nemesis Rhodopis with her ropes of golden hair, her rosy knees, her overflowing zone of honey with its golden thatch, her silver sandals and her ten pink toes—everyone would *see* her beauty. The priestesses didn't understand this. Does anyone understand a singer but another singer? They wanted to assure me that every amazon was perfect—from the dawn of time. But perfection is hardly inspiring. It is imperfection that sets our imaginations aflame!

"Surely not every amazon foremother was perfect?" I asked. "Some of them must have had foibles, failings. Some of them must have strayed from the path of virtue. You can't make an epic with all good characters! Even Homer couldn't do it!"

Hippolyta shook her head. "All our foremothers were virtuous," she said. "They taught us that in school."

"Was there no Elpenor, who fell off a roof in a drunken daze? Was there no Circe? No Calypso? No Helen of Argos? No Clytemnestra?

"Not among the amazons, Lady Sappho."

"Useless! You are all useless! Tell your queen I cannot write an epic made out of whipped honey! I must have nuts and raisins, even weevils to keep the listeners awake!"

The three priestesses went to huddle in a corner of my cave. Their whispering rustled at the porches of my ears, but I could not hear what they were saying. They came back and knelt before me.

"The old ones whispered of the black amazons who lived in Libya," Leucippe said.

"And castrated men with scythes so they could be eunuchs of the moon goddess," Hippolyta added. "Will that do?"

Leucippe interrupted, "There were also the gray-haired priestesses of Scythia, who rode into battle with men to cast spells for victory. . . . When the men opposed their judgment, they killed them and battled on alone, terrorizing the enemy."

"Describe them!"

"They were all beautiful," Artemisia said, "even the old ones."

"Amazons are always beautiful, even the Greeks say so," Leucippe added.

"How can I compose an epic in which everyone is beautiful? Who would want to listen to an epic in which everyone is beautiful?" I thundered. "Oh, go away! Leave me here to think!"

The priestesses withdrew, chattering among themselves.

. . .

IT WAS certainly a dilemma. If I retold all the honeyed tales they had told me of the amazons, no one would believe me. No one would even want to listen! But if I elaborated on the ancient stories of castrators and murderesses, the queen would surely have me beheaded or hanged or whatever it was amazons did. I could not compose a line.

What I needed was an amazon Odysseus—wily, clever, crafty, lustful, but with a good heart. A hero must be imperfect or how can she be tested? We accept imperfections in our men. We even dote upon their imperfections. But in women we want something else. We want perfection beyond humanity. And how can such perfection be real? Moreover, how can it inspire our love? Odysseus can be quirky, tempted by sirens, and too proud to be wise—and still we adore him. The more human he is, the more we love him. Not so with women heroes. Penelope is so patient we hardly believe our ears. Artemis is utterly virginal and Aphrodite utterly lustful. And then I realized if there is no female Odysseus, I will have to become her! The prospect was so exhausting that I put my head down on the floor of the cave and surrendered to the arms of Morpheus.

That night, as the moon rose over the land of the amazons, I slept deeply and dreamed of myself as an amazon priestess, flying through the skies on the back of Pegasus. I could see the stars twinkling in a black sky, the moon a sharp crescent, its points twinkling like a scythe. Down below me, I could see the earth laid out: Egypt, Babylonia, Lesbos, Lydia, Crete, Trinacria, Motya—all with their differing customs, gods and goddesses, all with their power struggles and wars. I knew there was no place on earth where all people were good and beautiful—certainly not Lesbos, which had banished me for seeking freedom. But I also knew that unless people *believed* there was someplace where everyone was good and beautiful, they would despair at the cruelty of the world. The singer had to tread a fine line between depicting Hades' realm and promising the Elysian Fields. I was not sure I was up to the task. Oh, it was easy enough to see earth as Hades' realm and dream of an Elysian Fields where all the gods were on your side, but what about the failings of human beings? "How mortals take the gods to task for their own failings!" Homer sang. But Homer was now safely dead. He was beyond being blamed for his words. A living bard was another matter.

Praxinoa awoke me in the middle of the night.

"Sappho, I must talk to you. Wake up! Wake up! Remember how you said I could choose my freedom when I would?"

I struggled awake. Why do people always ask the most important questions when you are half asleep?

"Yes."

"I want to stay here and become an amazon. I am even willing to sacrifice a breast so that I can be a better archer!"

I was stunned. I knew that Praxinoa wanted her freedom, but did she have to seek it in such an extreme way? How could she be so sure she was ready to make that sacrifice? I wanted her to think, but I had to be careful about my response. Though I was horrified by the thought of her losing even one of her sweet breasts, which I had kissed so often, I didn't want her to be afraid that I would go back on my promise to liberate her.

"Your breasts are so beautiful," I mumbled. "I'm sure you can be a fine archer without losing your lovely right breast."

"All the more reason why my sacrifice is important. If my breasts were misshapen, it would be a meaningless gesture to abandon a breast!"

"Think about it, Prax, don't make this decision in a hurry." Now I was truly awake. "Tell me all the reasons why you want to do this."

"I was meant to be an amazon! If I had been found as an abandoned baby, I would be one already. I love this land! I love the women here and I feel at home here as I have never felt at home anywhere before. I wish you would become an amazon too and stay with me. I think our destiny is here. Please say you'll think about it!"

"Prax—I think you have to consider your motives. This is a very hasty decision. We've been here only so briefly—how can you be sure? Wait until you know the amazons better. Then, if you want to become one, I'll give you all my blessings."

"I feel in my heart that I already *am* an amazon!" Praxinoa said. "But if you want me to wait and think, I will. But how long must I wait?"

"Until you are sure," I said.

"But I am sure *already,*" Praxinoa said. "I know I belong here. I think you do too."

When I had finally brushed all drowsiness away, I believed that I had dreamed this whole conversation, but it was not so. Praxinoa had already begun her training as an amazon while I slept in my cave. And now she wanted me to join her. She didn't even want to hear my doubts.

"I see no reason to return to the world of Rhodopis, the world of pharaohs and slavery, of Babylonians and conquest. I might have been an amazon had I been found as an infant and I'm sure I was *meant* to be one. The amazon priestess agrees. She has read my runes, even read the entrails of a great seagoing gull, and told me I am already an amazon at heart. Let her read yours too!"

"Not yet, not yet, Praxinoa, all in good time. I have to write *The Amazoniad* first. I cannot take a minute away from the task the queen has given me. I am to write the epic of the amazons—not an easy assignment."

"Have you started?"

"Well, yes," I lied. "I have begun at the beginning, with the most ancient legends of the amazons and their rise."

"They are hardly legends, but the only truth there is."

I looked at Praxinoa in disbelief. Was she already convinced of the absolute truth of everything the amazons had told her? I always cringe at the phrase "the only truth." I know I am in the presence of zealotry.

"It must be wonderful to have such an exalted subject given you— not like the frivolous themes of the symposia at which you used to perform in Trinacria and Naucratis. Now you can use your talent for something noble," Prax said.

"I was not aware I lacked noble themes before."

Prax looked at me ironically. "Aphrodite was all very well before we met the amazons—but now it is so clear that their goddess is greater."

"Is she?"

"Of course she is!"

"Then you are totally convinced."

"Totally."

"Is there nothing I can say?"

"Nothing. This is my destiny."

"And where is Aesop? Has he also discovered his destiny?"

"Locked in a cave, impregnating virgins. He seems to be having a good time, though he complains of the long hours. Ten virgins a day is tougher duty than slavery," he says. "They weep, they rage, they vie with each other for his favors."

"Then the amazons have not succeeded in abolishing jealousy and bickering among women?"

"It's because a *man* is there. Men bring discord. They just can't help it. They come from chaos and wish to return the world to chaos."

"Are you speaking of Aesop, the most rational man on earth?"

"The amazons believe there are no rational men."

"And what do *you* believe?"

"I believe what the amazons believe, of course."

"And you believe you have been liberated from slavery?"

"You promised me, didn't you? You're not going to take that back."

It is never profitable to argue with a new convert. I held my tongue while Praxinoa babbled on.

But whatever her beliefs were, they had certainly strengthened her. She no longer had any doubts about the future. She was sure she had discovered the only path to righteousness.

THE VERY NEXT night the amazons massed in a circle under the full moon. They performed the ritual in an apple grove with gnarled old apple trees whose fruit was pocked and wormy. A circle of mares pawed the ground under the trees. As the amazons sang and invoked their goddess, Melanippe, the mares joined in a chorus of neighs. Revelers rang finger bells and danced on drums with their bare feet. Infusions of herbs were brought in golden goblets and blessings were given before the strong-smelling liquids were drunk. The dancing and singing went on and on—amazons whirling as if in a trance.

Praxinoa astonished me by enduring the cutting and cautery of her right breast at the festival that night without a murmur or indeed a whisper of pain. The job was done by the forgetful Artemisia and I feared for Praxinoa's life. What if she confused her breast with her heart!

Attendants to Artemisia stanched Praxinoa's bleeding with herbs I did not recognize and bound her raw chest with linen. She lay at the center of the circle with a beatific expression on her face, immune to the pain. That impressed me more than anything. I did not know then that the amazons had given her powerful drugs all day long. They were great believers in alleviating women's pain and even had drugs for childbirth long before any other civilizations. Perhaps the excision of Praxinoa's breast should be a pivotal scene in my epic—but I wondered whether the queen would approve. That was the problem. The more I thought of the queen's reactions, the less I could write at all.

We had lost track of how much time we had been with the amazons. Was it only a few days? Or was it weeks? I would have given anything to speak with Aesop, but he and I were deliberately separated and Praxinoa was going through her own transformations. She was constantly busy learning the lore of the amazons at their school. I hardly even saw her after the initiation ritual.

Strange that the crew of our ship (which we had left docked in the harbor) had not found us yet. What had happened to them? Would they ever come and save me from having to write the history of the amazons?

I WAS SUPPOSED to stay in my cave and compose my stirring amazon epic full of only good and beautiful people, but since I was stuck, I requested permission to wander. This was not so easy to come by. The powers that be think you can squeeze a singer and songs will burst forth like pus from a lanced boil, but the muse is not always so cooperative. Sometimes it is necessary to move the feet in order to move the mind.

The island was full of long beaches and rocky hills. The ruins of great King Minos' palace were somewhere on the island and I was determined to find them.

Every morning I walked and walked until I was exhausted and then I returned to my cave and tried to write. Useless! But one morning, I pushed myself to walk on, even as the sun grew hot at noon. Eventually I came to a place where piles of rocks on the ground looked as if they had been set in a pattern, which I traced with my weary feet. I walked around and around concentric circles of stones, one leading into the other. At first I walked idly, thinking of nothing in particular, but when I came to the center, the wind began to whip and howl about my head, the sky grew overcast and black, and I seemed to be standing on a precipice, although the ground was flat. I walked out of the circle and the wind died down, the sky cleared, the sun was hot again. And then I walked back in and once again it seemed I had come to the center of the earth where Hades' realm plunged and the Elysian Fields beckoned.

The labyrinth! Had I found the ruins of the labyrinth that Daedalus built? It had that power—as if thousands of young men and maidens had perished in this place between the hungry jaws of the minotaur. I kept walking the pattern of stones to test what happened when I reached the center and it happened again and again. The ground seemed to open beneath me. The Land of the Dead seemed to yawn and I ran to the outer edges of the circle as quickly as I could.

And then I heard laughter and little shrieks of joy.

Where were they coming from? There was a thicket of shrubs nearby and the voices seemed to come from there. Then they seemed to come from behind me. Then I was not sure. I was standing very still at the edges of the labyrinth. I waited. Only birds and insects stirring in the hot sun. A lizard crawled over a rock at my feet.

I heard the laughter again.

I tried to follow it. It was farther away than I had thought. Suddenly it seemed closer. Sometimes it seemed to recede and then to get louder. The trees rustled in the wind. The lizard suddenly darted into the ruins of the labyrinth.

These are the ghosts of the girls and boys sacrificed to the minotaur, I thought. Then the first two lines of a lyric came into my head: *Ghosts of girls fed to the minotaur / Seek out the ghosts of boys who*—

Another burst of laughter. I saw a naked amazon run from behind a bush, pursued by an Egyptian sailor. Then another couple emerged—a Nubian slave and an amazon. And another couple. And still another.

These were no ghosts! The sailors from my ship were courting a bevy of beautiful young amazons, who seemed more than happy to be courted.

I sensed danger in their delight. Were young amazons allowed to play without permission from their Demeters, whose word was law? I doubted it. But their laughter and playfulness had stirred my soul at last. The sounds of love moisten the soul like love itself. I ran back to my cave, hoping that now I could write.

I WAS NOT used to composing on papyrus or wax-covered wooden tablets—much less dictating to helpers. I was used to composing orally, with my lyre in my hand and with a warm and waiting audience inspiring my song. If my poems were later learned by others, later written down by other hands, that was not my business. As Aesop said, the more people repeat, even imitate you, the more likely you are to be immortal.

At first I ground out the lines like sausage, not much liking them, wishing I were writing about maidens and the minotaur. I had a curious sense of foreboding. Images of Praxinoa's raw and bleeding chest kept coming back to me. I doubted I would ever get to Delphi. I missed Alcaeus. I longed for Cleis. I worried that I'd be trapped forever with the amazons, writing only what their queen decreed.

Would I ever get away? How? The sailors were otherwise engaged. Aesop was shut away in a cave doing his duty with the virgins. I was condemned to labor on, writing an epic when I was no epic poet—trying only to please Queen Antiope so she would not kill or enslave me.

I wrote for hours, until my hand was weary—for I had refused the help of the priestesses who wanted to write for me while I dictated. It was hard enough to write alone, but with the priestesses in my cave, it was impossible.

Just as I was thinking of them, Artemisia, Hippolyta, and Leucippe appeared.

"We are sent by the queen," Leucippe said, tossing her curls. "She longs to see your verses."

I looked up, annoyed. "Not finished yet. Only a fool shows half-finished work."

"But look at all these papyri," Hippolyta said, peering over my shoulder and the piles of scratched-out texts. I was not satisfied with anything I had written, certainly not *Wild women astride their horses' wings/Ride on the moon's pale rings.*

"Fits and starts," I said, "nothing to show yet."

"The queen will not be pleased," Artemisia said. "She is waiting impatiently."

"Then let her wait!"

"Oooooo," shrieked Leucippe, snatching a scrap of papyrus. "But this is good!" She had focused on that dumb line about amazons flapping around the moon on winged horses. "Let me at least show her this!"

"Not on your life!" I shouted, but before I could stop her, she bounced out of the cave with my papyrus scraps. The other priestesses followed at a gallop.

The queen will hate it, I thought. She will want to behead me or imprison me or something. I will never see my daughter again, or Alcaeus, or my damned mother. I will never sing again. What's the use? For the first time I discovered the pain of having unfinished work snatched out of my hand. I felt it was no longer mine and could not grow or blossom. It seemed a bird's embryo snatched from its shell: it would never fly. I wanted to cry.

Soon there was a stirring outside the cave. This time Penthesilea led the priestesses.

"The queen is ravished by your words," Penthesilea said. "She thinks they are immortal. She begs me to ask for more. She believes you have been sent to rescue the amazons and you will not fail her. She wants you to finish the epic as speedily as you can and then to pen an anthem to amazon victory that we can use in battle. We may have to go to war against the Egyptian sailors who are ravishing our maidens!"

So they had been caught!

"And what of the maidens?" I asked.

"We will wait and see if they are pregnant, and if not, they will be put to death," said Artemisia with great satisfaction.

"I cannot bear that," I said. "Tell the queen I will not permit it."

"I cannot tell the queen that," Penthesilea said. "No one has ever told the queen that. She will be furious. The goddess alone knows what she will do!"

"I am not afraid of her," I said. "If my words are immortal, perhaps *I* am immortal."

"Lady Sappho, I cannot give your message. You must face the queen yourself. I would, however, advise you to come to the queen bearing an epic and an anthem."

"Then I must get busy," I said, bending down to write.

I WROTE incessantly for ten days and ten nights. Good or bad, I would finish this epic to spare the maidens' lives. Inspiration often arrives when life hangs in the balance. I had my motivation now and I was fast. I scarcely stopped to drink water or eat a bite of bread. The cave was littered with papyrus scraps—all out of order.

When I thought I had done all I could, I summoned the priestesses to help me recopy the epic on papyrus scrolls. That took another week. The queen kept sending Penthesilea to check on our progress. Meanwhile, they had rounded up the offending virgins and most of the sailors and were interrogating them—for all the good that did. Apparently some sailors and virgins had escaped and were preparing to set sail. Time was short.

14

The Coming of Pegasus

Her pure delight in holding the branch of myrtle
And the flower of the rosetree,
Moved me as she sang,
Tossing her long hair
Over her bare shoulders
And beautiful back. . . .
—ARCHILOCHUS

IT WAS EARLY evening. The amazons were assembled in the same ominous apple grove where Praxinoa had her breast cut. Invisible cicadas sang and birds chirped on the low-hanging boughs. From time to time a heavy apple fell from a weighted bough. The queen had called this convocation so I could read my epic to the assembled throng. Even the ravished maidens were there, with bound ankles and wrists. The sailors who had been caught ravishing them were also prisoners and had been dragged out of the prison caves wearing their wooden and bronze shackles.

Praxinoa was there, sitting among the priestesses who had attended me in my writing cave. She held hands with our guide Penthesilea. On her face was the most beatific expression I had ever seen her wear. She was happy. Why, then, was I so uneasy?

The whole floor of the grove was littered with rotting apples, which gave a deep but not unpleasant aroma. To this was added the perfume of applewood fires and incense. The air was heavy and so was my heart. Yes, I was happy that Praxinoa seemed so happy, but I still had my misgivings about her conversion to the amazon cause and I wondered how I would ever weather the loss of still another loved one. As the sun set below the horizon, as oil lamps were lit and tended, I wished Alcaeus were here to guide me and I wished my darling Cleis were in my arms. The amazons did not believe in clinging motherhood, but what I wouldn't have given for a bit of clinging now!

I began to recite the history of the amazons from earliest times. The words poured out as if I believed them—and of course, in many ways, I did. I believed in the power of women to make their own lives. I believed in women's strength and ingenuity. So I recited with deep conviction. But as I read from the papyrus the priestesses had prepared, I realized that not all the lines were mine. Where I had attempted humor, it had been deleted. Where I had attempted wordplay, it had been changed to literal statement. Where I had joked, there was only seriousness. Everything was so heavy-handed! Nevertheless, the queen appeared delighted. She laughed and sighed and clapped her hands. She repeated several lines after me. The convocation and reading appeared to be a great success.

When I came to relate the visitation of Pegasus to the land of the amazons, there was a noise overhead. The sky was so cloudy that at first it was not possible to see what was happening. The sounds might have been thunder or the rumbling of a far-off volcano. I went on with my presentation without daring to look up. I described the immense iridescent wings of Pegasus, his golden hooves and his wild fire-colored eyes, his mane and tail of stars. I described his origins in the wise blood of the moon goddess, his sacred mating with the white mare Aganippe, *"the mare who destroys mercifully,"* and his digging with his crescent-shaped hoof the famous Hippocrene—the well of poetic inspiration. On Mount Helicon, the home of the muses, was the sacred spring from which all poetic inspiration was fed, and Pegasus had opened it up for all the singers of the world. It was said that whoever could ride Pegasus through the skies would possess forever the key to poetic power. I longed to gallop on his back and hold the secret reins of the muses in my hands. My longing fueled my performance and I entranced the audience with the rise and fall of my voice, so like the galloping of this mythic steed.

Then, all at once, looking up, I seemed to see golden hooves flashing and a tumult of two immense wings parting the clouds! Was I dreaming? Had I gone mad? Was I the only one who saw this? No. All the heads of the spectators were thrown back in wonder.

Pegasus himself flew low over the gathering, snorted mightily, nearly knocked us all over with the hurricane generated by his huge varicolored wings, alighted momentarily on the ground in a thunder of metallic hooves, and flew off again in the direction of the mares' quarters. We all fell silent with awe. The cicadas stopped singing, as did the birds, as if there were a hole in time.

Then I began to read again. I read about the good and beautiful amazons, about their conquests, their achievements, their art, their architecture, their goddesses, their revolutions in child-rearing, horse-breeding, warfare. We could all hear the neighing of mares in the distance. When I came almost to the end of my epic and the listeners were hanging on each word, I took a long pause.

"Go on!" the amazons cried. "Go on!"

I stood very still and silent, knowing that I had to take this opportunity or forever regret it.

"I command you to continue," the queen said.

I did not move. I did not speak.

The amazons looked frightened. They had never seen anyone defy their queen before.

"We have been sent a sign," I said very softly, so softly that everyone had to strain to hear.

"What sign?" asked the queen.

"The return of Pegasus."

"That is because of your epic," said the queen. "That is why we plan to keep you here to compose for us."

"With all due respect, great Queen Antiope, I disagree with you," I said.

Praxinoa put her hand over her mouth in shock. There was a common intake of breath from the amazon priestesses.

"How dare you disagree with me?" Antiope roared.

"I dare," I said softly, "because I hate to see winged horses with withered wings."

"Let me worry about that!" said the queen. "Our wisest advisors are studying the mares even as we speak!"

In the distance, the mares were whinnying softly. They almost sounded like Aphrodite's doves cooing.

"Your Majesty, I think Pegasus has returned not because of my epic but because of the joy and happiness of these amazon maidens."

"You mean the prisoners?"

"I mean the lovers among us, Queen Antiope. The lovers have brought Pegasus back with their pure joy and delight. When Aphrodite inspires us, flowers bloom and maidens laugh and mares give birth to winged foals. This is not my doing—it is Aphrodite's. Banish Aphrodite and your horses will all be born with stunted wings. It was Aphrodite who sent me here—and even the sailors who seduced the maidens. Without her mischief, nothing flies!"

"Heresy!" said the queen. "Aphrodite makes us weak, makes us succumb to the blandishments of men. We do not need her! And we do not need men!"

"But you *do*! Pegasus was drawn back by Aphrodite's laughter. It is Aphrodite who gives us wings. Without lust, life has no juice! Without lust, we cannot fly! Unless you release the sailors and the maidens, I will not finish reciting my epic of the amazons."

"Defy me and you die!" screamed Queen Antiope.

The amazons gasped. The queen summoned her guards to bind me.

"Bind me if you wish, but you cannot bind Aphrodite—she comes and departs when she will. Even the gods obey her!"

"Finish the poem! Finish the poem!" the amazons chanted.

"Queen Antiope, will you agree to liberate the maidens and the sailors and to let me go? I cannot be a poet in captivity."

The queen hesitated. She furrowed her brow, balancing absolute power with the need to please the populace.

"Sappho should be our queen!" Penthesilea declared, coming forward. "She is in closer touch with the gods and goddesses than you are. She can give us winged horses. You cannot." The crowd of amazons began to cheer, *"Sappho, Sappho, Sappho!"*

The queen directed that Penthesilea also be taken prisoner. This was a moment when even apples stopped falling from the gnarled branches.

"I can guarantee nothing," I said. "I can only try to lure the gods with words. Poetry is not a science. Winged horses cannot be broken to the bridle."

As I argued with the queen of the amazons, I was sure I was digging my own grave but somehow I did not care. Why should she tolerate my defiance? Where had I found the courage to question her power? Well, if I was to die, I might as well die here and now in the midst of a performance. If I died defending Aphrodite, wouldn't she take pity on my tortured soul?

"Perhaps it is time to bend the rules a little," the queen finally said. She knew her power was in peril. "Perhaps Sappho should complete her epic and be on her way."

"Not without the maidens and sailors, and not without Aesop! And not unless you agree not to punish Penthesilea!" I said.

"Stay, Sappho, stay!" the amazons pleaded. "Stay and rule us as our queen!"

Now Queen Antiope was truly alarmed. "When Sappho finishes reciting her epic, I shall decide."

This was plainly a mistake. The amazons were restless. They were gathering around Penthesilea to ask her advice. Some were chanting my name over and over. The happy neighing of the mares formed a background to their chants.

I proposed a compromise, for the sake of my amazon admirers if not the queen. "I shall leave you Praxinoa as my emissary. She knows everything I know and she is wise beyond her years and loyal to your cause. If Queen Antiope agrees to share her power with Praxinoa and Penthesilea, I can leave you in their capable hands."

The queen hesitated again, and I hesitated myself, imagining myself queen of the amazons, with Praxinoa and Penthesilea as my highest ministers and Pegasus as my steed. I saw myself as the amazon queen, dispensing justice and song in equal measure and galloping through the skies. I even saw myself giving up poetry for power. I would make a far better queen than Antiope! I nearly seduced myself with my own vision, but I pulled myself back from the brink. My nature was too restless for ruling a nation and I needed to find my daughter. I loved the adulation and applause, but administration bored me. Besides, I would have to kill the queen—I who had never killed anything in my life. Did I have the courage to kill the queen? I disliked her heartily, but was that a reason to kill? Poets prefer to kill with words instead of knives.

"Unbind the prisoners!" said the queen. "Continue with the epic!"

"Do you vow to share your power with the populace and with your wise advisors?"

"I solemnly swear," said the queen.

So I performed the last stanzas of my epic with tears in my eyes and heresy in my heart. The audience was weeping as well. The epic was hardly as subtle as my lyrics, but it certainly set the amazons to roaring.

There is nothing like flattery to please the crowd. There is nothing like telling people what they want to hear. People love it when you say that they are good and true and beautiful. They love it even if they don't believe it.

When my recitation was complete, crowds of young amazons led us down to the shore, carrying both me and an exhausted, flower-bedecked Aesop on their broad shoulders.

We were just in time. The sailors still on board were making ready to sail at dawn. The just-released sailors and their unbound amazon mistresses swam to the ship as fast as their arms could carry them, but even the loyal amazons who were staying celebrated all night on the deck. Everyone reveled except Aesop, who collapsed in exhaustion the moment we came aboard.

The sky was orange and lavender as we bade farewell to the land of the amazons at dawn. Praxinoa and Penthesilea were waving from a small boat bearing the farewell party. The queen sat in it, pretending to weep over my departure. As we hoisted our sails, the farewell party threw flowers and streamers.

All at once, above us there was a hurricane of wind. Our sails bellied out and our ship sped on. There was whinnying and the flash of golden hooves. Pegasus was overseeing our departure.

The little boat with Queen Antiope, Penthesilea, and Praxinoa nearly foundered in the tossing waves. But soon they bobbed up again and began to row back toward shore against the tide.

They struggled with the oars. The waves rose and fell around them. Then a barge full of younger amazon maidens came to their aid. The two boats went up and down in the waves as they made the perilous transfer. Queen Antiope nearly fell into the sea, but Penthesilea caught her. I couldn't help but wonder what might have been if she had not.

I blew kisses to Praxinoa, whose chest was still bandaged, and who was waving and waving until she seemed a tiny speck on the water. I knew how much I missed her already.

15

Ghosts

Here was great loveliness of ghosts!
—HOMER

WE WERE SAILING north into stormy weather after many months
with the amazons. Delphi was still our destination, but I had begun to
understand that this journey would be no more predictable than those
that had preceded it. The gods were in charge, not I. Perhaps they had
something else to teach me.

ZEUS: *Well, at last she's learning something!*
APHRODITE: *I told you she was worth saving.*
ZEUS: *I'd hardly go that far.*

We had rams and ewes aboard, and chickens and pigs. We were
stocked with amphorae of wine and barrels of barley and grain. If our
luck held, we might reach several safe anchorages on the way back to
Delphi. And if it did not? Best not to think about it.

Deeply troubled about my experiences with the amazons, I was hardly sure I had done the right thing by refusing to be their queen. I missed Praxinoa, who had been my only lifelong witness. It was as if, with her disappearance, my whole past had vanished as well. Alcaeus suddenly seemed a distant myth. Did he really exist at all? And Cleis? How old was she now? Two? Three? She was definitely not a myth. Her baby smell came to me whenever I closed my eyes. But how would I ever find her again? Perhaps if I had accepted being queen of the amazons I would have had a better chance. I could have ridden to her on the back of Pegasus! And carried her away.

Aesop slept as we sailed away from the land of the amazons. He was impossible to rouse. Had he been drugged? He knew nothing of my discussions with the amazons, nothing of my epic, nothing of Praxinoa's conversion, nothing of Pegasus. What a pity! He had missed all the greatest adventures.

Days passed. We sailed and sailed. Once I was able to rouse Aesop, I regaled him with everything that had transpired. While I was in a cave forced to compose, while Praxinoa had her breast removed, he had been fed and bathed and cosseted by the amazon maidens and urged to feast endlessly on young amazon flesh. He hardly seemed happy about it.

"Men *dream* of such things—a cave of virgins and you the only stud! Didn't you at least enjoy it?" I asked.

"Let me answer you with a fable," Aesop said. "A hare was very popular with the other beasts, who all claimed to be his dear friends—even his lovers. But one day he heard the hounds approaching and expected to escape with the help of his many admirers. He went first to the horse and asked him to carry him away from the hounds. But the horse refused, claiming that he had important work to do for his master. 'All your other friends will come to your assistance,' he said. The hare then approached the bull, hoping that he would repel the hounds with his horns. The bull replied, 'I am very sorry, but I have an important appointment with a beautiful young cow; I feel sure that our dear friend the goat will do what you want.' But the goat feared that his bony back might harm the hare if he balanced him on it. He suggested that the ram was the proper friend to apply to for help. So the hare went to the ram and told him his predicament. The ram replied, 'Another time, my dearest hare. I do not like to interfere on the present occasion, as hounds have been known to eat sheep as well as hares.' As a last hope, the hare went to the little calf, who in a baby prattle said that he was unable to help since he did not like to take the responsibility upon himself when so many older and wiser animals had declined. By this time the hounds were quite near, and the hare took to his heels and escaped like the wind."

"And what is the moral?"

"*He that has many friends, has no friends,*" Aesop said.

"The story you have told does not prove that," I said. "You will have to come up with more appropriate fables if you wish to be immortal. I think the amazon maidens have addled your brain. Perhaps you should write a tale about the amazons and the fable-maker, about a good man locked up in a cave, assigned to the tough duty of impregnating virgins, and how he goes a little mad. What a fable that would make. It would make your name for all eternity."

"I have vowed to write only about animals in the future," Aesop said.

"Why?"

"Because when you write about people, you inevitably offend—but if you write about animals, the evil do not recognize themselves but the good understand immediately."

"Since when should the fable-maker worry about offending the subjects of his fables?"

"It is human to care," said Aesop.

"It is godlike not to care," I said, "and a fable-maker must imitate the gods."

"So must a singer. Yet you care," Aesop said.

"I wish I didn't."

"Ah, so do we all!"

"Then you feel like a hare among fair-weather friends?" I changed the subject.

"I did not say that."

"You implied it."

"That is the beauty of speaking in parables," Aesop said, his black eyes burning. "I was only giving you an example of how someone might feel surrounded by too many sweethearts and suitors. Love is singular, by definition. The great king who has a harem has no real lovers among the ladies."

"And why do you think this is?"

"Because they are all thinking of each other and not of him. By eliminating risk with numbers, you create another sort of risk—no one really feels loyal to you. They are all worried about the others and how to get the better of them. This can be very tiring. Instead of being a lover, you become a diplomat. You spend your time arbitrating disputes among your suitors. That leaves little energy for making love. Eventually you have to take to your heels and escape."

"So it was no fun at all?"

"I didn't say that," Aesop said, "I only said it was not what it seemed to be. Or one man's pleasure may be another man's pain."

"Hardly pain, I should think."

Aesop smiled slyly. I was never able to get a straight answer out of him.

The atmosphere of the ship was much changed, with so many of the amazon maidens aboard. The men seemed much happier—even if there were not enough maidens to go around. Just the presence of women cheered them. One of the most beautiful of the young amazons, Maera, she of the red ringlets and eyes the color of young emeralds, of the sun-freckled nose and rosy ankles, took me to task for having left the queen alive.

"You should have killed her while you had the chance," Maera said, "she'll never be able to share her power with the others. She'll revert to her wicked ways soon enough. If you were going to refuse to *be* queen, you should at least have appointed Praxinoa in your stead. A three-woman team will fall apart bickering. The amazon ideals are good in theory, but in practice, they don't work. For example, I'm sure they never showed you the graves of the boy babies."

"What boy babies? What graves? I thought the amazons had eliminated all boy babies."

"And how would they do that, Sappho?"

"I thought they had pessaries to filter out the male seed. Or so I was told by the priestesses."

"Rubbish! They kill them or expose them, just as girls are exposed in the Greek world. Surely some of them survive, nursed by wolves who prowl the ruins of the labyrinth, but then they grow up more brute than human—which justifies the amazons hunting them down as beasts."

My mouth hung open. "Why did no one tell me that?"

"Why indeed. You were our honored guest. The more you are honored, the more people tell you lies."

Now I felt like an idiot. Why had I not seen? Had I been lulled by the foolish tales of the priestesses? Was I too busy writing my epic? Or was I just too hopeful that somehow, somewhere, peace and justice could exist between the sexes?

"I thought the amazons had solved the problem of warfare between men and women."

"Well, if you kill all the boy babies, that's a kind of temporary solution. But remember the stunted winglets of the foals? You yourself pointed out to the queen that true flight is impossible without love!"

"So what are we to do about the two sexes?"

"Why *do* anything?"

"Because otherwise men dominate women or women get even by dominating men. Two sexes seems to be a recipe for grief and warfare."

"Then we should invent *more* sexes—just to confuse everyone! That will solve the problem!" Maera said, laughing. "Let's have men with breasts and women with phalli! Some men should have *more* than one phallus so as to love a woman and a boy at once! And some women should have deltas all over their bodies!"

The gods had arranged the world rather poorly. Even Zeus and Hera couldn't get along—so how could mere mortals? And poor lame Hephaestus was always catching Aphrodite in her adulteries. Zeus wanted a womb and Athena wanted a phallus. Why should we mortals be content with our limited equipment when the gods *themselves* weren't?

ZEUS: *Now she is criticizing us again—what hubris!*
APHRODITE: *Perhaps she needs a stronger lesson.*

ZEUS: *There's only one place for that—the Land of the Dead.*
APHRODITE: *Only if you promise to spare her life!*
ZEUS: *Why should great Zeus promise anything?*

Maera ran back to her Egyptian sailor. "Right now he loves me and follows me like a dog with his tongue hanging out! If he ever stops, I'll become an amazon again! I can fight as well as he can—maybe better. I'm certainly not afraid of him—or any of them!" Her laughter echoed after her.

I was vexed about the amazons. Was there no land free of violence and pain? Or was Maera lying about the slaughter of the boy babies—in order to justify her own escape from the amazons? Was she lying to herself most of all? And what would become of Praxinoa? Had I freed her from bondage only to see her become Antiope's slave?

THE WEATHER was stormy, but the crew rowed on. Endless days and nights we rowed and sailed. There were bone-white islands stuck in misty seas where we could not stop because it was said they were inhabited by fierce monsters.

"Fiends with the heads of birds of prey and the claws of tigers inhabit these islands," one sailor said.

"Snake-headed goddesses," said another. "They turn men to stone."

IT WAS TRUE. Ravenous birds followed us, hovering, screeching, and threatening. We saw bloody parts of sea creatures dangling from their sharp yellow beaks. Sometimes drops of dark blood fell upon our decks or spotted our sails. The waters themselves seemed ever more treacherous.

We rowed straight on. Often the fog grew so thick that we didn't know whether we sailed in the sky or on earth. The ship rocked so hard that we had to tether ourselves to the rails with rope to stay aboard. We lost three sailors overboard and watched in horror as birds of prey dove down and plucked out their eyes.

"Never have I seen such a sight," I cried to Aesop.

"The gods are angry," Aesop said.

AT LAST, lacking fresh water, we were forced to stop, however inhospitable the shore.

A conical volcano topped the island we found. It was spewing smoke and lava. Gray dust hovered in the air.

"We should turn back!" the sailors said.

But as we drew closer in, we saw that the island's shores were verdant as those of Lesbos. The weather cleared for a while, revealing a huge lagoon surrounded by green hills. The island was shaded with trees of all description. At first I thought it might indeed be my native isle and my heart leapt, thinking I might soon see Cleis. Even if Pittacus had condemned me to death, at least I'd clasp my child before I died. But I was wrong. This island was not Lesbos. My mind was playing tricks.

We sent our scouts ashore to look for fresh water. We planned to stop only one night before proceeding to Delphi.

It was almost sunset when the scouts came back to the ship to tell us the coast was clear. No vultures or raptors or mythical beasts had been seen ashore. The island appeared to be uninhabited. But the sailors and maidens were frightened by what they'd already seen at sea and they refused to join us. While the rain held off, they romped and swam around the boat like sea sprites and dolphins. Then the sky darkened again and they clung to the boat, refusing all blandishments to come ashore.

Aesop and I rowed in with the water-bearers just as the sky opened up with rain.

The rain was full of ash and grit—almost as if it were a solid substance. It stung our faces where it fell. We wrapped our cloaks around us for protection, but we were already soaked and our capes were heavy with this wet dust. Up ahead, there seemed to be a clearing where a few last rays of red sun still shone. We ran to it as if that were the way to get out of the gritty rain. It led us up a narrow path on the slippery side of the volcano. The stone was pumice and it slid under our feet. We went around and around the conical sides of the volcano, losing our bearings.

Then suddenly the road dipped down and we seemed to be under the mountain as well as on top of it. How this was possible, I don't know. I reached out for Aesop's hand and clung to it. Darkness fell very swiftly. There was a rushing river under our feet that appeared out of nowhere. We waded across it, thigh-deep in the freezing water. A shadowy ferryman put out his oar.

"Come aboard," he said. It was Charon and his boat was full of souls.

"I'd rather walk," I said, thinking that if I refused Charon's ferry I could return to the Land of the Living.

He laughed at me. "Whether you ride or wade or swim hardly matters," Charon said. "If you don't believe me, ask your guide." I turned to Aesop, who was climbing into the boat. He shrugged his shoulders.

"I've never been here before either," he said, "and Homer never warned me of a boat of souls or indeed of any boatman to ferry them."

Suddenly a red-gold cat with one blue eye and one agate leapt into my lap, crying like a human baby.

"Sesostris!" I shouted, recognizing Isis' beloved lost cat from her description, but when I put my hand down to stroke him, my fingers felt only air. Here was the magical cat I had searched for all over Syracuse, and I could not stroke his beautiful fur.

I looked down into the black water. Under the rippled darkness, the pale face of my little brother Eurygius stared up at me. Pink fingers reached up to grab the side of the boat.

"Eurygius!" I called out.

Charon brought his oar brutally down and smashed the tiny hand. I screamed as if it were my own.

"He can't feel it," Charon said. "But he has the power to keep you here forever."

My brother disappeared again in the inky water.

We reached the other side. A tumult of forms came surging toward us as if they would be taken back to the Land of the Living. I remembered Odysseus in Hades' realm feeding blood to the ghosts so they could speak to him.

"Where is the pool of blood?" I asked.

"What pool of blood?" Charon asked.

"The one that allows the souls to speak."

Charon laughed bitterly. "Homer was blind. What he thought was blood was only water—the thick, frigid water of the rushing river, sticky with souls."

I was astonished to hear that Homer had been wrong. If great Homer was wrong, anything was possible! The souls surged forward. As they came toward me, I could make out familiar faces.

"Ignore them," Charon said, "if you ever want to return to the Land of the Living." But I could not ignore them. At the front of them all was my father, Scamandronymus.

"Sappho, little whirlwind," he said, "what are you doing here? Don't tell me you are dead. I cannot bear it."

I ran to throw my arms around my father, whose battle wounds still oozed dark blood, but he pushed me away.

"Do not embrace the dead," he said, "if you want to go on living. Lord Hades will take it as a sign you wish to stay. I did not willingly run to my death. I was sent by Pittacus to the Troad to fight the Athenians. Only he and his cohorts came home alive. If I had died to keep Mytilene free, I would not grieve, but I died for him and his vile satyr's lust. Sometimes I think he and your mother planned the siege just to get rid of me."

"No! Impossible!"

"All too possible. Husbands have been dispatched in war from the dawn of time. Why should I be immune? The fates decreed it and my wife's lover carried it out."

"But she loved you so—were you true to *her?*"

"Never untrue—to my dying day—except with meaningless slaves and concubines and pretty boys. My love for your mother was the ruling passion of my life. I loved her as you love the father of your only child."

His words went through me like a knife. Alcaeus! How did he know? And he had betrayed my mother too—with meaningless slaves and boys, just as Alcaeus betrayed me.

"I have been watching as your life unfolds, unable to do anything to help. I would never have married you off to an old sot, nor taken away your only child, nor let your brothers come to grief in Egypt, following their foolish pricks. Your mother always thought first of herself and how she could best survive—but do not blame her. Women make strange compromises with power and Pittacus served her better than I did. The old aristocratic code is dead. Gold rules the world today. Your mother was as quick to take advantage of the changing winds as I was blinded by antique ideals of glory. But never forget that you have some true friends. Alcaeus is one. Aesop is another. Praxinoa will always love you. As queen of the amazons, she may do you much service in the future. Treasure your friends. They will bring you home. Stay true to your tutelary goddess, Aphrodite. She is tricky and fickle, but she will bring you lasting fame. Good-bye, my daughter, I am watching over you. I will not let you die before your time."

"Don't go!" I shouted, but he was fading fast. "Stay!" I cried, embracing the air where he had stood. He had slipped away. I whirled around, looking everywhere for him. I stared deep into the cold black water for some trace of Eurygius, but he and my father were nowhere to be seen. Aesop too was gone, and Charon and the boat of souls.

In the crowd of shades I saw tall Jezebel, the Motyan priestess, holding the sacrificed slave baby in her arms, stroking it tenderly. I saw Sisyphus rolling his rock everlastingly uphill. I saw Tantalus bending down to drink from a stream, only to see the stream dry up. I saw him reach over his head to pick a red apple, only to see its branch bounce out of reach. I saw paunchy Cercylas, my unlamented husband, holding aloft a cup for wine on which lewd scenes were painted. He was still drinking, even in Hades' realm—though he could not taste the wine. I saw vulgar Cyrus of Sardis, who had drowned with all his gold. He waved limp fingers at me and winked a shadowy eye.

"Gold is no guarantee of eternal life, alas," he muttered. This I already knew.

I had nothing to say to any of them. I knew their sad stories. Sesostris jumped like lightning from one shade's shoulder to another's.

Let me not find my soul mate Alcaeus here, I prayed, looking at the pale, transparent faces. *Let me not find my darling Cleis. Let me not find dear Praxinoa.* Was she indeed queen of the amazons? Good for her! Long may she reign!

Orpheus was there, holding his head in one hand and his lyre in the other.

"The reward of poetry is to be torn to bits," he sang. "But all the bits still sing."

I remembered the Orphic lyre kept in a temple on my native isle, how all the poets worshiped it because it was said to bring immortality.

"Even if they tear you limb from limb," the headless Orpheus said, "your songs remain. You whirl in bliss through eternity to the music of the spheres." Then, behind Orpheus' fading headless form, I saw Antiope, the amazon queen.

"*You!*"

"*You!*" she shouted back. "You brought your slave to overthrow me! My priestesses revolted when you left and put Praxinoa and Penthesilea in my place. Until you came, no one would have dared. You corrupted my followers with your quaint ideas of justice. Now they nurse their boys instead of throwing them to the wolves. They suckle their own doom!"

"Let them train their sons to justice, then."

"Justice is the dream of philosophers. It cannot exist. I drank the hemlock willingly rather than remain in a world where women share their power with men. It will come to no good. Their own sons will overthrow them! Mark my words!" She began to fade.

I was walking in circles around the smoking mountain. I looked around and could not find Aesop anywhere. The river and the ferryboat were gone. The ground was gray with pumice pebbles. I looked up at the sky and saw the lyre of Orpheus outlined in glittering stars. The sky was black. Out in the middle of the bay, there was a ship from which sweet singing rose. I wanted to go home.

Finally, I reached the base of the slippery mountain, and there, on the rocky beach, Aesop slept, wrapped in a woolen cloak. I shook him awake.

"Did you find fresh water?" Aesop asked.

16

After Hades' Realm

Home is sweet as honey.
—HOMER

YOU MIGHT WONDER how I could even think of suicide after my
trip to the Land of the Dead. Those who have seen the shades close up
generally do not wish to join them. It is not that the punishments there
are so severe. I saw no frozen canyons, no burning lakes, and no spikes
to pierce the heart more sharply than motherhood pierces it. To be dead
is to lose the power of physical feeling. Whatever wisdom comes to
replace that bittersweet ability is not enough. And the dead still long for
life—that much I knew. They cannot feel the warmth of human flesh,
yet they can feel regret.

We had left Hades' realm—or whatever glimpse of it I had been
granted. (Perhaps, not being truly dead, I could not really know its
essence.) Much time had elapsed during my brief travels there. I knew
this when Aesop and I came back to the ship—for some of the amazon
maidens were now mothers of three-year-old children, and there were
many younger children as well. I had wandered among the dead, mar-

veling at how much they looked like their living selves. Aesop had slept and slept and the whole ship had become a nursery! I saw these newly hatched children with an aching heart, missing Cleis more than ever. She would now be five years old!

Some of the sailors were happy to be fathers and doted upon their children, but others were restless and jealous, feeling themselves displaced in the affections of their women. These had begun to court the other amazons and the community was hardly as harmonious as it had been when last I left it.

In my absence, all attempts at sailing had ceased. The ship had been dragged up on land and the sails had become tents. The animals we had carried aboard now roamed free on the strand—at least those that hadn't been eaten. The amphorae of wine and grain were empty and it was time to stay and plant crops or move on to another island. But nobody seemed to have the discipline to make any decisions. Between the squalling babies, the wooing and courting of the amazons and the sailors—chaos had come again.

The Nubian galley slaves had also become full members of the community and had intermarried with the amazon maidens. The captain's power over his mariners and oarsmen was at an end. And he was in love with an amazon maiden who had borne him two sets of twins. He had become such a passionate father that he wished only to babble at them in baby talk and stare into their bright eyes.

I'd emerged from Hades' realm to find a sprawling settlement at the edge of the sea—without laws, without sufficient food, without peace or serenity.

Maera was now the mother of two—an infant and a two-year-old. She had banished her lover from her tent for wooing another young amazon called Leto, who had no children and was liberally entertaining those sailors who'd grown tired of fatherhood. Leto, named for Apollo's mother, had become a sort of Rhodopis of this uninhabited island, luring sailors into her pleasure tent on the edge of the strand for orgies.

I had returned from Hades' realm, in short, to find a mess that nobody had sufficient power or authority to end. The amazons were used to being ruled by their queen; they saw no reason to obey a man—even if he had been appointed captain by a distant pharaoh.

Who was the pharaoh to them? Simply a man in curious robes and a double crown. They had no fear of him—or any man.

As for the Nubian slaves, they saw no reason why they should row the ship rather than steer it from on deck—but the Egyptian mariners refused to row, being unaccustomed to the task. While the slaves and masters fought over their future duties, the ship moldered. Its hull had not been tarred, nor its sails—those that had not been cut up for tents—mended. It was rotting even as we watched. Clearly, we would all perish on this rocky island on the edge of the Land of the Dead unless something was done. Water had been found, but food was running low. You cannot live on fish forever—at least without oil, without grain, without fruits and vegetables. We had goats' milk and cheese, but no fruits. The island grew none and its rocky soil was inhospitable. The ale and wine were gone and some of the men found life without these anodynes intolerable. The babies had milk, but their mothers were malnourished for lack of fresh foods. Some beautiful amazon maidens were losing their teeth from nursing.

Already several amazons had died in childbirth and babes had perished in infancy. Beyond Leto's pleasure tent was a little graveyard by the sea that grew daily. Its grave markers were made of driftwood and shells. It was open to the wind and bodies had to be buried quickly before the wild seabirds could feast on them.

I consulted Aesop.

"A leader is needed—and a strong one," he said.

He was right. But who could claim authority over this disparate crew? The amazons were used to one form of society, the Egyptians to another. They had worshiped different gods, followed different ways of life, different sacrifices, different rituals. The Egyptians believed the body must be preserved after death. The amazons fed their monthly blood to their goddess. And yet, no matter how various their ways, they had common needs: for order, for feeding themselves and their children, for educating their young.

I thought about the amazons and the rules they had lived by. They had accepted a world without men, but as soon as the joys of sex beckoned, they converted quickly enough to the worship of the goddess of love. What was the answer here? A world where love was free or a world where love was chained? Where was happiness to be found? In freedom or in deprivation? Had my brothers found happiness in Naucratis? A city of rampant luxury and sin—and they fall prey to a courtesan who enslaves them. Some people will turn freedom to slavery and others will turn slavery to freedom—like Aesop. Aesop understood all these paradoxes better than anyone.

"You must become the leader of these people," Aesop said, "or they will never survive. They are confused. They have no rules to live by."

"Why not you? You have a beard. A beard is always helpful to those who wish to rule!"

"Sappho, you jest. You know that a beard is no sign of authority to amazons."

"How shall I—a mere musician—command the Nubians, the Egyptians, the captain, the navigators?"

"By making them think you have the gods on your side, as kings and queens have always done. You have returned from the Land of the Dead. Surely that gives you authority!"

I wondered. By what right could I seize command? I wavered as I had with the amazon queen. The only power I knew was the power of song.

"You must seize your right with words. Either words or swords win leadership—and words are your best weapon."

"I have no idea how to begin."

"How did Pittacus take over Lesbos?"

"He was the leader in the war against the Athenians, but he subdued the aristocrats of Lesbos more by guile. He seduced the leaders to his side and little by little took over their power."

"Then so must you. You must use the power of Hades' realm and prophecies you learned there to get the attention of the natural leaders of the populace."

"Who are they?"

"That we will only learn by going among them. Sappho, we must begin, or we will all be buried in that graveyard, except for the last to die, who will be torn apart by wild seabirds. There is no time to waste!"

So Aesop and I began to go among the people, to take a tour of the domain we sought to conquer. We would listen to their hopes and grievances and start to learn how to bring order to our little land.

The amazons were angry with Leto—who was no titaness. Not only Maera of the red ringlets, but many of the other young mothers wanted Leto's pleasure tent closed down. Leto had been joined in her enterprise by a few of her sisters, but most of the amazons were disgusted by her exploitation of their men.

"Men are weak," Maera said. "We all know that. Seducing them is no trick. But try getting them to take care of their children! Oh, I wish that I had never left the land of the amazons, where women band together instead of fighting among themselves for men! I would go back if I could!"

"Antiope would have had you killed after your first child was born," I reminded her. I did not say that I had met Antiope in the Land of the Dead and knew that she had perished.

"Even Antiope looks good to me now!" Maera fumed. "Antiope was a moral force compared to Leto!"

"Listen to her!" Aesop whispered to me. "Even an unjust ruler is better than no ruler at all."

That night, Aesop and I went to find Leto at moonrise. The sea lapped at the shore. Birds rustled in the dark leaves. A fume of incense rose out of the opening at the top of Leto's tent. Within we heard the music of pipes and stringed instruments. The flute sounded its low melancholy tone. Leto emerged from the tent briefly to lure the admirers who waited outside looking like stray dogs.

Perfumed like a goddess, she wore a cape of woven sea grass, which shimmered as she moved; under it were multicolored silks. She had borne no children and still smiled with all her white and shiny teeth.

She now had dropped the sea-grass cape, and her rippling rags of silk fluttered as she danced. With great skill, she unpeeled the silk streamers one by one.

Now she ushered us all into her tent.

Eros loves disguises more even than touch and perfume. Leto knew this. She had to be all things to all men and she had constructed cunning masks for the purpose. She had bird masks and animal masks, masks with horns and masks with long gold hair. She had fashioned them herself and her movements transformed her into any creature she wished to be. A dancer can transport her audience by movement alone and Leto had that gift. She could become a cat, a panther, a snake, a horse. She could impersonate any mythical being she chose. Perhaps she was a titaness after all.

The men were rapt and silent at her performance. They were transported to a world of magic. Whatever the blessings of children, they make magic seem far away indeed—and Leto also understood this. She was slim and lithe. Her eyes were gray-blue and her lashes were long and dark. Her long hair was almost the color of silver with gold threads. She draped it over her chest where one breast was missing. The sight sent a shiver down my spine. She was joined by her two amazon attendants—as beautiful as she, though one was dark and plump, with olive eyes, and the other had blazing red hair the color of polished copper and eyes the color of that metal when tarnished. The three began to dance together, fondling each other's single breasts, kissing each other's lips, exchanging masks and then acting mute pantomimes in which they seduced each other.

I watched them in a trance, remembering how long it had been since I had tasted ripe flesh, since I had kissed a living man or woman. In the Land of the Dead no one could fuse flesh to flesh. That was the paradox of that place: endless yearning, endless deprivation. In the Land of the Dead, everyone was cursed like Tantalus. I had been chaste among the lovely amazons—what a waste! All I did there was write! And in Egypt, I had pleasured the pharaoh rather than having him pleasure me. (That's the problem with pharaohs!) How long had it been since I and a lover had gifted each other with our liquid love? My legs ached and my belly throbbed. I thought of Alcaeus and Isis, thought of the joy of clasping a friend who is also a lover. It had been too long!

There were far too many men for three women to receive in love. What could Leto possibly have up her sleeve? Or under her silken rags?

Soon enough, she produced a rude clay pipe. One of her maidens lit it. A strong smell filled the tent. The men leaned forward to inhale. They clapped and stamped their feet.

As the dancing continued, the pipe was passed from one spectator to another and its fumes were inhaled deeply. There was so much smoke in the tent that even I, without puffing the pipe, began to get light-headed. I thought I saw swirling rainbows in the smoke.

Aesop and I left the tent for a few moments to breathe fresh air. We gulped it hungrily.

"Somewhere on this island, she has gathered mushrooms," Aesop said. "I know the smell. Leto should be careful. In small doses, some of these mushrooms are intoxicants, but some are lethal as hemlock."

"The amazons studied herbs—both anodynes and stimulants. They know far more than any people I have met. I am from Lesbos—I know only wine."

We went back into the tent. Now the men were sprawled on the floor, dreaming in the smoke-filled air. The amazons continued dancing. They danced over the men triumphantly, linking hands and weaving around their prostrate bodies. They laughed.

"Well, that was a great beginning for our interviews of the populace," I told Aesop when he and I were alone together.

"Information is always useful."

"You and your damned epigrams! *You* govern this island! I'm not interested."

"All right. But where will you go? Back to the Land of the Dead? To sea without a boat? Sappho, you have no choice. Either govern this island or let it govern you!"

I thought about this. Aesop was right. He was always right! I kicked a stone. I walked into the sea and swam in the darkness. As I swam to and fro, to and fro, wishing the nereids and Poseidon would save me or drown me, I had an inspiration, and the inspiration became a plan.

17

Demeter and Osiris

Mortal immortals, immortal mortals,
Living their death and dying their life.
—HERACLITUS

"AESOP," I SAID, "you call a convocation of the tribe for this evening at sunset and I will address my people."

"I *knew* I could count on you," Aesop said.

That night, as the sun sank below the horizon of our mountainous island, the whole population began to assemble. I had sent word via Aesop that we should assemble in the graveyard at the edge of the sea. I knew of no better way to summon serious thoughts.

Nearly everyone came—women burdened with two or three children, pregnant women, men dragging goats behind them or carrying baskets of fish. They were a ragtag lot as they seated themselves on the ground near the graveyard. They looked a great deal more tired and bedraggled than they had been when we sailed away from the island of the amazons. They were exhausted from the toil of child-rearing and scrounging for food. Everyone but Leto and her maidens looked exhausted. They flounced in last and stood at the back of the crowd, preening. But the men were shy about flirting with them while their women and children were present.

Wearing the only chiton I still had that was not in tatters, I stood up before them at the edge of the water under the rosy rays of the setting sun. I had no idea what I was going to say. But I was brazen. If you can compose lyrics at a symposium, it inures you to any kind of stage fright.

"Sit down, Leto," I commanded. "I'd rather have you sit than fall down when I say what I have to say."

At first Leto stood defiantly. But I waited, my eyes boring into hers. Then she sat, with her maids around her.

"I wonder if you have missed me or have thought about where I'd disappeared. I doubt it. You have all fallen into a black sack of trouble, though some of you hardly seem to know it. Your stores are exhausted, mothers are losing their teeth and dying in childbirth, children are dying, and men are straying. The gods have abandoned you. And I know why."

Now all the listeners looked rapt. I had their attention at last—even Leto's.

"I went to explore this isle and slipped—it was the will of gods, not men—into Hades' realm. The Land of the Dead is very near. We are always on the edge of it, whether we know it or not. There I met my long-dead father, my little brother, hordes of gray dead souls with no hope of eternal life. I rode in Charon's boat. I interviewed the dead. I met great Osiris and eternal Demeter. I learned the secrets of the future. Shall I share them with you? Are you worthy? Or shall I let you perish?"

The sun had slipped below the horizon. Babies were squalling. Mothers were nursing. My listeners stared at me as if they too saw dead souls.

"Osiris bade me go back to you and warn you of the danger you are in. You have forgotten his worship and your flesh will crumble into dust beyond the promise of resurrection. The divine father is angry with you—and so is the divine mother, Demeter. She is the door of birth and rebirth—never forget that. If you ignore her, all your generations will perish."

I paced before them—taking a long pause. I could feel their anxiety and questioning. I used these for my own ends.

"Why should I care about your future?" I continued. "My immortality is assured through my songs. If I died now, my songs would still be sung, my daughter would still grow to womanhood on my native isle. But you are in dire straits. You have lost the guidance of the gods." I paced some more. I looked as if I were not sure whether to continue.

"What did Osiris say?" one of the Egyptian sailors called out. "Tell us!"

"If I tell you, will you take it to heart?"

"We will!" cried another of the sailors.

"Osiris is not my god," Maera of the red ringlets protested. "Who cares what he says? Tell us what great Demeter said."

"In Hades' realm, the gods do not care what we call them. They sit in an immortal symposium drinking exquisite wine and viewing our doings with detachment. They do not care if we live or die. They barely smell our puny sacrifices. They wait for proof of our worthiness to live, and if we fail they are happy to reduce us to clay and start all over. The gods are like potters at the wheel. If a pot is crooked, they throw it back into the bin. They can start again as many times as necessary. To them we are only broken, leaky pots. We must prove ourselves by being straight and holding water. Otherwise we will be thrown upon the heap. Our very names perish and our individual souls are lost forever."

"What shall we do?" Maera called out in distress.

"What indeed? You must win back the favor of the gods. You must purify yourselves for Demeter and Osiris. You must worship them again and heed their rules."

"But how shall we *know* their rules?" Maera asked.

"You shall know them by me," I said. "They have told me how they wish to be worshiped. I have been given The Way. The gods themselves have entrusted me with their divine papyrus. I have decoded it and I can tell you how to save yourselves."

Leto shouted, "Why you, Sappho? Why are *you* our leader? Prove you have the favor of the gods! Show us a miracle! Bring Pegasus again! Bring Persephone from the house of Hades to vouch for you!"

I paced before them. I did not at once respond. Could I summon Pegasus again with my verses? Could I bring ghosts from the Land of the

Dead back to earth? I was not sure. But from under my himation I produced a thick papyrus scroll. I waved it in the air for all to see.

"This scroll was dictated to me by the gods. If you are respectful, I
shall share its teachings. Otherwise, I shall throw it in the sea." I paced
at the edge of the water and let the wavelets lap my toes.

"It's up to you. If you are happy with the way things are, you have no
need of me or the gods' papyrus." I began to walk deeper into the water.
Waves were breaking just beyond where I stood.

The crowd seemed agitated. They whispered among themselves.

"Prove you come from the gods!" Leto shouted.

"Yes! Prove it!" echoed her maids.

I ignored them, saying nothing but gazing intently at them. I waded
into the sea up to my waist, then up to my chin. I held the papyrus aloft.

"I have nothing to prove to you," I shouted. "If you are happy with
the way things are, you have no need of me or this papyrus. If you are
not, then hear what the gods have decreed."

"Let's put it to a vote!" Maera shouted. "And only mothers get a vote!"

"Absurd!" said Leto. "Why not fathers?" But nobody seconded her, so
she kept silent after that.

I stood in the sea holding the papyrus of the gods above my head. I
was determined to drown rather than enter another foolish argument
about the nature of men and women. Aesop smiled as if to encourage
me, but he didn't come forward with a fable. Damn him. I would make
up my own fable! I walked slowly out of the sea and stood before them,
all dripping wet.

"Demeter is the mother, the divine delta, the door of life, the door
of birth, the door of death, the door of rebirth. Cross her, anger her,
and no babes will be born to you ever again. No crops will grow. The
whole earth will be barren as a grave. Osiris is the savior-king, consort
of the great mother, the king who dies so that the crops may grow.
Without harmony between these two sacred beings, life will cease.
Demeter and Osiris must dance together like perfect lovers or the
world ends. All of this is in your power. I can bring you the harmony or
the discord of the gods. How many wish harmony? I will not ask again."

Hands shot up all over the assembly. Maera and Leto might argue, but the majority wanted harmony and life.

"Well, then, if you will live and prosper, hear me well."

Deep sighs were heard in the crowd. As darkness fell on the island, I outlined what the gods had decreed.

"Mothers and fathers will share the care of children equally. They will also share hunting, fishing, farming, and weaving."

"Weaving!" cried a sailor. "Men can't weave! It's women's work!"

"You will learn to weave so as not to anger the gods. The gods decree that all labor will be shared as Demeter and Osiris share the world between them."

"What about holidays and feasts?" Leto asked.

"There are four a year—the summer solstice, the autumn equinox, the winter solstice, the spring equinox. On all these turnings of the year, men and women may make love freely with all members of the tribe, but only as sacred homage to the gods and only to make the crops grow. The rest of the year the gods decree chastity."

"Chastity!" Leto exclaimed. "Who wants a world of chastity?"

"A world of chastity is better than a world of chaos," I said. "Eros brings chaos in his wake." Clearly, I was thinking of my poor benighted brothers, but was I also thinking of myself?

"But the gods are not chaste," Leto protested.

"That is why they are the gods," I said. "People do not have enough discipline to make love like gods. Eros brings madness with his poisoned arrows. He must be restricted to the celebrations of the gods or his mischief will destroy the earth."

"And what will happen if we break these commandments?" Maera asked.

"Something so terrible I cannot even describe it. I urge you to follow what the sacred papyrus decrees. I am only the messenger of the gods—not the author of the sacred papyrus. But I fear for your lives if you anger the gods." The water still dripped from me. I shivered in the gathering darkness as though the breath of the gods were upon me.

"I say we try what Sappho says," cried one of the Egyptian sailors.

"Aye! I agree!" cried another.

Before long, the commandments of the sacred papyrus had been adopted by proclamation and the tired assembly straggled back to their tents. I was glad to return to my tent, change to dry clothes, and get warm.

Later, I sat with Aesop and handed him the sacred papyrus. He carefully unrolled it. It was blank. He laughed and laughed.

He was full of admiration for my guile. "How clever you've become since your trip to the Land of the Dead," he said. "But did you have to be so severe about men and women making love? Life is hard without the little anodyne of love. Love and wine are all most humans have to make their short and wretched lives bearable. Just because you are chaste, must everyone be chaste?"

"Nobody despises chastity more than I do, but I can only couple with those who set fire to my heart. My love is far away, so I am chaste."

"So you would impose chastity on everyone?" Aesop asked.

"Why not? They will love love more when they have to wait for it. If they make love only to honor the gods, love will mean more to them than when they couple for lust alone."

"So every sensualist is a sacred virgin at heart?" Aesop teased.

"Go make a fable of it," I spat angrily.

"I think I will," Aesop said. "What animal would you like to be?"

"Damn you, Aesop. What help were you to me when I was searching for the gods' commandments? You simply sat there grinning."

"That is because I trust you utterly. You may think you made it all up like a song at a symposium, but I know the gods dictate to you. Someday you may know it too."

I gathered my blanket around me and slept. Translating the will of the gods is nothing if not exhausting.

18

Sirens

Sea rovers here take joy.
—HOMER

WHETHER MY ORDERS came from gods or mortals, they worked. People are happy to have rules to live by, however arbitrary. The island became a buzzing hive of industry. Men learned to weave and women learned to hunt. Children depended on their fathers as much as on their mothers. Leto's brain-fogging symposia were no more. Eventually we found another use for her tent as a school for the growing flock of children on the isle, and she became their schoolmistress. She fulfilled that role quite as enthusiastically as she had played the siren. People are nothing if not adaptable. I also found another use for her magic mushrooms.

Because I had interpreted the gods' commandments, I was forced into the role of priestess. People would come to me with disputes and I would resolve them. For this I needed some solemn ceremony. I confiscated Leto's store of mushrooms, toasted them in a golden bowl perched on a high tripod set over the fumes, and pronounced as if I were the Pythia herself. I had studied her in Delphi, and since I was a born performer, I could play her. People require drama from their emissaries of the gods and Aesop and I provided it. We had seen enough rituals in our travels to know that belief is enhanced by theatrical display. The mushrooms certainly helped. Aesop would sit through the rituals somewhat woozy from the smoke. I would go into a trance and rhyme whatever came into my head. The islanders had so great a need to believe that the gods were nearby and doted on them like fond parents that they had no problem accepting me as priestess and Aesop as my priest. We did our civic duty—with a little help from the mushrooms.

Months grew into years. The lowering volcano that had belched smoke and lava was silent. It seemed to have gone into hibernation. Our little island on the edge of Hades' realm prospered. But when our children reached the age of adolescent restlessness, would we be able to go on like this?

Our children had been carefully educated in Leto's tent. We wanted them to love learning, to eschew war, to understand that exploration of the unknown was the highest good. Aesop had taught them his fables about wise and foolish animals. I had sung them my songs of love. The Egyptians had given them their hymns to Osiris and the amazons had taught them the stories of great Pegasus and the glories of the moon goddess, the white goddess, who, they claimed, was merely another aspect of Demeter. We taught both boys and girls to be warriors and weavers. We did not make any distinction between the sexes. Girls slaughtered heifers for the sacrifice and boys cooked them. Boys shaped pots and bowls on the wheel and sewed garments of skin and of linen. Girls built houses and learned to sail ships. It was part of our faith that girls and boys could do everything equally.

We had allowed the children to explore each other's deltas and phalli when they were little. We told them that pleasure and knowledge were the greatest goods earth had to offer and that pursuing them would lead to happiness on earth. We even stole a motto from the Oracle of Delphi: "Know thyself." The children were given utter freedom in sexual matters. Only the adults had to accept a life of near-chastity. Leto had devised didactic rhymes to teach the boys and girls:

> *The divine delta*
> *Is Demeter's doorway.*
> *And the precious phallus*
> *The scepter of Osiris.*
> *As a glowing torch lights up a dark cave,*
> *The powerful phallus floods the divine delta*
> *With sacred knowledge.*

All this had worked wonderfully while the mountain was silent and the children were small.

But then the mountain began to make its presence known again. From time to time it would spew smoke and rain down pumice stones, and then it would grow quiet. At the same time, the children were growing older and some were beginning to itch to see the world. The island was too small for our burgeoning population; it was clear at least to Aesop and me that we couldn't stay here forever.

So I had the youngsters begin to build a boat. Using their elders' knowledge of the sea, they improvised a great galley with many sails and many oars and prepared to set out to sea.

The boat took longer to build than anyone could have foreseen. It was necessary to reinvent the art of shipbuilding there on that desolate isle. Just as the galley was nearing completion, just as the parents were starting to grow anxious about the imminent departure of their children, the conical mountain began to rumble and spew showers of stones at shorter and shorter intervals.

The sky would grow black, the waves boisterous—as if Poseidon were angry with our islanders. I was asked to pronounce on the future. So I dutifully roasted mushrooms in the golden bowl and pronounced. But it hardly took the gift of prophecy to see what was happening. The conical mountain that concealed Hades' realm was trying to tell us something. We would have to build our departure ship large enough and stout enough to carry us all away.

As I watched the great ship being built, I thought of Antiope's prophecy: *Their sons will overthrow them.* The boys on our island were gentle and kind and had been raised to consider fighting and feuding unmanly. But their temperaments had never been tested. They had not yet succumbed to Eros in his purple cloak with his tiny pointed arrows of bronze and his eyes the color of rain-drenched hyacinths. The girls had been taught to speak their ideas and opinions openly, not to defer to their brothers and cousins, and to solve all problems by rational discourse rather than flirting or fighting. We had created a society of peaceable children—but would they be as peaceable when they grew old enough to fall in love?

And how much time did we have? When the mountain threatened, it seemed to me its warnings were thunderous and the sky was often crimson with molten fire. Nobody wanted to think about this. The boat was under construction as if we had all the time in the world.

Maera had produced two boys, now ten and thirteen, and she had named them Hercules and Prometheus. Like most of the amazon mothers, she was besotted with her boys. She loved them more than life. Boys were a novelty among the amazon maidens who had mated with the Egyptian sailors, and as a result they were coddled. Girls, on the other hand, were given early responsibilities: taking care of younger siblings, organizing feasts and sacrifices, preparing for the quadrennial orgies—when the adults were allowed to mate. The girls' training for life had made them far more resilient than the boys.

But Hercules and Prometheus were born leaders. They rose to challenges other boys shrank from. Hercules had apprenticed himself to our aging captain to learn everything he could about sailing and he longed to see the world.

And the mountain was cooperating with his wishes. Its threats had become a daily occurrence. It had taken to spewing molten lava, which coursed down its sides. Aesop and I wanted to climb to the top to look into the volcano's aperture and predict when it would explode, but we never even got halfway up without having to turn back. The eruption was clearly imminent. There was nothing for us to do but to sail away.

It was not the best month for sailing. The *zephyroi* blew and the sea was full of whitecaps. The birds had gone south and the dolphins had followed. The rainy season was upon us, yet we had no choice but to set out to sea. As we embarked, the mountain was spewing lava. The sky was darkening and red fire gleamed against the storm clouds. The ship was much too small for us all. Men, women, and children crowded into the hold, sharing quarters with rams and ewes and chickens. There were boys and girls hanging over the decks and older folks hanging on to the masts for dear life. As priestess, I had to invoke Osiris and Demeter for their protection. Neither Aesop nor I was sure we would not be wrecked before we even started.

Our strongest girls and boys were at the oars, belowdecks. As we saw the mountain spew fire, they rowed. We watched the lava engulf our beloved farms and homes. We watched our mountain implode and sink into the sea, sending huge waves that nearly toppled us, that crashed on our decks, sweeping animals, food, and aged parents into the devouring waves. We could not turn back. Our mountain had become a seething pit surrounded by a rocky donut of land. The Land of the Dead had slipped beneath the sea and all the souls were drowning. I felt utterly desolate. I thought of my baby brother gone forever, of my father's bones scoured by the salt of the sea. I feared for Cleis. Hades' realm was a *place*! The vast sea bottom was *nowhere*. Or so I thought. But I could not show my fear. I was the priestess now. I had to be strong.

So I stood on deck and raised my arms in supplication to Demeter, Osiris, and finally great Poseidon. I pleaded. I begged. Despite the lurching deck we attempted to make a sacrifice, but the wind kept putting out the fire. Then I remembered what Alcaeus had said to me in Pyrrha when we were fleeing Pittacus' cohorts: "You are praying to the wrong goddess!" *Aphrodite!* In my enforced chastity, I had forgotten Aphrodite and her vast powers. That was why these disasters were befalling us! Without the life force Aphrodite embodies, there is only barrenness and despair. So I invoked my own goddess. I called on her for the first time in years.

Come to us from Crete, my lady,
We, your poor supplicants, call on you to be our ally.

Come in your chariot of flames
Drawn by your swift sparrows with whirling wings.
Leave Zeus and Ares and the other immortals
And come to us! Come to us! Come!

As I invoked my tutelary goddess, I imagined a great convocation on Mount Olympus. Demeter the great mother was arguing with Aphrodite about whose power was older and more indispensable. Poseidon was arguing with his brother Zeus, as usual, about everything. And Osiris, the ancient Egyptian god, was calling them all upstarts:

I am Osiris, oldest of old,
Savior from worms and corruption.
When I mate with my bride, my mother, great Isis,
Crops rise up under the bright light of day.
When I retreat from the earth, crops wither
And night covers all.

"Outrageous!" said Demeter. "He is usurping my ancient function. *I* make the crops rise and the babies burst forth from the delta of life."

"Ah—but without me there is no lust, no desire, no current of life!" said Aphrodite. "Try making crops or babies without me! Try!"

Zeus lounged on a cloud with the disdain of the almighty and taunted Aphrodite:

"What has become of your darling girl now? She's at sea again with the *zephyroi* blowing, with her boat of souls sinking, with her foolish dream that she can save the world through song and invocation! Absurd!"

Just then, Poseidon drew Aphrodite close and whispered in her ear: "Ally yourself with me and we shall humble Zeus and make a fool of him. I'll lend you peaceful seas if you will lend me all the love you keep in your golden girdle. There is a maiden I would have as my lover— Maera of the coppery ringlets, the amazon maid with the two strong boys. Do we have a deal?"

So Aphrodite lent Poseidon her golden girdle—which he fastened around his stout blue waist—and, as the gods looked down and watched us bobbing on the sea, as the gods looked down and laughed at our travails as if they were a play, the epic of the amazons and the Egyptians sailed to its watery conclusion.

As I FINISHED my invocation to Aphrodite, the seas began to grow calm. A fair wind filled our sails and we began to sail out of darkness, into light. Three strong girls slew a ewe upon the deck and roasted its thighbones to please the gods. Then we all ate heartily.

Maera hugged her two strong boys to her chest and cried out, "Praise be to Sappho for our deliverance!"

"Hear! Hear!" cried Aesop, leading the others.

Was it possible Aphrodite had heard?

For several days and nights the seas were calm. The *zephyroi* had died down. We sailed the broad back of the sea as if it were a flat road between green pastures. Sometimes the sea was so calm you could see your reflection in it.

Maera looked down onto waters from the prow of the ship and said, "At times I dream of living in a castle beneath the sea, a castle made of glittering precious stones and coral. Mermaids would arrange my hair and seahorses serve as footmen at my table."

"You are mad, Maera," I said.

"It's only a dream," she answered.

Prometheus and Hercules had climbed the masts, looking for land. They were so high above us, they could have been birds or squirrels. The children rowed on, changing shifts every five hours, working in perfect harmony. Often, we sacrificed a ram or a ewe to thank the gods for their favor and pray it would continue.

I don't know how many days and nights were like this before we heard the sounds of singing over the waters.

"Whales are singing to each other," Maera said dreamily.

"Or dolphins," said Aesop.

Then the sounds would go away and we would hear only the wind singing.

I was agitated. I thought often of Odysseus and the dangers he had braved. Would we encounter Scylla and Charybdis to drown our young or another earthquake to roil the waves or mythical monsters more terrible than even Odysseus knew?

The sea's calm was unearthly. It would not last. That much I knew.

THEN THERE WAS the distinct sound of female voices singing. They came over the sea as if they could charm the waves themselves.

> *Where is knowledge to be found*
> *If not in love?*
> *Rowers, row this way,*
> *Into our loving arms.*
> *Bring your boat, your shipmates*
> *To our magic isle*
> *Where love alone*
> *Is the lesson,*
> *Where love alone*
> *Propels your questing arms,*
> *Where love alone allows*
> *Knowledge of the gods.*

An island appeared in the midst of the clouds. On it sat beautiful young maidens with bare breasts. They were opening their deltas with their fingers—as if the voice of their song came from deep within.

The boys began to rise from their oars. Hercules and Prometheus shimmied down the mast.

"Plug your ears! These are the sirens!" I screamed out. But the wind carried my voice away. Young men began diving over the prow and sides of the ship and swimming in the direction of the unearthly voices. One after another they left their stations and jumped overboard to swim in the direction of the song.

Hercules and Prometheus held out longer than the other boys. They looked dreamily at the horizon and stood still, listening, but eventually they too began to clamber over the side of the ship.

Maera became hysterical. She grabbed at her sons' clothes, screaming, "Nothing awaits you but death!" They refused to heed her. Bewitched, they stood on the side of ship and prepared to dive into the sea.

The music became louder and louder. A strong smell of sex wafted over the waves. Now only girls were left at the oars. I went down to join them and we all rowed madly, hoping to catch up with the swimming boys. We threw spars over the sides for them to grab on to. We threw lines to them—all in vain. We begged them to turn back, but they could not hear us.

We rowed after them as long as we could, but finally they outdistanced us. From where I sat rowing at my station, I saw a huge blue arm rise up out of the water and seize Maera in its hand. The voices of the sirens dissolved into the wind as she was dragged under the waves. Maera should have been terrified, but at my last sight of her she was smiling. Aphrodite's laughter filled the sky.

19

Air, Fire, and Water

One story is good until another is told.
—AESOP

LEFT ALONE ON a boat filled with grieving old men and women and girls who feared they would always be husbandless, Aesop and I wondered what we had done wrong.

"You can educate boys against war, but clearly you cannot save them from sirens," I told Aesop.

"All creatures must respond to reason," he said.

"Except young men," I said. "Reason hardly governs their world. Aphrodite does. It's my own damned fault for calling on her!"

"How could you not? She is your tutelary goddess. But you cannot blame yourself. We were unprepared," Aesop said. "We had no beeswax for their ears, no ropes to bind them to the mast. We were helpless. Odysseus was prepared by Circe the sorceress. We were not. I must make a fable of it."

"You and your fables! Can a fable undo Aphrodite's power? I doubt it."

Aesop scratched his curly beard. "We thought about every aspect of their education, but we did not think what would happen when they heard the sirens."

It was true. Once again the gods had outwitted us.

"It is in the nature of the gods to outwit mortals," I told Aesop. "If I've learned anything from my travels, it's that. They play with us as little boys play with flies—ripping their wings off. We amuse them with our dreams and desires, our vain hopes of improving the world."

Aesop looked perplexed. Reason was his god and reason had failed him.

The ship sailed on.

THE GIRLS WERE strong rowers and the winds continued fair. Aphrodite was still in our corner. Poseidon was quiet. Was he in love? From time to time I thought of Maera and her sons transported to the grottoes of the sea god, living among starfish and sharks, octopi and seahorses, bedding down on seaweed, subsisting on sea grapes—those tiny succulent gifts from creatures of the deep, that burst on the tongue and are delicious without cooking.

We sailed and sailed. The girls wept and rowed. I tried to comfort them.

"Now we shall never be married!" cried Arete—one of the prettiest girls and only fifteen. Her shoulders were like dark honey softened by the sun.

"Never mind—there are better things in life than marriage. Marriage is not the beginning of life—it's the end. Trust me, I know." And I told them about Cercylas and his paunch and his drunkenness. I recited my ironic epithalamia until they laughed and laughed.

Then they remembered their lost boys and they cried again.

Each night, I would take one of the girls to bed with me and teach her about pleasure—a priestess' prerogative.

How beautiful they were!

Arete was dark, with a delta that turned plum with pleasure. Atthis was blond; you could see her pink nether lips through her golden fuzz.

Gongyla was coppery colored; her zone of pleasure was speckled like an undersea creature's shell.

I taught each girl not to be afraid of joy and to know how to please herself so as never to be dependent on a man. How sweet they were, with their deltas salty as the sea. Some of them had merest buds for breasts. But deep within them, Aphrodite dwelt.

Atthis was my favorite. Shy at first, she woke to pleasure quickly. I would place her high on the ship's rail and lick her till she throbbed within, grasping my probing finger with the pulse of life. Then I would bring my lips to that nub, gleaming like a wet ruby, half veiled in cream, and flick my tongue against it till she screamed.

As long as I seduced the maidens, Aphrodite sent us gentle seas. But when Aesop put a stop to my seductions, the weather turned and we were rocked again by ill winds.

"Sometimes I think you're glad the sirens lured our boys away so you could have the girls all to yourself," said Aesop.

"Are you jealous?"

"Maybe I am," said the fable-maker. "I wish you loved me even a little."

This statement came as an arrow to my heart. I looked at Aesop, with his broad chest, his commanding height, his tawny brown skin. He was a fine specimen of a man, and yet I never thought of him as a lover. Why?

"Is it because I was born a slave?"

"Not at all. Any of us could be enslaved at any moment. I think of you as mentor, guide, and friend—not lover."

"Cannot a friend be a lover?" Aesop asked. The question hung in the air, waiting for Aphrodite to come answer it.

I TURNED and paced the deck. Around and around I walked. Aphrodite was a capricious goddess. Yes, she was indispensable, but chaos came in her wake. I thought of the sirens in their bloody meadow surrounded by the clean white bones of the men they had seduced and devoured—the heaps of shinbones, the pelvises like bows, the femurs like arrows.

"O Aphrodite! Moderate your awesome powers a little! Let us live to see home again!"

THE NEXT MORNING we awoke to see an island on our horizon. It was mountainous and green and at first sight it seemed to be uninhabited. We looked for a harbor in which to land and saw none, so we stood off and waited. Then we circled the island again and again. Soon a small craft came up, seemingly out of nowhere. Three stout young men were rowing it. They were followed by other boats with other young men. Their chests were muscled and their arms were thick as tree trunks. The girls looked out their oar-holes and melted with desire. The men gestured for us to follow them. And so we did. They led us to a hidden cove between two tall white cliffs and bade us tie up there.

Dry land! We couldn't wait to leave our foul-smelling boat and feel our feet upon the earth again. The maidens leapt from the galley, followed by their elders. Aesop and I hastily engaged some of the strong-looking young men to clean and provision our boat. They were more than willing. Some of the maidens lingered, watching them.

"What is this place?" I asked one of the young men.

"You have come to the Island of the Philosophers," he said. "Here we ponder truth and beauty and study how the world is made. Don't judge by us." He gestured to his companions, one handsomer than the next. "We are only the philosophers' slaves. The philosophers themselves are next to the gods."

"If you are the slaves, I imagine the philosophers must be blindingly beautiful."

"You'll see," the young man said. He put his fingers to his lips and whistled shrilly. Down from the hills they came—more beautiful young men with broad shoulders and muscled backs. They wore only loin-cloths of snakeskin and seemed as unaware of their own beauty as the maidens were transfixed by it.

The beautiful young men began to clean and provision the boat. Their leader, Creon—for that was the name of the golden young man who first had greeted us—inquired if I was the captain of the ship.

"Priestess," I said, "and this is my priest, Aesop."

"Then come with me," said Creon, "to the Cave of the Philosophers."

"Must we go with you?" wailed the maidens.

"Stay and help with the ship," I said, seeing that they longed to.

Aesop and I followed Creon up a rocky path that led to a narrow staircase cut into the chalk-white rock. Creon leapt ahead of us like a mountain goat. Aesop and I puffed and clutched our pounding hearts. We had to stop often to catch our breath. Weeks on the ship had left our legs feeble and we still expected the ground to pitch under our feet like the ship's deck. The climb seemed interminable. Up and up and up we went. I was beginning to wish I had stayed on the ship myself.

Near the top of the cliff there was a carved archway. Creon had bounded into it and was lost in the gloom.

"Shall we follow?" I asked Aesop. "Is it safe?"

"Safer than this climb," said Aesop, panting and wheezing.

We followed Creon into a long corridor cut into the rock. Again we struggled to keep up with him. He rounded a corner in the rock and disappeared into a dark cave.

"Come!" he called, urging us on.

As our eyes slowly adjusted to the gloom, we could see three withered old men sitting cross-legged on the floor around a fire that flickered like the tongues of serpents. They had been sitting there so long that they seemed to grow out of the rock itself.

"The earth is made of fire," the first one said. "Great rings of fire from which the light shines forth. As light is truth and truth is light, fire set this world in motion and will be its end."

"No—it is made of water," said the second. "A waste of waters spawned this world and, as all living things are made of moisture, water is the essence of the world. At the end of time we shall all merely float away."

"No—it is made of air. Without air, no fire burns, no waves pound, no lungs breathe. Air is the essence of creation."

Creon flattened himself on the ground before these sages.

"They have been arguing for decades," he said. "They commune with the gods and tell us what the gods desire of us. We would be lost without them. As long as they sit and debate the nature of the universe, we are safe. Should they stop, chaos will come again."

"I'm a priestess too. I know that game." I stood brazenly before the three philosophers, arms akimbo.

"I say the universe is made of love!" I said.

"Who is that?" said the first philosopher, blinking.

"This is heresy!" said the second.

"Do I hear a woman's voice?" said the third.

"Yes! You hear the voice of Sappho of Lesbos. How can you know what the world is made of if you live in a cave and never see it?"

Creon was apologetic. "Forgive her, fathers, she doesn't know what she is saying."

"The world is made of love, you say?" asked the first old man.

"Yes, love."

"And what is love?" asked the second old man. "Is it an element?"

"Yes," I said. "It is at once a force, an element, a whirlwind. It is pure as gold and fierce as war. It is joyous as birth and melancholy as death. It is all these things."

"Is it made of air or water or fire?" asked the third old man.

"It is made of all these things," I said.

"Can you bring it to us?" asked the first old man.

"No—you must go in search of it," I said.

Creon was ashamed. "Excuse me, sirs, she is mad and merely a woman."

"Perhaps we have been in this cave too long," the first old man said.

"That is possible," said the second.

"Lead us to love!" said the third.

Leaning on me and Aesop and Creon, shielding their old eyes against the light, the three philosophers carefully descended the stone stairs to the harbor. There they saw a vision out of paradise—beautiful young men and maidens provisioning a boat together.

The old men looked and looked. Then they gathered in a huddle and whispered together for some time.

"The gods demand you listen!" shouted the first philosopher. "It has long been prophesied that maidens would come to our island and make it bloom again. We shall choose the most beauteous to be our wives."

"Each of us requires only seven wives," said the second old man.

"Ten," said the third. "And they must all be virgins."

The maidens looked horrified, but the young men accepted this requirement unquestioningly.

"Let me examine the new recruits," said the first philosopher. He walked up to beautiful Gongyla and began to touch her breasts. I was outraged. So was Aesop. Creon and his men stood there passively.

"How can you tolerate this?" I shouted at Creon.

"The gods will otherwise be angry," he muttered.

"How do you know this?"

"The philosophers said so."

"Philosophers say a great many things. That hardly makes them true. Let's try a little experiment," I said. "Let's refuse the philosophers and see what happens."

"We cannot," said Creon. "They have always made the rules."

"Then it's time for new rules," Atthis said, stepping forward. "I for one refuse to be married to an old man. Let's put these three ancients in a boat and float them out to sea. Maybe their gods will save them."

With the help of Gongyla and two other maidens, she dragged the three old men to Creon's skiff. Without oars or sail, the boat drifted for a time between the beetling cliffs, then the tide floated them out to sea.

"Let your philosophy save you!" she cried merrily. "We'll take the young men!"

We could see the philosophers shaking their fists at the sky and we could hear them screaming as the currents caught them and they drifted out between the high white cliffs. The maidens, meanwhile, paired up with the beautiful young men and led them away. They dispersed among the rocky caves to celebrate Aphrodite.

Aesop watched all this in fascination.

"What are the gods, after all, but another name for our deepest desires? And what are our legends of the gods but ways of celebrating those desires?" he asked.

"But this is to deny the gods," I said.

"Sappho, look at what we have just beheld. We lost our boys to the sirens on the sea and now we have lost our girls to the sirens of their own desires. These girls want babies. They will worship Aphrodite till it's time to worship Demeter. It hardly matters what we call the gods. The gods are within us. The gods are our deepest dreams. Let me tell you a story. A man and a lion went out walking in Naucratis. They saw a great wall painting on the side of a temple showing a man standing astride a wounded lion.

"'See how my species subdues yours!' exulted the man.

"'Wait till you see the pictures we'll paint of you in the jungle!' said the lion. 'One story is good until another is told.'"

"But if the gods do not exist at all—then we are lost," I said.

"On the contrary—we are found!" said Aesop.

"But when we are afraid, who can we turn to, if not the gods?"

"Ourselves. We turn to ourselves anyway. We only pretend there are gods and that they care about us. It is a comforting falsehood."

"Then who created the world, if not the gods?"

"I can't answer that, but I do know that what we have beheld since we left the amazons is the work of people, not gods."

I thought of Pegasus, of the Land of the Dead, of the erupting volcano that drove us across the sea. I thought of the sirens, of Poseidon's great blue hand, of the coincidence of finding an island of beautiful young men to mate with our maidens.

"I am not ready to give up the gods just yet," I told Aesop.

Aesop laughed. "Perhaps when the gods give *you* up, you'll be ready." That chilled me.

"Without the gods, how would I sing?" I asked.

"With your own voice," he said.

20

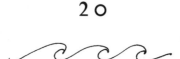

Of Love and Serpents

What life, what pleasure is there
Without golden Aphrodite?
—MIMNERMUS

FROM THE TIME Aesop declared his love for me, things between us began to get difficult. Say what you like about love and friendship being the same—once it is clear that one person feels passion and the other does not, friendship begins to fade.

"Who have you loved the most in your life?" Aesop asked. The question gave me pause. Was it Cleis, or Alcaeus? How could I choose between them?

"Why do you ask?"

"Because I must know. If you truly believe that the world is love, as you told those poor moth-eaten philosophers, you must have a reason for saying so. You sing of love as if you knew it. Do you?"

Like so many of Aesop's questions, this one gave me pause. "Do you?" I asked.

"I believe I do," Aesop said. "Once, long ago, I accepted slavery so that another could go free. That, I believe, is love."

I was astonished as I often was by Aesop. "Who was that other?" I asked.

"I'll tell you," said Aesop. "But I must object when you use love as a banner under which you march. Love is a quieter thing. It lives in deeds, not words."

"Aesop—you amaze me. First you tell me you do not believe in the gods, then you tell me I know nothing of love. Then you refuse to tell me why."

"First I will tell you why I do not believe in the gods—then I will tell you the other. Come, sit with me at the edge of the sea."

We sat on a rock overlooking the sea. Before us were the high chalk cliffs through which we had sailed. Behind us the chalk caves into which our maidens had vanished with their swains. From time to time sweet singing wafted from the openings of the caves. Aesop began:

"The gods never die, so nothing can matter to them. Time is not important. Their lives go on and on. They sit in the marble halls of Olympus and look down on us. Our troubles look petty to them, but we entertain them. Without us they would be utterly bored. We are their amusement, their way of passing the endlessness of eternity. It is *our* lives that matter—and why? Because of death. When I say I don't believe in the gods, what I mean really is that our lives matter in a way theirs do not. We invented them, rather than the other way around. That's why I never tell fables about the gods. All my fables are about human foibles—even if I disguise them in animal skins. People can learn as the gods cannot. People can change as the gods cannot. I would not tell my fables to the gods. They'd be of no use to them whatever."

ZEUS: *Get rid of this man! He's dangerous!*
APHRODITE: *And leave Sappho without her only friend?*
ZEUS: *Why should I care?*
APHRODITE: *The future will care!*
ZEUS: *Past, present, and future are all the same to me!*

"Whom did you give up freedom for?"

"My mother. She was one of the black amazons who lived on the shores of the River Hermus and panned for gold for the Lydian kings.

Thinking they were weak because they were women, the Lydian traders swooped down on their encampments and stole all their gold. Then they captured the amazons and their children. I was ten. Without my mother's knowledge, I bargained with the chieftain to go into slavery in her place. I was carried away to the island of Samos and sold to a goldsmith named Xanthes. There I met Rhodopis, who was enslaved in that same household. When Xanthes went to Naucratis to sell his wares to the wealthy Greek merchants, we went too. There we earned our freedom. Rhodopis became a courtesan and I became a sage. The fact that we were former slaves gave us a certain fascination both to the Egyptians and the Greeks."

"Then you never saw your mother again?"

"Never. Not since I was ten."

"Do you suppose she is alive?"

"I have a feeling that she is. But perhaps I do not want to believe my sacrifice was in vain. I delude myself just like other mortals—though I make fables out of my delusions."

A POWERFUL voice boomed out behind us. "Delusions!" it echoed. We looked around. There was a tall, beautiful woman wearing a crown of live snakes that hissed alarmingly.

"You must be the two who took my husbands and gave them to the maidens who came from the sea. You had no right to do that. They were mine. They were perfectly happy with their lives before you brought those maidens. Now I will have to kill them—or turn them into snakes. My sister Circe would, of course, turn them into swine."

"Your sister? Circe? Then who are you?" I asked.

"Who are *you*? After all, this is my island. I should not have to identify myself on my own island!"

"We were told it was the island of the philosophers," Aesop said.

"Well, you were certainly told a lot of things that were wrong," said the snake woman. "I am Herpetia—I can turn even *you* into snakes and add you to my crown. Medusa was also a sister of mine. But I never saw the point of turning men to stone when there are so many more interesting things you can do with them. Why turn more than one part of a man to stone? If I should ever have a problem, I'll call on my sister, but so far her intervention has not been needed!"

She draped her arms around Aesop, who shrank back from the hissing snakes. "If you were mine, I'd leave you just as you are. I wouldn't change you at all. But you are wrong about the gods. They *do* exist. I myself am the daughter of a god and a serpent. The gods would not be happy to know how you doubt them. They hate disobedience. The only thing they hate more is the defiance of death."

She gestured with her hand and the ground was alive with multicolored snakes. They crawled everywhere—out of the caves the maidens had retreated into with their swains, all over the ground, all over each other. She gestured again—and they were gone.

"Tell me again that you do not believe in the gods," she said to Aesop tauntingly.

"Trickery and magic do not prove that the gods exist," said Aesop calmly. "You can turn the men into snakes—turn me into a snake, for all I care—and still it doesn't prove anything . . . except that you are adept at magic."

Herpetia frowned fiercely. Her snakes hissed. "Usually this sort of thing silences everyone," she said. "Now I meet a man who is not afraid of me. Who *are* you?"

"Aesop at your service, madam," said Aesop.

"The fable-maker?" Herpetia asked.

"The very one," said Aesop.

"Oh, good!" Herpetia said. "It has been so very boring on this island without fables. I have had to turn myself into various things just to keep from dying of boredom. It was I who became those three philosophers in the cave debating the nature of the universe. I have been turning men into snakes just for the fun of it, then turning them back just for the fun of it. It tires them out. Actually, it tires me out too. The truth is that for centuries I have been looking for a husband who is not afraid of me. Maybe I have found him."

Herpetia linked arms with Aesop and hurried him along to stroll by the sea with her. What was he up to? Was he trying to make me jealous? As Aesop romanced Herpetia, her snakes became docile and hung at her cheeks like limp curls. She kissed him passionately. He appeared to reciprocate. I went to warn the maidens that we were all in danger.

I found them in their caves still making love to their beautiful swains. Clearly, we were still in Aphrodite's power. I directed the maidens and men to return to our ship while Herpetia was busy courting Aesop.

"She is a mistress of transformations. If you like your present form— then come along with me! She loves to turn beautiful young men into snakes!"

The men knew I was speaking the truth. The besotted maidens hesitated. They doubted me. Honey-skinned Arete, my erstwhile playmate, challenged me.

"What do you mean, my lover will turn into a snake unless I go immediately?"

"Please don't fight with me about this. Just obey me. We have only a little time to escape the power of this sorceress. Aesop has disarmed her. While she's docile, we must sail away."

But Arete was so intoxicated with her lover that she could not hear me. The other maidens also ignored me.

Aesop somehow broke away from Herpetia and met me on the beach.

"Now I understand Medusa, Circe—all the great sorceresses. They're simply women in search of love. Medusa, furious at being unloved, turned men to stone. Circe turned men to swine. All this could have been avoided if they were properly loved. They turned to black magic for lack of love."

"You say you don't believe in the gods, but even *you* are in Aphrodite's power!"

"Absurd," said Aesop. "I am reason itself. If I love Herpetia, she will turn gentle and mild. You've seen it with your own eyes. I plan to stay here on this island and be her consort. It's my duty."

"I will not let you make this mistake," I said.

"It's no mistake," said Aesop. "It's my destiny."

How I knew to do what I did next, I do not know. But I did. I picked up a piece of driftwood from the beach and brought it down upon Aesop's head, knocking him out. Then I dragged him down the beach and called for help to get him to the boat. The parents and grandparents who had remained on the boat quickly came to my aid and helped me bring Aesop aboard.

Some of the maidens who saw what had happened followed me down the beach, their swains in pursuit. Some stayed on the island lost in love; all I knew was that we had to get away as soon as possible. Whoever Herpetia was—whether a goddess or a projection of Aesop's need for love—she had the power to end our odyssey. Ever since we left the realm of Hades, we had been in lands of myth and delusion. We needed to get back to the real world.

I will never forget the view from the stern of the ship as we hoisted sail. The entire beach was a writhing mass of snakes entangling the legs of the maidens who had ignored my warnings. They tried to get away, and as they ran, the snakes twined around their legs and brought them down. When they stood up, the snakes bit them until they fell motionless in the sand. A few of the strongest maidens gained the ship. Atthis wrestled her snake to the ground and stabbed his throat with her golden clasp. Gongyla outran hers—but Arete, beautiful Arete, lay in a purple python's power, gasping with pleasure as he made love to her again and again. Her gasps and sighs brought other rainbow snakes to watch. She was embraced in the coils of the largest python I had ever seen and he was killing her with love. I was sorry I had taught her about pleasure. My lovemaking had prepared her doom.

Herpetia stood atop a mountain of writhing snakes and cursed us as we sailed away between the two white cliffs.

"Cowards!" she shrieked. "I thought I had found the one man who was not afraid of me—but even he turned out to be a coward! I should have transformed him into a snake before he escaped!"

That frightened me. Would I go below to find Aesop turned into a writhing snake?

"I will be here forever!" she screamed. "And you will all be dead!" With that, the skies opened and the rain poured down until we all ran belowdecks for shelter.

I checked on the sleeping Aesop. He was still himself.

2 1

Among the Centaurs

Thracian filly, why do you look at me and flee?
—ANACREON

AFTER OUR ENCOUNTER with Herpetia, I felt responsible for the fate of Arete and my other maidens. I was their priestess and I should have known better than to linger on such hostile shores. Pouring rain, thunder, and lightning accompanied our departure. It was no weather for sailing, but we had little choice in the matter.

Atthis and Gongyla sat with me belowdecks and tried to wake Aesop. He had a huge bump on his head where I had struck him and his eyes were ringed with black and plum.

When he awoke, he was not angry with me. "You saved our lives," he said.

"Our numbers are much reduced," I said. "We have lost most of our maidens to the serpents, our men to the sirens, and their parents to withering grief. I fear it is my entire fault for invoking Aphrodite's power. Our boat is hardly seaworthy, our rations few. The seas are rough. We have been punished for our arrogant disregard of all the gods but Aphrodite."

"Perhaps I have sinned by denying the gods," Aesop said. "Or perhaps, by calling forth Osiris and the most ancient gods, we also summoned ancient serpent-headed goddesses from the deep. Or perhaps the ancient Egyptian followers of Akhenaton were right. Perhaps there is only one god—the blazing sun."

"Aesop, you amaze me."

"Archilochus said, '*All things are easy for the gods*.' Perhaps we have just been praying to the wrong *idea* of god. Akhenaton was called a heretic for worshiping one god—but another desert people took up his creed. They claim they are the chosen people of the future."

"One god? How can one god command all the various things in the sky and the earth?" I asked.

"Because god is a force, not a personage," Aesop said. "God is wisdom, light, life."

"What a strange idea!" I said.

Our damaged ship braved the waves. Some of our older passengers succumbed to seasickness, starvation, despair. Even when we saw islands on the horizon, we were afraid to stop for fear that serpents—or worse—lurked there. We were forever committing bodies to the waves. Our ship smelled foul as death. And those who remained on board grew thinner and thinner for want of food. I was sure this was the end. With no place to land and nothing to eat, the sea would eventually swallow us. No trace of us would remain—not even our names. Once I had been so sure the future would remember my name and my songs. Now I despaired.

Aesop and I, along with Atthis and Gongyla, had taken the habit of sheltering under a canvas in the very prow of the ship so we could scan the horizon for possible rescuers. Wind and rain did not daunt us. The slap and splash of seawater did not discourage us. We were determined to be the first to recognize a friendly ship. The sailors had taught me how to shimmy to the top of the mast and from time to time I did this—my heart beating in my throat—then I'd slide down. Whenever I saw distant lightning flashes in the sky or heard thunder, I'd descend the mast as quickly as I could.

We had no idea where we were. We might have strayed beyond the

Pillars of Hercules, for all we knew. We had disrupted the calm order of the amazons' lives and perhaps were being punished for that. We had questioned the gods we grew up worshiping. Would I ever see my child again? Would I ever see Alcaeus?

There was a huge crack of thunder and a bolt of lightning. It split the mast and brought it down, with all the tattered remnants of our sail. Around and around we spun, out of control in a cauldron of seawater. Another bolt, and our prow was severed from our stern. Boards, broken amphorae, shipmates bobbed in the waves. I last saw Atthis and Gongyla paddling the bottom half of an amphora as if it were a toy boat—then they disappeared behind a towering wave. Aesop and I must have inspired pity from Poseidon—or from his companion Maera—because we were swept up upon a sandy spit where, unconscious, we rolled half in and half out of the sea.

We slept—for how long, only the gods know. When we awakened, it was to the thunder of horses' hooves. A pack of wild horses with the torsos and the heads of men encircled us. They advanced on us slowly, and seeming to know they could not prod us with their hooves, their leader, who had a bushy white beard and bright green eyes, knelt down and touched me gently with his hands.

His touch was tender—even for a man. Aesop leapt up as if to defend me.

"No need," said the leader of the centaurs. "Zeus may have thought us beasts and banished us to this rocky isle, but I know how to treat a lady, as do my misunderstood brethren. I am Chiron—older than Zeus, older than Poseidon, older than them all. When the upstart gods decided to cast out the animals in themselves—or hide them, rather—they sent us far away. We were an unpleasant reminder of the past—like the harpies and the gorgons."

"We have met Herpetia. We know."

"My horrid stepsister," said Chiron, "but we are far more civilized than she. We taught the gods all they know. For that, they hated us. We live in perfect harmony, eating only apples and grasses. We kill no other creatures. We study herbs and healing. We spend our lives grazing and contemplating. We have discovered the perfect stillness that reveals the secrets of the universe. It was a centaur who first observed that you never step into the same river twice."

Chiron led us to a grove where we could feast on apples, drink clear cold water, and rest. The babbling brooks that traversed the centaurs' island home were amazingly restorative. After a short time, the shipwreck seemed as distant as childhood.

What did the centaurs do all day? They galloped all over the island to exercise their muscles. They danced in elaborate patterns to marvelous wind instruments. They bathed in the cool streams. After a lunch of apples and grasses, they briefly slept. They spent long hours standing perfectly still in contemplation of the horizon. In the evening they shared the wisdom this had brought.

But there was a problem. All the centaurs were male and they could not reproduce. They were getting older and older. Being part deity, they could not die, but Zeus had cruelly decreed that they would grow old forever. Who would replace the ancient centaurs, no longer good for anything but grazing in the pasture? Who would take care of them in their endless decrepitude? There was no younger generation.

"We need mares," Chiron said. "Otherwise our great philosophy will come to nothing."

"Too bad the maidens perished in the sea," said Aesop.

"Maidens?" asked Chiron. "What maidens?"

"They were the daughters of amazons and Egyptian sailors. Some were entrapped by Herpetia's serpents, some were lost at sea."

"Are you sure they all perished?" Chiron asked.

"As sure as anyone can be sure of anything after having been fished out of the sea! If any remain alive, I'll be astonished."

"That's what they said of Persephone—yet we found her in Hades' realm and were able to revive her. Alas, we had to give her back for half the year because of those pomegranate seeds she ate. In those days we served Demeter, the great mother, and learned her most secret rituals for making the crops grow. Those were the days." And with that Chiron gave a series of loud whinnies that rang through the groves and across the beaches. The youngest, fastest centaurs galloped madly into the sea. They swam so ably you would have sworn they were dolphins.

"What did you shout?" Aesop asked.

"I cannot tell you with a lady present," said Chiron, blushing. "It's too indelicate. Let me just admit that centaurs are very sensual creatures. We meditate to tame our passions."

I walked with Aesop on the beach.

"The whole world is Aphrodite's province," I said. "Even these noble animals who spend half their days meditating will jump into the sea if their phalli stiffen. I give up. Say what you like about gods old and new. Aphrodite rules the world."

APHRODITE: *What a clever girl!*
ZEUS: *A contradiction in terms. Women are only good for one thing!*

Aesop and I watched while the remaining centaurs danced at the edge of the sea, playing their strange pipes and treading very gracefully for such large beings. Horses fascinated me with their agility and their muscular beauty. No wonder the amazons worshiped a mare-headed goddess and prayed for the return of Pegasus.

"If only these creatures could mate with the amazons," I said, "what a powerful race of wizards and witches they could create."

"I think they did once in the mists of time," said Aesop, "but Zeus sent the lapiths to prey on them and undo their magic."

"If we could reunite them, what wonders they might give the world!"

A commotion on the beach. Several of the strong young centaurs galloped out of the sea, dragging nets of seaweed. Tangled in its greenery were Atthis and Gongyla, who seemed to have turned the same color as the seaweed. I would have sworn they were dead.

Then Chiron and his cohorts laid them out on the beach with great tenderness. First they washed their bodies with fresh water. Then they anointed them with oils suffused with herbs. They danced around them, playing those breathy instruments that sounded half like birds and half like the snorts of horses.

"O Demeter, great mother, we have brought your daughters back from the house of Hades like your own Persephone," they chanted.

Then they neighed and whinnied and galloped in circles around the two green girls.

"The next part of the ceremony is not fit for your eyes to see," Chiron said. "You must retire to the Cave of the Elders." He gestured to a low entrance in a great rock that stood half in and half out of the sea.

Aesop and I did as we were told. We had to bend very low to crawl into the rock cave, where it was very dark and the stench was unbearable.

"What is that putrescent smell?" I cried out.

"The smell of death that will not die," came the whinnying reply.

When our eyes grew accustomed to the darkness, we saw all around us creatures who had once been centaurs. Some lay outstretched. Some leaned against the walls, examining their rotting hooves with their human hands. Some of these fearsome creatures curled on the floor of the cave in piles of shedding skin. They groaned and winced at the light.

"Have you come to grant us death?" one toothless centaur asked. "We crave the blessings of death, which Zeus has denied us as punishment."

"What terrible crimes did you commit?"

"Shape-shifting magic, instructing the gods. They want to pretend they learned it all themselves!"

"If only we could grant you death!" cried Aesop. "But we are only humans."

Unable to stand the smell, I fled the cave.

There on the beach I saw each of the centaurs stroke the maidens with his enormous phallus. An arc of fire went from that organ to the maiden.

Atthis was the first to stir. Next Gongyla came to life.

"Aesop!" I cried. "Our maidens are revived!"

Aesop dragged himself out of the Cave of the Elders. "Now you know why death is a blessing," he said.

"Now you know in which organ the magic of the centaurs resides," I answered.

There was no question that Atthis and Gongyla were coming back to life. Atthis stretched her arms above her head and stared at the circle of centaurs in astonishment. Gongyla sat up too.

"Chiron—if you can so restore these maidens with your healing, why are your elders rotting away?"

"Another trick of Zeus. We can heal all creatures but our own kind."

"Why did Zeus so hate you?"

"We had the power of horses and the brains of men. We knew the healing arts, all magic, and had the power to turn ourselves into any shape as he did. But above all we were more potent than he was, more irresistible to women. Zeus in particular hated that. We had taught the gods all they knew and Zeus wanted to forget where this learning originated. In our early days we were beloved by Poseidon and could gallop across the sea. Zeus took that from us as well. You know that he hates whatever his brother loves."

Atthis and Gongyla were now fully awake. They leapt on Chiron's back and bade him take them all over the island. I heard them laughing with delight as they galloped away.

"Let's bring the amazons and the centaurs together," I said to Aesop. "Women love horses better than they love men."

"How on earth will we accomplish that?" asked Aesop.

"With the help of the gods," I said.

"If only they could gallop across the sea again," Aesop said dreamily.

"That's the only I hope I have of ever getting home again," I said. "On some centaur's back."

But I was wrong.

2 2

The Eye of Horus

I am that Eye of Horus, the messenger of the lord.
I am he that created his name.
—Ancient Egyptian prayer

SOME DAYS LATER, a great Egyptian ship with a huge eye painted on its side sailed into the harbor of the island of the centaurs. Since the centaurs had no docks or provisions for landing, the ship had to anchor out in the deep waters. Chiron studied it with suspicion, thinking it was another punishment visited by Zeus on those beloved by Poseidon.

"Perhaps we should sink the ship," he said to Aesop and me while his circle of centaurs looked on, awaiting his orders.

"It is called the *Eye of Horus*," said Aesop, who could read hieroglyphs after his long sojourn in Egypt. "It might presage something good. For the Egyptians the eye is the symbol of the Great Mother. We humans are merely tears of the great eye. This may be just the redemption you are seeking."

"I doubt it," said Chiron. "Zeus has tricked me in so many ways that I know how cunning he can be. I say sink it."

"And stay here with your rotting elders, your helpless isolation? Perhaps this ship can carry you to a better fate."

"All right, then, Aesop, I delegate you to swim out to the ship and speak to them. If you do not return swiftly, we will know they are enemies and we will sink the ship."

"But I thought you killed no living creature," Aesop said. "Would you so betray your own philosophy?"

At that moment a small speck began to bob on the sea near the great Egyptian ship. As it came closer, we saw that it was a tender from the *Eye of Horus*. It had a canopy of gold, which glinted in the sun. Four powerful Nubians in white linen rowed it. Under the canopy sat what appeared to be an Egyptian nobleman. But as he rowed closer, we saw that this Egyptian nobleman had golden hair.

I stood transfixed. The boat rowed closer and closer. Two powerful Nubians leapt out and dragged the boat up on the strand. Then they helped the nobleman out of the craft. The two other Nubians detached the canopy of gold and held it over the blond head of the Egyptian lord.

Perhaps it was because he was clean-shaven in the Egyptian fashion, perhaps because so many years had elapsed, but I did not recognize this man until he began to speak in the soft syllables of my native land:

"What land is this, where men are horses and horses are men? Does anyone speak Greek?" It was Alcaeus! I hid behind Chiron, worrying that I did not look good enough to meet my old love. My hair was a mess. I had no paint, no perfumes, and no elegant clothes. In all my dreams of this moment I never expected to look like a castaway.

"Do you come in peace?" Chiron demanded. "Or are you another hostile emissary of Zeus?"

"You flatter me if you think I come from Zeus himself, but the pharaoh sent me, not the king of the gods. I'm afraid my mission is more mundane. My pharaoh seeks a certain Greek singer who has captured his heart."

"Who might that be?" Chiron asked.

"A woman who sings so sweetly she might be one of the muses. A woman whose hair is so shining and black it might be ebony. A woman who smells of all the perfumes of the East. . . ."

"We have no woman like that here," said Chiron, who had never heard me sing. I shrank behind his huge flank, praying that Alcaeus would leave before he saw me in this state. I had dreamed of him for years and now all I wished for was his departure.

"I have heard the singer that you speak of," Aesop said. "She became a legend in Naucratis. She is Sappho of Eresus."

"The very one," said Alcaeus.

"We have no Sappho here," said Chiron.

Alcaeus looked downcast and turned to go. "But perhaps I might refill my water jugs before I sail again?"

I debated with myself. Should I crawl back into the cave of the ancient centaurs and avoid being seen by Alcaeus? Should I make myself known even in my hideous state? My vanity warred with my love.

"You may have water," Chiron said.

Alcaeus turned away to instruct the Nubians.

"I will return to my ship," he told Chiron, "and then send my men back with jugs for water. Thank you for the courtesy." And he turned his back to us and began the short walk to the skiff under his canopy of gold.

My heart was pounding in my chest. The sweat poured down my face.

I could not stay and could not go.

Aesop stopped Alcaeus. "May I sail with you back to Egypt?" he asked. "I may be of some service."

"And who are you?"

"Aesop the fable-maker."

"The pharaoh also mentioned you as friend and advisor. Surely you must know what became of Sappho?"

Aesop hesitated. I saw myself abandoned on the island of the centaurs while these two sailed away together and I panicked.

"Alcaeus—I am here!" I shrieked and ran to him, throwing my arms around him. He embraced me warmly, then stood back and looked at me with amazement.

"Well, you certainly look the worse for wear!" he said.

"If you had been to Hades' realm and back, you might not look so good either."

"Hades' realm! You always did have a tendency to overdramatize your life. Being the favorite of a pharaoh is hardly so horrible."

"So you two know each other?" asked Chiron.

"We certainly do," I said.

Later, on the *Eye of Horus,* he took me in his arms and kissed me to make up for all the years of kisses we had missed. Kisses—the sweetest fruits of love—can be lyric or epic. Our kisses were epic. They were the weavings and unweavings of the gods. We caught up on the years. Alcaeus told me about Sardis, about Delphi, about Naucratis. I told him about Syracuse, the amazons, and Herpetia. We told all—or almost all. Yet we clearly left things out. I did not mention Isis. He did not mention Rhodopis.

"I wish you could have shared the court of Alyattes with me," Alcaeus said.

"I wish you could have seen Syracuse," I said.

"I wish we had met at Delphi instead of constantly missing each other," Alcaeus said.

"Let's make up for it now," I said, "with the prophecies of kisses to come." And then we were lost again in each other's tongues.

Alcaeus and I were two of a kind. We were too much alike—vain, sensual, wanting to be admired for our cleverness. We always held something in reserve. One lover was not enough. There had to be another waiting in the wings.

"So, Sappho, you are a widow now. Will you marry me? Or shall I carry you back to your besotted pharaoh?"

"One marriage is more than enough for a lifetime. I hope never to do *that* again. Cannot I just keep you as a plaything?"

"And what about the pharaoh?"

"Let him pay the bills. Pharaohs are good for that."

WE CRUISED ON the great Egyptian ship and made love day and night as if we were the newest of new lovers. We wrote each other songs—all of which have been lost. We devoured each other's bodies hungrily. While we did, the Nubians sailed eastward in the direction of Egypt and Aesop worked busily transcribing his tales on papyrus in the captain's quarters. The centaurs were also aboard, for Aesop had sworn to take them to the island of the amazons. But for all that, Alcaeus and I might have been alone.

There is nothing sweeter than to be on a boat with the love of your life. You inhabit a private world—a world made only for your love. Alcaeus described the court of Alyattes for me and the interminable wait for the Oracle of Delphi. I told Alcaeus of my marriage, of the birth of Cleis, of my adventures with Cyrus, with Praxinoa, with Penthesilea and Antiope.

When I spoke of the amazons and Pegasus, of the Land of the Dead and the failed utopia that followed it, I am not sure Alcaeus believed me. He looked at me quizzically, as if I had made it all up. But I no longer cared. Lost in the sweetness of sex, I had no energy to argue with him. Desire is its own country and we were its king and queen.

AT NIGHT, Aesop would tell his tales on the deck, greatly amusing the sailors. Every tale ended with a pithy moral. If only life were as simple as that.

If lovers could live forever in the land of desire, life would have no problems. But desire, once satisfied, makes room for other things. I longed to see my daughter, my gold flower, my darling Cleis. I put it to Alcaeus that we should return to Lesbos—whatever the cost.

"In Egypt, we are royalty," he said, "in Lesbos, outcasts. Why on earth would we return there?"

"So I can see my child," I said.

Alcaeus was not convinced.

"And if Pittacus executes us—what good will that do your child?"

"I'm sure Pittacus will be reasonable," I said.

"How little you know him!" Alcaeus countered. "You cannot go back as long as Pittacus lives."

We were bound for Egypt, and that was that.

We would stop, of course, in the land of the amazons—which Alcaeus had agreed to because he didn't really think it existed. Aesop had somehow convinced Chiron that the amazons were their natural allies—and Chiron, who desperately sought mates for his men, was ready to attempt this radical solution to the barrenness of his land.

Chiron himself had taken both Atthis and Gongyla as his brides and the other centaurs were restless to have brides themselves. They paced the deck while Chiron cavorted below with his maidens.

"If you will not return to Lesbos," I said, "I'll escape at the island of the amazons and make my way from there." But Alcaeus—perhaps because he did not believe any such island existed—was undisturbed by my threat.

My longing for Cleis became the worm in the golden apple of our love. I wanted Alcaeus to want Cleis as much as I did. Nothing but that would do. I planned to tell Alcaeus that Cleis was surely his daughter, waiting for the right moment to make this revelation. I wanted the atmosphere to be perfect. Was I afraid that Alcaeus would somehow regret both me and Cleis if he knew? Was I afraid he would not be a father like my own father? Did I still long to be the 'little whirlwind' of my earliest days? So much memory flows between lovers. So much time passes in our lives, and yet so little. From childhood to maturity is the blink of an eye—the eye of Horus!

"I want you to myself," said Alcaeus, stroking my cheek, my breast, my thigh. "I want to feast on you forever. If we could sail away to our own island and never see anyone but each other for all eternity—that is what I would like best."

"That is what I want too," I said. But I was thinking of Cleis.

AT NIGHT I would lie awake next to Alcaeus and yearn for Cleis. I saw her always in a religious procession, wearing a string of figs around her neck. I saw her weaving gowns to robe Athena. I saw her carrying a basket on her head—a basket full of objects sacred to Aphrodite.

The truth is I didn't know whether she was alive or dead. I didn't even know whether my mother had safely made the journey from Syracuse to Lesbos. Nor did I know whether my mother was alive or dead. Nor whether Pittacus was still in power. If my daughter lived, she would be a woman by now. And if she hadn't lived? It was unthinkable!

"Sappho," Alcaeus would say, "we can have other children. Cleis is not the only child you'll ever have."

Somehow this rankled more than if he had said nothing. He didn't understand my longing. Again, I put off telling him that Cleis was his daughter. I hesitated and the right moment never presented itself.

In all the years I had yearned for Alcaeus, I thought him my double, my twin, the only soul to penetrate my heart. His lack of understanding pained me. I wanted to tell him that I was sure Cleis was his daughter as well as mine, but something held me back. I wanted him to love her without proof of paternity—love her simply because I loved her. It was a kind of test. But why did I feel I had to test him? Was it that I wanted him to know without my telling him? Was it that I wanted him to read my mind? Surely he must have heard Cercylas was such an impotent old sot that he could never have fathered anything! Yes, I wanted him to understand without being told. This was the ultimate proof of love I required.

LATER, I WOULD ask myself why we allowed so many rifts between us. There were so many ways we could have reassured each other and built our love on a sounder foundation. Why did I keep procrastinating about telling him that Cleis was his daughter? Why did I never tell him how much I resented his intention to deliver me to the pharaoh? I don't know the answer to these questions. Many nights I lay in bed with him with Rhodopis on the tip of my tongue. Why didn't I confront him with her boast that she had bedded him in Delphi? Why was I afraid?

If I could have answered these questions then, wisdom would have been mine and my odyssey would have been at its end. But I didn't know myself well enough yet. I loved Alcaeus, but I didn't know how to love myself.

It was on the *Eye of Horus* that I thought again and again that perhaps I should have stayed with the amazons and become their queen. I wanted to tell Alcaeus that too, but I was afraid he would mock me. He thought the amazons were a myth.

Aesop understood my longings, but I loved Aesop only like a

brother. Alcaeus was my destiny. Between my wild passion for him and my deep maternal yearnings, I didn't know which way to turn.

I do not know what to do.
My mind's in two.

It was then that Aesop made his move. He came to me one night when I was pacing on the deck to stave off insomnia.

"Sappho," he said, "all these years I have agreed to be your faithful shadow. I have asked nothing for myself. I have honored your love for Alcaeus. But now I see how you long for your child, how troubled you are by Alcaeus' indifference to your plight. I must declare myself. Whatever you wish shall be my command. If you desire to return to Lesbos, I shall accompany you. If you desire to rejoin the amazons, I am yours. If you want to go back to Egypt, likewise I will take you. Say the word and I shall do it."

"Don't tempt me, Aesop. My condition is weak. My mind's divided."

"He is not good for you, Sappho. All these years you have been strong and brave. Alcaeus returns and you do not know your own mind. Love has made you childlike and unsure. With me you were a goddess. With him you have become a slave."

I knew there was some truth in this. I took Aesop's arm and we paced the deck together.

"I cannot bear to see you weaken," Aesop said. "I want my valiant Sappho back again."

He led me to a small skiff, which sat on the great deck like a babe at its mother's breast. It was covered with its own sail. Behind the boat he kissed me. Within the boat he made love to me and gave his whole soul to me. When Alcaeus found us, we were still clinging to each other.

23

Home

Far more sweet-sounding than a lyre.
More golden than gold.
—SAPPHO

"DAMN YOU! Sappho," Alcaeus shouted, "you are the first woman I ever trusted and you betray me like a common harlot!"

I looked up and there was Alcaeus. How long had he been watching us? I grew defensive, when an apology would have been what my heart dictated.

"You mean like Rhodopis? I know all about you two! She herself boasted of your prowess as a lover. How clever of you to forget to tell me!"

"She meant *nothing* to me!" Alcaeus raved.

"Can't you think of a better excuse?"

"I made love to her and thought of *you!*"

"And you expect me to say 'I made love to Aesop and thought of *you!*'" I shouted. We were still inside the little skiff, perched on the afterdeck, and Alcaeus was leaning over the edge, staring at us hatefully.

"Well, it's true. I *did* think of you. Only of you." This I whispered.

"You never told *me* that!" said Aesop from his supine position in the skiff. "I thought you loved me a little."

"Forgive me, Aesop, I *do* love you as a brother, but Alcaeus is my destiny. I know that now. I've known it from the first moment I set eyes upon him!"

For a minute nobody said a word. All we could hear was our own labored breathing. Aesop was clinging to me like a baby clutching at its mother. I struggled out of his reach, clambered out of the skiff, and tried to follow Alcaeus as he stormed off the deck. He went below to hide himself among the centaurs. By now I was sobbing desperately.

Why, after all this time, had I chosen to do the deed with Aesop? Had I needed to provoke Alcaeus? I was enraged at myself. I would have done anything to undo my foolishness. The regret I felt was the regret of the damned. I had seen it on my father's shadowy face in Hades' realm. I felt that I was back across the rushing river with the dead. Better *be* dead and numb to all sensation than to feel the way I felt!

I pursued Alcaeus belowdecks. He refused to see me. He sent Chiron to inform me that he was too ill to speak to me. The wise old centaur shook his shaggy white mane and said, "You broke his heart. There's nothing for it."

"Help me, Chiron!" I begged. "Tell Alcaeus how much I love him!"

"How can I dispute what he just saw with his own eyes?"

"Tell him it meant *nothing*. Tell him it was a momentary lapse of judgment. Tell him I love only him. Please. I beg of you." By now I was on my knees in supplication.

"He will not believe me. He refuses to share you with Aesop. He is a proud man and you have humiliated him."

"But Chiron, you can cure *anything*. You know the secrets of healing. Heal his broken heart. I know you can do it. Besides, you have two wives *yourself*. You'd happily take three and think nothing of it. You love more than one woman. How can you fault me for loving two men? It's not impossible to love two men!"

"It's different for men. The phallus can accept no competition. You women are used to it. Deltas are less discriminating."

All I could do was fall to the deck and wail like one in mourning. I pounded my fists and tore my chiton. But still Alcaeus did not appear.

ALCAEUS PUT BOTH Aesop and me off the boat at Samos. As I watched under the deep blue Aegean sky as the *Eye of Horus* sailed away bearing all my hopes and dreams, I knew I had lost the love of my life a second time. The first time is heartbreaking, but the second time is like an evisceration.

Why had I brought disaster down upon myself? Perhaps I was afraid to give myself entirely to Alcaeus because I loved him so utterly. And abandonment seemed as inevitable as death. I had broken three hearts—Aesop's, my own, and Alcaeus'—and I knew I was doomed to live with regret forever.

I remembered the legend of Leucas. It was said that lovers who jumped from the Leucadian cliff either got over their hopeless passion or died trying. In either case they were cured. Now I understood what always seemed so desperate before.

So here we were in Samos, Aesop and I alone together, and desolate. Aesop knew Samos well from his slave days, but he hated the place as crass and gold-loving. He was despondent about what he perceived as my rejection of him. You would have thought that with Alcaeus gone, Aesop would have claimed me as his own, but both of us were devastated. Something was deeply wrong between us. We both now knew we were friends rather than lovers, but we had tainted that long friendship with unrequited love. Sometimes you have to couple to uncouple. Unfathomable, the mysteries of love!

Why is it that you can love two men but love them in totally different ways? Why is it that one may claim your fealty and philosophy and the other your desire and your delta? Why is it that love is so damnably various? And why are men so unprepared to grant that women are as various as they? We are more various, in fact. Little good it did me to philosophize like this! It did nothing to ease the pain. Men were blind and narrow-minded, but I loved one of them!

Aesop and I stayed together for a while, chewing over the past, growing gloomier and gloomier. The more we talked about our dilemma, the less we could resolve it.

One evening we were crying into our wine in a little tavern in a back alley of Samos and we noticed a group of Lydians watching us, listening for every word.

A great gray-bearded fellow with sea-green eyes surrounded by innumerable crinkles finally rose from his table and came over to Aesop.

"Is it Aesop the fable-maker?" he asked.

"Why do you ask?" muttered Aesop grumpily. Then he looked up and his face spread with a smile. "Syennesis!" he exclaimed. "My dear old friend!"

They began a spirited conversation about things and people in the past I had no knowledge of. It turned out that Syennesis was a philosopher and a friend of Aesop's former owner.

"I always knew you'd become famous!" he said to Aesop. What about me? I thought. Was I a cipher? The man did not recognize me at all, nor did Aesop remedy the slight.

"We are bound for Delphi," said Syennesis.

"Of course you are!" I said peevishly. "Whenever anyone in this part of the world is at a loss for anything—Delphi is the answer."

"And who is this?" the Lydian asked Aesop, as if I could not speak for myself.

"Why, this is the famed singer, Sappho of Lesbos," said Aesop.

At that, the hairy, wrinkled Syennesis fell to his knees, clasped his hands, and began to sing, "*I have a daughter like a golden flower. / I would not take all of Alyattes' gold with silver thrown in for her!* I'll never forget where I first was when I heard that. If you are the divine goddess who first composed that song, then I am at your service, Lady."

I must admit this softened my mood somewhat—though he had misquoted me.

"Thank you," I said simply. And then the accumulated tears I had been storing up began to flow. I thought of Cleis as she had been as a baby and great sobs shook my body.

"Forgive me," I mumbled. Aesop put his arm around my shoulder.

"I think it is time for you to go home," he said softly. And I knew he was right.

So Aesop went with the Lydians to seek the wisdom of the Oracle of Delphi (that charade again!) and I steeled myself to return to my native isle despite the order of exile probably still in force against me. Aesop and I said farewell sadly, knowing the gods had made us tools of each other's wisdom but not lifelong partners. Aphrodite had asserted her power over me again in a new and tricky way.

Damn you, Aphrodite, I thought. I knew now how Chiron had felt about Zeus, how angry one could be at the gods, but I humbled myself before Aphrodite, knowing now that she was far shrewder than I. You win, Aphrodite! You've ruined my life! You've taken me to the edge of the cliff!

ZEUS: *Do you intend to let this insult pass unpunished?*
APHRODITE: *Of course not! Phaon will be waiting to humble her once more.*

Then I made my way to Lesbos secretly, not disclosing my identity. I crept upon my native island like a ghost.

I went first to Eresus, not Mytilene, hoping to conceal myself as long as possible. As far as I knew, Pittacus' minions would dispatch me for daring to return. No doubt I was still under sentence of execution. And yet it was sweet to be home. If I was meant to die here, so be it. I had reached the end of my winding road. I could smell death waiting in the wings.

At the little town where I was born, there was a strange hush. The hills were green as ever, the olives silver, the sea sparkling, but the people were subdued, as after an enemy attack. Everyone seemed to be waiting for something to happen. I asked the boatman who brought me what the trouble was.

"The tyrant's love is dying," he said. "Cleis, beloved of Pittacus, may be breathing her last."

Somehow, I had sensed this. Perhaps it had drawn me back to Lesbos as surely as my longing for my daughter.

"Where does she live?"

"Here in Eresus. . . . A great lady."

He rowed me to my grandparents' house—it seemed so much smaller and more modest than I remembered it—and into a courtyard filled with people weeping. I had the feeling I was back in the Land of the Dead. Everything seemed hazy and insubstantial, as if I walked among ghosts.

I drew my veil over my face, still not wanting to be recognized.

Then there was a commotion—guards pushing the people aside, myself included—and a great paunchy man with a white beard sailed in, a golden-haired young woman at his side.

The man was clearly an aged Pittacus. But who was the young woman?

I pushed through the crowd and found myself borne on a sea of sobbing humanity. Two guards restrained me and held me painfully by the arms. But now we were in a chamber where a woman lay dying, and she recognized me.

"Sappho!" she whispered. "Forgive me!"

The grizzled man and the golden girl stood aside in surprise. The man indicated to the guards that I might be released.

I ran to my mother's bedside and fell to my knees. Her face was gray. Her eyes had lost their luster. She smelled of mortality.

"Forgive me," she said again. "Is it really you? Am I dreaming? If it is really you, I can die. The pain is so terrible that all I want to do is sleep. Sleep has become my only blessing."

I knew now that my mother's dying had somehow reached me even on the *Eye of Horus* in the middle of the sea.

I thought of so many things I wanted to tell my mother—of meeting my beloved father in the house of Hades; of living with the mythic amazons whom she had so revered; of losing Alcaeus again because of Aesop; of understanding now that a woman could love two men, that a mother could follow her destiny and still love her child more than life itself, that the gods were capricious and uncontrollable—but all I could do was hold her in my arms and weep. She wept too. "Forgive me, forgive me," she kept mumbling.

"There is nothing to forgive," I said. "The gods decreed it all—even my return. The gods are in charge, not we."

We stayed like that for a long time. How long, I don't know. Little by little her body, which I caressed, began to smell as it had when I was a child—fragrant with the perfumes of the East. Hours, days, and years went by—or seemed to. When I lifted my head, my mother's mouth was slack and a shining filament of light fell to my hand from her lower lip. Was this my legacy? Her eyes were open but gone. She had left me an orphan, holding her in my arms.

Pittacus and the young woman were standing utterly still and staring at me. Something in the young woman's eyes reminded me of those that had just closed. Could this be?

"Hang me from the rafters if you must," I whispered to Pittacus. "But what I want is to see my daughter before I die."

"Sappho—I pardoned both you and Alcaeus months ago when your mother fell ill. And your daughter stands before you."

The beautiful young woman came forward to embrace me. I drank her beauty with my thirsty eyes, then sank to the floor in a faint.

When I awoke, it was in the women's quarters of my daughter's house in Mytilene. My daughter was caring for me. She was so beautiful that had I met her without knowing of our relationship, surely I would have tried to make love to her. Whenever I looked at her, my breath caught in my throat and a subtle flame heated my blood. Her teeth were straight and white and slightly buck—a sign of sensuality. Her golden hair tumbled over her flushed pink face as she nursed me.

"I forgive you for everything," she said, "even abandoning me."

So that was the story she had been told! I did not contradict her—not yet.

My mind journeyed back to the events that had brought me here. I saw myself on the boat with Alcaeus, living in rapture. Then I saw myself ruining it all with Aesop. And then I understood. Had I stayed in the arms of Alcaeus, my mother would have died unforgiven. There was a divine plan, after all—but one I could only see looking back.

My mother was dead. Larichus was dead. My grandparents were long dead. My brother Charaxus was running the family vineyards with the help of his wife—Rhodopis! The beautiful courtesan was now a harridan, everyone said, but she still thought herself bewitching. She, no less than my mother, had perpetrated the story of my supposed abandonment of Cleis. Charaxus had not contradicted her—but then he was afraid to contradict her about anything.

As the adopted child of the tyrant, my daughter had had her choice of men, but had chosen badly and seemed unhappy. Her husband was rich, but he was not clever enough for her. And because he was not clever, he was not kind—for kindness is the highest wisdom.

My son-in-law was called Elpenor—after that fool who fell off the roof in a drunken haze in Homer's epic of Odysseus. Who calls his son Elpenor? Only the most foolish or venal of fathers! And Cleis' husband lived up to his name too. He bumbled and stumbled with his tongue if not with his feet. No wonder his wife couldn't stand him!

Because she was so unhappy, she had fallen into the habit of consulting soothsayers and asking them the unanswerable, but not one of them had predicted my return.

Each day a bird would be sacrificed and brought to her to tell her the way the day would go.

"You'd be better off listening to their song, Cleis, than allowing their slaughter. The unhappy always fall into the traps of soothsayers."

"Why are you so wise?" she asked.

"Pain and shipwreck, shipwreck and heartbreak."

"Will you stay with me forever?" Cleis asked.

"I'll try," I said.

OF COURSE, it fell to the women of the family to wash and perfume my mother's body for her funeral rites. There I stood in the courtyard opposite my nemesis Rhodopis while we tenderly washed my mother's corpse in seawater, attached the golden strap to hold her chin, closed her beautiful eyes, and put a coin in her mouth to pay for her journey to Hades' realm. We dressed her all in white and pointed her feet toward the door as she lay on her bier. We placed a wreath of gold upon her head to indicate that she had won her battle with life and we placed a ceramic bird on her chest to represent her singing soul. We gave her her mirror and *alabastron,* a little vase for perfume, to take to the Land of the Dead so that even there she could be beautiful. We set *lekythoi* of perfumed oil about her crowned head. Then we sang all manner of dirges for her, assisted by all her female friends and a chorus of professional mourners sent by Pittacus.

"I loved her so!" Rhodopis wept. "That was why she promised me her jewels!" She was eyeing the golden crown as if she felt it was a shame to bury it.

I said nothing. At one time, I would have done battle with her over the jewels my mother left behind, but I was too exhausted for that now. However little you depend on your parents from day to day, however you expect their deaths, their final departure is a cataclysm. It is as if you stand on solid ground and suddenly the earth gapes beneath you.

I thought of the Land of the Dead where my mother and father would be reunited.

"At last!" my father would exclaim.

"At least here you have no body to betray me with!" my mother would snap. Then she would be glad to be with him for all eternity. And with baby Eurygius.

Pittacus had prepared a monument for my mother in which she appeared, sculpted in all her youthful beauty, holding a small girl child. The epitaph read: *"I hold the dear child of my daughter. May we never be parted in this world as we were inseparable in the world where the sun shines."* Under the little girl's feet was written: *"I am Sappho beloved of Cleis as Cleis is beloved of Sappho."* A riddle worthy of the Oracle of Delphi.

No expense was spared for my mother's funeral. My mother was carried to her grave in a hearse drawn by four white horses. Even the horses were sacrificed and entombed with her as if she were a great warrior.

"You have dealt the death of my soul by dying!" Pittacus exclaimed at my mother's graveside. Cleis wept and wept as if she could never be comforted. I took her in my arms, but she subtly pulled away.

• • •

THE WHOLE ISLAND was sunk in official mourning. I was beginning to admire Pittacus for the care he took with my mother's passing. It was not surprising that the long struggle of Lesbos against Athens had created such a leader. At times of war, people turn to heroes and strongmen and happily give them extraordinary powers. People talk of loving peace, but war cements the powers of tyrants and the military. It will never be abolished as long as men are men. The need for domination is in their blood. We women could bring peace if we did not live as an occupied nation in the world of men. But having seen how even the amazons could be corrupted by evil rulers, I did not hold out much hope for humanity of either gender. Why did the gods let us kill each other so readily? Was it all an entertainment for them in their vast boredom on Olympus? That was the only explanation that made any sense at all.

The war between Lesbos and Athens had dragged on and on for years. Just as it seemed peace was imminent, another expedition of war ships would arrive to skirmish on our shores. The populace feared peace after so many years of war. People would retreat inland from Mytilene to wait out the bloodshed. Then calm would come again. Then another skirmish would erupt. But after so much bloodshed, even the Athenians were exhausted. As the war had receded, both Pittacus and the people had mellowed. Now that he was supreme ruler, secure in his power, Pittacus could be kinder. He could become a Wise Man. In fact, he was promoting himself as such through patronizing minstrels and artists and filling his court with philosophers. He wanted to be known as one of the Seven Sages after he died.

"Even Alcaeus might now come home with no fear," he told me. "But it seems he prefers Egypt. He was always a wanderer at heart." When he said that, I began to sob. He put his arms around me as if he had decided he was my real father.

"It is time for you to sing again."

"What's the use?" I said. "Song changes nothing. It does not stop war or bloodshed, or raise the dead, or prevent children from being snatched from their mothers, or allow love to last. All my life I have made songs. Now I am ready to be silent."

And I meant all this in my despair, but the muses still nudged my elbow from time to time and bade me try to sing. All my efforts came to naught. My heart was no longer in my craft.

I tried to write a song for my mother's passing, but I could not. I kept struggling with my farewells.

As we commit you to Persephone's dark bedroom, I began. *As wind shakes the mountain oaks, grief shakes my heart,* I attempted. But nothing was adequate to the pain. I was not an elegist after all, but a love poet, and love had fled forever.

When it came time to divide up my mother's jewels, Pittacus put them all out on a Lydian carpet in the courtyard of his house. Cleis, Rhodopis, and I were to take turns choosing pieces that we wanted. But whenever I selected a necklace or a ring, Rhodopis would stamp her foot and shout, "I was promised that!" Then she would fall down on the ground, screaming and pounding her fists.

"Don't tell me you would cry over a ring, Rhodopis," I said.

"I loved her! I loved her!" Rhodopis wailed. "I am crying for her— not for her jewels."

What did I care who got the majority of golden trinkets? I gave Rhodopis a necklace and ring she wanted and earrings that matched them. I gave her a golden dolphin clasp encrusted with jewels that my mother had often worn. I gave her earrings cunningly made as leaping dolphins and a diadem of gold that resembled olive leaves. I gave her earrings with rams' heads crafted in gold. No matter how much I gave, she screamed for more. At last, there was a golden snake necklace with ruby eyes and a tail that could cunningly affix to its neck. I remembered my mother wearing it when I was a child. She had worn it with matching snake earrings that Rhodopis now wore day and night.

"She was *my* mother!" I shouted. "Give them to Cleis at least. For myself I'll take nothing."

"I loved her like a mother!" Rhodopis wailed. "Besides, the earrings and the necklace belong together!" Now even I had to laugh. Rhodopis found nothing funny in her words. Instead, she fell to the floor again and pounded it. Eventually Pittacus had to come in and make the division himself. I got the golden chain with the tiny quinces dangling from it. I wear it every day. I often sleep in it.

But even death recedes in time. Sad as I was, I was happy to be back on my native island. I walked among the olive trees with Cleis, telling her of all my adventures, of my love for her father, Alcaeus, of my despair when she was taken away. I related the whole story of her fever and Isis' spell— leaving out my love story with Isis. (Children never want to know these things.) Did she believe my version of events? She wanted to, I know.

I visited the family vineyards—which Rhodopis had revived. I took over my grandparents' house in Eresus where my mother had died.

I had almost forgotten my calling. But my fame had spread as my songs were sung all over the Greek world. Families from Athens and Syracuse, even Lydia, wanted to send their daughters to me to learn the lyre and the art of making song. I became an accidental mentor to the next generation.

Cleis hated this. She had missed me so long that she could tolerate no loss of my attention now. She made fun of my students. She wanted me to live with her and care for her child—Hector, a beautiful little boy who was dark like me—rather than care for making songs. My grand- child melted my heart. I adored him. But I could not do what my mother had done and woo my grandchild away from his own mother. I loved him, but I knew he needed his mother more. Cleis could not understand my reserve. She thought I was holding back my love some- how. That was where our rift began.

But of course it did not begin there. It began with the slander that I had abandoned her—a slander perpetrated by Rhodopis. I had told Cleis the true story, but she only half believed me. She struggled with her feelings. She wanted to love me but she was afraid to be abandoned again. Very well, I told myself, she will come to it in time. She will real- ize how much I always loved her.

But no, as I settled into the role of mentor to beautiful young ladies from abroad—Dica, Gyrinno, another Anactoria, another Atthis, and another Gongyla—Cleis seethed with envy. I tried to explain to her that my students were no match for a *real* daughter, but she did not believe me. She wanted me to worship her body and soul and worship her child. And I did! But teaching saved my life. Without it I would have pined away for lack of the love of Alcaeus.

"You love Dica and Gyrinno more than me," Cleis would accuse.

"Absolutely not. I love you best, I always have."

"Then why do you need these silly students?" Cleis protested. "Anactoria will play you false. Gyrinno is vain as a peacock. Atthis has no talent for the lyre," Cleis protested.

"But if I am nothing but a grandmother, I will pine away," I said. "I need song to keep me whole. My teaching is my calling."

"Your grandchild is calling you," Cleis said. "Listen to his cries!"

"I will not neglect him, I promise you," I said. And Cleis sniffed resentfully.

I built a small temple in the grove behind my family's house and there we danced and sang our songs to Aphrodite. I had no doubt after my travels that she was the most potent of all the goddesses and I instructed my students in her worship.

"The gods hardly care about us," I told my students. "We must attract them with the beauty of our song and dance, tempt them with our sacrifices, and make ourselves worthy of their attention. To them our lives are so temporary that we are little more than leaves on a tree. They are concerned with their own intrigues. They love, war, build, destroy, blink and we are gone. If we wish to be more than falling leaves to them, we must sing so divinely they cannot but hear us.

In the grove behind my grandparents' house we burnt incense to Aphrodite and honored her with song and dance. We sacrificed the first fruits of our vineyards and olive trees. We piled up apples and peaches in her honor. We roasted the fat thighbones of white heifers bedecked with flowers and sprinkled with barley. We had contests for the most beautiful songs, the most beautiful dances, the most beautiful robes. On the warmest summer nights, we flung off our robes and danced naked under the moon, invoking Aphrodite.

From Sappho pressed is this honey I bring thee,
Sticky as love, nourishing as breast-milk to a baby,
Beautiful to Zeus as a maid who is not Hera,
Pleasing to Aphrodite as the stiff phallus of her lover.

How could we know we were being observed in our devotions? Rumors of our naked dancing drifted across the hills from Eresus to Mytilene. One line—*Mnasidica has a lovely body, lovelier even than soft Gyrinno's*—was quoted as proof of our debauchery. Rhodopis spread the rumor that I was training maenads to tear men and children apart with their bare hands. It was said that I had seduced my own daughter and now had moved on to the daughters of others.

Songs of mine were always quoted out of context. *My desire feeds on your beauty* was repeated all over the island. *May you sleep on your soft girl-friend's breasts* was another. It was true that some of my students evoked the greatest tenderness in me and wanted to die rather than leave me. But it was the suicide of Timas that started all the trouble.

Timas came to me from Lydia when she was thirteen. Plump, with reddish curls, she had a natural talent for singing and for the lyre. I poured all that I knew of my art into her. She blossomed under my care. It was as if nobody had ever encouraged her before, and she lapped it up as a cat laps milk. This was true of so many girls outside Lesbos. How much freedom I had taken for granted living here—even during the long war. There were so many places where women were treated little better than slaves.

Timas would look at me and say, "Sappho, when I grow to be a woman, I want to be just like you."

"You don't know the griefs I've tasted. Don't wish for what you cannot know."

"You are simply being modest. You are my hero. When I think the world is cruel to women, I think of you and how you've overcome all the adversities of a woman's life. You even have a beautiful daughter and a grandson who looks just like you. I wish with all my heart I were lucky enough to be your daughter!"

This excess of emotion worried me. When a heart is so open, it can accept arrows as well as honey. I was torn between my need for Timas' adulation and my fear that it would come to a bad end. Yet I loved her and she loved me. I taught her about pleasure as I had done with the amazon maidens and she gave her whole heart to me. I worried about how unstintingly she gave it.

• • •

TIMAS FLOURISHED in Eresus. She stayed with us for two years, growing in skill and courage. At first she imitated my style as they all did, but soon she came to have her own voice so that her lyric meters were crisp, playful, and lilting.

Then word came from her father in Sardis that she was to be married to a courtier who was a friend of his. The man was old and rich and loathsome—that old, old story. Timas wrote to her father, pleading to be allowed to stay in Lesbos. He wrote back that she was a disobedient daughter and had disappointed him.

I saw her struggle with this. Her mother had died bearing her and she was sure the same fate was to be hers. She was afraid of marriage and childbirth and she was afraid of losing her freedom. Who could blame her? Female education always provokes this paradox. We teach maidens to be free and then we enslave them to marriage.

"I do not want to disappoint my father, but I can't do as he asks," she wept. "I'd rather die than leave you!"

"You must pray to the gods and do what is in your heart," I said.

"But what did you do when you were young?" Timas asked. "It's said you ran away with Alcaeus."

"I cannot deny that."

"Then if you were a rebel—why do you expect obedience from me?"

"I only expect that you will be true to yourself. No one can ask more of you."

Timas threw her arms around my neck. "Sappho, help me to escape my father!" she cried.

"I can do everything but that," I said.

And then I told her what I always told girls of that age—that life is unpredictable, that the future cannot be calculated, that life is full of amazing surprises, good and bad—that death comes soon enough. I sounded like my own mother talking to me when I railed at being married to Cercylas! The irony of it! My mother was dead and I had become my mother! As I aged, I was even beginning to look like her. I would catch a sidelong glimpse of myself and think—there goes my mother.

Timas only *seemed* to be comforted by my words. She went down to the sea to swim with Dica. She braided herbs and flowers for Atthis' curls. She brought me as a gift an embroidered headband from Sardis. It was all an act.

We found her in the apple grove, hanging from the oldest tree by one of her gold-embroidered sashes from Sardis. Her feet bounced slightly as if they were dancing in air as they pointed down to a bed of purple hyacinths. On the highest branch of the apple tree, there remained one red fruit nobody could reach.

We cut her down, washed her lovingly, and threw locks of our own hair into the funeral pyre with her. They sizzled and burnt with an acrid smell—the smell of sacrificed youth.

The girls were desolate. They demanded a song for her, which we could sing as we sent her home. We put the urn aboard ship with this inscription:

> *This is the dust of Timas*
> *Who was led unmarried*
> *Into Persephone's dark bedroom.*
> *Her life was cut short*
> *Like our hair,*
> *Which, with newly sharpened steel,*
> *We, her companions, gave up.*

Word leaked out all over the island that one of Sappho's students had killed herself. That was the beginning of the end.

MY BROTHER CHARAXUS had become rather pudgy and was losing his hair. Rhodopis had grown into her soul and now looked on the outside the way she was on the inside. Not a pretty sight.

"Sappho," she said, "we are troubled by the rumors we hear about you and your students. It's said that one young woman hanged herself for love of you. We worry for your own good. We worry for your reputation."

"My reputation!" I spat out. "My reputation, like yours, has long been ruined. You know what they say in Naucratis: *'If your reputation is ruined, might as well have fun!'*"

Rhodopis batted her eyes innocently. "Nobody ever said a bad word about me till you included me in your indiscreet songs. Now it's not so easy to clear my name. But as a respected married woman and the wife of your brother, I must ask you to be more circumspect."

"Get out of here!" I screamed at Rhodopis and Charaxus. "And never come back again!"

If only Aesop were here to make a fable of it: *There is no more perfect prude than a reformed whore.*

24

After Timas

Being above the earth
Holds no pleasure anymore.
I long for the lotus-covered banks
Of Acheron.
—Sappho

THE FIRST DEATH of a contemporary strikes a group of friends like lightning. Grandparents die, parents die, warriors die in battle and wives in childbirth, but when a girl of fifteen takes her own life, her friends suddenly feel their mortality. Death was a myth before. Now it is a reality.

Dica asked, "Why did we not save her, Sappho?"

"Because we did not realize how deep was her despair," I said. "We cannot save everyone."

"Why? Why? Why?" Atthis cried.

"Because the gods are capricious and the spinners both spin and snip. Life is distributed unequally."

"Tell us we will never die!" cried Anactoria.

"If I told you that, I would be lying, and as your teacher I will never lie."

We huddled together for warmth in my big bed and reminisced about Timas' winning ways.

"Why did the gods allow death into the world?" asked Atthis.

"Because they are jealous of mortals and want to control our fates," I said. "Accept it and make songs about it. That is your best revenge."

Perhaps Timas' suicide shattered us because it was a harbinger of everyone's fate. My students tasted freedom, only to have it snatched away. The plan had been to make them skillful adepts of the arts before they turned good wives. But wives in those days were little better than slaves. And art teaches liberty. It is a paradox. We teach maidens to sing and then we give them husbands to silence them. This breeds a desperation that leads to clinging crushes, simultaneous menstruation, hysteria, melancholy. A group of young women together is sweet yet incendiary. There is so much smothered passion threatening to explode.

The more we closed ourselves off from strangers, the more the rumors flew about us. Rhodopis had been poisoning all of Mytilene against us. Charaxus was using her slanders to keep from paying my share of profits from the family vineyards. Whatever dangers I had braved among strangers, my family was a more insidious foe.

Even Pittacus came to call on me in Eresus to warn me of the trouble I was courting.

"Your mother loved you, Sappho, and I swore to her to pardon and protect you, but the rumors that now fly about you in Mytilene make my promise hard to keep. Your fame is the glory of Lesbos, but it is turning to scandal as I watch."

"Since when is it a crime for girls to sing together? In my youth we were always famed for our swaying choruses of young girls."

"Sappho, you've been away a long time. While you explored the world, many changes occurred in Lesbos. There was an outbreak of fever that carried away half our citizens. Some said the Athenians and their poisoned spears caused it. In the Troad they were reputed to anoint their spearheads with offal from rotting corpses. Some said the fever was spread by the influx of slaves brought home from the war. Thousands died of this fever, vomiting blood, their faces turning black as earth. Those of us who remained—all of us—became less carefree than in former times. Symposia began to be seen as dangerous places of infection. Songs were snares. Even the pageants of dancing maidens were curtailed. People became less fond of the lyric art and saw it as a danger. They wanted patriotic songs, songs of war and battle, songs of righteousness and revenge. Your mother and I bemoaned this—but we understood. The carefree Lesbos we had known was gone. The climate here has changed. Once we were famed for our easy and luxurious life, now our people are more careful. A long war changes everything."

"Then we must bring back the Lesbos of old!"

"You can't bring back the past. The carefree Lesbos of my youth, where girls sang to girls and the entire world was made for wine and song, will never come again. We have other struggles now. We have to repopulate our island. We can't afford the luxuries of old. Oh, nobody regrets it more than I do. But we must be realistic."

"Does that mean song is superfluous?"

"Not all song, Sappho, but the sort of song that celebrates love alone is old-fashioned. We need songs now to inspire the people to community solidarity and unity, songs that celebrate the great *polis,* not songs for lovers alone. Love is selfish. Rebuilding our city is of the essence. Pray teach your girls to sing of civic pride, of Mytilene and its glory, of the joys of wars won and peace achieved. Such songs are needed now—not silly love songs. Look—you are a great singer—you can sing of anything."

Had I not heard all this before?

"Pittacus—what would you have me sing?"

"Songs about my triumphs in the war—that sort of thing."

"And if I go on singing of love?"

"I'm afraid I'll have to banish you again—and all your girls."

WHEN I WENT to see Cleis, it was no better. I began to see that my fame embarrassed her. When fragments of my songs were quoted, she blushed.

"I wish you could write *other* kinds of songs, Mother—or else just be a grandmother. Hector needs you. Why do you have to write songs *at all?*"

And I tried to be a good grandmother. I would stay in my daughter's house, trying to make myself useful, trying not to offend—and suddenly she would explode at me:

"All through my childhood, I was mocked for being your 'golden flower'! Everywhere I went, your words preceded me. I hated it! I hated you!"

The longer I stayed with Cleis, the sadder I became. I loved her with all my heart, but my love embarrassed her. The world had changed. The love I offered her was out of fashion.

She would explode at me. I would apologize to her. Then we would both cry and embrace each other and promise to love each other forever. She looked so much like Alcaeus that just being with her made me long for him. I would go back to Eresus and my students with a heavy heart. Of all the people in the world I needed to have understand me, Cleis was the one. There had been a time when I sought my mother's love—now I sought my daughter's. It eluded me.

I bounced back and forth between Eresus and Mytilene, dreaming of winning my daughter's approval. When I was away from her I ached, and when I was with her I ached even more.

We were so different. She was a beauty and she knew how to manipulate men to do her bidding. She could toss her blond curls and smile to get what she wanted. I had always won love with my songs, with my fierce energy and soft sensuality. And now my songs were suspect, and so was my sensuality. They were both aspects of each other, both aspects of Aphrodite—and now they were banned!

My students tried to comfort me. I would take to my bed in despair and they would try to lure me to get up:

"Sappho—if you will not get up and let us look at you, I shall never love you again!"

So said Atthis (I used her phrase in a song). She urged me to walk with her and Anactoria in Mytilene "like a mother surrounded by her daughters." Sometimes we did and people would stop and stare. They would rush up to me to tell me about my songs and how the songs had affected them, about the lovers they had seduced with my words and the way they had sung my song to Cleis to their own daughters.

"See, Sappho," Anactoria would say, "you are loved still. People have your words by heart. That is the true test of your genius—not the tyrant's criticism. You write for the people, Sappho, not for your daughter or Pittacus." But her words only half comforted me.

Atthis had grown from a graceless monkey-faced child with wild hair to a beautiful young woman in the time she had been with us. She had learned to make songs and sing them. She had learned to please her listeners. And I was proud of her. She had begun to comfort me for the loss of Timas. But just when she was beginning to mend my heart and make me mourn less for Cleis' coldness, she left me for a rival teacher called Andromeda and renounced everything I had taught her.

> *Andromeda in her vulgar finery*
> *Has put a torch to your heart!*

Andromeda had given up writing of love in order to write political songs that pleased Pittacus. When Atthis went over to Andromeda's side, she too began to spread ugly rumors about me. At first I thought it was because she could not stand to share me with the other maidens; she was jealous like my real daughter. But little by little I began to understand that she had gone over to Andromeda's side out of naked ambition. She saw that my songs were out of favor with the tyrant and she wanted to trim her sails to a more favorable wind. Andromeda was asked to sing at all the patriotic festivals and I was not. Andromeda's songs were in fashion and mine were not. Andromeda was given honors and prizes and I was not. What did anyone care that Andromeda had no talent? She reflected the vulgar spirit of the vulgar age. Oh, the people loved me, but the powers had decreed me irrelevant. The people sang my songs, but they could not do so publicly. Atthis saw this unfold and she fled to Andromeda.

Men could break your bones, but girls could break your heart. That was what I was discovering. The fierceness of women was not found only among the amazons.

Timas had loved me truly, but Timas was dead. Anactoria was engaged to be married and would be leaving soon. When I had seen her talking and laughing and flirting with her intended, my heart cracked in my bosom.

> *The man who sits opposite you*
> *Seems fortunate as the gods*
> *Listening to your sweet voice,*
> *Your lovely laughter*
> *Which sets my heart trembling*
> *In my breast.*
> *When I so much as glance at you—*
> *My tongue goes numb.*
> *I cannot speak.*
> *A subtle fire*
> *Steals beneath my flesh.*
> *My eyes are blind.*
> *My ears hum.*
> *Sweat pours from me.*
> *Trembling seizes me all over.*
> *I am greener than grass,*
> *And I seem to be*
> *A little short of dying.*
> *But I endure it all*
> *For love of you.*

Atthis had defected to my rival and Rhodopis made sure everyone in Mytilene knew it. New girls would come and go. They would suck me dry and leave the husk. No sooner would a girl blossom in song than she would be snatched away by some unworthy man who appreciated nothing I had taught her.

When I thought of this, I wanted to die, to see *the lotus-covered banks/ Of Acheron* as I sang in one of my most melancholy songs. Death beckoned to me. I felt I had lived long enough. I had lost everyone I truly cared for—my mother, my daughter, Alcaeus, Isis, Praxinoa, Aesop. My life seemed soaked in sadness.

Then Phaon appeared, with his agate eyes and his voice like molten honey. The first time I clapped eyes on him, something in me said: *Beware*. I listened to that voice and pretended that his black ringlets and shoulders like an Adonis did not move me. I played the game of indifference so well that he increasingly humbled himself before me.

Phaon was a rough youth, who plied a ferry between Mytilene and the mainland, but he was beautiful and he knew it. He put himself entirely at my disposal and would ferry me and my students around the island from Eresus to Mytilene and back again. He refused all pay.

"It is an honor to be your boatman," he insisted. "Your songs are payment enough." And he would sing to us as he rowed. He always sang my love songs, and he sang them so well it made me blush.

He slept in his boat pulled up on the Eresus beach near my family's house. He did little favors for us—cutting firewood, carrying heavy things—but he refused to come inside. Sometimes we would offer him food and he would take a crust of bread and go and eat it in his boat. He was crafty. He was biding his time.

One night, when the moon was full and was spilling blue moonlight all over the beach in Eresus, I walked down to his boat, which he had tented with a ragged sail. By the light of an oil lamp, I saw him scratching on an Egyptian papyrus with a reed. When I looked closer, I saw he was copying my songs.

"What are you doing?" I asked.

"Making you immortal," he said. Then he realized at once how conceited that sounded and he corrected himself: "The gods made your songs immortal—I am only copying them. The more I copy them, the more I see their genius."

"I fear you are flattering me," I said, enjoying it even as I complained of it. The boy looked up at me with a tear in his eye. "These songs will last forever."

I gave a deep sigh and strode away. Oh, I wanted to believe this was more than flattery, but I knew better.

There is nothing like a pretty boy who adores you to mend your heart when you have been undone by the treachery of women.

I have loved men and I have loved women and I can say that men are more transparent to love. Men are ruled only by their pricks, which are simple and blunt—but the moon rules women. And the moon is a body that gives back borrowed light. Bodily lovemaking with women is tender and sweet, but the minds of women are tricky as moonlight. Men do not scheme in love as women do. What am I saying? Phaon was both tender as a woman and twisted in his scheming. He sweated moon-dew. The drop of moonlight that swelled on the head of his phallus when he became aroused must have been made of magic potion. When later I licked it off, I grew weak as Circe's sleepy beasts. He schemed so patiently it didn't seem like scheming. I resisted and resisted and resisted until I could resist no more.

APHRODITE: *The gifts I have given Phaon will test her to the limit and—*
ZEUS: *She will fail!*
APHRODITE: *Not this Sappho! My follower is strong—stronger than all the mortal women you have raped.*
ZEUS: *I'll win this bet. I always win.*
APHRODITE: *Not this time, Father.*

I had gone back to see Cleis and my grandchild again. Little Hector would throw his arms around my neck and cling until I could hardly breathe. I understood the desire to kidnap a grandchild then. But I would never do it. Grandsons and grandmothers have such a strong and simple bond, while the link between daughters and mothers is often so convoluted. I felt rage toward my mother for leaving us with such a legacy. She had no right to do that! She had taken the prerogatives of the gods upon herself.

I thought of a woman I had once met in Syracuse who had allowed her husband to take her newborn daughter out on a hill to be exposed to the elements.

"How could you have permitted such a thing?" I asked her.

"Because I knew that without her father's love, she would never thrive and blossom into a good life."

"But he would have *come* to love her—how could he *not*? She would have won his heart. Daughters always win their fathers' hearts in time."

And the woman began to weep disconsolately. I had broken her with my blunt words. She had found a way to live with her sadness and I had snatched it from her with my unwelcome truth. Lies are sweeter.

Then I thought of Isis and how she had saved Cleis' young life. I thought of Alcaeus, who had never really known his daughter. And I cried and cried, clutching my grandson to me, wondering if I would ever have a granddaughter with whom I could remake this sad legacy—and the world!

My beautiful daughter Cleis strode in.

"Mother, whenever you come to see Hector, he clings and will not let you go. And when you leave, I can do nothing with him for days and days."

"Are you telling me not to come?"

"Not at all, Mother, but I wish you would be less emotional with him, more disciplined. I wish you would not encourage all this emotion. It makes my life difficult. It makes the nurses complain. You stir him up and then you go away."

"I will try not to stir him up."

"You can't help it. It's your nature. You aren't happy unless people are weeping and raging around you. You have no moderation in you. Your mother always warned me about that. She said that I should learn calmness, as you never did. Your mind is like a tempest stirring up the whitecaps on the sea. Even Pittacus said that about you."

"I will try to do better, Cleis," I said, "but I come from a different world."

"Then join this world," Cleis said.

"Perhaps I cannot—what then?"

PHAON WAS WAITING in his boat, so I left Mytilene and I started back to Eresus without thinking very much about it.

It was dark. We sailed by moonlight. The sea was full of little white-caps, but I didn't care. I almost wished to drown and be at the end of my troubles.

"You seem sad, my lady," Phaon said.

"All my dreams have come to naught," I said.

"But look what you have given the world."

"It's not worth it to live with so much pain."

"Your songs make everyone happy but you," Phaon said.

I bowed my head.

"Andromeda is a fraud," Phaon said.

At this I perked up.

"She goes around Mytilene in that hideous purple chiton emblazoned with gold embroidery and sings those idiotic songs about the greatness of Pittacus and the wonders of war. People laugh at her privately, but they are afraid to do so in public when the tyrant has so honored her."

"They know nothing of song. All they know is about honors and prizes," I said.

"Not true, my lady. The people of Lesbos have always loved song. It is in their natures. We are all the heirs of Orpheus."

I thought of Orpheus in the Land of the Dead, holding his head in his hands and speaking of the fate of singers. "Torn to bits—but all the bits still sing!" Prophecy!

"I think you are too trusting in the wisdom of the people, Phaon. They don't know good from bad, beautiful from ugly. All they know is what is anointed by power. If Pittacus says Andromeda is a great singer, then she's a great singer. If he says she has true genius, it doesn't matter what she sings. The people bow down to power, even in song."

"But in their homes, they sing *your* songs. In their heads, they sing your songs. In their hearts, they sing your songs."

With that he reached out and touched me on the back with such tenderness it set me aflame.

His touch was lightning. You always know a future lover by touch even if he or she only touches you in the most innocent of places. Phaon looked at me as if I were Aphrodite.

"You are so beautiful," he said.

"Beautiful I am not," I said.

"Your beauty is within, but it still sends a subtle flame under my flesh."

"I seem to recall having written that somewhere. Phaon, be wise, do not romance a woman old enough to be your mother."

"It seems you are younger than *I*!" he said. Oh, what a smooth talker this one was!

"Take me back to Eresus," I said. "This is no time for love between a gray woman and a green boy."

"Then when?"

"Probably never," I said. "Cast off."

On the moonlight sail around the island I refused to speak to Phaon. I looked at the beauty of the sea, the beauty of my island, and thought of all my travels, all my loves. The last thing I needed was a pretty boy who thought to ensnare me with flattery. So what if he was my enemy's enemy? Maybe he was honest when he spoke slightingly of Andromeda. Maybe he was trying to win my favor. Who cared? He was not Alcaeus.

When we arrived at Eresus, he helped me out of the bark.

"I fear I have offended you, my lady," he muttered, eyes downcast so I could admire his shiny black lashes on his tawny cheeks.

"Not at all," I said.

"I would die rather than offend you," he said.

"Don't offer to die so readily. It comes soon enough."

Phaon fell to his knees and kissed the hem of my chiton.

"Please, get up," I said.

"I cannot. I want to be your slave," he said. "Brand me, chain me, command me, all I want is to serve you. My life is meaningless unless I serve you."

"Get up, Phaon, I hate this sort of talk," I said. "I freed the only slave I loved. I don't want another one."

"Then is there a chance that you might love me?" he said, leaping to his feet. He stood above me. His muscled arms were tan from working on the water. When he smiled, the little crinkles at the corners of his mouth seemed to have smiles of their own.

He took me in his immense arms and stroked my back again and again. The flame under my skin grew hotter. My eyes glazed. My fingers trembled. My ears hummed as if a swarm of bees flew toward them. Sweat poured from my armpits. I wanted to say no, but I could not speak. His touch had made me dumb. I shivered and burnt at the same time. Greener than grass? No. But all logic was gone. It was as if my tongue were amputated at the root. Why not? my delta asked. And there was no organ to refute it!

That was how we began. He wormed his way into my life. I had thought I had had enough of love, was sick of love, sated by love—but this beautiful young creature gave a freshness and carelessness to my life I thought I had lost forever. Since my mother died, I had wanted to die myself. Phaon banished that cloud.

He copied out my songs, cut firewood, and sailed me here and there. He pruned the olive trees and vines on my property. He made himself useful in the most cheerful way. And he warmed my bed. Oh, how he warmed my bed!

Shall we talk about that? All lovers are different and all lovers are the same. This man knew his power and he had honed it. He could have seduced Aphrodite herself! Perhaps he had!

He was not Alcaeus, but he had his own sweetness—the sweetness of youth. If he was false or conniving, he hid it well. But he had something I had never known before except in maidens. He had the most powerful drug—the drug of youth. His skin seemed as fresh as my grandson's. His hair was as shiny as a young centaur's mane. Phaon made me understand the seductions of Zeus. Phaon made me know why Aphrodite loved Adonis. In fact, I *felt* like Aphrodite with Adonis. *Tear your garments, maidens, and weep for Adonis!* Phaon was so beautiful, he made me weep.

And then there was the matter of his potency. A boy of twenty never tires. The phallus empties and fills again. The phallus stands up, lies down, and stands up again before you know it. No wonder even Alcaeus loved pretty boys. I was beginning to understand the attraction.

ZEUS: *You see! True wisdom dawns in our heroine.*
APHRODITE: *Wisdom comes before the fall, you think—but she will surprise you!*
ZEUS: *Never! Not with this boy and his indefatigable implement! Hah! Even the cleverest women are brought low by love!*
APHRODITE: *You'll see!*

25

The Binding of the Babe

As long as there is breath in my lungs,
I shall love—
And even after
—Sappho

Was I happy with Phaon? Perhaps I was distracted from my grief more than I was happy. And he made himself indispensable to me. Copying out my songs was the least of it; he really did make himself my willing slave. He took over all the things in my life I hated to do—arguing with Charaxus over my share of the wine crop, defending me with Rhodopis when she tried to take the furniture that had belonged to my mother and grandparents, ferrying my students around the island, organizing their travel home, dealing with their parents on my behalf. He made my life easier. In fact, he coddled me.

"If you ever left me, how would I survive?" I used to joke to Phaon. It was only half a joke.

And I did not give up visiting Cleis and trying to make peace with her. That was my deepest desire.

Every week I would sail to Eresus in Phaon's boat and stay with Cleis for three days until Phaon came back to fetch me. In the meantime, he took care of the students and their needs.

Hector was five by now and Cleis desperately wanted a daughter—but she kept losing babies. It seemed she could not keep a pregnancy. I privately thought this was because she was unhappy with her husband, but I never said this to her. We consulted midwives together. The best midwife in Mytilene was said to be a woman who called herself Artemisia after the goddess Artemis, who protected women in childbirth. (Immortal Artemis was a fierce virgin who hated intercourse and consequently the men who subjected women to the perils of childbirth.) Her devotee Artemisia was about my age—old!—and she lived in a great house on the harbor in Mytilene. She was famed far and wide. Her practice had made her rich. But she did not hate men. Quite the contrary.

Artemisia was not easy to see, even if you were the adopted daughter of Pittacus and the daughter of the singer Sappho. She had many women waiting for her counsel. I had sent Phaon again and again to plead with her for an earlier audience. He must have bewitched her with his beauty, because finally we were to be given one.

Artemisia was tall and handsome, with a square jaw and flashing dark eyes. She wore her dark hair coiled in serpents of gold. Her clasps were fashioned like gold serpents and her golden sandals were entwined with golden serpents. At first sight she reminded me of Herpetia the snake goddess, but I tried to put that out of my head. We needed her—Cleis and I.

CLEIS TOLD Artemisia her sad tale of lost pregnancies while I sat silently, listening. Artemisia asked questions that Cleis found embarrassing.

"After your husband makes love to you, do you lie still without jumping up out of bed?"

"What do you mean?"

"I mean—do you run away? Do you run back to your own quarters?"

"Why would I do that?" Cleis asked.

"I don't know," Artemisia said. "Some women don't like their husbands very much."

"But I love him like a dutiful wife!"

"But are you *fond* of him?"

"Why does this matter?"

"Some doctors believe that the male fluid determines a boy, while the female determines a girl. If you are nervous or jump up after love, your fluid may not be sweet enough."

Cleis leaned forward in wonderment. "Astonishing," she said. "Mother—will you wait outside?"

"Of course," I said and I left to wait outside among the desperate young women—one of whom recognized me.

"I dream of a golden flower like your Cleis," said the woman. "I sing that song each night before bed, hoping for a golden girl. I already have three sons—but who shall be with me when I am old if there's no daughter?"

"I am grateful for your words," I said. "Thank you." The woman seemed crestfallen that I had not said more, but I had heard this so many times from strangers while the same song embarrassed my own daughter. Silly me. Families never appreciate what comes from your muse. Why should they?

Everywhere I went, this sort of thing happened to me, and yet my songs were still out of favor with Pittacus and forbidden to be sung at public festivals. Andromeda had risen like a terrible goddess over us all. She and the maidens who followed her sang her dreadful songs at every festival, at every symposium. Yes, they had revived the symposium in Lesbos, but even *there* no one dared to sing anything but songs to Pittacus and his warrior glory. Glorifying the warrior-ruler is such an easy emotion. It covers a multitude of sins. And a multitude of clumsy songs with witless words.

I waited while Cleis confided in Artemisia. Better that I was not there to hear. Finally I was called back into the room.

Artemisia was instructing Cleis about a magic spell involving red binding thread and birds' eggs. It seemed that if you bound three sparrows' eggs in a nest with red thread and invoked Aphrodite and Artemis, you might persuade a pregnancy to last.

"Eggs bound to the nest will never fall," said Artemisia. "But your intention must be pure. You must cleanse yourself for seven days before you perform the ritual; you must gather only the largest eggs of sparrows, sacred to Aphrodite for their fecundity. If you cannot find sparrows' eggs, you may, in special cases, use the eggs of doves. Both sparrows and doves are sacred to the Cyprian. You must spin the red thread at your own loom. You must gather the nest from the highest tree on your land. If you will do these things and lie still after love, perhaps I can help you, but only if it is the will of the gods."

Cleis said, "I will do all these things."

"Then come back in two weeks with the eggs, the nest, the thread."

"I will," said Cleis.

I sent one of Artemisia's slaves out to fetch Phaon and the bag of gold we had brought for Artemisia.

In a little while, Phaon appeared, bowed low to Artemisia and gave her the bag. A look passed between them that made me think they knew each other intimately—or perhaps I was imagining this.

Artemisia looked in the bag, saw that it contained gold coins from Lydia, and seemed not wholly pleased. "I shall also require *oboloi* to be sent to me. Send them with the boy!" She nodded at Phaon, who lowered his head.

"How do you two know each other?" I asked.

"What makes you think we do?" said Artemisia. "Return in two weeks with the objects I have commanded! And purify yourself before you come!"

I STAYED in Mytilene then to help Cleis prepare for her next audience with Artemisia and sent Phaon back to Eresus to fetch the *oboloi* and attend to my students.

The red thread was not a problem to spin, but it was the wrong time of year for a sparrow's nest and sparrows' eggs. We would have to wait months for sparrows' eggs! And doves' eggs too! Was this part of Artemisia's intention? Cleis was frantic.

"Why didn't you think to tell her that sparrows' eggs could not be found this time of year?" Cleis fretted.

"It slipped my mind. I just never thought of it! Sometimes the most obvious thing is impossible to remember."

"Mother! Don't you care about me at all?"

"More than life itself."

"Then we must find sparrows' eggs out of season!"

"Where will we find sparrows' eggs out of season?"

"I don't know! Perhaps your *boy* can find them!" She said this with considerable derision.

We went back to Cleis' house, where she proceeded to weep uncontrollably. I had sent Phaon away to Eresus, but Phaon was the only one who could scour the island of Lesbos for me to get sparrows' or doves' eggs out of season. I ran to the harbor and commandeered a boat to follow Phaon to Eresus. We encountered fog and rough seas and when we finally arrived in Eresus we were much the worse for wear.

Phaon was not there. None of my students knew where he was. I remembered the look that had passed between him and Artemisia and I had a sickish feeling, but I suppressed it. The next morning he appeared, begged forgiveness for his lateness—the storm! the fog! the seas!—and we sailed back to Mytilene so that I could see Cleis and try to comfort her.

In the boat I looked at Phaon coldly and hated myself for having gotten involved with him. He was no Alcaeus! No Aesop, even. He was a vain boy who was much too proud of his indefatigable phallus. He was no man. He was no hero. He was any woman's plaything for a price. My coldness penetrated the air between us. He felt my disgust.

"What can I do to comfort you?" he asked.

"Nothing," I said.

"Sappho, please, I cannot bear your anger."

"Why do you think I am angry? I am more sad than angry."

"What can I do?" he asked, stroking my back as he had that first time.

"I fear there is nothing you can do to melt my mood. I am angry at myself, at fate, at the gods," I said.

"Then give me a task. May I fetch the golden fleece? May I stare down the gorgon? May I kill a cyclops? May I climb to the top of Olympus and plead with the gods on your behalf?"

"It will do no good," I said despondently. "What I need most in life, I have carelessly thrown away. When love is gone, nothing can make up for it, not even the elixir of sweet youth." Alcaeus was in my mind then, as he always was. He was the emptiness in my heart, the queasiness at the pit of my stomach, the throbbing pain in my temples.

"But I love you so," Phaon said.

"Even if it were true," I said, "it would not matter."

We spoke no more on that trip and we parted in silence.

In two weeks Cleis and I returned to Artemisia with the red thread but without the nest and eggs.

"There are no sparrows' eggs in this season," Cleis said. "Nor doves'."

"If this is the strength of your intention, you will never be a mother again!" Artemisia said. Cleis began to sob.

"Don't cry," Artemisia said. "I have the nest of eggs, but it will cost you twenty *oboloi*.

"I have no *oboloi* here," I said.

"Then send your boy with them," said Artemisia.

She produced a sparrow's nest with three eggs in it and, taking the red thread from Cleis, began to bind each egg to the nest with Cleis' red thread, chanting:

> *Bind me a babe.*
> *Bind me a daughter,*
> *Give me your heart,*
> *Immortal Artemis!*
> *Bind me a heart,*
> *Bind me a daughter.*
> *Babes can be bought*
> *But I would hatch mine.*
> *Let her be blond,*
> *Let her be beautiful,*
> *Let her sing like her grandmother,*
> *Have wit like her grandfather.*
> *May the blessings rain down!*

May the harvest be rich!
Bind me a daughter!
Bind me a babe.

"How do you know the grandfather of Cleis' babe-to-be?" I asked Artemisia.

"Everyone knows it was the witty Alcaeus and not your witless husband Cercylas who begot your babe! Alcaeus is a legend in Mytilene. He has long been banished, but the people still speak of him—and privately sing his songs, though they are publicly forbidden."

"Mother! You are interrupting the spell!" Cleis hissed. "Hush!"

Artemisia repeated the spell, twice. I knew we would have to pay for it thrice.

When the spell was done, Cleis took the nest and eggs and secreted them under her chiton. She was to sleep with them under her pillow for seven nights.

Artemisia took me aside. "Would you have news of Alcaeus?" she asked.

"Gladly!"

"Then come back to me alone!"

"When?"

"As soon as you can!"

"Let me escort my daughter home and I will return!"

Artemisia winked at me. She really did look like Herpetia the snake goddess. My blood froze. Had she transformed my dear Alcaeus into a serpent? I wanted him back in any form at all!

26

The Curse of Beautiful Men

Some say a line of ships
Is the most beautiful thing
On the dark earth—
But I say it is what you love!
—SAPPHO

OH, TO HEAR news of Alcaeus! I wanted to return to see Artemisia immediately, but first I was pressed into grandmotherly duties. Cleis was upset and needed me to take care of Hector. Of course I complied. It was my joy to take my darling five-year-old grandson out walking in Mytilene.

We went to the harbor to see the boats from all over the world. Boats from Egypt and Phoenicia, boats from Lydia, Samos, Chios, Crete. We stared at the sailors working in the whipping winds and I thought about my seaborne adventures. I missed my old soul and sea mates Alcaeus, Praxinoa, and Aesop, but I also knew I was lucky to have had such a variegated life. I thought of my travels and I smiled to myself. A singer must have something to sing about and the gods had given me a cornucopia of loves and adventures. Ah, if only I could have kept Alcaeus! The more time elapsed, the more I missed him. Phaon was a callow boy. He was skillful in bed but lacked the cleverness to keep me.

He was no Alcaeus. Alcaeus was a philosopher and singer as well as a lover. Phaon was just an ambitious youth. When the lovemaking was over, he bored me.

APHRODITE: *You see, a woman like Sappho needs more than a stiff phallus!*
ZEUS: *She needs a touch of my thunderbolt. That's all she needs. I'd take the daughter, but the mother's too old for me now!*
APHRODITE: *You old goat! What makes you think the daughter would want you? Besides, Sappho loves Alcaeus; she'll never play him false again. I'll see to that!*
ZEUS: *Both Hephaestus and I know how much you value loyalty!*
APHRODITE: *Like father, like daughter!*

Wasn't it possible Alcaeus and I would meet again somewhere, somehow? This *could* not be the end of so great a love! Great loves have legs and wings. They are substantial. They do not dissipate so easily. Great loves do not end because of a callow boy or a callow girl. Great loves have staying power. Or so I told myself.

We wandered around the quay in the whipping wind. Hector could not take his eyes off the boats.

"When I am big, I will sail the seas!" he said, less in baby prattle than big-boy speech. "I can say a poem about the sea. Want to hear it?"

"Yes, my darling boy."

Hector stood tall in the furious wind of the harbor and recited:

This wave repeats the one before!
It will take much time
To bale it out!
Let us strengthen the ship's sides
And race into a safe harbor!
Let not soft fear
Seize our strong hearts!
Let every man be steadfast!
Our noble fathers

Who lie beneath the earth,
The earth, the earth, the earth . . .

Here he faltered and spoke baby prattle again. "Grandmother, I can't remember!"

"Splendid! You take my breath away! And do you know the way the song ends?"

He shook his curls.

So I sang out:

Let us not disgrace our noble fathers
Who lie beneath the earth.
They built our city and our spirits!
Let us not bow down to tyranny!

"And do you know who wrote that song of valor and the sea?"

Hector shook his head. His baby cheeks wobbled.

"It was . . ." Here I stopped, suddenly afraid. Should I tell the child it was his own grandfather, Alcaeus—or might that get the boy in trouble? I decided to wait till Hector was older to tell the whole tale. Perhaps by then Pittacus would no longer be in power. Oh, Pittacus had said he pardoned Alcaeus, but Alcaeus had still not returned. Did he know something ominous I did not?

"It was a great singer of Aeolic Greek—but his name I cannot remember! Where did you learn that song, my beautiful boy?"

"From my nurse! She taught it to me when we first sailed to Pyrrha."

So it was true that the people still sang the songs of Alcaeus! Thank the gods!

Already my darling boy was getting ready to be a man. Next year, he would leave the women's quarters and start his education as an aristocrat of Mytilene. He would be a cupbearer like my brothers and go on to study statecraft and war, how to be eloquent at a symposium and in the agora, how to defend the *polis* and subjugate women! Impossible that this sweet little boy should grow up into a tyrant.

"Hector—do you know how much I love you?" I asked.

"How much?" he asked.

"More than sunlight and honey!"

"More than fish?"

"Much more than *fish*!"

"More even than eels from over the seas?"

"*Much* more than eels!" I picked him up in my arms and hugged him. What a dear little boy!

At that moment, I saw Phaon coming out of Artemisia's house on the harbor. He ducked his head and tried to avoid me, but I boldly ran up to him with the child in my arms.

"What are you doing here? I thought you were to look after the students!"

"I had come to deliver the *oboloi*. I will return to Eresus right away."

I looked at him skeptically. "How could you get to Eresus and back again in this wind?"

"On the wings of love and duty, my lady," Phaon said.

"More love? Or more duty?" I said cynically.

"Equal measures of both."

"Fine, let us return to Artemisia's house and see if what you say is true."

Was I jealous? I asked myself. How could I be jealous when Phaon actually meant so little to me? He had hurt my pride with his lying. It was clear that he thought he could romance my students and Artemisia without my knowing. I suppose I was angry to be taken for a fool.

We entered her house, where I demanded to see Artemisia at once. At first her slaves demurred, but then, realizing it was *I*, they ushered me in with the child in my arms and Phaon by my side.

Artemisia was surprised we had come back so soon.

"Show me the *oboloi* Phaon brought for you! I want to be sure they are the right ones!"

Without a pause, Artemisia produced the *oboloi*.

"Good," I said. "I am happy Phaon is so efficient."

"He is a *good* boy," Artemisia said, without a trace of irony.

"Go back to Eresus," I said to Phaon, "and tell my students I will be back soon. Come to fetch me in a week."

"Very well, my lady," said Phaon, bowing low and taking his leave.

"A beautiful fellow," said Artemisia.

"*Too* beautiful," I said.

"He looks like a *kouros* made by the greatest sculptor," Artemisia said.

"Agreed," I said, "but I worry that he knows it all too well."

"Ah," said Artemisia, "beautiful men are a blessing and yet a curse. When we find them beautiful, so does everyone else. It is said that Alcaeus suffered that fate when young."

"What *of* Alcaeus? You promised to tell me." Artemisia was quiet for a moment, simply gazing at me. I could hear the abacus clicking in her head. Should she sell the information like her sparrows' eggs or give it for free, hoping for even greater future gain? She paused and thought. Then she decided on the latter.

"A client of mine has just now come from Delphi, where she saw Alcaeus. He spoke of yearning to return to Lesbos. He spoke of you, Sappho, with great longing."

"He did?"

"Yes. He was seen in Delphi traveling with two friends—one a dark-skinned former slave who makes fables and another former slave, who tells the world she is queen of the amazons and needs to know the future of her people. It is said that a centaur accompanied them— which must be rubbish, since there are no centaurs except in legend."

"I know some very wise centaurs—wiser than men."

"Remarkable," said Artemisia, clearly taking me for a madwoman but refusing to battle on this account when more *oboloi* were at stake.

My heart began to flutter like a trapped bird. Sweat poured from my armpits. My skin prickled. A shiver raced down my spine.

"Tell me more!"

"More I cannot tell. All I know is that the woman seen with him had but one breast and a brand on her forehead like an escaped slave. She was no mistress, but a boon companion to Alcaeus. And this other man—he had a dusky complexion and a long white beard. As I said earlier, he is a fabulist."

"Aesop—the famous maker of wise fables—do you not *know* him?

He is famed throughout the Greek-speaking world! As famed as Alcaeus."

"I can make my own fables," Artemisia said with a laugh. "Who needs a *slave* to make them?"

Artemisia was a rather vulgar woman who thought song and fable were quite superfluous unless they earned political power. Or *oboloi*.

"Is this your grandson?"

"Yes—the joy of my life!"

"And now all you need is a granddaughter!" Artemisia laughed and laughed—rather cruelly, I thought. "What will you pay for one?"

"I have already paid dearly."

"Yes, but there is one more thing I might do to grant your wish."

"What is that?"

"I cannot say. Power spoken dissipates like fog."

"How much?"

"I will not charge you until the babe is born and it is a daughter. I will take that risk."

Surely this was a trick. Surely the treacherous Artemisia had something up her sleeve. Still, I decided to risk it.

"I am a betting woman. So be it."

"Sappho, you will not be sorry."

"Whenever anyone says I will not be sorry, I *know* I shall be! But do your magic! I will take the chance. With the help of the gods, all will turn out well!"

APHRODITE: *You see! She puts her life in our hands. Let us not disappoint her!*

ZEUS: *What do I see? I see a poor deluded woman! An* old *woman! Who cares about an old woman?*

APHRODITE: *I will* make *you care when I win my bet!*

ZEUS: *Daughter, I doubt it. When you have lived as long as I have and had as many silly women, you know the species far too well to have any illusions about their common sense.*

APHRODITE: *Sappho is* different *from other women.*

ZEUS: *Hardly. She is just like Leda with whom I played the swan,*

Europa with whom I played the bull, and even Metis the titaness. I fooled even her! She was said to be invincible, yet I conquered even her. And my daughter Athena, born from my own skull, is here on Mount Olympus to prove it!
APHRODITE: *Sappho will surprise even you!*
ZEUS: *No woman surprises me—not even Hera—that scheming bitch.*
APHRODITE: *Did anyone ever tell you that you* hate *women?*
ZEUS: *Me? I love them. Look at how many I've bedded!*
APHRODITE: *But none of them twice—or so I've been told.*

"Very well," said Artemisia, rubbing her hands together. "Do I have your word on this?"

"My word is golden."

Hector and I went out and walked to the harbor again.

"I do not like her," Hector said. "She's mean."

"What a clever boy you are!" I said and pressed him tight. We returned to the house of Cleis and her husband.

CLEIS' HUSBAND was repulsive—at least to me. He was large and square and he could not utter a sentence without stumbling over his words like a peasant. Oh, he was rich. His family grew and pressed all the olive oil in Lesbos and from that they had branched out to buy more and more land from the old aristocratic families who had fallen on hard times. In a war, food is necessary for armies, and Pittacus had patronized the family of my son-in-law and made them rich; after that he made them new nobility.

My daughter might be angry with her mother, but her mother's hot blood ran through her veins. She could not quash *that* heritage. Aphrodite ruled her even if she did not yet know it.

"Welcome, honored Mother," said Elpenor.

"Thank you, honored son-in-law," I said. I could hardly look at him without being revolted. How could this boob have produced this beautiful boy? Hector had all his mother's beauty and none of his father's bumbling. He was a golden boy, as Cleis was my golden girl. The blood of Alcaeus ran in their veins. Wit and beauty were their legacy. So what if Cleis found me troublesome now! So what if I irritated her as much as she irritated me! She was my bone and blood. Someday she would have a daughter and understand everything I understood. Then we would be friends—the better friends for having been so prickly to each other. This I knew.

"Elpenor," I said, "your boy is a prodigy. He knows poetry and song and story. Someday he will do you proud at the symposium.

"And on the battlefield!" said Elpenor.

He scooped the child up in his arms and ruffled his golden curls. "And what a beauty he is too! Golden like his mother! Ah, he will make a fine cupbearer to Pittacus the Great!"

Hector wriggled out of his hamlike arms and ran away to his nurse in the women's quarters.

"A fine boy!" said Elpenor. "Now all we need is a girl to take care of us when we are old! Will you excuse us, honored mother-in-law? Of course you will. You know the heat of the blood! All your songs prove it! Though only serving maids and common folk sing 'em, they still have *something* to 'em. Why, I used to use your songs myself to sing maidens into bed! Don't tell Pittacus I said so! Come, my girl, to bed!"

Cleis winked at me conspiratorially. This was a change! Someday we would laugh about this! And about Elpenor who could not tell my songs from Andromeda's—but then neither could my daughter!

I sat down at the loom and thought and thought. Suddenly a line took me and I ran for papyrus and reeds. *No matter what Aphrodite promised me / There is no road to Olympus / For mortals . . .* I scrawled.

I paused, then began again:

> *When I think of my love*
> *Far across the seas . . .*

No good, too banal.

> *Let us sacrifice to Aphrodite,*
> *Inconstant, constant goddess,*

Let us bind our locks with dill
And all sweet-smelling herbs
And praise the power of Aphrodite
And her sparrows with whirling wings
Who bless us with fruitfulness and love!
Holy mother Cyprian
And the nereids,
Awake with varied notes
The down-rushing wind of desire
And send Eros as your messenger
To fill our hearts with love,
Our loins with lust,
And shower us
With . . .

At that very moment, Rhodopis, my sister-in-law, rushed in.

"Sappho! Do you know that two of your students are with child? And that Phaon is the father?"

I can't say I was surprised. There are certain things you know without knowing them. And I knew from the start who Phaon was. It was only a question of time.

"A fox in the chicken coop!" said Rhodopis, as if she were a virgin herself. "Oh, the shame of it! The scandal! Now your school is ruined and I am afraid you are too!"

I stayed calm—if only not to give Rhodopis the satisfaction of seeing me shaken.

"I'm sure we can deal with this," I said. "Who are the girls? And who knows about it?"

This latter was a foolish question, since, if Rhodopis knew, the entire isle of Lesbos knew!

"Dica and Anactoria. But Atthis may be pregnant too!"

"The whole henhouse! My, what a sneaky fox he is!"

"And they say Artemisia *too* is his lover—but not with child, since she is well past it! Like you!" Rhodopis smirked at me—though in truth she was older than I, claiming to be younger. She and Charaxus had gotten a son somewhere—but I doubt it sprang from those sullied loins!

Rhodopis was not happy with my unruffled demeanor. She'd expected me to be more upset. She'd expected that I would be distraught.

"Calm yourself, sister-in-law," I said (it was the first time I had acknowledged her as such). "I'm sure we'll figure out what to do with the girls. Artemisia has potions to bring on abortion and she'll have no choice but to help us if she herself has been poaching on Phaon's staff."

"And a very lively one it is too."

"Have you tried it *also,* dear sister?"

"How dare you insinuate that I would be false to your brother! I am an honest woman! What slander!"

"Oh, forgive me, Rhodopis, I forgot that you were a virgin when we met!"

Rhodopis grimaced. She had rewritten her history here in Lesbos, but she could not fool me and she knew it. She had lost her looks and now was puffy and fat, with treble chins—so of course people believed her to be virtuous. But I had known the *old* Rhodopis. In Naucratis she was no virgin, and she was already over thirty then! Ancient! The gods alone knew how old she was now!

"I will go back to Eresus and see about my maidens, and then we'll see what we shall see."

"Sappho, I cannot believe how calm you are!"

"What use will it be to become frantic? Will it end their pregnancies? Or will it keep Phaon from poaching in my coop? I doubt it."

"Don't you care? I thought he was your lover. I thought you'd throw yourself off a cliff if he deceived you!"

"Hardly. He was the plaything of a month, a week, a day. Come, Rhodopis, you don't think that I would throw my whole life away for a lively prick! Once, when I was young. But now? Other things are far too important. And life goes on. It is not long, but it *is* long enough to see through the follies of men. Pleasure is good, but it is not all of life. Lovers like Phaon are rare but not extinct. If not him, another. A girl's first love is the only one she'd die for! And I am no longer a girl, as you pointed out!"

"But what about your girls? And what about the parents of your girls? Their fathers will call for your head!"

"Or so you pray. Rhodopis, spare me your false concern. I can deal with all this. After my travels—not to mention my return home—these are very minor troubles. If necessary, I'll raise the babes myself. I always wanted more children. Go—tell Charaxus I need his help and send him to me in Eresus. You can stay here and tell the whole of Mytilene about my troubles."

"I would never do that!"

"You probably already have!"

"Never, Sappho, I am true to you."

"Rhodopis, I know who you are and you know who I am. Let us not delude ourselves with lies."

"I don't know what you're talking about!"

"You know perfectly well. Go—go to your silly husband and tell him I am ready for him to repay my generosity to him in Naucratis. He will know what I mean. Go!"

Rhodopis scurried away like a rat surprised in the granary.

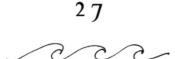

27

A Sacrifice, a Prayer, a Ring

Crazy girl, do not boast about a ring!
—Sappho or Alcaeus

I WAS ON my way back to Eresus in the frigid wind to see about my students and my poacher in the henhouse. What to do with Phaon? Kick him out summarily? Pretend I didn't know and let him stew for a while? My revenge would be all the sweeter for my delaying it. The boy had gone too far. Seducing Artemisia was one thing. (She had probably seduced him!) Anyway, that could be handled discreetly—though Rhodopis had by now trumpeted it all over Lesbos. But seducing green girls who could get pregnant? What a reckless cock of the walk Phaon was! I had been right to be suspicious of him. He was a trickster and a lowlife. He had never really fooled me—except in bed. No wonder the wisest philosophers considered love a sort of derangement. When the loins grew hot, the brain grew fuzzy, and when the delta yearned, the intellect took a leave.

Phaon had, of course, told me the whole incredible and absurd story of having met Aphrodite and having had her gift of irresistibility bestowed upon him.

"Sappho," he had said, "I met someone who appeared to be a wizened old crone and I ferried her to the mainland and refused to charge her. After we stopped on the coast of Lydia—she was bound for Ephesus, I think—she gave me a magic *alabastron* full of magic salve. Ever since then, women young and old have looked with favor upon me. But I never wanted any of them till you."

"A likely story," I had said.

"It's true," he had protested. "She was Aphrodite in an old woman's disguise. I know it. Her eyes were young and beautiful—like yours."

I faced him down. "A boy like you! Why, you've been taking women and boys since you were twelve. And getting paid for it too, I'll wager."

"Not true! You hurt my heart by saying that. I always saved myself for you. I knew someday I'd meet the love of my life."

I should have known then what a liar he was! *I* was the idiot for taking him into my bed. And yet. And yet. He was a sweet distraction after my mother died. And he was a good ferryman. Where was he now when I needed him? Or had I sent him back to Eresus to further raid the henhouse? Idiot! We *both* were idiots! Aphrodite had maddened us—both of us. Love is a sort of madness, as all singers know. It is a bitter madness that inspires sweet song!

Back to Eresus. There was work to do.

The wind was fierce. The boat I had hired had a far less skillful helmsman than Phaon. I half expected to be blown away. That would be too easy. Odd how much more precious life grows when you are old. In youth we'd throw it all away for a pretty boy or ripe girl. In old age, we long to live if only to see how it all turns out.

Circles are completed. The innocent are rewarded and the guilty are punished. Sometimes the innocent are punished and the guilty rewarded. It's all up to the gods. But you want to be there to *see* it all. And laugh!

No, having survived so many shipwrecks in my youth, I did not want to die now in the waters of my native isle. I would confront this wind— and Phaon! I would confront Rhodopis and Artemisia and all of them.

I knew who mattered to me. My daughter. My grandson. Alcaeus. Praxinoa. Aesop. My students. Aphrodite. All the rest could fall into the sea, as far as I was concerned. Phaon could jump off a cliff! Let him kill himself when I unmasked him. Yes—that would be a just revenge. But maybe there was one more service he could do me before he died. I would pray to Aphrodite and offer up a fine white heifer when I returned to my grandparents' house in Eresus.

And that is what I did. Before I even bade hello to my students or unmasked the tricky Phaon, I went to the apple grove outside. In the little temple to Aphrodite I myself had built, I sacrificed a fine white heifer—the very best and fattest on my property.

My farm slaves helped me with the sacrifice. I sprinkled barley over the heifer's lovely head while she lowed mournfully and bowed her head as if she knew her fate. Then my farmhand, Cleon, swiftly slit her throat so the bright blood pulsed below the altar. We caught it in a golden bowl. Cleon and another farm slave, Castor, butchered the beautiful heifer, then built a blazing fire on the altar. We reserved the fat thighbones for Aphrodite. We burned them heavenward with this prayer:

> *Hither to me from Crete*
> *To this holy shrine,*
> *In this encircling grove of apple trees,*
> *Bare now, but soon to bloom again*
> *Despite this whipping wind,*
> *Come, Cypris, daughter of Zeus,*
> *Born of the waves,*
> *Of the soft sea foam*
> *Gods secrete in their sacred loins.*
> *Descend from heaven,*
> *Beloved Aphrodite*
> *To help me and all those I love!*

APHRODITE: *She calls!*
ZEUS: *Let her call again!*
APHRODITE: *She needs me!*

ZEUS: *Silly girl! Are you really my daughter, or are you the daughter of Uranus? You are far too attentive to the mortals! Gods should be above all that. Let the mortals stumble on their stupid way while we delight ourselves above! They are the creatures of an hour, a day, a week! Their lives hardly matter!* We are the ones who matter!

APHRODITE: *Sappho's life matters! She is not just another mortal. Her body may be dust. But her voice is divine. Someday she will be called the "tenth muse" by a great philosopher, not yet born, named Plato.*

ZEUS: *Plato, schmato! These mortals are no more than dust!*

APHRODITE: *I tell you, it is her* voice *that is divine!*

ZEUS: *Because it is* your *voice, my girl, but it issues through* her *mouth! And you love the sound of your own voice!*

The sweet smells of the sacrifice brought two of the students to the altar.

Atthis and Dica arrived, knelt down, and blessed Aphrodite as I had taught them to.

"Sappho! Thank the gods you are back!" said Dica.

"Shhhhh!" said Atthis. "Sappho is sacrificing!"

I repeated my prayer. Now the two girls joined in.

Come, Cypris, born of the soft sea foam! sang Dica.

Come, Cypris! sang Atthis. *Daughter of Zeus!*

I repeated my prayer as the aroma of meat curled skyward with the soul of my beautiful heifer.

The pungent aroma filled the sky and drifted into the apple grove, where I now saw Phaon working, collecting fallen applewood branches for our fires.

NOW PHAON joined us, carrying an apple log, which he added to the fire. The fire sputtered and hissed from the dew on the log. In a few minutes, the lovely smell of applewood was released into the brisk air.

I glared at Phaon. Dica stared at him with big eyes as if she had never seen a man before! Then it was true that he had bedded her and stolen her virginity! But Atthis was wholly indifferent to him. She was concentrating on the sacrifice. He had not yet poached on her. Was it only a matter of time?

I saw that Dica wore a new gold ring on her finger. It had a central stone that was blue as the skies.

We continued to sacrifice to Aphrodite. Now Phaon sang a song of Mimnermus, which I'm sure he wanted Dica to think was his own composition:

> *What life, what pleasure is there*
> *Without golden Aphrodite?*
> *When I no longer care for her gifts*
> *Let me die!*
> *Clandestine love,*
> *Persuasive presents,*
> *A scented bed*
> *Are the blooms of youth!*
> *When a man grows old,*
> *These gifts are fled!*
> *He takes no pleasure*
> *From the radiance of the sun!*

"But you will never grow old, Phaon. Aphrodite has seen to that!" I said coldly.

"I don't know what you mean."

"You know perfectly well," I said. "Phaon—you and I must talk."

"With joy, my lady!"

"Don't *my lady* me! Come to me later in my library, after the midday meal."

"With greatest pleasure, my lady Sappho."

He betook himself in all his beauty back to the apple grove to continue gathering wood.

Dica and Atthis stayed with me on bended knee. I caught Dica gazing after Phaon dreamily. Then she looked down and twisted the new gold ring on her finger.

We finished the sacrifice, bade Cleon and Castor tend the fire and roast the meat for our meal later that day. I put my arm around Dica and walked with her into the house. Atthis returned to her chamber in the *gynaikeion*.

In my library, beside another applewood fire, I questioned the shy Dica.

"My girl, what is that ring?"

"Sappho—I am so glad you asked! Phaon loves me! We are to be married!"

I looked at silly Dica with love and pity. "And how do you know this?"

"He *told* me! He plighted his troth to me. He says he loves me above all mortal women. He says that only Aphrodite is more beautiful."

I looked at Dica, with her lovely curly reddish hair, bound in a gold-embroidered ribbon from Sardis. I saw her round, swelling breasts, the blush that rose on her cheeks when she spoke of love. The tenderness with which she pronounced the name *Phaon*. I didn't know whether to laugh or cry. Poor darling! Poor sweet girl! I saw *myself* when I first fell for Alcaeus. I saw the whole tribe of maidens back to Hera. Back to Helen. Back to Leto, mother of Apollo. I saw Europa mastered by the bull and Leda seduced by the swan. I wanted to hold her and kiss her and at the same time slap her!

"Dica, Dica, Dica," I said.

"What is the matter, Sappho?"

"What is the matter? What is the matter? The matter is *Aphrodite*. The matter is love and madness. The matter is Eros with his poisoned arrows. The matter is youth. The matter is fire in the blood."

"I don't understand, my teacher, my mother, my beloved singer."

"Of course you don't. It will take another twenty years before you even *begin* to."

"Sappho, I am scared. Doesn't he love me? He gave me this ring. It is pure gold."

"And did you ask him where he *got* the ring?"

"Why should I ask? That would be ungrateful."

"Give me the ring," I said.

"I swore never to take it off," said Dica. "It is bad luck ever to remove it, Phaon says."

"Don't worry. The spell cannot so easily be broken."

Reluctantly, she gave the ring to me. I looked inside it. Engraved in tiny letters was this sentence: "*Panaenus made me for the great Artemisia who plights her troth to beautiful Phaon beloved of Aphrodite.*"

"Dica, did you *read* what it says inside?"

"That would be bad luck!"

"That would be *smart*! Let me read it to you." And I slowly read the awful inscription aloud. Dica looked confused. Then she looked stunned. Then she began to cry. She blubbered, "But it can't be true! He now loves *me*!"

"Then why did he give you the ring Artemisia gave *him* without even bothering to have her inscription scratched out? Surely that would have been an easy enough thing to do."

"Then he *doesn't* love me?"

"I'm afraid he loves no one but himself."

"Sappho—I may be pregnant. What shall I do?"

I took the girl in my arms while she sobbed and rocked her as if she were a small child.

"We will worry about the baby soon enough. First you must weep out all the tears you have inside you."

"That will take years! I will never stop weeping!"

"You think that *now*, but the truth is you *will* stop weeping. I promise you, you will even *laugh* about this one day. Love is not a fatal disease but a powerful lesson. It will never stop teaching you about yourself."

"I will never stop weeping."

"You most certainly will—and sooner than you know. You will stop weeping and start laughing. Love is tragic at first, but in time it becomes comic. All you have to do is *wait*."

"My father will kill me if I come home pregnant!"

"Then you will not come home pregnant!"

"What will I do? I cannot kill his baby, I love him!"

"It's yours to do with as you will. It hardly belongs to Phaon. If you have it, you will never regret it. If you lose it, it's the will of the gods. All in good time, all in good time we will understand what the future has in store."

"How can you be so calm?"

"Because I am old. I have lived through many shipwrecks. I know what I know. You will too, someday. Let me tell you a story. When I was just the age that you are now, I also fell in love with a beautiful young man."

"Who was it?"

"He was a great poet and a great warrior—Alcaeus of Lesbos."

"The one who wrote the legendary songs?"

"The very same."

"What happened?"

"I fell in love—precipitously, disastrously, completely."

"And then what happened?" Dica had stopped crying. Now she was curious about my story.

"Ah, Dica—I will tell you the whole story if you will dry those pretty eyes. I will tell all—but not just now."

"When, Sappho, when?"

"I will tell you all after I have attended to some other business. Go and be calm. Trust in the power of Aphrodite. I will come to you soon and tell all."

Dica ran off to the women's quarters with dry eyes.

AFTER OUR MIDDAY meal of heifer, rice, olives, all washed down with wine from our family vineyards, I met with Phaon as I had promised. He came into my library, looking as beautiful as ever.

"You called, my lady Sappho?"

"I think you know why," I said.

Phaon opened his big eyes at me as if he knew nothing. Innocence. His look was pure innocence.

"*What life, what pleasure is there without golden Aphrodite?*" I said, quoting him, quoting Mimnermus.

"I don't know what you mean," the boy lied. "I worship you, my lady, above all other women."

"Come, Phaon, truth is the only love we owe each other. We have shared the pleasure of the bed—one of Aphrodite's greatest gifts. Let us not insult each other with lies after such intimacy."

"I don't know what you mean," said Phaon, fluttering his long black lashes.

I gave the boy a swift slap on the cheek. "Do you remember now?" I asked.

There was a red mark where I had struck him. Now he began to cry great round tears, which only made his eyes look more beautiful. He sobbed more than Dica. Oh, it was an awful sight, to see this grown man cry!

"It's not your fault, Phaon. Aphrodite decreed all this. She is the queen of madness and lust, of aching loins and throbbing deltas. She makes the phallus stand and the mind relax into submission. I cannot blame you entirely. But I can exact payment. I can demand justice."

"What sort of justice, my lady?"

"You will never see Dica again, or me, or Artemisia. You will leave this place, but you will be bound by my wishes until I release you."

Phaon looked frightened. Was I about to enslave him? In my own way, yes.

"You will go to Mytilene and seduce my daughter Cleis. You will stay with her until she bears a beautiful daughter. Then you will bring her and the baby and my grandson to me and disappear forever!"

"Never to see you again? I cannot bear it!"

"You'll manage—with Aphrodite's help!"

"What shall I do with all the papyri I have transcribed?"

"Leave them with me! They are the least you owe me."

"But I love you. I love you with all my heart."

"Then show your love with your obedience to me."

Phaon knew now he had no choice. He took his boat, and before sundown was bound for Mytilene in the frigid wind.

28

Kinship

I am not one of those with a spiteful temperament.
I have a gentle heart.
—SAPPHO

AFTER PHAON left for Mytilene, my brother arrived. Charaxus had not aged well. He looked as puffy as his wife Rhodopis. And he was getting old. Was it possible I looked as old as he? I was the elder, and yet I felt much younger! Song keeps you young, I suppose. Or perhaps it was love. Aphrodite had breathed her hot breath on my life and kept it warm!

> APHRODITE: *That's for sure!*
> ZEUS: *Oh, you credulous girl!*
> APHRODITE: *Why credulous? No one escapes my power for long. Even you succumb to desire, Father.*
> ZEUS: *Had I ravished you, you'd be more compliant and less arrogant!*
> APHRODITE: *You revolt me.*

"Rhodopis bade me come, my sister. She said I must help you in any way I can!"

"Well, there's a change!"

"You underestimate Rhodopis, Sappho. She has grown. She is no longer the Rhodopis of Naucratis. She's a good woman now. My influence, I think."

"She certainly has grown," I said. "Sideways."

"It must have been our baby. Her pregnancy quite distended her. She will get back her shape in time. I know it."

I looked at my brother. Was it possible the gods had given all the brains to women and had none left over for the men? Or was it simply that the phallus drained the brain of wisdom? No. Alcaeus was clever. Aesop was clever. Even Chiron was clever. Only my brother had forfeited his intellect.

"Let us not discuss your lawful wife, nor the baby she bought off some slave and pretended had come from her sullied womb."

"Sappho, that is my own dear son."

"I would not lie to you, Charaxus. Honesty is kind. It is the only kindness we know. I will honor my nephew however Rhodopis got him. He is my kin as you are. Do you know why I have called you here?"

"No."

"Let me take you back to your slavery in Naucratis many years ago. You promised to be forever in my debt and to repay in time. Will you keep your word or die and go straight to a traitor's grave?"

Charaxus looked perplexed. Then, slowly, recollection dawned. Mnemosyne, goddess of memory, found him.

"I remember, sister. What do you require of me?"

"Take my student Dica to Artemisia in Mytilene and do it privily. Tell no one—not even your wife Rhodopis. Can you manage that?"

"What if she presses me?"

"Be strong. Be silent. Keep this one secret in your life. Are you a man or not?"

"Of course I am a man!"

"Then *do* something for once without consulting her! I was your sister before she was your wife! Do you remember how we played in Eresus when we were small? Do you remember how we played that the Athenians would come to enslave us?"

Charaxus looked down. He could not look me in the eye. "I do, sister."

"Then for the sake of loyalty, of kinship, of all the gods, take this girl to Artemisia without telling Rhodopis!"

"I will, Sappho."

"Do you swear on our sacred father's honor?"

"I do, Sappho."

"Do you swear on the ghost of our beloved mother?"

"I do, sister."

"Do you swear on the blessed lives of the next generation?"

"I do, Sappho."

"Then here is what you must do."

Whereupon I carefully instructed him to take Dica to Artemisia in Mytilene and pay for the cleaning of her womb. Charaxus looked at me wide-eyed. Women's mysteries somewhat embarrassed him. He knew *of* Artemisia, but naturally he had never been in her inner sanctum, seeking counsel, and like many men, he believed her to be a witch, like Circe.

I read his mind, hardly a difficult task. "She is no witch, my brother, but just a greedy woman who has grown rich off other women's desperation. She will not bite you."

"I am not afraid of her!" my brother snapped.

"Just as you are not afraid of your wife," I smiled.

"Sappho—do not mock me."

"Did I mock you when you enslaved yourself willingly? Hardly. But I see it has taught you nothing. You will always be a slave to someone—if not to the enemy, then to some woman. Come, Charaxus, your good sister Sappho will save you."

I put my arms around him and kissed him tenderly. Charaxus shed a tear, then quickly wiped the corner of his eye.

"Oh, Sappho—how can I repay you?"

"You know perfectly well how! Pay me the lawful share of the wine crop! Send me the *oboloi* you owe. Give me a fair accounting. Did I quibble about payment when I liberated you in Egypt?"

"But Rhodopis claims she has *saved* our wine trade and therefore deserves the lion's share! She spends and spends! I can never make enough to keep her!"

"The lion's share! Would that Aesop were here to make a fable of it! And you? Are you a lion or a mouse? Would you cheat your sister for your whore? Many men have done this, but I thought you were more honorable. Now I see I was wrong!"

Charaxus looked sheepish. He wavered between family honor and his fear of Rhodopis. I knew him so well. I could see the conflict on his face.

"Go, Charaxus, never darken my door again! I see you are neither the son of Scamandronymus nor the daughter of Cleis the elder. You must have been a changeling! My true brother would not cheat his kin for a trollop!"

I sternly turned my back and walked away.

And then I heard it. Charaxus was sobbing. He was sobbing great choked sobs. Then he was raging, and he attacked: "You insult me, sister! You have always torn me down! You have always made fun of my passions! At least Rhodopis loves me truly!"

"If you cannot tell the difference between a sister's loyalty and a whore's greed, then I pity you! *Go!*"

"Damn you!" I muttered under my breath. "A fool from birth will always be a fool." My mind instantly ran ahead to other plans. I would take Dica to Artemisia *myself.* I had no doubt that Artemisia would find a use for Dica's pregnancy. Either she would end it for gold or sell the child to the highest bidder. She knew how to do all these things. She fattened on the fears of women—as Rhodopis fattened on the fears of men. Who needed Charaxus or Rhodopis! I would manage all this myself. Then I would disband my school and go to find Alcaeus, Aesop, Praxinoa—my real kin. I was already making plans to do so when Charaxus returned. He fell to his knees and kissed the hem of my chiton.

"Sappho—you are right. I will do as you ask."

"Be kind to the girl—she is shaken. Is that a promise?"

"I swear on my son's life."

So he returned to Mytilene with Dica in tow while I prayed to Aphrodite that he would not weaken when he saw his awful wedded wife.

• • •

WHY ARE MEN so weak? I wondered as I went about my chores. Why have the gods put all their power in their phalli? Why are they so unable to think clearly when a woman commands them? What can be the meaning of this madness of lust? Why do we need it? Why does it so distort our world?

Because of lust, Helen sparked the Trojan War. Because of lust, Odysseus lost his men. Because of lust, Demeter lost her daughter half the year. Wild lust has convulsed the earth too often and killed too many mothers' sons. Why?

APHRODITE: *Because of my father's fury! Know that when I ruled the world with Demeter and Hestia and Hera and even great Gaia and the other goddesses, the world was a gentler place. Then Zeus came with his overwhelming lust and chaos was here again!*

ZEUS: *So I suppose women are never cruel!*

APHRODITE: *Less cruel than you!*

ZEUS: *And what of the way they flirt with and frighten their young sons? And what of the way they taunt and torture us?*

APHRODITE: *Our only remaining power. Love is a weapon because we have no other. Beauty is a dagger only when you disarm us. Sex becomes a spear when you vanquish our mothers. When Isis ruled supreme, the world was just. But when the consort overpowers his mother, war comes to the world. And burns it in fierce flame.*

ZEUS: *So have your blessed matriarchy. Rule the world. You will see how hard it is to rule, and how thankless.*

APHRODITE: *When women retake the world, we will prove you wrong!*

ZEUS: *I doubt it.*

I sent the girls home to their families one by one. I closed up my grandparents' house, leaving the caretakers in charge. Then I went to bid farewell to my daughter in Mytilene.

Cleis was glad to see me this time, as if she knew she might never see me again. Hector threw his little arms around my neck and would not let go.

"Tell me the song of Alcaeus again, Grandmama!" And I sang it, slowly, sonorously. He clapped his hands in delight.

"Never forget that you are the grandson of singers, Hector. Perhaps song can't cure the world, but it is the only consolation the gods have given us."

Cleis looked different. She had a sort of gleam in her eye, a golden radiance of serenity. Had Phaon come to call? Had he taught her the secrets of love's sweet madness? I hoped so. Phaon had his uses. Every girl should have a lover like that before she becomes a contented matron. Every maiden should be aroused by Aphrodite's chosen swain. Then good riddance to him!

"Mother," Cleis asked, "did you ever find pleasure with a man who was not your lawful husband? Or with a woman?"

"Why do you ask?"

"Just curious."

"Pleasure is good—wherever you find it, Cleis, just as long as no one is hurt by knowledge they would rather not have."

"That's what I thought myself, Mother," Cleis said, almost singing. Oh, Phaon had been here all right.

As I was bidding farewell to Cleis and Hector, dreaming of Alcaeus and determined to set out to find him, I once again remembered the legend of the rock at Leucas. The wise ones said that if you were possessed by an impossible love, you must go to the isle of Leucas, climb to the shrine of Apollo, and jump off the high white cliff above the sea. If you survived, you would be cured of yearning. And if you did not, you would also be cured!

On my last night in Eresus before departure, I sat alone in my grandmother's bedchamber and thought about this legend. Then I wrote a song about it.

> *O Aphrodite, is it true*
> *That hopeless love*

Drowns in Leucas?
I must climb to the top
Of that white cliff
And throw myself into
The roiling sea
Because I have lost my one true love!
If you cannot bring me love,
Then bring me death.
I have served you long enough.

I sang that mournful song on the boat that was to take me from Mytilene to Delphi. And the people who heard it cried, "I must learn that song before I die!" How could I know that my fellow passengers would learn it and sing it to Alcaeus and Praxinoa and Aesop in Delphi and that my old friends would come in search of me?

29

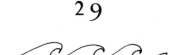

The Great White Rock

Death is an evil,
Otherwise the gods
Would die.
—Sappho

WOULD LEAPING really cure hopeless love? So the legend went. I stopped on the isle of Leucas to see the fabled great white rock, which I had never beheld with my own eyes. I knew only the myths that swirled about it like mist on Mount Olympus. Some said in ancient times prisoners were hurled from the rock to purge the island of evil. Those who perished were presumed to be guilty. Those who survived were pardoned. Later, in the curious way legends are transformed, the place became a lovers' leap. I had always dreamed of seeing it. But equally I feared it.

The cliff was prodigious. One sheer side of naked rock beetled over the sea. The rock seemed jaggedly torn and the wind howled around it. I planned to visit the shrine of Apollo on the promontory, then continue on to Delphi, where my old bones knew that Alcaeus would be waiting for me. And if he was *not?* Then I would do whatever I would do. I refused to fret about it. My life was in Aphrodite's soft hands.

As usual, nothing worked out as I had planned. The ship on which I had sailed from Lesbos waited for another cargo, which was late making the crossing from Naucratis. So I remained on the isle of Leucas far longer than I would have wished, but I kept postponing my visit to the shrine of Apollo on the cliff.

It was good to be in Leucas on my own. Everywhere I went, people sang my songs to me with great emotion. I came to realize that though I was no prophet in my own land, I was beloved all over the rest of the Greek-speaking world—which was, of course, the only world that mattered.

Women came to me weeping. They told me that "gold flower" had made them love their daughters more. Men came to me and said that my songs of passion had won them love time and time again.

So I had not been forgotten—except on my native isle! I was born to be an exile. Lesbos made me, but Lesbos was no longer my home. The world was.

I stayed in Leucas, waiting for the boat to Delphi—delayed and yet again delayed. While I waited, I was asked to sing at many symposia—and I did so, performing all my old favorites. The audiences loved me and my spirit soared.

I could stay in Leucas, I thought, if it were not for my longing for Alcaeus.

After I had been in Leucas several weeks, I finally found the courage to visit the famed shrine to Apollo on the jagged cliff.

Climbing alone in a whipping wind, my whole life passing before me, my thoughts begin to darken. What if I get to Delphi and, as before, Alcaeus has already left? What if the dream of Alcaeus is as vain as in times past? What if Artemisia's tale of Alcaeus, Prax, and Aesop traveling with Chiron to see the Oracle of Delphi is not even true? What if I am doomed to have my hopes dashed yet again? I cannot bear it! To lose him once, twice, was bad enough, but the third time will surely kill me.

Up. Up. Up. I climb and climb. Seeing the bleached white bones of small creatures makes me mutter under my breath, *May the gods bless the souls of the animals.* My golden sandals skitter on the white pebbles.

Crawling up the mountain, I seem to be in an endless nightmare. Sometimes I stumble forward and skin my knees and palms.

Below me the sea boils as in a cauldron. Above me the winds shriek like furies. I strain to see Alcaeus in the mist that rises from the rough landmass above the wine-dark sea. I think of all the great singers before me who have sung and died. Homer was not spared by the gods, though his words were. What is the use of life after all? It is a litany of disappointments and regrets. Love cannot stay. Life cannot stay. Better to die than linger on, an old woman at the mercy of her daughter. I remember the chest in which I have carefully stored my papyri in my family's house in Eresus.

"Guard this treasure with your lives," I had told my caretakers. "When he is grown to manhood, see that Hector gets these papyrus rolls. He will understand his grandmother. He always did."

Perhaps, when I reach the top, I will test the legend of Leucas. I do not believe I have planned this, but visions of jumping crowd into my spinning brain. As I look down the mountain, I see little boats bobbing below. Lovers would leap to get over unrequited loves as their friends waited below to pull them out of the drink alive or dead. Some leapers surely died upon impact with the water. But many survived, to be rescued. It was all in the hands of the gods. Perhaps I should make my obeisance to Aphrodite and jump. If I were meant to, I would live. And if I were meant to die—so be it!

Now, at the cliff's white top, I look down. My knees want to buckle under me. My breath grows short. I flirt with the edge. Lean over, lean back, lean over, lean back—imagine myself donning wings like Icarus and flying over the foam. Balanced between life and death, I teeter, imagining the icy waters of Hades' realm licking my toes. I tease the gods and myself by thrusting myself over the edge and then suddenly pulling back. I think I am in control, taunting the immortals. But this time I lean too far. And then, without entirely meaning to, I stumble forward and I fall.

The fall seems to take forever. As I fall, I call out to Cleis and Hector. I see a vision of a granddaughter whom I will never hold. I think of

Alcaeus in all his youthful beauty and I reach out to him. I think of my mother and how much I loved her. I think of my warrior father, whom I will soon see again in the Land of the Dead. I think of my grandparents—and then the fury of the water rushes up to greet me.

Down, down, down I plunge into the sea. The brine fills my nose and eyes. My chiton grows heavy and drags me down. My golden sandals float away. Am I dead or soon to be dead? Is death Poseidon's realm or is it Gaia's? Am I to plunge forever? Will I drown in the sea or ascend through clouds? Will I find myself in Hades' realm with all those shades who feel nothing and long for the deliverance of touch?

After a long breathless while, I rise up to the silver surface of the water. I see above me the bottom of a little bark. Coming up into the rippling light, I gasp and fill my lungs with sweet sea air. I swim into the sun.

Leaning over the edge of a little boat are three familiar faces: Alcaeus, Praxinoa, and Aesop.

"Thank the gods who bring us together again!" Alcaeus cries.

"Blessed be Aphrodite!" shouts Prax.

"My heart nearly broke when I saw you leap!" shouts Aesop.

Half drowned but keenly conscious, I draw the air into my aching lungs. Utterly naked, dripping with seawater, I climb into the boat with my three true kin.

EPILOGUE

Of mortal creatures, all that breathe and move,
Earth bears none frailer than mankind.
—HOMER

SO WE LIVE on this small sunny island with the centaurs and amazons. Chiron wants to call our island Centaurcadia and Praxinoa wants
to call it Amazonia—but otherwise they have no quarrel. Unable to
decide on a name, we call the island nothing, which keeps people away.
Apparently, if you are nameless, no one wants to visit you. We like this
very much.

Alcaeus and I have mended our love. Aesop is our dearest friend and
lives with us in perfect harmony. Prax rules the amazons justly and
wisely, sharing her power equally with Chiron. We live in peace, make
songs and fables, and cultivate our gardens. We grow grapes and olives
here and catch fish from the rich seas and make cheese with the milk of
our goats. We lack for nothing. Nothing is missing in our lives. Except.
Except . . .

Alcaeus knows Cleis is his daughter and that he has a grandson
named Hector. He learned that in Delphi from the oracle. Apparently

the oracle appears as each one imagines her. Was my oracle really Aphrodite in disguise? Alcaeus and I discuss this often and can never decide. Alcaeus longs to see his grandson.

But I say, "Do not go to Lesbos. Home is no longer where you think it is and life is happier here among our friends." Sometimes Alcaeus frets and will not be comforted. Then I take him in my arms, saying, "You and I are true kin. Children must have their own lives. When they are ready, they will come to us."

One day in summer, we are walking on the strand of our green island and we see a sail in the distance. Nobody ever comes to visit us— so Alcaeus and I are fascinated. We watch the sail as it comes closer and closer. When the ship is almost at our strand, a ferryman leaps out and tows it closer. He looks for a place to beach.

"Not here!" I scream. "The rocks are lethal! You will tear your hull!"

"Then swim to us!" shouts the ferryman.

"Who are you?" Alcaeus bellows. But the wind carries away his words.

For a while, the little boat bobs with nobody on deck.

"Shall we swim to it?" I ask Alcaeus.

"How do you know he is friend, not foe?" he asks.

"I don't, and yet I think he comes in peace."

"Then I'll swim out, Sappho. You stay here."

My heart stops.

"I cannot bear to lose you again!" I tell Alcaeus. But before I can stop him, he leaps into the water like a dolphin and swims like mad to the unknown sailboat.

I see him pull himself aboard. I see the ferryman help him. I see a beautiful golden-haired woman come on deck with a golden child in her arms. I see a brave boy at her side who can only be my own Hector!

My heart! My heart!

I leap into the water and swim to the boat.

"Grandmother!" Hector cries.

Alcaeus is on deck, weeping tears of joy.

"I've come to introduce you to my daughter, Mother."

On her hip is a child of six months. She gurgles at me happily.

"I have named her Sappho after you!" Cleis says. "There is so much to say to you, Mother."

Dripping wet, I take my dry granddaughter in my arms. I think I have never felt anything so tender before, greener than grass, so newly made, so blessed. I see the light of the sun in my daughter's eyes, the same sun that sparkles on the sea and spreads to the distant horizon.

"In truth nothing more needs to be said," I say.

Author's Afterword

Aeolian earth, you cover Sappho, who among the immortal muses is cele-
brated as the mortal muse, whom Cypris and Eros together reared, with
whom Persuasion wove the undying wreath of song, a joy to Hellas and a
glory to you. You fates twirling the triple thread on your spindle, why did
you not spin an everlasting life for the singer who devised the deathless
gifts of the muses of Helicon?

—Antipater of Sidon

SEVEN YEARS AGO, Sappho set her delicate sandaled foot in my life and
since then I've never been the same.

I had read her fragments before, but they had not struck me with the
force they later carried. She'd seemed so remote. The world of the eastern Aegean 2,600 years ago had seemed so remote. But now it seemed
suddenly close. It is in the nature of those books we call classics to wait
patiently on the shelf for us to grow into them. I read Sappho again in
my fifties and suddenly I understood. I saw that her legend had been
confabulated with the legends of Aphrodite. And I began to write a
sequence of poems in Sappho's voice, in Aphrodite's, and in my own.

The poems, which follow this afterword, led me to *Sappho's Leap*.
Poems, like dreams, are a sort of royal road to the unconscious. They
tell you what your secret self cannot express.

I wrote these poems and then went on to other things. I continued to
read Sappho from time to time, but the novel I dreamed of writing about

her was stalled. Perhaps it was growing what Nabokov called "wings and claws" in secret. I began a play about Sappho in which she is about to jump off the Leucadian cliff to her death but stops to tell her story. I never finished it.

I don't know why books come in this zigzag way. The great Polish poet Wisława Szymborska says, "Whatever inspiration is, it's born from a continuous 'I don't know.'" That has been my experience. The poems presage the novels, but why the subject goes underground for a period of years while life catches up to it, I have no idea. Perhaps all mysteries don't have to be solved. Perhaps the mystery of how novels emerge is better left unplumbed.

As I say in my prefatory note, not much is known about Sappho's biography other than that she flourished in Lesbos circa 600 BCE. Even the date of her birth is uncertain. There are, however, many traditions and legends about her life—including the most famous one: that she threw herself off a cliff in middle age for the sake of unrequited love for a beguiling young ferryman called Phaon. Aphrodite, the goddess of love, had granted Phaon the gifts of great beauty, sensuality, and irresistibility in love—and Sappho fell.

Aphrodite is the goddess most passionately and frequently invoked in Sappho's songs. Could sending a beautiful young man to tempt the greatest singer of love between women have been a trick of the gods? Was Aphrodite testing Sappho? These questions provoked my story.

A novel always begins with a "What if?" What if Sappho was about to jump but stopped to tell her story? At first that was all I had. Yet I strongly felt that the tradition of her suicide was wrong. It seemed a myth attached to Sappho by those who wanted to mock her. I decided that she had thought of jumping but changed her mind. Could she have toyed with suicide and fallen by accident? Now my research began. The more I read, the more I realized that there were remarkably few agreed-upon facts about Sappho. For a historian, this is an obstacle; for a novelist, it may be a blessing.

Sappho is an icon to women everywhere despite the fact that so little is known about her. She is associated with women's sexuality and gay rights—but she may not have been homosexual at all; or she may have loved both women and men, as was common in the ancient world—and is in ours. The concept of homosexuality as a distinct lifestyle did not exist in classical antiquity. People were bisexual, free of sexual guilt as we know it; it was a pagan world. Attitudes toward love, toward sex, toward conquest, toward slavery, toward money, toward social climbing were uncannily like our own—and yet fascinatingly different. Women were sexual chattel, yet, as in all times, there were rebellious, adventurous women. This is the fun of setting a story in the world of 2,600 years ago.

But who was Sappho really? Every age that fell in love with her made her its own. Since she became a muse to later poets, they fashioned her in their own image.

We have few facts, but we do have the sound of her voice. Sappho's is one of the few female voices that has come down to us from antiquity. Passionate, personal, searingly erotic, the fragments of her songs that have reached us show how much women of 2,600 years ago were like us. Yet there are immense gaps in our knowledge. You might say that our knowledge is *mostly* gaps—surrounded by tantalizing legends.

Sappho comes from a time in which the oral tradition was only beginning to give way to the written. Her songs were learned by other singers and performed throughout the ancient world. She was widely heralded and imitated. If you wanted to be glib, you could say she was a cross between Madonna and Sylvia Plath—like Madonna in her huge fame and like Plath in her ferocious truthfulness and legendary suicide. In fact, there has never been *anyone* like her. She became an inspiration to the singers who followed her. She has remained a muse into our own time.

Plato called Sappho the "tenth muse." Ovid fell in love with her songs and paid tribute to them, bringing her into the Roman tradition—which eventually delivered her to us. Every modern poet, from Rainer Maria Rilke to A. E. Housman to Thomas Hardy to Edna St. Vincent Millay to Robert Lowell to Sylvia Plath, has fallen for her combination of voluptuous sexuality and fierce honesty. Her subjects were: erotic love, the hypocrisies of marriage, the ecstasy of motherhood, bisexual passion, the fickleness of Aphrodite—the goddess of love whom even the gods obey. Her work still seems modern today.

She may never have transcribed her own songs. Perhaps other singers learned them and passed them on. Of these, many were lost—because of prudishness, the burning of ancient libraries, destruction caused by wars—but the fragments that remain have cast their spell over succeeding generations.

USING SAPPHO's surviving fragments, the few biographical markers—all of them disputed—my own reinvention of archaic Greece, and the songs, epics, and histories of her contemporaries, I began to imagine Sappho as the greatest singer of all time.

I saw her as an adventurous young girl who got involved in political intrigues, fell in love with the handsome rebel poet Alcaeus, and then was married off to a drunken old husband to keep her out of trouble. She gets into plenty of trouble anyway—no trouble, no story.

Sappho's life is a story of love, adventure, and heroism. It takes us from ancient Lesbos to ancient Syracuse (a Greek colony then) and throughout the Mediterranean world. Sappho was contemporary with Pharaoh Necho of Egypt, Aesop of the fables, Nebuchadnezzar of Biblical fame, the philosopher Heraclitus, and the legendary Alyattes of Lydia, whose court in Sardis was the most luxurious the world had ever known.

Sappho's contemporaries consulted the Oracle of Delphi before they made a move either in love or battle. They were obsessed with witchcraft and magic. They were trained for war and conquest, but they also worshiped the muses and valued song above all the arts.

It was an age of inspired amateurism in which a well-educated aristocrat was expected to be able to make up songs and perform them at a symposium (the classical term for an elegant dinner party), play musical instruments as accompaniment, and converse brilliantly of politics, philosophy, and love.

Not the world of fifth century Athenian male chauvinism we know from Plato's *Symposium,* not a world that excluded women—though it did limit them to certain roles—archaic Greece (circa 800 BCE–500 BCE) was every bit as cosmopolitan and international, in its way, as our own world. People traveled widely for trade, for war, for love. They regularly traversed the Middle East, from Lesbos to Sicily to Gibraltar to North Africa, from Persia and Egypt to Etruscan Italy, in their small, rudderless boats with square sails.

They traded Lesbian wine for Egyptian grain. They used windmills to pump seawater in order to garner salt. They navigated by the stars. They were fascinated by the customs of other cultures, learned much about art from the Egyptians, about coinage and trade from the Lydians, about the alphabet from the Phoenicians. They thought their world as advanced and modern as we think ours. They worshiped many gods and disputed about the creation of the universe even as we do.

A slave society that invented our basic ideas about democracy, a world in which women were valued primarily as breeders, which nonetheless produced the singer who gave us the imagery of erotic love that has lasted until this day, a world of magic that gave birth to our world of science, Greece is the very foundation on which our civilization is built. Sappho is at once the voice of ancient Greece and a voice we recognize as ours.

In naming the characters in the novel, I decided to use the most familiar, usually Latinized spellings—Alcaeus not Alkaios, Cleis not Kleis, Pittacus not Pittakos. These spellings are still used in most dictionaries and encyclopedias. Though it is sometimes fashionable today to play with pseudo-Greek spellings—Kronos, not Cronus—my aim was to make the reader as comfortable as possible with Greek names and to be as consistent as I could in transliterating from another alphabet. Occasionally, where Greek words seem particularly beautiful, I have used them in the text, defining them on first appearance.

Translations of Sappho have always reflected the age in which they were created and the personalities of the translators. My reading showed me that different translators tend to produce different Sapphos. After much deliberation, I decided to attempt my own versions—not literal translations but adaptations of Sappho's verses in a style appropriate to the flow of the novel. In my versions I have tried to capture the essence of Sappho's ideas, in a way that approximates (as much as possible) the original Greek. If the reader is inspired to go back to Sappho herself, I will be delighted.

I have also taken the novelist's prerogative of adding some pseudo-Sapphic texts. It must be acknowledged that the historical novel is an artifice. The ancient Greeks did not speak English. Moreover, this is a novel that incorporates myth and fantasy into its plot. The novelists who inspired me—from Robert Graves and Marguerite Yourcenar to Mary Renault and Gore Vidal—all were aware of the contradictions built into the making of historical fiction. One writes of the past in part to hold a mirror up to the present and in part to honor one's literary ancestors.

It is my pleasure to express my gratitude to Robert Ball, the classics scholar who vetted the manuscript and translations for errors. His generosity has been a great gift. I would like to thank the intrepid Star Lawrence of Norton, exceptional editor and fellow novelist, as well as freelance editor Leslie Schnur. My agent Ed Victor encouraged this daunting project from the start. Ken Follett, Susan Cheever, Shirley Knight, and Naomi Wolf gave me valuable notes and criticism. Lucilla Burn of the British Museum guided my early research. Linda Brunet helped me plunder the rich resources of the libraries of Barnard College and Columbia University, as well as the New York Society Library. Carolyn Block and Lisa Wright transcribed the ultimate edits. Patrick and Narelle Stevens sailed me all over the eastern Aegean on two occasions. I hope I have captured something of the light of those islands and seas in these pages.

Talking to Aphrodite

I. The Priestess Attempts to Retire

Aphrodite, I have toiled
in your service forty years
& I am still alive to tell it.

Those I have loved—bandy-legged smiths
& lost boys,
defrocked shamans,
warlocks of the left,
doctors who could not heal themselves,
poets whose lives did not scan,
gigolos tangoing on tossed bedsheets—
I have mostly forgotten,
but your service I have never regretted:
it has brought me
all the wisdom I have earned.

Once a woman came to me in your likeness—
eyes blue as the sea on a sunless day,
skin pink as the dawn
rising over my Connecticut ridge
at four when I awaken to your worship.
I knew her as your stand-in
& loved her as if she were
myself in a mirror—
all for love of you.

But now I want to quit
this worship,

give up my priestess' robes of red,
my gold chokers, my silver bells, my black pearls,
& go naked into simplicity
becoming poetry's crone,
a white witch of rhyme,
a tree-hugging pagan philosopher,
grandmother to my daughter's
new green passions.

But you—joker Aphrodite—
send me another man
to worry my pulse
& fill my eyes with mischief,
my skin with false dawn.
What is another man
but trouble?

Sappho, being fifty & past mothering
her precious Cleis,
loved a ferryman
who ferried her to the cliff
from which she jumped—
or so the story says.

(But what could Ovid & Menander
know about the heat of a poet's heart
tangled in a woman's breast?)

Take away this Phaon!
This agate-eyed aging Adonis
wooing me with words!

But even as I say this
your most secret eyes meet mine:

"Just one more tumble into ecstasy,"
you tease. "Who knows what hymns to my glory
you will write now,
at the peak of your powers?

What are the lives of poets
but offerings to the goddess they adore?
Do you think such worship is a choice?
Even immortals
obey her capricious laws."

II.   Blood of Adonis

In April, when the blood
of Adonis blooms
on every slope above
the Mediterranean,
my blood blooms too.

You do not love like that
without exsanguination.

Even Aphrodite bleeds
where the great tusked boar
gored her love.

But she remains alive
forever to her pain—
the curse of goddesses.

Adonis sleeps.
Lethe is the milk
of mortals.

III.   Aphrodite Explains

Some say Phaon
was no ordinary ferryman
but a daimon
who plied the glittering waters
between Lesbos & the mainland.

One day I arrived
in the guise of an old woman:
hairs sprouting from my chin,
collapsed jaw, a few brown reeking teeth,
sad dugs with nipples pointing earthward,
feet yellowed with calluses,
an Aeolian lyre with broken strings
in my brown-dappled hands.

But Phaon greeted me
as if I were a girl of twenty.
His bright eyes revived me,
made me young again.

Asking only a kiss
he ferried me safely back to Lesbos.
& for his pains
I gave him the fabled alabaster box
filled with the magic unguent
that makes women love.

Phaon could have his pick
of young buds.
If he loved Sappho,
he loved her truly,

not for her youth

but for her poetry & prescience.

But Sappho was
a mistress of imagined slights
like all you self-singers.

& when he rowed in late,
his muscled arms gleaming,
his ferry decked with flowers,
she cursed me, daughter of Zeus,
for a fabricator of falsehoods,
& cursed him for deceit,
pelting his cheeks
with fiery menopausal tears.

She imagined maidens her daughter's age
spread upon his bed of seaborne flowers—
& leapt to her death
from the Leucadian cliff
simply to spite him.

I am Aphrodite
& I sail the skies
in a golden chariot
drawn by sparrows
that beat the air into submission
with their wings.
I see the past & what is yet to come
& I can bend the hearts of men
to passion if I choose.

But here my power stops:
I cannot save a singer
seduced by her own song.

IV.   When?

When do we give up love?
My daughter begins her adventures
with that cock who crows so insistently
morning, night, high noon,
& neither I nor Aphrodite
can undo its upstanding magic
with moon-dew at its tip.

But I am wise
if not yet quite old,
wanting the poem
more than the lover,
wanting words
more than the sticky dew
men secrete in their
private places.

I teeter on the edge
of love—deciding whether or not
to give the body sway.
My blood boils
only for poetry or power.
My black trance of night
does not need a man to fill it.
& you, golden Aphrodite,
with your swans,
mean more to me as muse
than as harbinger of love.
The rose-ankled graces
will dance for my pen
even if I dance alone.

"Not so fast, priestess,"

you admonish me.

"Would Orpheus have sung
so sweetly
had Eurydice come home
from Hades on her own?
Would Persephone still be
'the maiden whose name must not be spoken'
if she spent all the year
picking daisies with Demeter?
Would Pygmalion have made Galatea
so beautiful without
that last deep debt to me?

Heifers with gilded horns,
snowy goats with silvered horns
stampeded through the streets
on my feast day,
& maidens burned incense
of vanilla & myrrh,
strewed petals of the rarest Lydian roses—
blue & lavender—
& still I did not bless
every lover unrequited
on bended knee.

I give my favors sparsely, if at all.
I give my favors only to the brave."

V.   Aphrodite's Laughter

A sudden thunder
of sparrows' wings
& I am awake.

The sky is streaked
with ruby, tangerine, pimento—
lavender banners
divide a molten core
of cumulus clouds—
& suddenly she is there
rolling across the heavens
in a chariot of burnished gold,
her crown of towers burning
like a city set ablaze
by incendiary armies,
her forehead a show of
scenes of the Trojan War.

My lady, Aphrodite, Venus,
fairest of goddesses,
sticking one shell-colored toe
in the Aegean,
paddling long, thin fingers
in the Baltic,
your sex a great South Sea
of liquid pearl—
you cover the world
with your mischief,
making populations burgeon
beyond our poor earth's power to bear.

You laugh, uncaring—
a goddess' laugh.
Hecate attends you
with her jet-black panthers,
her gleamless jewels of night.
Poets die to become
speaking instruments
to sing your praises.

Maidenheads fall
like hyacinths grown
too heavy to stand.
Purple stains streak the skies.
Too-persuasive goddess,
visit other planets for a while.
Earth has had enough
of your beneficence.

The scalloped foam at the edge
of the shore
is full of dying creatures,
lost limbs of crab,
turtles without shells,
oysters drying out
in crumbling sandcastles. . . .

Go to the moon, Aphrodite,
& make it breed!
Go to Mars, your lover's
red planet, & raise
the Martian plankton
into spacemen & galactic women!

If anyone can do it,
you can!
But leave us alone
on earth
to catch our breath.

You laugh again,
putting a torch to my heart,
lifting your robe
above your rosy knees
& whispering, almost hissing:

"Death is
good enough for mortals,
not for gods.

The planets are my playthings
& their inhabitants my toys.
& who are you to question it?

Sappho, for her pains,
jumped off a cliff;
& Sylvia stuck her head in the oven,
leaving her mate to become poet laureate.
Anne wrapped herself in furs
& fell asleep forever,
leaving daughters
to decipher
her coded messages.

But you want to be a poet & not die?"

Aphrodite's laughter shakes the sky.

VI.   Aphrodite's Day

I have always loved Friday,
your day, my lady, the night
the week erupts into love. . . .

"Venerdì" says my small, red
Italian calendar
perpetually rounding
off the days
as they tumble

upon each other
like worn pebbles
in a rushing stream,
as they blur into bitter blue,
round red, rushing gold.

Where do the days go—
each one irretrievable,
each one full of silver seconds,
moments of the purest fire.

Is life much too long
for an immortal?

Do you scan the skies
looking for trouble
because of the boredom
of being beautiful
forever?

Do you play with your people—
placing a Sappho
before a Phaon,
Sylvia & Ted
just so—
& wait for the disaster
you know must happen
to amuse you?

Life is very long
for gods & goddesses,
& mortals are their movies,
their soap operas.

Is that what I am, to you—

a soap opera?
Perhaps even less.
I would like at least
to be a long novel
layered with subplots.

& so you play with my heart—
setting a fire in one ventricle,
a flood in another,
a hurricane in my blood—
"the touched heart madly stirs"
as Sappho said. . . .

Ah, Sappho's soap opera
reverberates down
through the centuries
touching even our own
antipoetic age.

Poets are pebbles in a stream
animated by your laughter.
Everything we do
is your proclamation.
A man looks at a woman
& she sets him above
the gods & heroes.
A woman looks at a man
& he sees her as Aphrodite.

You merely pass the time,
making millennia fly by.

You are the prow
of the ship called Poetry

&you smile
your antic smile
as the world explodes
in your father's skies,
making nebulae

for your name's sake,
amen.

Both here on earth
& in the skies
every day is
Aphrodite's day.

VII.   Conjuring Her

Mandarin oranges,
love apples,
honey in a jar,
last year's rose petals,
dried gardenia whose pungency
lingers in the air . . .
& a shred of brown paper
burned at the edges
with his secret name upon it
in heavy grease pencil,
my name, too.

Love has ignited
the edges of my life
& the honey
saturates his name
at the bottom

of the round, clear jar—
a little womb of wishes.

I have kissed the lid,
lit incense sacred
to you, my lady,
& now I wait
for him to fill
my honey jar,
if it pleases you.

It pleased you to see
Arion rescued by his lyre,
clinging to it in the stormy sea
as if it were a dolphin's back.

It pleased you that Sappho's
fragmentary verses
went to make sarcophagi
for the sacred alligators of Egypt—
thus were saved,
—a papier-mâché patchwork
quilt of poetry
spared by time.

Lady of papyri & sarcophagi,
lady of lovers' jumps,
lady of spells & incense,
of goats & heifers
bleating to the sacrifice,
of maidens & madonnas
silently doing the same,
I bow my head
to your unending miracles—
I surrender to your power.

Some say love is a disease,
a fire in the blood that burns
every human city down.
I'll take my chances.

Before I curl
like incense to the sky,
before I study how to die,
drizzle the honey
of my wishes
on my waiting tongue . . .
teach me how to fly.

VIII.   Sappho: a footnote

A nightingale sang
at her birth,
the same nightingale
who sang
in Keats' garden.
She tried to hold
the sky in her two arms
& failed—
as poets always fail—
& yet the effort
of their reach
is all.

She understood
that her life
was the river
that opened into the sea
of her dying.

She understood
this river flowed
in words.

Her harp
buoyed her like Arion's
as she drifted toward
the all-forgiving sea.

Most of her words
vanished. Millennia
flew by.
The goddess she worshiped,
born of the sea's pale foam,
grew younger
& more beautiful
as the words of the poet
dissolved.
All this was foretold.

Sappho burned
& Christians burned
her words.
In the Egyptian desert,
bits of papyri
held notations
of her flaming heart.
Aphrodite smiles,
remembering Sappho's words:
"If death were good,
even the gods would die."

You who put your trust
in words when flesh decays,
know that even words

are swept away—
& what remains?

Aphrodite's smile—
the foam at her rosy feet
where the dying dolphins play.

IX.   Her Power

All around the crumbling
limestone shores
of the Mediterranean
there are traces
of her power—
the queen of Cythera,
foam-footed Aphrodite,
she who makes the muses
dance together,
plaiting poppies
in her golden hair. . . .

Temples to her capriciousness
stand everywhere
facing the sea
which is full of nereids,
dolphins, blue & gold tiles
of sunlight, & caves where
the moon hides between pregnancies.

I have always been drawn
to these shores
as if I knew
the goddess I worshiped
would be found

looping the ancient isles
made of limestone,
most soluble of rocks.

She took the moon on her tongue,
the silver wafer
giving a lemony light.
She watched the waves erase
her filigreed footsteps.

She is everywhere & nowhere—
provoking love in the least
recess of longing.
She is the goddess for whom
the earth continues to spin—
in her turning
all endings end
& all beginnings
begin.